PENGUIN CANADA

FIELD OF MARS

A native of North Carolina, STEPHEN MILLER graduated from Virginia Military Institute and obtained a master's degree from the University of British Columbia. He is a screen and television actor. Miller's debut mystery, *The Woman in the Yard*, was published in the United States and Canada. He lives in Vancouver with his wife and son.

STEPHEN MILLER

Field of Mars

PENGUIN
CANADA

PENGUIN CANADA

Published by the Penguin Group

Penguin Group (Canada), 90 Eglinton Avenue East, Suite 700, Toronto, Ontario,
Canada M4P 2Y3 (a division of Pearson Canada Inc.)

Penguin Group (USA) Inc., 375 Hudson Street, New York, New York 10014, U.S.A.
Penguin Books Ltd, 80 Strand, London WC2R 0RL, England
Penguin Ireland, 25 St Stephen's Green, Dublin 2, Ireland
(a division of Penguin Books Ltd)
Penguin Group (Australia), 250 Camberwell Road, Camberwell, Victoria 3124,
Australia (a division of Pearson Australia Group Pty Ltd)
Penguin Books India Pvt Ltd, 11 Community Centre, Panchsheel Park,
New Delhi – 110 017, India
Penguin Group (NZ), 67 Apollo Drive, Rosedale, North Shore 0632, New Zealand
(a division of Pearson New Zealand Ltd)
Penguin Books (South Africa) (Pty) Ltd, 24 Sturdee Avenue, Rosebank,
Johannesburg 2196, South Africa

Penguin Books Ltd, Registered Offices: 80 Strand, London WC2R 0RL, England

First published in a Viking Canada hardcover by Penguin Group (Canada),
a division of Pearson Canada Inc., 2005.
Simultaneously published in the U.K. by HarperCollins Publishers Ltd.
Published in this edition, 2008.

1 2 3 4 5 6 7 8 9 10 (OPM)

Copyright © Stephen Miller, 2005

*Publisher's note: This book is a work of fiction. Names, characters,
places and incidents either are the product of the author's imagination
or are used fictitiously, and any resemblance to actual persons living or dead,
events, or locales is entirely coincidental.*

Manufactured in the U.S.A.

LIBRARY AND ARCHIVES CANADA CATALOGUING IN PUBLICATION

Miller, Stephen E., 1947–
Field of Mars / Stephen Miller.

ISBN 978-0-14-301772-1

I. Title.

PS8576.I556F53 2008   C813'.54   2008-900675-5

ISBN-13: 978-0-14-301772-1
ISBN-10: 0-14-301772-1

Visit the Penguin Group (Canada) website at www.penguin.ca

Special and corporate bulk purchase rates available; please see
www.penguin.ca/corporatesales or call 1-800-810-3104, ext. 477 or 474

For Wendell

And down the embankment of history
Came not the calendar
But the real Twentieth Century

Akhmatova

The decadent Ottoman Empire is in retreat.

Poised on her northern borders, the Austrian and Russian Empires intrigue ceaselessly to further their own ambitions. For Russia it is the dream to possess Constantinople and guarantee herself an outlet to the Mediterranean. For Austria, it is hegemony over the Balkan nations, and naval domination of the Adriatic. Unable to restrain herself, in 1908 she annexes the province of Bosnia—a stroke that inflames Serb patriots.

By 1913 the Great Powers are locked into a frenzied arms race, spending themselves into debt producing dreadnoughts, howitzers, repeating rifles, experimental aeroplanes, and undersea boats. At the same time humans are connected as never before—by motorized vehicles on improved roads; by faster vessels, telephone exchanges, and telegraphic cables that girdle the Earth.

As the Ottoman tide ebbs, all the Balkan nations begin vying for supremacy over their neighbours. In a mad dance of betrayal and avarice, Greece, Turkey, Bulgaria, Montenegro, and Serbia fight a bloody war. Momentarily separated by an armistice in April, they are joined by Rumania to clash again barely two months later.

Although the wars in the Balkans are remarkable for their cruelty and casualties, the Serbs are doing well.

Their star is on the ascendant, but they are anxious that in a future war against Austria-Hungary they can not win alone. As fellow Slavs they look toward Russia for protection.

Everyone is afraid to provoke mighty Russia. Her multi-million peasant armies are thought capable of annihilating any opposition. But Russia's Tsar is more remarkable for his faults than his virtues. St Petersburg might be one of the great cities of Europe, but the court is in the grip of sycophantic corruption. Nicholas is an indecisive man who likes domestic life, who enjoys noting down the changes in the weather. The Tsarina Alexandra has given him four daughters and an heir—Alexei, afflicted with the barely-understood disease of haemophilia. Deeply religious, and despairing, the Romanovs are easy dupes for a series of faith healers and charlatans who promise a cure for the Tsarevich.

None of this is a secret. Indeed all of these topics are endlessly discussed in newspapers, cafés, and bars; in the streets and on trams, over expensive dinners in the finest restaurants, and over cigars and brandy in diplomatic salons, in bedrooms and bordellos. A whirlwind of gossip, speculations, and nightmares. Amateur strategies, and apocalyptic theories. All is known. All is pondered, all is anticipated.

Yet still there are secrets.

ST PETERSBURG
1913

ONE

St Petersburg shimmered like a vast hallucination. It was three in the morning, but on this white June night the sun flared like a beacon over the deserted boulevards.

Lost in their dreams, the innocents slept. It was the hour of the prostitute and her final client, the hour when the drunk had collapsed into his nightmare, the hour when the suicide ceased his pacing. It was the hour of the thief and the hour of the investigator, the hour when tears had dried and laughter was just a memory. The hour of the predator and the hour of the victim.

Petersburg was a premeditated city. A metropolis with artificial neighbourhoods and preposterously wide boulevards that ran arrow-straight to the horizon. It was a place even a peasant could understand, its avenues designed for military parades, bisected by canals whose bridges could easily be blocked by cossacks.

Three centuries of Romanov rule had not mellowed the city's master plan; there were the parks with their silent green foliage, cathedrals looming over statues of long-dead Tsars, garish sentinels protecting the most important circles and plazas.

An artist's eye might linger on the barges moored against the embankments, the golden flash of the Admiralty's spire, the leaden green light across the broad waters of the Neva, the row of red-painted government buildings interrupted by the gigantic yellow General Staff building. But no colours could enliven Russia's purpose-built gateway to the world—a city built upon the corpses of serfs enslaved to the horrific aspirations of Peter the Great. A capital born with its cord anchored to a swamp—beautiful, on the surface.

On this garish morning two carriages were drawn through the heart of the empty city. Leading was an opulent troika pulled by white horses. Beneath its luminous black lacquer one could still detect the ornamental crest of the House of Romanov. At a discreet distance a threadbare izvolchik followed, with three members of the Okhrana secret police crammed inside. Beyond boredom, they had nothing to look forward to and no plans, for anything might happen at such an hour. They had raised the top of the cab to protect themselves from the glare and two were sleeping while their superior leaned his head against the window post and fought to stay awake.

Pyotr Ryzhkov watched the city glide by—a long blur of apartment blocks, office buildings and markets, most of them built in identical style, from identical materials to an identical height. The slow pace of the carriage gave him the illusion that he was *falling*—sinking into an eternal void.

Ryzhkov was the most ordinary looking of the three. With unruly dark hair and strong brows, he looked like his father without the moustache. Eyes that were blue, but with dark pupils, as if always starved for light. He seemed a little older than his years, the hard life had done that. Here and there he had a scar; wrinkles of concern, and a slight frown that had etched itself into the mask he had worn as a face for too many years. He needed a shave and a few regular meals. He needed a vacation, some new clothes. To sleep. A new life.

Ahead of them the elegant troika slowed, turned off the embankment on to a narrow side street. Muta flicked his whip, and in a few seconds they reached the intersection in time to see the troika stopping at the entrance to an ornate office building.

'All right. He's decided to stop . . .' Ryzhkov nudged Konstantin Hokhodiev awake. Kostya was a big man. He yawned and stretched and tried to straighten his legs in the small carriage. 'Whose place is it this time?' he groaned without opening his eyes.

'I don't know. Someone with money to spend, just looking at it,' Ryzhkov said. Down the street a queue of expensive carriages and motorcars rested at the curb, their drivers sleeping or standing about smoking. The windows of the mansion were open and there was a wash of sound: music, laughter, groans.

Dima Dudenko, the youngest member of their team, yawned and also tried to stretch his legs in the carriage. His feet got tangled in Ryzhkov's and he woke with an irritated jerk, then realized where he was. 'Good Christ, this is insane. Doesn't Blue Shirt ever sleep?'

'Here he comes . . .' Ryzhkov muttered as the door of the troika opened and the mad monk—Grigori Efrimovich Rasputin, stepped down on to the pavement. The prostitutes were tipsy. They laughed and stumbled into the street behind him. Hokhodiev managed to blink himself awake just as Rasputin and his friends climbed the front steps. A sign hanging above the portico read Apollo Fine Papers & Binding. The front doors opened and Rasputin threw his arms wide as a blast of applause engulfed him. A clutch of men in formal dress stepped out to kiss his hand. Laughing, he was dragged inside.

They were in a fading neighbourhood, a little too far away from the canal, not close enough to the theatre, and much too close to the stench of the market on a warm day. Ryzhkov cleared his throat and spat out on to the cobbles. 'This is . . . Peplovskaya Street, yeah, Muta?' he asked the driver.

'Peplovskaya, yes, excellency. Only a small street,' Muta said in his thick Georgian accent. Ryzhkov had been along the little street dozens of times; still, he had never really noticed it. An uninteresting street, the kind that could only take you somewhere else.

'Well, he'll be in there for hours,' Dudenko muttered. 'Does anybody want something to eat? There's a place down the corner, they might have something?'

'Not me,' Hokhodiev said, got out and walked a few paces out into the street and began to urinate.

'Go ahead. I suppose he's probably safe enough in there.' Ryzhkov climbed out of the carriage to shake the stiffness out of his legs, took a moment to roll his head around on his shoulders.

Ostensibly the Okhrana were charged with watching over Rasputin to ensure that he did not come under the influence of foreign agents or revolutionary elements that might use him to gain access to the Imperial family, but really they were guarding 'Blue Shirt'—as the Internal branch knew him, from embarrassment in the newspapers. There was no detective work involved. Everyone knew the secret police were trailing the staretz, not because he was a threat to the Imperial family, but because he was their pet.

In less than a decade Rasputin had become a legend. He was thought to be a holy wanderer who could speak directly with God, a creature with unlimited sexual appetites who could cure illnesses with a simple caress. Everyone in the capital knew that if you wanted something—a posting to a particular ministry, special attention paid to your proposals, consideration when it was time to hand out military decorations—*anything* at all, you would need Rasputin as an ally. His favour was a necessity in order to ensure a successful career, his wrath could obliterate a cabinet minister in a single morning.

Thus, when their rotation came around Pyotr Ryzhkov and his men dutifully trailed Rasputin back and forth across the city. It amounted to a series of sleepless nights that only ended when Blue Shirt fell into his bed in the company of a final prostitute he would select from the group waiting at the entrance to his building. It was boring unless you enjoyed watching the upper crust humiliate themselves at the feet of a con artist, an exercise which Ryzhkov had long since ceased to find amusing.

His memory of the street gradually came back—apartments over shops down at the corner of Sadovaya, a couple of shabby wooden houses and a little warehouse up on the market end of the street—*Peplovskaya*. The only thing disturbing the peace of the street was the noise coming out of the Apollo Bindery.

'Look at this,' he said, shaking his head.

'Oh, yes, all you need is the money and you can buy a little taste of heaven . . .' Hokhodiev joined him as he walked along beside the carriages. Painted on their sides were the crests of some of Russia's most powerful families. At the head of the queue, the black troika of Prince Yusupov, behind it a carriage inscribed with the gold filigreed crest of the House of Orlovsky. A flaming fortress indicated the Evdaev family, next was the gleaming Renault of Prince Cantacuzène.

'Well, they must be sewing together some extremely rare books. A very literate clientele, by the looks of it . . .'

'High flying, even for our friend,' Hokhodiev said. 'You want me to get the numbers?'

'Oh, yes, whatever the circumstances we must complete our paperwork. Do you have enough space in your book?' The carriages and motorcars continued for the length of the street past the bordello, vehicles belonging to an assortment of devotees, perverts, aristocrats, power-mad debauchees of every stripe.

'If I run out of pages, maybe I'll go up and buy a new one from the management, eh?' Hokhodiev laughed and walked away down to the start of the queue.

Ryzhkov stood in the centre of the street, fiddled for his watch and checked the time. Nearly four in the morning. The sky above him was a pearly white tinged with streaks of yellow. From above one of the prostitutes was crying out in pretend-orgasm. The chauffeurs looked over and he shook his head and they laughed. Down at the end of the street he watched Kostya gathering the meaningless licence numbers.

'No point,' he said. He sighed and headed back to their carriage, the most unkempt vehicle on the street. 'No point whatsoever . . .'

Dima came back with rolls and a pot of tea. When Ryzhkov took a drink he flinched. 'Are you all right?' Dudenko asked, his narrow face frowning.

'Oh, it's just this tooth, it's started up again. I'm fine.'

He took a sip from the glass of tea that Dudenko gave him. The heat brought another jolt of pain to his jaw.

'You should do something about that, an infection can lead to serious illness, eh?'

'Yes, yes, yes . . .' He held the hot liquid on his jaw and waited for the pain to go away.

They sat in their shabby little carriage and shared out the food among themselves. Muta took the opportunity to fall asleep with the reins in his hand. After a few minutes Hokhodiev returned, opened the door of the carriage, sat on the step and smoked. They talked about the schedule for the next day. It should have been the end of a hellish week of Blue Shirt surveillance, but the Tsar was in the capital and the three of them were to augment the Imperial Guard at the Marinsky Theatre. What that meant was—less sleep all around.

Dudenko gathered their glasses and had taken only a few steps down the pavement when they heard the screams.

There was a sudden crashing that came from the end of the street. All the drivers and chauffeurs looked up. It sounded like one or two women—angry. A man's voice, lower. Something crashed into splinters and shards.

'What . . . what is this? Tell me he hasn't gone and got into something stupid . . .' Ryzhkov stood up in the carriage. Muta woke up and his pony took a nervous step forward. There was another long scream from the upstairs of the building.

'It's down there—' Dudenko stooped and placed the glasses on the pavement, stood and peered down the street. Ryzhkov could see the drivers at the end of the queue looking at something masked by the edge of the building.

'Something going on in the lane down there,' Hokhodiev said.

Ryzhkov jumped out of the carriage, ran across the cobbles and down to the corner of the bindery. There at the beginning of the lane a group of drivers were standing still, serious expressions on their faces. In the distance sounded the shrill blast of a police whistle. He rounded the corner and saw what he first took for a bundle of clothes tossed on to the pavement.

And then—

One of the drivers had covered her with a jacket, but it was too small and Ryzhkov could see the fan of her blonde hair across the stones. Reflexively he moved closer and one of the drivers reached out to stop him. He shook the man off and held his Okhrana disc up for them to see. From the back of the building the cooks and servants had come running out. An old man was standing over the girl, rubbing his hands on his apron.

'She *fell* . . .' the old man said in a weak voice. He looked at them as if he hoped someone would help him find a better explanation for the dead child on the cobbles, for the sparkling wreath of broken glass all around them. 'Yes, she fell, excellency,' the old man, said again. 'From up there someplace—' The old man pointed to the windows above them, and they all craned their necks trying to see up to the top floors of the building and the yellow sky beyond.

He walked forward and pulled the jacket off her, brushed the long blonde hair away from her face. An angel, was the first thing he thought of. An angel tumbled right out of the heavens.

Pale white body, tall for her age, he thought. Wearing a little night-dress that clung to her, a gossamer wrapper that had ridden up, making it look as if she were dancing. Leaping, with her arms to the sky, a pink satin ribbon around her waist, celebrating something that she'd never seen before. A long smear of blood down both of her legs, but nothing else. The long blonde hair wreathed around her, half-undone. All that was missing were the wings.

He pulled her hair back a little and, looking closely, saw marks around her neck. Rubbed, raw. Her face was smiling, almost. Only a little blood at the corner of her mouth. You might mistake it for lipstick gone awry.

Her eyes were open; eyes, rimmed with dark orbs of kohl, rouge that had been brushed on, too dark for her skin. Skin pale as milk. An angry gash on her forehead that hadn't bled very much, he thought. Her clear blue eyes open and staring out at the glass like diamonds sparkling all around.

'Pyotr . . .' he heard Hokhodiev behind him. 'We have to find him and get out of here, eh?'

Behind him there were more whistles and the drivers scurried aside to let a St Petersburg Police Ambulance manoeuvre into the narrow lane. Ryzhkov pulled his eyes from the girl and saw three officers had run up from the other end of the alley.

'Hey . . . Blue Shirt, Blue Shirt, Blue Shirt . . .' Hokhodiev prompted, giving him a little tug. He realized now that he was standing over her in a daze, staring at all of them, the officer, the servants, the drivers who had crowded into the lane.

'Yes,' Ryzhkov said. 'Let's find him and get him out.'

He started back on to Peplovskaya Street, his heart beating like a racehorse, Dima running ahead. Rounding the corner they saw a gallery of men in formal dress and varying states of intoxication leaving the building, pushing their way towards their carriages as quickly as possible. Men with money. No blood on any of them. None of the gendarmes was doing anything.

Right in front of him there was an angry shriek and Ryzhkov saw a young woman being pulled away from the gate. She was strong and she fought her way down the steps and out to where the men were trying to escape. There was the crack of a whip and a carriage bolted away in front of her; at the last moment someone jerked her out of the path of the wheels and she stumbled and fell into the gutter.

She got up, 'No, no . . . *no!*' Slapped her way free of the gendarmes, and started running down the pavement toward the lane. '*Murder!*' she called with her face lifted to the high windows of the building. And then the police were upon her, wrenching her arm back so that her face contorted in pain.

On the entrance stairs a uniformed officer from the Life Guards was in conversation with a clutch of police. He was laughing, his hand extended to offer the overawed policemen cigarettes from his silver case. The madam of the house was there on his arm, her dazzling red hair piled up with feathers, a beaded dress with a décolletage that provided an easy view of her ample bosom. She was smiling through it all as she wished everyone goodnight.

Behind them Ryzhkov saw Hokhodiev and Dudenko pushing Rasputin out of the foyer towards the street. A little mob of aristocrats were jammed up there, all patting each other on the back and moaning their goodbyes.

'Let them through!' Ryzhkov growled at a gendarme sergeant who was smiling and bowing and apologizing for the situation. The man's eyes suddenly went wide with fear and he backed up two steps when Ryzhkov held up his disc. Suddenly the knot of pleasure-seekers parted and Rasputin was right in front of him.

'Unfortunately, we must be leaving, Holy One,' Ryzhkov said, trying to take the sarcasm out of his voice as he reached out and grabbed Rasputin by his satin shirt. The man smelled of tobacco, body odour, and lavender perfume.

'But, I thought we were here for the music?' Rasputin was saying to the woman behind him. Ryzhkov had Rasputin by the shoulder and steered him down the steps towards his carriage. There was an enthusiastic chorus of goodbyes and blessings for a safe journey. The guards officer watched them go, smiling faintly.

'What happened in there, Holy One?' Ryzhkov asked Rasputin.

'I don't know. We haven't even started and boom it's all for nothing.' He seemed genuinely perplexed by the whole thing. Hokhodiev looked over at Ryzhkov and shrugged. 'But there's always another party going on somewhere. Who knows? It's probably for the best, eh?' Rasputin said.

'Perhaps, Holy One. Go, now . . .' They pushed Rasputin into his carriage and the driver flicked his whip. Around them the policemen were helping the guests on their way. He and Hokhodiev stood there for a moment, looking down at the end of the building, both of them thinking about the girl. He didn't want to go back down there.

'Whoever did it has had lots of time to get out,' Hokhodiev said quietly.

'Yeah, yeah . . .' Ryzhkov took a sharp breath, shook himself like a dog. His fingers had cramped around the knife he carried in his trouser pocket.

'But Blue Shirt certainly was under control. I found him at the table, just like a gentleman.'

'He has a sixth sense.'

'Exactly, he can sniff trouble. He *knows*, I'm telling you . . .' Hokhodiev frowned, put a big hand on Ryzhkov's shoulder. 'Are you all right?' he asked cautiously.

'Yes . . .' he said, but he wasn't and they both knew it. A St Petersburg police officer was a few paces away and Ryzhkov walked over, flashed his disc. 'Hey, who owns this place?' The lieutenant shrugged, gave a thin smile and pointed to the sign over the portico. 'Well, this isn't a book factory, there's obviously some kind of apartments up there. What about those?'

The lieutenant was still smiling. 'Yes, a Finnish gentleman has leased the entire building. Unfortunately, he's not on the premises. Tonight appears to be a private party, some friends of his.' The young officer shrugged. He wasn't going to give Ryzhkov much help no matter what service he was from.

'Hey, who's paying you off, pal?' Hokhodiev stepped forward to intimidate the gendarme, but the lieutenant didn't budge.

'It's a suicide, from what I've heard,' he said. 'Some little *vertika* tail-twister jumped out of one of the windows around the corner.' They all looked down to the lane. 'It happens more and more,' the lieutenant said with a sad smile.

Suicide. Ryzhkov thought about it for a moment, tried to put it together with what he had seen in the lane. Maybe suicide was becoming fashionable, but he hadn't realized that children were doing it. The whole thing was a lie, transparent as the dead girl's dress. He turned and looked at the officer for a moment, gave him a smile of his own. 'Sleep tight, little fellow,' he said and walked back towards the alley.

The gendarmes backed away as soon as they rounded the corner.

Ryzhkov stood there, a little unsteady, looking down at the girl, memorizing it all. Maybe he had been thinking she'd wake up, or move, or say something. Maybe he'd been thinking that he could heal her somehow. He looked up to the opened windows on the top floor. There was still gramophone music playing up there, crazy, jangling 'negro music' that filled the street.

'Ah . . . if we hurry, we can catch up with Blue Shirt . . .' Hokhodiev said gently. Dudenko only shrugged.

'Pyotr, she's gone, and we have to go too,' Hokhodiev said.

'Yes,' Ryzhkov said finally, backing away so that the attendants could free her from the pavement and roll her onto the stretcher.

A crowd had formed now; neighbourhood residents who had heard the commotion and had rushed to their windows, then thrown on their robes and come out on to the street. As they headed back through the crush he saw officers from both the Preobrazhensky and the Grenadier Guards regiments, and what he supposed were uniforms of at least two foreign countries. There was even a pair of court pages there, boys not yet grown into men, who strode away nervously, heading towards the busy intersection of Sadovaya Street.

'Excuse me, sir—' a nervous gendarme rushed toward the gates where several women were being briskly escorted off the property. Ryzhkov saw the same angry one among them.

'There you have it, Pyotr,' Hokhodiev mused. 'An entire flock of whores, judging by the feathers . . .' Six or seven of them, pulling on their brightly coloured robes, being rushed out of the building before they had time to finish dressing, hair undone, clutching their bags.

Ryzhkov saw that the angry one had fallen behind the others; she was spent now. No longer screaming about murder, just standing there alone. Hat jammed down over her head, clutching her bag across her breast, just staring down towards where the ambulance attendants were doing their work. He thought he could see her lips moving, talking to herself.

'Are we ready, now? Have we done our careers enough damage now?' Hokhodiev said, trying to make it all go away, trying to turn it into a joke.

'Yes . . . why not?' Ryzhkov said.

'Good, while we all still have jobs, eh?' Hokhodiev steered him out of the lane. Ahead of them Ryzhkov saw their cab drawn up at the corner by the teahouse.

It was a scruffy place, there was no sign above the shop, just a long arc of painted flames that spanned the width of the establishment. Muta was sitting there pretending to be calm, taking a pull from his pipe. The ejected prostitutes had gathered at the door and were talking with some of the customers and angrily pointing back to the bindery.

Hokhodiev pulled him across the cobblestones to avoid his being trampled as an expensive carriage glided by—inside Ryzhkov could hear the passengers laughing. Now that they had got away without arrest or embarrassment the whole event had become an exciting, giddy experience. Not something to tell their wives and children about, but nevertheless, a most unusual night. A thrill, even though somewhat frightening for a time, surely, but invigorating for all that, and even fun . . .

'Hey!' Dudenko suddenly cried out and rushed ahead to their cab. Two of the prostitutes were now angrily demanding a ride from Muta. Dudenko began waving them away but the girls simply parted and neatly circled him.

'Thank you . . . thank you . . . ladies, I'm sorry we are full.' Hokhodiev pushed the girls away, yanked Dudenko up on to the step.

'This place looks like your home for the night, girls,' Hokhodiev called out to them. The men at the door of the café laughed and one of the girls slung her bag at Hokhodiev as got into the cab. Ryzhkov saw it was the angry one again, the same girl he had seen staring down the street. He watched as she pirouetted on the pavement: in a complex negotiation between her friends and the laughing men in the doorway.

He could see her closely. She was even more dishevelled now, certainly intoxicated, hysterical from the shock. Her tears had made dark rivers down her cheeks. Her nose was red, from crying. Attractive, if you went for women of that type. On the thin side. Yes, certainly, somewhat attractive. Even beautiful in a lewd, trashy way.

Then suddenly there was the crack of Muta's whip and she was gone.

TWO

Led by the splendid figure of Prince Nestor Vissarionovich Evdaev, two thousand horsemen proceeded along the embankment of the Yekaterininsky Canal, a route which took them past the Church of the Resurrection, a short way from the capital's huge parade ground, the Field of Mars. It was a great plain, a huge rectangle with one end sliced off by the Moika and the Mikhailovsky Gardens, a corner defined by the Marble Palace, and one long flank bounded by the Summer Gardens.

A breeze billowed down the canal, thick with the heat of an early summer and the many fragrances of soldiery. Prince Evdaev's mount was Khalif; snow-white, his mane shorn and ribboned with satin—a perfect animal. For two weeks Zonta, his groom, had trained Khalif, fed him a secret diet devised by the old equerry. In preparation for today's ceremonies Evdaev and his officers had returned to the gymnasium and he was hard now, his skin browned by the hot Russian sun, his legs strong, his moustaches waxed, freshly bathed and barbered that very dawn, his cheeks stung with a mint lotion. His valet had spent an hour polishing his helmet, his breeches were newly tailored for the occasion, his gloves chalked to perfection.

Oh, and were the streets not glorious! No expense had been spared for today's celebrations, only one of a year's worth of events marking the 300th year of the Romanov dynasty. Oh, it was wrongheaded, of course. An extravagance. A veneration of incompetence. But nevertheless, Evdaev thought . . . glorious.

Golden double-headed eagles, flags hanging from every lamp standard, decorations in every shop window. The evening before (only a few hours ago!) he had been here in the throng, giggling at the amazing fireworks overhead—a display especially designed by talented Spaniards, a gypsy family that specialized in the beautiful and the dangerous.

They clattered along the cobbles that curved beneath the Church of the Resurrection. Evdaev looked up to the mosaics set into the bricks, the arms of the great royal families of Russia. Above he saw his own family's arms—a burning flame suspended over a bloody stockade wall—the House of Evdaev. He bowed his head, made the sign of the cross, a small act of contrition as he rounded the site. The next time he raised his eyes he saw the ikons of the saints staring down at him and for just a moment he could see his own image there—his face transformed into a grinning skull, with eyes burning hellfire for eternity.

Treason! I am committing treason!

Was God watching him, protecting him? The church was new, only completed a few years earlier, and known as the Saviour on the Spilled Blood, because it had been built on the exact spot where Tsar Alexander II was killed. On that bloody day a terrorist had thrown a bomb as the Tsar arrived to visit his aunt. Alexander had escaped injury from the blast, and had even attempted to help wounded bystanders, truly a saintly act.

But there was a second assassin lurking with a second bomb and Alexander had died in his palace, the bedroom preserved as it was when he'd succumbed; the bloodstained sheets, his last lists to himself. A water glass, reading glasses. Could Alexander's ghost see into his traitor's heart?

There was still time, he thought.

He could dismount, crawl up the steps to the church, confess and make his penance atop the bloodstained cobbles. Still time, still choices to make.

But . . . thousands of hooves clattering on the road blended with the cheers of the bystanders—a buoyant, jittery torrent of sound. The crowd was screaming, their faces upturned; smiling red-faced shopkeepers off for the day, families dressed in their finest marshalling their children into some sort of order, newly arrived peasants transfixed with amazement, girls laughing with their hands covering their mouths, boys running ahead to keep the pace.

Everything was too quick, everything was irrevocable. Evdaev held his breath, waiting for the dead Tsar's revenge, waiting for a Romanov curse to strike him from the saddle.

But it did not come.

They rounded the church and gradually the apparitions vaporized behind him. Nothing ahead of him but cheering citizenry. No curse, no ghost, no revenge.

'God give his blessings to you, sir!' his young adjutant shouted to him, and Evdaev turned and saluted. 'And to you, Lieutenant. But we are late, we'd better hurry along!' He smiled, raised his sabre, and spurred Khalif into a canter as they reached the bridge. A scream of trumpets heralded their arrival and an immense cheer went up from all sides of the field.

Evdaev sighted the blaze of lime spread across the ground ahead, all but eradicated by the caissons of the artillery and the herds of infantrymen who had shuffled across the field. By the time the trick riders of the Caucasian Regiment had done with their acrobatics— diving beneath their saddles to retrieve handkerchiefs tossed by the young grand duchesses—there was nothing but a chewed-up field of stubbly grass. Then, because of the extraordinary heat, his guardsmen had been delayed yet again by a comical team of sprinkling carts unloading themselves in a futile attempt to keep down the dust.

Finally the whistles blew. Now his guardsmen waited— two thousand gleaming statues as the priests finished their blessings. There was no way that a regiment of cavalry could charge across the field and bring their mounts to an abrupt stop without some accident taking place. It could happen to anyone, a horse would certainly go down, bringing others with it. There would be blood, broken bones, fractured spines, death. Certainly it would occur here in just a few moments. Somewhere inside he was praying.

Afterwards, after he had celebrated with his officers, he would go to meet Sergei.

Somewhere secret, somewhere utterly safe. They would feast, and drink toasts to the success of their camarilla. Things were progressing well, he'd been informed. There was not much longer to wait. Surely before the year was out.

Across the holy ground, soil that was consecrated with the blood of generations of Russia's soldiers and their animals, sheltered within a gingerbread-trimmed pavilion, sat the man he was destined to supplant. Nicky. The Tsar. The Tsar of all the Russias. One sixth of the world's surface. They had been children together, cadets. Courted and bedded the same ballerinas. A lifetime of memories.

And soon . . . surely before the year was out. He would have to die. And the boy.

Evdaev could see the royal family, Nicholas shuffling into his seat. The pretentious lieutenant's dress uniform that he wore. Flouting his power by dressing as a junior officer. Absurd. The dull eyes, the invisible smile beneath the moustaches that covered up his rotten teeth. Smiling and blinking. He'd grown into a silly, even weaker version of his childhood self.

Soon.

Besides, the money continued to arrive. Money and even more money, for longer than a year now, ever since he'd agreed to the Plan. Under Sergei's astute direction he had invested most of it, and the returns had been spectacular. They were building a war chest—funds to purchase arms, to purchase men, to purchase allegiance.

Khalif twitched between his legs, pawing the dust. The horses always knew, they remembered from one year to the next. They could smell the excitement, the smoke, and the blood. It had been bred into them for generations. Drums began to pound and the artillery fired a rippling salute. Now he was screaming a command and his men drew their sabres . . . the sudden gleam of sharpened steel against the white sky.

He had hardly to touch the spur to Khalif, and they were off.

THREE

Sergei Andrianov sat in his box in the dignitaries' grandstand that spanned the long eastern dimension of the Field of Mars. The enclosure was a wooden creation with finely turned filigree along the eaves of the roof, wide awnings freshly painted in the Imperial colours. Pennants flew from every flagstaff, from every post—a rush of red, white, and blue. The men surrounding him were in summer suits, some with straw hats and coloured feathers pinned to their lapels. The women were fanning themselves against the heat, chattering and cheering. Almost everyone had opera glasses.

There had not been time for him to take his private car and he was exhausted because he had been forced onto the express, then had spent a sleepless night mulling over the chaos that had taken place at the bindery. In the hours before dawn he arrived in Petersburg, and took a carriage straight to his house; a mansion inherited from his father and refitted with all the modern conveniences, built upon the rise of the Kamenoovstrovsky Prospekt, giving onto a fine view.

Andrianov, except for the quality of his clothing, was the kind of man that was overlooked, until he moved. He knew that it was his energy people first noticed. Business, pleasure, whatever he did, it was like that. Not stopping was attractive to some women, not attractive to others. He couldn't help that. The rules of life were made for ordinary men, not someone like him. A cultivated man, a man with money. A fine nose, even features. Perhaps more Teutonic than Slavic in his appearance, with blond hair and eyebrows that emphasized his brow and the shape of his skull. Looking out over the field below him, as the gleaming cavalry regiments organized themselves into multi-coloured patterns, he was glad he had elected to come alone, mainly because he could make an easy exit when the festivities were finished.

Unfortunately he had to share the box with Dr Lemmers and they'd found themselves beside the repulsive Brogdanovitch who was wedged into his seat, red-faced and sweating. The moment Brogdanovitch had laid eyes on him, he'd abandoned his wretched family and leaned across to hector Andrianov about the new electric engines he was experimenting with in his mills.

Andrianov listened and nodded, pretended to be more interested than he was. But inevitably it was too much; he let Brogdanovitch's theories on oil transport fade away, turned his attention to the field and watched Prince Evdaev as he wheeled his horse and took his place at the head of his cavalrymen. Behind him the regiment cantered smartly to their stations.

Andrianov looked along towards the military enclosures, the ornate uniforms, the splashes of gold braid and feathers creating a perfectly ironic display of romantic traditionalism. A lesser man would be laughing at the absurdity. All around him in the capital he could see the chaos mounting. How many others on the Field of Mars had the blessing of such sight? A dozen?

Less than a dozen, he decided.

He had only reached out to a select few of these visionaries. He could bring the others into the Plan later, when the time was right.

He shook his head at the plumes, the polished brass, gold, and silver—the huge lie that was being paraded before him. Evdaev's beloved military had grown soft under the command of an inherited elite, unable to project Russia's will even within her borders. It amounted to a supreme obscenity to which this horde of perfumed aristocrats was utterly blind. The best rifles in the world were British, the best light howitzers French, the best heavy ones German, the best General Staff, German again. So much for Russia as the great military steam-roller.

Domestically? The economy was as thin as paste-board; he knew its fragility intimately, and, yes, he had taken advantage of the markets, why not? The police were ineffectual and corrupt. And all of it ruled by a teetering autocracy—Nicholas held in thrall to Alexandra, his German-born Tsarina, and her grotesque companion, Rasputin. Throughout Russia were cries for reforms that would never be granted until it was too late. And Andrianov was supposed to simply sit on his hands, put his holdings at risk while the Tsar and his sycophantic ministers dithered? They were like a pack of blind children, stumbling towards the brink!

The looming threats were there for anyone to see, but none of this crowd had ever visited the darker quarters of the city, none of them could begin to grasp that surrounding their perfect palaces and sculptured gardens was a rising tide of revolutionary ferment.

If the Tsar did nothing, sooner or later someone would take matters into their own hands. And Sergei Andrianov had long realized that the future belonged to the one who struck first.

That morning he had struck over breakfast.

Breakfast was with *Bear*, otherwise known as General A.I. Gulka, head of the Third Branch of the Imperial Chancellery, the Okhrana. Alexandr Ivanovich was a large man, more porcine than ursine, with puffed, watery eyes. Like all military men he was fond of his uniform and decorations, and he wore them at all times. He wheezed, and ate his meal enthusiastically while Andrianov listened.

'I can assure you there is no cause for worry, excellency. It is an insignificant death,' Gulka breathed.

'You're certain? Nothing that would put Gosling in jeopardy?'

'Mmmn . . . absolutely nothing at all.' Gulka chewed reflectively for a moment, knife and fork standing at attention, and then, after having decided that he believed what he'd just said, returned to his plate. When Andrianov had not made a comment after several seconds, he looked up. Innocent. Unknowing.

'You didn't have to intervene . . . send anyone to take care of it?' Andrianov asked quietly.

'Mmm, no, no. Nothing could be simpler. It's purely a municipal police matter. Some little whore, she's disgusted by her life, lovesick, homesick, who knows? She throws herself out a window in order to end it all. It's plausible.' Another shrug.

'And no relatives have come forward, no one to look under the rugs?'

Gulka half-laughed, shook his head. 'Girls like that, Sergei. No one wants them back, eh?'

Andrianov stared at him. Gulka was one of his most valuable assets. His resources were infinite. The coup would be impossible without his cooperation. If he had not been brought into the Plan, Andrianov would have been forced to kill him. Appropriately, Andrianov's payments for his services ran to thousands of roubles each month. What made it more difficult was that fat man knew his worth, exploited it at every opportunity, constantly tried to raise the stakes. Not for the first time Andrianov reflected that Gulka's greed might bring the entire scheme crashing down.

'Good. I'm glad there's no trouble, because *Gosling* is important, very important, Alexandr Ivanovich. He may seem like a small bird, but we need him, eh?'

'Mmnn . . . Yes, if you say so, Sergei. He's our holy grail if you say so.'

'He's the one who signs the papers, and he doesn't know us, cannot be traced back to us, yes? He's the one who's in front. He doesn't know it yet, and we've taken these steps to ensure that he will never turn on us. That was the rationale all along, that was Ivo's big idea. To isolate *Gosling* from the rest of us, yes? I've never met the man. You yourself said it was a good idea. I'm sure you understand his value, and I'm sure you are aware of the danger. If something were to go wrong—'

'Nothing is going to go wrong, Sergei . . .' Gulka was laughing and eating at the same time.

'But . . . *if* something were to go wrong, better Gosling than one of us, eh?' he waited for Gulka to comment, but the man only kept on eating. A waiter appeared, refreshed their champagne. The windows were open against the heat and the noise of the traffic along the embankment wafted into the restaurant. Andrianov stared at his own untouched plate, reached into his jacket for his wallet. 'That's why he's important. He's our insurance.'

'I promise you, Sergei. I'll take care of it. I have taken care of it. It's all been taken care of,' Gulka said without looking up from his plate.

Andrianov stared at him for a long moment. One day he would erase Gulka, he promised himself, if only for his patronizing attitude. 'Well, good. That's excellent, wonderful. I suppose, Alexandr Ivanovich, no news is good news as they say.' He forced himself to smile, extracted a fifty-rouble note and slipped it under the edge of his plate. 'Just remember, if anyone makes enquiries we shut them down, and quickly.'

'Mmm . . . but of course . . .' Gulka nodded, his mouth full of food, waving his fork in an ornate salute as Andrianov headed out of the room.

He met *Heron* inside the arched entrance to the Summer Gardens at the Alexander Nevsky Chapel, a particularly ironic spot, Andrianov thought. The chapel had been built in memory of Alexander II's survival of an assassin's bullet, and there was a warning inscribed on the walls—'Do not touch the anointed sovereign.' It had taken the People's Will terrorist group eight attempts to get him.

It wasn't the same these days, he thought.

Andrianov only had to wait for moment or two and then a carriage pulled up and Count Ivo Smyrba, the Bulgarian military attaché, leapt out, smiling. *Heron* was a little man, meticulous with his dress and toilet,

always in fashion, utterly disorganized and distracted by
his ready eye for the ladies. In some ways Smyrba was a
tolerable presence, but in others vastly more disgusting
than General Gulka.

Andrianov had recruited him carefully, mindful that
he might be loyal after all, and funnel information
straight back to Bulgarian military intelligence. Using
him was delicate; valuable because Andrianov made
frequent trips to Sofia, and hoped to make more. His
business interests were expanding there, there was
money to be made even during the recent fighting, and
Smyrba had cooperated over the months, helping with
introductions, information, rumours, gossip—in short,
the grease that turned the wheels of industry more
efficiently, war or no war.

Andrianov reminded himself to stay in control of his
emotions, to maintain an even temper as they talked, yet
everything that had gone wrong had been Smyrba's fault
as far as he could tell.

'Please, I had no idea, I assure you, that the Baron . . .
I mean, that this *Gosling* was like that . . .' Smyrba
waggled his hand to indicate an instability of mind.

'Violent, you mean?'

'Of course. He showed absolutely no indication. You
would have never thought. A distinguished man of that
sort, a man of taste. Naturally we all knew he was a
paedophile. He liked children, fine. That was always the
basis, the entire basis of the . . .'

'Yes, your idea was good. Blackmail him, bind him to
us for as long as we need him. Tell me about the photographs.' Andrianov said quietly.

'Oh, yes . . .' There was hesitation in Smyrba's voice.

Andrianov stopped, there on the walkway, grabbed
the little man by the sleeve. Now he could see the fear in

Heron's eyes. He kept his expression muted, his face calm.

'It's best, Ivo, if you tell me everything,' he said quietly. He even smiled. Perhaps that was why Smyrba was so frightened.

The little Bulgarian cleared his throat, his eyes flicked down the pathway. 'Yes, excellency, we do have the photographs, but they are barely useable. Blurred, you see . . .'

'Blurred?'

'Well, he was moving very quickly and there was insufficient light . . . I brought these . . .' Smyrba reached into his jacket, extracted an envelope and handed it to Andrianov. 'As you instructed, the negatives have been placed in a box for safekeeping.' Smyrba smiled reassuringly.

Andrianov tipped the envelope and extracted a sheaf of photographic prints. The paper was thick and textured, the kind of thing you would use if you were giving your mother a sentimental portrait.

All of them were abstract shapes. He could make out the slash of a door, the spill of light from a window, the line of someone's back and shoulder. He was drawn immediately to Smyrba's own face, blurred yet recognizable, as he stood in the doorway, his hands on the shoulders of a child. Another photograph showed the hallway in the background, prostitutes running out of the rooms, what looked like a man's raised arm.

He shuffled through the photographs, but the only one that showed *Gosling* with clarity was a shot taken over his shoulder; the man's white hair and side whiskers showed clearly. There was a wild expression on the face. Terror? Ecstasy?

Smyrba fumbled in his jacket for his cigar case, offered Andrianov one. Together the two men lit up.

'You see what I mean, Sergei. I'm sorry but I'm not sure they are any good, eh?'

One by one Andrianov slid the photographs back into their envelope. 'But still, Ivo, if we showed just *one* of these to him, let's say this one where you can see his face . . . he wouldn't know about the quality of the others, yes?'

For a moment Smyrba looked up at him with confusion, then he understood. 'Yes, of course. I see. No. And we could perhaps add something . . . perhaps there is a police photograph, something of the dead girl that might be added—' Smyrba giggled and sucked on his cigar, '. . . for spice.'

'Yes, Ivo. That's very good. Let's look on the bright side. *Gosling* won't put up a fight once he thinks we've got photographs of him strangling a child. You will approach him, and it's simple, either he cooperates entirely, or that photograph is all over the press. And we have the police to threaten him with.'

'Yes . . .' Smyrba was smiling now. Relaxing.

'Good. So, now we have to clean up the mess. Did anyone see him do it?'

'No,' Smyrba said quickly. Maybe too quickly. 'No, excellency. No one.'

'Fine. What's his condition? Is he composed, is he falling apart? What?'

'I saw him only yesterday. Naturally, he's nervous. He tried to get away from me. It is as if he blames me for everything that happened, you know? I think he is sinning and sinning, and now it is time to repent, and I am the one reminding him of his sin.'

'Well . . . we'll perhaps send someone around to question him, or put a little scare into him, you know?'

'A policeman?'

'A policeman. I don't know. Perhaps . . . just something so that he doesn't think he is off the hook. Perhaps we can organize it so it happens just when you are passing by, or visiting . . .'

'He may not wish to see me.'

Andrianov smiled. 'Oh, he'll see you, Ivo. And when it's all over a day or two later, you return and tell him not to worry, that he has friends, eh? Tell him that you'll take care of him. Tell him that. Tell him that he's in great danger but you know people who can help.'

'I know someone who can help.'

'That's right, Ivo. If he plays along you can make it all go away. No one will ever know.'

'Yes. Yes. Go away. Absolutely,' Smyrba nodded.

Andrianov pointed to the last photograph, the one where *Gosling* was shown in a sweating profile, used his finger to etch a box around *Gosling*'s face. 'Have this one made larger.' He smiled. 'So he can get a good look at himself.'

His last meeting was with Prince Evdaev and it took place at Evdaev's mansion, an older building on Kronyerkskaya just above the Aquarium, not that distant from his own house. He was less anxious now, after seeing Gulka and Smyrba. It appeared that the crisis had been managed. They would continue with the Plan.

'An event like this, Sergei, I don't mind telling you, it makes you worry,' Evdaev said quietly. At heart the man was a coward.

'It's been taken care of, Nestor.'

'Yes, but . . . weren't you saying that he, ah . . . *Gosling*, that he was the key? The key to the whole thing, yes?'

'One of the keys, Nestor. One of the keys.' They had been drinking. It was the only time to meet with Nestor. After the marches and inspections. After the parades and the endless war games were over. He wanted to leave and see Mina, but she would be asleep by now.

'What about the detectives?' Evdaev seemed nervous.

'There were no detectives. She's been delivered to the morgue.'

'Suicide?'

'Yes, Nestor. Not to worry.'

'No witnesses, no names?'

'You were there, did you see anything?'

'I was downstairs. I stayed away.' Evdaev was squirming in his seat. If he hadn't been holding a glass of schnapps, he would have been wringing his hands.

'Good. You did the right thing, and I didn't want you anywhere near *Gosling*.'

'Yes. I have no idea.'

'That's not your role. And you shouldn't concern yourself further.'

'Yes, thank you. I don't mind telling you, this whole business . . .' Evdaev sighed, wiped his hand across his brow.

Andrianov smiled. The man was an utter coward, a baby. The whole day had been like that. All through his conversations he had become less and less impressed with his recruits into the scheme. Yes, they were all important men, necessary parts of the conspiracy; yes, they had all screwed up their courage to commit treason. Yes, they all had the necessary sentiments and ideological underpinnings to carry them through the storm, but underneath they were weak, ineffectual. They loved the romance of the code names, the secret rendezvous, and, of course, the payments. But for anything difficult, anything that might involve a little dirt or blood, all of them were play-actors. He even had his doubts about how Gulka would react in a crisis. Evdaev was fit to sit on a throne and take orders, fool enough to charge into battle, but for anything dangerous he had no will whatsoever. It was one more symptom of the dry rot that had disabled the whole of Russian society.

'We have nothing to fear, Nestor. There are no names and no witnesses. Certainly no one reliable. It's only a whorehouse, after all.' Andrianov laughed and after a glance at him Evdaev did too, a little self-consciously. They touched glasses.

Andrianov smiled. On the night of the consummation, he had pushed the first envelope across the surface of Evdaev's table. Eagle, the great warrior, had been afraid to take it, recoiled from the thing as if it were a viper. By rights the prince should have reached for the telephone, called for the gendarmes. But he hadn't. Instead he had listened, he had let Andrianov's words draw him in, subduing his reason like the narcotic smoke of a genie's lamp. Hardly believing as the logic coiled around him, overwhelmed him, seduced him.

'I know what you love, Nestor,' he said, and waited. 'But me? I love my businesses. I have love for Mina, of course. My father's house is one of my greatest treasures. But more than all of those . . . it's Russia that I truly love.'

Evdaev was nodding at him, staring into his glass and bobbing his head. Tears starting to form in his eyes.

'And, yes, sometimes, when we love something, and it means everything to us, and it's been hurt or broken, well . . . we have to repair it, restore it. So it is with Russia . . . we have to sweep out the cobwebs, break out the rot, and glue things back together. Is this not true, Nestor?'

Nodding that big head.

'We are not alone, you're not alone, Nestor. Indeed, you are surrounded by secret friends and believers. And we offer you the world. We offer you the chance to be the saviour of your nation. We do this because honour prevents us from doing otherwise. I am here, and I devote myself to you, brother, and to our cause. And as a brother, I pledge my life to you.' He let himself laugh a little. 'But, I don't have to tell you, you know. You're a soldier. One small life, one life is nothing, not really.'

'No,' Evdaev said. Trying to make his voice courageous. It only came out as a burbling sound of drunken assent. Andrianov reached into his jacket, pushed a new envelope across the table. Nestor reached out quickly to save it from the spilled wine.

'There will be more expenses. Men will have to be compensated. We will have to entertain, persuade, blackmail. There will be blood. It will not be pretty . . .'

'I know,' Evdaev said, serious now. Sobering up.

'It's not treason, Nestor.'

And now the big face looked up at him. Stricken. A scared stupid boy waiting for the lash.

'No . . . Is it treason to see? Is it treason to realize that we're surrounded by enemies! We've been humiliated by the Japanese. Who's next, the Turks? Meanwhile our brothers in Serbia are fighting and dying to stave off conquest by Hapsburg pigs and the Jews of Vienna! We watch and dither and sit on our hands. No one is doing anything about it except us. We are the true patriots!'

'Does Nicholas ever listen to God?' Evdaev suddenly blurted.

'He listens to her.'

'Yes . . .'

'And she listens to that fucking monkey Rasputin, with his chants and his séances. We need to get rid of him, all of them . . . It's obvious, isn't it?'

'But the boy . . .'

'Yes, yes. It's terrible. It's unsavoury, I admit, but the boy will be dead before he reaches the age of twenty whatever we do.'

'Yes, I know, Sergei . . . they must all go, they must die, I know that, but . . .'

'Yes, all of them. But our hands are clean. We're sitting on a powder keg primed and ready to blow. When this little revolution comes, well . . . what they do is not our fault. They might spill some blood, but they won't last. They're too fragmented. One cell believes this, another believes that. But by doing this, we will clean out the stables and leave them empty and waiting for us, Nestor . . . Then when you become Tsar, we will hold Russia for all time. But we need a little war, a little revolution. First create a crisis, Nestor. Then control it.'

'To the death of the Romanov dynasty,' he said and Evdaev smiled more broadly. They drank. He looked around the room. Dark, draped with carpets and tapestries found in the most distant corners of the East, a Japanese flag and crossed axes Evdaev had brought back from Port Arthur, all of it ringed with stuffed heads of boars, panthers, stags, pheasants and fish—prize specimens that Evdaev or one of his ancestors had taken at the hunt. A pair of crossed spears above the fireplace, a sooty canvas of a sixteenth-century noble in full boyar costume posed in front of a sulphurous horizon of burning trees and defeated barbarians.

Andrianov had a happy moment. How far would these sanctimonious idiots go? He shook his head, gave a worried sigh.

'What?' Evdaev looked up, suddenly nervous all over again.

'Well, I've been wondering who is paying for the vertika's funeral? Someone should. We can't just let her be thrown into a pit. In a way, she's part of the Plan after all . . . She's our sister.'

'Ah . . . yes, I suppose so.' Evdaev looked suddenly sad. Almost as if someone had taken away his puppy.

'She's our first real casualty. I suppose that in a way she's fallen in the service of our battle, yes?'

'Oh, yes. Very true, very true, very true, she's a heroine.'

'I suppose the bindery might cover the costs, that would be appropriate.'

'Yes, you're right, Sergei. I'll telephone. The company will take care of it. I'll personally see to it.' Suddenly Evdaev was gone all pious, a tragic note had crept into his voice like a bad actor.

'Yes, by all means. Let's be seen to do the decent thing,' Andrianov said, marvelling at the gullibility of 'patriotic' men.

FOUR

Barely awake, Pyotr Ryzhkov was the last one to climb out of the carriage that had drawn to a halt on the shady side of the Nevsky Prospekt. It was his team and he had the training, the seniority, the responsibility . . . and the list. Hokhodiev and Dudenko waited while he fished it out of his pocket, and then stepped back to look at the numbers on the building. Behind him a troop of cavalry passed noisily down the wide boulevard. It was only the beginning of what would probably be an excruciatingly long day—a series of extravagant military ceremonies designed to ennoble the Tsar's dedication of a new dock on the Admiralty Quay, a break for tea, followed by a special performance at the opera—all of it more of the tercentenary celebrations.

'This is it, right here,' Ryzhkov told them. It was a storefront with ornate bars that protected the glass windows: *Nevka Fine Sterling*. There was a pair of golden double-eagle warrants painted on the glass to show that the shop served the households of the Tsar

and Dowager Empress. He went over to the door and
tried it. Locked. He tapped with one knuckle on the
glass as he looked through the window.

Ryzhkov thought he saw a light inside. He tapped
again, harder; held the list up to the window. The silversmith was a little man, maybe in his sixties, perhaps
older. White wisps of hair that had come astray and a
black apron protecting his white shirt.

'We've closed for the celebrations, excellency.' The
old Jew was bowing and backing through the
showroom as Ryzhkov pushed his way into the shop.
An equally old woman peeked out from the back. The
daughter came down the stairs. She was dressed in black
and held a pair of binoculars in her hand.

'You have to leave, Father,' Ryzhkov said, smiling.
'Sorry.'

'But we're closed, and . . .'

'Hey!' Hokhodiev said sharply from over in the
corner where he was inspecting a display of silver
samovars. The family had taken all of their merchandise
out of the window for the day. There was an extra rack
of bars that closed over the window from the inside of
the shop. They probably had a safe in the back
somewhere, Ryzhkov thought.

'We've got you on our list. You have to clear out, eh?'
Ryzhkov held up the list so the old man could see it. As
if the presence of the paper explained why a Jewish
silversmith might be suspected of wanting to murder the
Tsar.

'We're closed,' the girl on the stairs said.

Dudenko walked over to the bottom of the stairs.
'You have to close and lock the upstairs windows, too.
Didn't they tell you that?' The mother came out from
the back and scurried over to put herself between

Dudenko and her daughter. 'I'll do it,' the girl said to her mother.

'Go up with them,' Ryzhkov said. 'Don't worry,' he said to the old man. 'He's from Kiev.'

'We were going to watch from upstairs, where will we go?'

'Go home, or watch down on the corner, what about that?' Ryzhkov said, trying to help a little. There were a lot of things about his job that he didn't like, things he couldn't escape, things that were just part of the atmosphere.

'Yes . . .' the old man said, staring at Ryzhkov's chest, his hands clutching his apron. Upstairs Ryzhkov could hear Dudenko and the women shutting up the windows.

'How did a family of Jews wind up with a shopfront on the Nevsky?' he finally said, to break the silence while they waited.

The old man looked up at him, a little confused. 'We inherited from my wife's uncle. We were very fortunate,' the old man trailed off. Ryzhkov shook his head. Why they wanted to watch the Tsar ride by when an Imperial eye-blink could exile them all to the Pale mystified him. 'Well, just go for a walk somewhere. Anything. But you can't stay here.'

Hokhodiev had lifted the samovar and was checking the workmanship on the base. The old man was watching him with alarm, one hand floating out, too frightened to ask him to put it down. The girl had come back down.

'How long is this going to take?' she said. Her voice was sullen and her face was red.

'Well, how can I say? It's not up to me. You know these priests, they go on and on. No one knows. When the Tsar is ready to go home, I suppose. Come back around two, that ought to be long enough,' Ryzhkov said, trying to smile a little so she'd go along with the dance.

'Yes, yes, of course. Two.' The old man had overcome his fear, slipped around Ryzhkov and was heading for Hokhodiev, who had turned his attention to the valves on the samovar, screwing them this way and that. 'Are you interested in this item, excellency?'

'What? Oh, no. Just looking. Nice stuff, some of this.'

'Yes, thank you, thank you.' The old silversmith settled the samovar back on its base.

'They can't pray for all that time,' the girl was still complaining. She had put on a jacket.

'Probably not, but just lock up, now. We'll stick around to make sure, eh?' Ryzhkov said, and headed for the door.

'Everything's closed upstairs,' Dudenko said, looking the girl over as he passed behind her at the bottom of the stairs.

'Look,' the girl started, still not giving up. 'This doesn't make sense—'

'*Don't*,' said Ryzhkov, tired of it all, tired of cajoling. The girl stopped when she heard the edge in his voice. All of the policemen were looking at her. Ryzhkov reached into his pocket and pulled out his disk. He held it up so the Jews could all see that they weren't just ordinary cops. 'We don't want to make any trouble. It shouldn't be that hard for you to find somewhere to spend the day. Go and sit in a restaurant, but hurry up. We have others. We have a whole list to do before the procession starts.'

He turned to the old man. 'Tell her what's what,' he said quietly.

'Yes. Yes, of course.'

They went outside and stood around watching the street start to fill up. Women, children, families all dressed up for the occasion. Little flags on sticks for the children to wave when the Imperial family passed by. Dudenko looked around and saw Ryzhkov's sour expression and then looked away out into the street. Sometimes it was better to just leave Ryzhkov alone when he was looking like that.

'What's wrong?' Hokhodiev asked, seeing Ryzhkov's expression and watching him reach up and rub his jaw. 'Are you sick? Toothache?'

'I don't know, maybe.'

'Hmm. You're not going to make a mess, are you?' Hokhodiev asked, frowning.

'No. It's not like that,' Ryzhkov muttered. The pain went away as fast as it had come.

Ryzhkov consulted the list and they moved further down the wide limestone pavements of the Nevsky. They followed the Jews to make sure they didn't just come straight back. Dudenko still had his eyes on the girl. Hokhodiev looked over and nudged the young man out of his reverie. 'You could convert, eh? I think she liked your dominating personality back there, you know? Having you visiting her bedroom, and all,' he laughed.

'Go screw yourself Kostya,' Dudenko said, but he still kept looking at the girl.

'Here we are. This place here.' Ryzhkov had found the next address. They ascended a narrow staircase that led to a set of offices used by three different suspect newspapers. The names of the publications had been painted on one of the glass doors, *Beacon, Russian Alert!* and *Popular Knowledge*. They banged on the main door that was marked as the entrance, and then went along the corridor banging on all the doors but no one answered. Ryzhkov got Dudenko to find the dvornik, a kind of combination caretaker, porter and concierge for the building, and extract him from his shack in the courtyard. Absurdly the dvornik had forgotten his pass keys, so Ryzhkov fished out his picks and in a few seconds they had broken into the offices.

Inside was a musty collection of desks, writing lamps, battered typewriting machines, and cluttered bookshelves. There were piles of paper on every surface. In one corner was a small hand press, something you could use to whip off a few hundred radical leaflets in half an hour and then wipe clean.

'We ought to seal this place, eh?' said Hokhodiev, but Ryzhkov shrugged. If the editors of the collection of newspapers had managed to pass the censors, who was he to shut them down? Maybe they were paying someone off. Whatever it was he didn't want to fool with it.

There was only one more address on their side of the Nevsky, a café, supposedly a centre of well-heeled, intellectual, hot-blooded anarchism. When they got there the owners had already closed. Ryzhkov stepped down into the street so that he could see the topmost windows. Everything appeared to be shuttered.

'Knock anyway,' he told Dudenko. 'Go around the back, Konstantin,' he said to Hokhodiev. 'See if they left anyone up there.' He had started to fantasize that some assassin was waiting in an upstairs room for the Tsar's carriage, a marksman with a hunting rifle and a lot of tangled ideas about starting a Slavic version of the French Revolution. He waited while they went about their tasks. Stood there and had a cigarette and watched the street.

The Nevsky: one of the great thoroughfares of
Europe. Nearly two miles long, running arrow-straight
from the golden spire of the Admiralty to Moscow
Station where it turned, angling south towards the
domes of the Alexander Nevsky monastery.

Ryzhkov loved the street at the sudden start of spring,
when the pedestrians came out to promenade; all of
them drawn to the bustle, the elegance, and the energy
of the great boulevard. Along the sides of the street the
cobbles had been replaced by hexagonal wooden blocks
in an effort to dampen the noise of the carriages. Still,
on a busy day it was the sheer cacophony that defined
the prospekt—the shouts, the whistles, the clattering of
the horses' hooves, the carriages flying past, the splutter-
ings of the motorcars, the yelping blasts of their horns,
the ringing of the bells on the trams. The murmur of
thousands of conversations, the buzzing of the throng as
they moved from shop to shop; laughing, arguing,
complaining, lecturing. Shop assistants mingled with
soldiers, who mingled with priests, who mingled with
tea-sellers and princesses. Some walked briskly, desperately about on some pressing business, faces grim.
Others simply idled along, content to be part of the
great stream of humanity with no place better to go,
admiring their reflections in the shop windows. An
endless promenade; a blend of the ultra-rich in silks and
feathers, with newly-arrived peasants clutching their
hats in their grimy hands, staring up at the fantastic
buildings. That was life on the Nevsky; it was the spine,
the vibrant centre of modern Russia.

But this morning all that vigour was restrained,
forced off the balconies, and out of the windows, everything cordoned off to allow the Tsar free passage.

'I got in up there. Nothing,' said Hokhodiev from behind him. Dudenko was talking to a man on the corner. They were pointing to the café. The man was smoking, trying not to show his nervousness at being grilled by one of the Okhrana. Dudenko nodded and the man smiled with relief and ran back across the street. Coming back to them Dudenko looked happy, almost blushing, Ryzhkov thought. Like a spring bride. Young, alive, and maybe even delighted to be pushing people around who were too scared to fight back. 'Everything's fine,' he reported.

Hokhodiev looked over at Ryzhkov again. 'Are you sure you're feeling up to all this?'

'I'm fine,' he said. 'Fine for now anyway.'

FIVE

The upper tier of the Marinsky was more sauna than theatre; a miasma of stale perfume, cigar smoke, and sweat. After the procession, Ryzhkov and his team had been able to return to the dank dormitory that Internal kept in the basement of their headquarters building on the Fontanka. He was able to wolf down some soup, took just enough time to file a request for a St Petersburg Criminal Investigation report on the Peplovskaya Street murder, and then they were rushing across the city to the theatre.

The toothache had diminished in the late afternoon, but now he was in real pain, the throbbing in his jaw keeping pace with the tempo of Glinka's score for *A Life for the Tsar*. All he could do was lean against the carved walls of the opulent blue-and-gold dress circle corridor of the Marinsky and feel the sweat trickle down his spine into his underpants.

Hokhodiev and Dudenko were pacing up and down the corridor, locked into one of their sporadic arguments. On this occasion it was over the ruthlessness of the fighting in the Balkans, the various armies like a pack of crows picking over the carcass of the Ottoman Empire and the waning hopes for peace. Dima was doing most of the talking, since he fancied himself a great critic of kings and politicians.

The bad tooth was his own fault, Ryzhkov decided. He had made more than one appointment to have it fixed, but had been scared of what his dentist would find. The molar had been cracked for years, the result of a violent confrontation with a group of metalworkers who had surprised him as they'd poured out of a clandestine meeting where they had been preparing strike plans. He had been caught right in their path, incriminated by the revolver he was loading. He hadn't even got it closed before one of the metalworkers hit him with something hard, like a brick. He didn't remember anything after that.

They had taken his gun, of course, and left him with a cracked jaw, swelled to the size of a coconut for nearly three weeks. Drinking through a straw. Listening to Filippa berate him a dozen times a day about his choice of occupation before she left for her uncle's, tired of playing the role of nurse.

And so, yes, in typical Russian fashion, he *deserved* to carry a little bit of hell around with him. He had made mistakes, he had committed crimes. He had sinned, he had sinned repeatedly. He had never, never been good, never lived up to expectations, not really. So, then. All the pain was justified. Perhaps his father had been right all along. He should have tried to accomplish more, to have made more of himself. But he hadn't. He'd either been too distracted or too lazy, and when he'd finally picked a vocation it had been for all the wrong reasons.

He'd ended up being the one who cleaned up the trash, swept the mess of the empire into a corner, and then saluted his betters as if nothing had ever been there. He could have been someone of worth, someone of substance. Instead he had become a kind of necessary rat, a creature devoid of status, respect, or glamour. Something vile, ruthless, and efficient.

Not just a policeman, but *more* than a policeman.

Pyotr Mikhalovich Ryzhkov was an Okhrana investigator, a member of the dreaded Third Branch of the Imperial Chancellery. He had advanced in his career to the point where he led a section of investigators, all of whom were supposedly elite policemen. They were charged with the task of suppressing all forms of dissent against the Tsar, the Imperial family, its property, or its policies.

Okhrana was divided into three branches. The Foreign Agency, sometimes called 'The White Branch', held the portfolio of international espionage. Its work was conducted by men and women whose annual budget for clothing exceeded Ryzhkov's income by thousands of roubles. Their battles were conducted in the glittering salons of embassies spread around the globe.

Closer to home was the External Agency, responsible for the active policing of threats to the state. External rigorously monitored the activities of any organisation that might have reasons to bring down the empire. They studied reports of terrorists' comings and goings, read their letters, deciphered their codes, sifted through their rubbish, and analysed their publications. No cell was too small to avoid scrutiny. Thousands of External clerks maintained a vast system of files containing information and photographs of anyone charged with a crime; dossiers on all labour leaders, prominent members of the liberal and radical political parties, exiled or expatriate politicians, editors and journalists of magazines, books, or seditious literature of all kinds.

But Ryzhkov and his men were gorokhovniks—members of the Internal Agency. The nickname was a slur derived from the slang term for their long raincoats named after Petersburg's famously drab Gorokhovaya Prospekt.

Internal investigators were considered little more than thugs and informants by the more genteel External agents. They operated out of safe-houses and flats, often used multiple identities and routinely dealt in conspiracies, blackmail, bribery, and assassination. They were on call twenty-four hours a day, filled in when the External needed them, snatched sleep and meals when and where they could.

There was no such thing as a normal day for an Internal investigator. Within the branch, marriages were doomed to failure; Ryzhkov's was on its last legs. Children were neglected. He thought himself lucky that he had none. To relieve the futility, Internal investigators often fell prey to drink or the kind of low level corruption that came with nearly unlimited police power. It was more than a job, it was a way of life, a way of behaving. A way of thinking and existing to which Ryzhkov had grown accustomed. And gradually he'd come to accept that the purgatory of being in the despised Internal branch, like the pain in his tooth, was something for which he was uniquely suited. Something he deserved.

A man content to give his life for the Tsar.

'. . . and the next thing is that the Hapsburgs are going to use the excuse and step in to protect their empire, and then it's everyone rushing to be manly, eh? To protect the home and the hearth, eh?' Dudenko was lecturing as the two of them paced by Ryzhkov, who had been propping up the wall.

'Be quiet. Be quiet, for Godsakes,' Ryzhkov said weakly. Neither of them could hear him. 'Just, please . . . be quiet,' he mumbled. Even moving his tongue hurt. Inside the theatre he could hear an alto singing desperately:

> *Oh, I wish I were a knight!*
> *Oh, I wish I were a hero!*
> *I would break down the gates be they of cast iron!*
> *I would rush to the chamber where our Tsar reposes,*
> *I would call 'Servants of the Tsar!*
> *Wake up!'*

There was a commotion down the hallway and reflexively all three Internal inspectors straightened as the Chevalier Guards Officer-in-Charge came striding along the carpet. He was resplendent in his shining silver breastplate, skin-tight breeches and gleaming helmet. Beside him Hokhodiev looked like a small-town magistrate in a borrowed tailcoat.

The guardsman's eye settled on Ryzhkov and he frowned. 'Has this one been drinking?' he asked.

'Toothache,' Ryzhkov muttered. The officer nodded sympathetically. Everyone had been pressed into service today. Normally a section of Internal men would be nowhere near the Marinsky, but extreme times called for extreme measures.

'Bloody hell,' the officer said. Ultimately he was in charge of the security precautions at the theatre. 'Well, stay here. I'll get you something.' He headed back down the carpet toward the Imperial boxes.

Ryzhkov relaxed, took up his place against the wall and let his eyes shut. His dentist had a surgery on Vasilevsky Island, but after-hours he had no idea how to find the man. And now he'd lose the tooth. Yes, it was his fault for ignoring it, but before the pain had never really been unbearable. A little twitch every now and then, but nothing like this.

'Why don't you sit down? If you hear me whistle, they're coming,' said Hokhodiev.

He began to pull Ryzhkov across the carpet to one of the satin covered benches that ringed the corridor. No one sat on the benches. They were strictly ordered never to sit on the benches while on duty. 'Sit, for Christ's sake Pyotr Mikhalovich,' Dudenko had slipped an arm around him, and he suddenly felt his knees collapse as they heaved him on to the settee.

Immediately he heard the guards officer's voice. 'Has he collapsed? Here, make him take this.' He pressed a round silver container into Ryzhkov's palm.

'Put it right on the tooth.' The man grimaced. Beneath the moustache Ryzhkov could see that the officer had very few teeth beyond his incisors. Evidently he knew what he was talking about.

The officer stood back and appraised the three of them for a moment, then went back to his station. Ryzhkov screwed open the salter and found it full to the brim with cocaine.

'Well, well, well,' Dudenko sighed.

'I expect that should do you for a bit, eh?' said Hokhodiev with satisfaction, and he and Dudenko moved along the corridor so they could cover for him.

When he began dabbing cocaine on his tooth the relief was instantaneous, a wave of cool water that spread through his swollen gums. He made a mental note to repay the officer for his courtesy, and sat there sighing with gratitude. Maybe the cocaine would provide him with enough relief to get up and do his job before the end of the act. It wouldn't do to get a citation on the Chevalier Guard nightly report, no matter what branch he was in. Ryzhkov's career as an Internal agent might not be glamorous but it was, nevertheless, all the career he had.

A smart young man with no connections or noble blood, Ryzhkov had come into the Police Department in 1897, at what seemed to him to be the absurdly distant age of twenty-one. His first job had been to shadow the great Tolstoy while he visited St Petersburg. It was a bizarre introduction to policing, following an ageing writer as he browsed through the bookshops and markets of the city. But Ryzhkov conscientiously recorded Tolstoy's every movement, the time and content of his meals, his conversations, and the numbers of the cabs he took across the city.

Now Ryzhkov caught sight of himself in a mirror. For a split second he thought it was someone else. One side of his face was swollen. He looked like a hamster or a man with a wad of tobacco in his cheek. His hair had come awry, his eyes were droopy and dull as if he had not slept in several days; perspiration had soaked his shirt front and the collar was stained and limp. Still, he had managed to restrain himself from pulling loose his cravat, and his suit was reasonably immaculate.

With a graceful flick of his fingertips he straightened up and shook his arms so the suit would settle across his shoulders. He tried to smile, tried to be debonair for a moment. The effort sent little spikes of pain across his jaw. He shook his head waggishly, as if he had just heard a naughty joke, made a smooth pivot, and with

astounding grace began ambling down the corridor
toward his men.

'We should get into our places. Isn't this the aria?'
Ryzhkov strolled toward the centre of the house.

'Are you sure you're feeling well enough, Pyotr
Mikhalovich?'

'Everything's under control.' He tried his debonair
new smile out on Dudenko, who was obviously upset.
Well, it was a very involving opera, a very emotional
story, especially for a Slavophile.

He led them nearly halfway along the long curving
corridor. At each entrance to the theatre two shining
Chevalier Guards were posted, their gleaming helmets
pulled severely down over their eyes. The golden chin
straps, originally meant to keep the helmet on during the
fury of a cavalry charge, had atrophied so that they fell
ineffectually below each young guardsman's lower lip.
Now they couldn't even bend over without losing their
hats. Something about the young, blank, obedient faces
of the guardsmen suddenly caused Ryzhkov to feel
weary. A fresh wave of depression flooded over him and
his step faltered on the carpet.

Suddenly there were footsteps behind them. 'Shit,'
hissed Dudenko. Ryzhkov felt Hokhodiev tighten his
grip, trying to hold him up straighter.

'All right, that's enough! Enough!' It was the guards
officer's voice, angrily taking charge. 'You people are
disgraceful! Get him out of here . . .' His diatribe got
lost in a wave of applause. Suddenly there were young
men in tailcoats rushing past them.

'God Almighty!' the officer spat. The young men in
tailcoats flung open the doors to the boxes and instantly
came a screamed command. The guards snapped to
attention.

And then . . .

The very atmosphere began to hum. It was as if an electric charge had been sent through the corridor. A rustling of silk, a dazzling flash of white as a fan of eagle feathers flicked in Empress Alexandra's hand as she swept out of the dark tunnel to the Imperial boxes. Simultaneously all of the men bowed, but Ryzhkov, caught dazed and unawares, could only stare at the Tsarina.

Empress Alexandra's features were frozen, her expression was a metallic mask—as dead as an ikon, her skin nearly as pale as the white lace she wore. Only the impatience of her step betrayed her emotions. Her eyes were dark and glazed, focused on nothingness, blankly staring ahead. Immediately behind her came a Cossack bodyguard carrying the young Grand Duke Alexei, heir to the House of Romanov. A few steps behind them, the Tsar strode out, deep in conversation with the Minister of War. All sound ceased except for the Tsar's voice softly fading as the Imperial entourage moved down the carpeted corridor between the ranks of gleaming soldiers, ranks so solemn that they could have been on parade for the dead.

Then, as abruptly as they had come, the Romanovs were gone, through the great doors and down the golden staircase, heading for their carriages at the front of the Marinsky. The tension instantly evaporated.

'Finally.' The officer turned on the Okhrana men, pushing them back against the wall so they would be clear of the swarm of Russia's elite rushing toward the staircase. The corridor was suddenly full of gowns and jewels and bright uniforms. 'What's your name?' the officer hissed. His face was red, angry.

'Deputy Inspector Hokhodiev, sir.'

'Get this one out of here. And you!' Now the guardsman whirled on Dudenko. 'You make sure he does it! Now go!'

'Take us to Glasovskaya Street then,' Dudenko called out to Muta.

'Not all that far, eh, Dima?' Hokhodiev said sarcastically. 'Only a few hundred miles across the Fontanka, way down there by the gasworks, tucked in beside the race track.'

'God,' Dudenko sighed.

'It's a nice *new* place, though, right? A little noisy, but still a nice place, eh, Pyotr?'

'Yes. Nice,' Ryzhkov said underneath the rushing trees. Filippa had picked it out, the family had bought it for them. The best apartment in the best building on a second-rate street. Being from Moscow they'd known nothing about the neighbourhood.

'You can keep this until the morning then, I suppose,' said Hokhodiev as he shifted the salter full of cocaine back into his pocket. Ryzhkov sat up a little, unscrewed the lid and stuck his finger in for another dab of painkiller. They were manoeuvring around a park and for a few moments he tried to decipher their location by the undersides of the trees as they clattered along.

Ryzhkov succumbed to a reverie that kept pace with the rhythm of their horse's hooves, only surfacing when he heard Hokhodiev tell Dudenko that the gendarmes' official explanation was that the girl at the bindery had been drunk and imagined she could fly. She had jumped out of the window in a fit of hysteria.

'But she had marks,' Ryzhkov said. 'Right around . . .' he tried to make a little circling gesture around his neck. 'Marks,' he said again and closed his eyes, musing on the nature of suicide. She might have been sick. Lonely. She might have been tired, tired of the bad life. Tired of being a toy for any man with twenty roubles. There were plenty of reasons for the girl to want to die, but she hadn't strangled herself first, he knew that.

And now officially they were saying he should forget all about it. Forget the smeared lipstick, the transparent dress. Forget.

At Glasovskaya Street they helped him up the stairs, helped him fish for his key, helped him open his great creaking door. 'It's almost time to wake up and go to the dentist . . .' he mumbled.

'All right, have a good night then,' Hokhodiev said, Dudenko's hand halfway rising in salute as he closed the door behind them.

Ryzhkov started undressing but he ended up just taking off his shoes and socks, walking out to the front room, covering himself with a dressing-gown and collapsing on the chaise. After only a few minutes he got up and moved to the writing desk. Under the blotter was the running letter he had started a week earlier. He pressed the nib of his pen into the blotter and made a series of dashes over the paper until the ink began to run, then he began to finish the letter.

. . . *only just returned now from the theatre. Unfortunately I have come down with a severe toothache* . . .

His pen hung paralysed at the end of the sentence. The clicking in his jaw was the only sound he could hear. He let his eyes travel up an empty frame on the top of the desk. He had removed her portrait months earlier, unable to live with Filippa's relentless staring. What to say? What to say to a wife who was gone, gone away for good, gone away to Lisbon for how long?

Too long. For longer than necessary. Yes. Unavoidable. Gone for all the right reasons: to help her sister and her children cope while their mother recuperated. Oh, yes. She'd *had* to go.

It had turned out to be an extraordinarily long illness. Filippa's mother was unexpectedly delicate. She had suffered from misdiagnosis, and quarrelled with her doctors. Filippa reported on her medical progress in letters that arrived every two weeks or so. He'd found that if he jotted something each day he ended up with enough for a return letter over the same time period.

. . . as regards the Tsarevich, now the rumours are confirmed and something is obviously wrong with the poor boy's health . . .

She had been gone for . . . how long now? Nearly a year. One of the neighbours was probably keeping count of the months. Ryzhkov sat there and drew little cross-hatchings on the blotter while he did the mathematics of her leaving.

The calculations got too complicated and he closed the curtain against the constant light. Of course the marriage had been a mistake. It was obvious, should have been obvious on the wedding day itself. They had 'grown apart' as one of their friends had said. I grow, you grow, we grow. Oh, yes, that's understandable. To grow apart, yes.

. . . there is an entire schedule of celebrations, so many that they will continue through the year . . .

He saw now that she'd always thought of him as a sort of *project*. Something that with a lot of work might one day be finished to satisfaction and mounted on the shelf. But after a dozen tearful attempts to push him into a series of more acceptable, more fashionable situations, she had abandoned him to the sordid world of policemen and criminals. 'You're like them, you're just like them. You admire them! You want to be like them!' she'd screamed at him when she'd finally had enough.

Now it was her idea that all should be forgiven. No one should be blamed, no one should even get angry. It was a modern world now. A woman leaving her husband, what was new about that? They would continue on as before, only on paper.

In one of her most recent letters she had mentioned a possible return to Petersburg at Christmas, but naturally this would be prevented if her mother's illness continued. Someone, then, would have to stay in Lisbon to manage things. If so, did he have plans to join her?

No.

So, gone for a year in March, then. And gone for a lot longer than that, to be truthful.

. . . *with my greatest consideration and respect, I remain* . . .

Gone.

SIX

It was a grey Bulgarian dawn and Sergei Andrianov woke from his sleep in the back of the Rolls touring car the railway had lent him. It came with a chauffeur, a quiet Italian named Mattei, who had gone inside the shed to talk with the signalman. He checked his pocket watch and there was a simultaneous hoot of an engine's whistle. Right on time, he smiled.

He straightened in his seat, found his case and extracted a cigarillo. He had been travelling throughout Europe for nearly two weeks through the dying summer and he was tired. This train, about to pull into the tiny siding, only kilometres inside Bulgaria across the Rumanian border, was the climax of all that work. He had spent his time moving from railway stations to hotels, in and out of telegraphers' kiosks, and then done it all over again. He had eaten catch-as-catch-can, passed envelopes to men who would pass them to others, assured the timid, threatened the weak. Not for the first time he had wondered if he should empower one of his confederates to take some of the task off his shoulders, but whom could he trust? Not Gulka, he had his hands full with security back in Petersburg, not Evdaev, he was more figurehead than tactician, and much too much the ditherer.

No, the Plan was a spider's web, each strand with its own discrete connections, but all of them leading to the centre, with him in control of everything. The smallest tremor in the web would bring his attention to bear, he would move rapidly to the troublesome situation, deal with any problem that might arise.

And to bring someone in at this late date would mean more risk. A jealous second-in-command would recognize the Plan for what it truly was—an elaborate strategy to preserve the Andrianov business interests. Ideology, while important and sometimes synonymous with his success, was mostly a smokescreen. What he had to do was to provide the leverage, the ideas, and the impetus to bring Russia into a war for which it was ill-prepared. Only Evdaev would have advance warning and would emerge as a hero, but Tsar Nicholas would be humiliated. And a second defeat after Japan would be the last straw. Losers always change their leaders, and that would be his moment. Publishers had been paid, articles already prepared, politicians cosseted, all of them standing ready to inflame the population. With the Duma a madhouse, the right men would come forward at the critical instant and call for abdication and arrest; stripped of its intricacies, that was the Plan.

He stepped out of the huge vehicle and peered around the corner of the station. Now he could see the train approaching along the tracks from Rumania; there was another careful whistle and at the signal box he saw the points change as the switch was thrown that would shift the train on to the line leading from Bulgaria to Serbia.

'Tea, excellency?' The chauffeur had come out. He was holding a tray with a single steaming mug on it. The fragrance of the tea was strong in the morning air, a scent of oranges and something darker. Everything was different in the Balkans . . .

He took the offering without a word and carefully sipped. Together the two men watched the train pull up to a watering tower. There was a great hiss of steam as the engine braked to a stop, a rumbling as the couplers collided with each other along the length of the train.

'Do you want your boots, excellency?'

'Yes, thank you.' They moved back to the car and he sat on the edge of the seat, took off his dress shoes, and laced up a pair of walking boots over his trousers. It was already getting warm, the mist was rising over the railway sidings and he could see clearly the trees beyond, the open fields extending to the east. The countryside was damaged from the recent movement of troops, even the station had not escaped. A fire had blackened one end of the building and there were holes where bullets had chipped the bricks around the entrance.

Andrianov fished into his pocket for the key and walked down the train to the first of the goods wagons. When he got to it he broke the Bulgarian military seals, and opened the doors.

He pushed his foot into a cleat and clambered up. Inside the wagon were two Schneider 122mm field artillery pieces nailed to the floor of the rail car and secured with chains and chocks. Their steel barrels were newly painted field grey. In the shadows at each end of the wagon, turned over with their wheels removed for cartage, were the guns' caissons. Andrianov checked the serial numbers, stood for a moment in the gloom, touched a finger to the lip of the muzzle of one of the pieces. It was raw metal, painted with thick grease to protect against rust. The finest product of the Putilov plants. The guns had been ordered to reinforce the Bulgarian army; only his money and Count Ivo Smyrba's willingness to betray his country had diverted them to this tiny shunting yard.

He turned to exit the wagon and saw a young man standing there. 'Welcome to Greater Serbia, excellency,' the young man said. His accent was Serbian and something else, maybe Galicia. His hair was matted and his white shirt was spotted with soot. He hadn't shaved for weeks and he clearly had been riding along in the engine. 'There's no need to check, further. Nothing's been touched.'

Andrianov stood there for a moment looking at the stranger. Then he climbed down. Together they slid the doors closed and started down the line of carriages. There were fifteen of them and a random inspection was enough.

'I am Krajic,' the young man said. He had taken out a cigar himself and struck a match against the side of a car as they walked. 'I've been with the shipment since it crossed the Danube. Well, too bad for Bulgaria—it's spoils of war, now. That will teach these barbarians to turn on us, just because they don't think they got enough in the peace settlement, eh?' The way he said it exuded self-satisfaction. A proud young man. Beneath the flap of his jacket, Andrianov saw the handle of a revolver. He stopped.

The young man caught the direction of his look. '*Apis* sent me, and let me tell you something, friend. If

I'd been planning to do you, you'd be welldone by now.'
He paused for a moment and then came the clear white
smile of the new Serbia.

'Good . . .' said Andrianov and together they
continued to the rear of the train. Andrianov stopped in
front of a wagon and broke a second set of seals. The
locks snapped open, the doors slid away. Another two
howitzers indistinguishable from the first pair except for
their serial numbers.

'The shells are stacked in the last two wagons, but it's
not enough. We'll need many more than that,' the boy
put in.

'I thought the war was nearly over? Haven't you
taken what you wanted?' Andrianov could not resist
prodding him.

'As long as we're winning I see no reason to sue for
peace. They can talk all they want to in London, but this
is our land and we will have it back. We don't call it
Greater Serbia for nothing. We were here running things
long before the Turks came along, long before the
Bulgarians took advantage, and we'll have it back. We'll
have all of it back,' the boy said grimly, looking down at
the gravel as they walked along the tracks.

Andrianov inspected the last two wagons—artillery
shells packed standing upright with wooden collars and,
alongside, separated boxes of fuses. There was an interval
of two empty flatbeds and behind them a last carriage
packed with crates containing bags of smokeless powder.
They put out their cigars and waited while the stationmaster undid the locks, terrified of making a spark.

Andrianov moved through the pallets and checked
the seals and when he pronounced everything satisfactory
and rewarded the sweating stationmaster with his
envelope, the man smiled and bowed profusely. A

second young Serbian had detached himself from the engine and had walked down the train to meet them. 'We can leave anytime,' he said to Krajic.

'Would you care to share some lunch?' Andrianov offered. The chauffeur had packed a hamper in case there had been some delay.

'The faster we get away from here, the faster we can kill some Bulgarians.' Krajic laughed and the second boy joined in. The stationmaster beetled on ahead of them, anxious to be done with the entire thing.

'You seem to be adept at difficult tasks. You certainly are courageous,' Andrianov said to the two of them. The second one nearly blushed. Andrianov reached out and grasped the young man's shoulder. 'Give *Apis* my thanks for taking extra precautions.'

'It's only logical,' the boy said. 'There's value here.' He looked back along the train.

Andrianov smiled. 'Maybe I will need you in the future. Occasionally I need men who can do difficult things. I look for men who can keep sight of the future, I look for someone with heart. Such men are valuable. I may call on you for a favour at some time. I am expanding my business interests here, eh?'

The boy laughed. 'Business? That's for later, eh? We are both from the action cell, and when the Bulgarians finally come to their senses and surrender, then we'll hide these guns until we can turn them on the Austrians and regain Bosnia.'

They had stopped by the engine. 'I want you to know that you're performing a great service, helping to steal these guns,' Andrianov said. The two young men were already climbing into the engine compartment. The driver and fireman looked at him for a moment and then turned their faces away, frightened.

The first boy leaned out of the cabin. 'We don't need to eat lunch with you and we don't need your kid gloves and your patronizing, excellency. Just keep the guns coming. Go!' he said pushing the driver in the back, and then turned for a moment, still smiling.

'Here!' Andrianov called. He pulled out a sheaf of bills and held them up to the boy. There was the sharp screech of a whistle and the great driving wheels began to slowly roll along the track. The boys were looking away—maybe they hadn't heard him. Andrianov started walking along beside the engine. He suddenly felt a wave of admiration for the dirty young men, for their courage, and even for their foolish bravado. He had met them here on the battlefield and they were the real thing. 'Here!' he called out again, holding up the money. 'For the cause!' he called to them.

The boys turned and saw him stumbling along, the banknotes drifting out of his fingers. For a moment they watched him and then turned away laughing with their eyes set on the track ahead. Then they were past him and the sound of the engine faded and was replaced by the clanking of the wheels of the wagons as they rolled over the joins in the rails, gathering speed, turning northwest towards its ultimate destination in Serbia.

Andrianov looked around at the little station. The whole place was filthy and there was a sour reek from the toilets. Now that the guns were on their way to Serbia, he might as well get back to Bucharest.

Mattei, the chauffeur had come out of the little house. 'Do you want me to set out something, excellency? Or shall we continue to the city?'

He turned to the chauffeur. 'Let's drive for a while. This place is tiresome.'

He settled himself in the rear seat, undid the boots and laid them on the floor, sat there in his stockinged feet as the big car gathered speed. There was no traffic to speak of, only an occasional cart. The road was too bumpy for him to read or do any work. He opened the windows and stared out at the torn fields. Every few kilometres they would see someone. A collection of huts in various states of collapse along the road. The soldiers had stripped everything, the fields had been harvested early and then abandoned. The landscape was bleak. At Novi Pazar they had to pause to cross a hastily built dyke where the road had been repaired.

The car slowed for a crossroads further along and they stopped waiting for a ragtag parade of Rumanian infantry staggering along in the dust. They were the heroes of the war, having rushed down to attack Bulgaria from the rear, and now they controlled this entire region. They were victorious, but you would never know it; they were caked with dirt, some had lost their headgear, others wore bandages. The chauffeur sat there, the engine idling along while they waited. The soldiers looked up at them as they walked past, grumbling abuse and curses in their direction. They were led by an officer who rode a brindled nag and appeared to be falling asleep in the saddle. His men's curses woke him up and he looked up and then saw their car there, marvelled at it for a moment, tried to peer through the darkened glass, then touched his hand to his cap in salute.

The soldiers took only a quarter of an hour to file by. There was a gap where the fighters left off and the walking wounded began. They were escorted by a single mud-caked wagon drawn by four mules. From the back of the wagon Andrianov could see the bloody splints on the legs of men who couldn't walk projecting over the lip of the tailboard.

The chauffeur put the car in gear and they wove their way across the bumpy intersection between the groups, shifted up a gear and continued along the road to Bucharest.

Only a few kilometres further there was what passed for an inn. Here there was no destruction. They slowed down to look at it; only a dilapidated house, stables, and a brace of privies set against the edge of the road, with a single acacia casting some shade in the courtyard. Mattei looked around at him and shrugged, Andrianov motioned in the mirror, and they pulled over.

It had grown hot and he had taken off his jacket. Now he undid his cravat and opened his shirt. Across the road there was a burned-out building, some telegraph poles that had been uprooted and pushed down into the ditch. A tangled coil of wire.

He was stiff from sitting in the hot car and he walked up the road to loosen his legs. In the distance he glimpsed a figure, someone working in the fields. As he got closer he saw it was a woman. She was bent over, grasping handfuls of straw and severing them cleanly with a short type of sickle, more of a knife. She was working her way along a row and then she would stop and hoe in the stubble. She had been doing this all day judging from the expanse of turned earth around her.

The wind was warm and he could smell the rot of the soil. The sun had arced towards the west. Above him a single hawk wheeled in slow watchful circles.

He walked closer until she saw him, then he stopped and gave a little nod, smiled. She straightened from her cutting. He could see now that she was possessed of that particular kind of peasant beauty that was so rare; a young woman with her husband gone to the war, a widow perhaps. Tall with strong legs and full breasts that pressed against the fabric of her simple blouse.

The light was rosy and it brought out her colour. She was deeply bronzed from her labours in the fields, and her dark hair was streaked with amber highlights from the summer's light. To gather her hair she had tied it back with a simple kerchief of lime-green cloth, imprinted with some tiny pattern. Her eyes were clear and blue as she looked at him, a blank expression on her face. The way someone would behold an angel, or an apparition.

She held her hand up to her brow to shade her eyes, and there was a flash of white as she grimaced to make him out in the flare of the sunlight. Exquisite, he thought. Pure.

From behind him there was a rustling and he turned and saw a cackling old woman approaching from the adjacent field. She ran up to him as best as her bowed legs could carry her—toothless gums, muttering a stream of unintelligible commentary to him, bowing, stooping, and curtsying as she hobbled out of the ditch.

As she reached him she began to extend her hands, her fingers wanted to tug at his rolled-up sleeves, but then would draw back at the last moment, afraid to soil the fabric of his shirt.

The girl looked at him for a long moment, then bent and continued with her crops. He watched her a little longer, then searched in his waistcoat pocket, dug out the banknotes the Serbians had refused, peeled one off.

'Tell her to come with me,' he said, handing the note to the old crone. She grasped it by the corners and stared at it as if there were an important message written across its surface, then began rubbing it to see if it would simply fade away. After a moment she looked up at him and then back out to where the girl was working.

'Tell her.'

Andrianov started walking back towards the car. Mattei had spread out the basket on the bonnet, but he had already made up his mind; they would leave right away, he would feed the girl on the way to the city, have her cleaned up and dressed. Buy her something, something she could treasure always. He could afford to spend another day or two in the city.

Just as he reached the stables there was the sound of a motorcycle rattling down the road, and he turned to see a courier approaching, a little man in leather riding-clothes, holding out a telegram.

The cipher was based on a short sequence of numbers that repeated themselves backwards. It was a code he used for financial matters and would not hold up to a thorough analysis, but it was quick. He climbed in the back of the car and worked out the solution in minutes. Business called, the pull of money triumphed over everything. Money was fuel, money was blood. One day there would be time for goddesses in fields, but not today. He sighed, called Mattei to start the car, flung some coins at the courier.

Mattei gathered the hamper up and put it in the back seat so that he could eat as they drove along, then ran around to the front of the car to crank the engine. When it sputtered into life, he climbed back in, set the gears and they swerved out on to the bumpy road.

As they raced away they passed the old woman; she was standing there in the ditch, and as they went by she spat and cursed the girl who had thrown down her hoe to meet him.

SEVEN

When Ryzhkov came back to consciousness he'd not only forgotten all about the tooth, he'd even forgotten who he was. He stared at the white ceiling until fundamental concepts began to filter through: that is a lamp, that is a ceiling. That is a nurse hovering over me. I am Pyotr Mikhalovich Ryzhkov. I am an investigator with the secret political police. Where am I?

He had to ask to find out that he was in a ward of the Military Hospital, and that he had been asleep for nearly a week. He could only dimly remember clutching the arms of his dentist's chair, being forced to listen a lecture from Dr Tchery on oral hygiene. Though he must have seen much worse, Tchery had claimed to be horrified at the extent of the infection: Ryzhkov should have taken better care of himself, he should have come around more often, he should have . . .

It all faded out with a warning about the danger of contracting blood poisoning as the dentist extracted from a drawer a long hose on to which was screwed a green rubber gas mask. The man continued to scold him as he fitted the straps over Ryzhkov's swollen face, pinching hair, bringing tears, and then moved behind the chair out of sight.

Ryzhkov blinked the tears away and stared out of the little office window. He could just see the bell tower atop the Academy of Arts, the masts of ships moored in the Neva beyond . . .

'*Just take a few deep breaths,*' Tchery said from somewhere behind him.

. . . and across the water, the red brick façades of the New Admiralty buildings, where undoubtedly some young naval architect was drawing up plans for Russia's latest dreadnought . . . where the wargamers were devising new ways of controlling straits, isthmuses, estuaries, peninsulas, archipelagos . . .

'That's *good* . . .' the dentist had encouraged him from a long way away.

Beyond that, it was all a fog.

He got up and walked along the beds, to the high windows that fronted onto the embankment. Stood there, shakily, awed by the constant traffic on the river below him. Walked to the end of the ward, explored the corridor down to the balcony, stood there until his legs grew tired. Stared out through the windows until he was focusing on nothing, then retreated to his bed and looked out of the top of the windows at the indistinguishable white days and nights.

It seemed the world had gone on without him. Barges and schooners were busily steaming to and fro. On either side of the hospital were the great factories; names painted across their brick façades—*Nobel, Lessner, Phoenix, St Petersburg Copper, St Petersburg Metals, Andrianov-Parviaine*. Their names were so huge that you could even read them in the distance, where the Neva curved around the Petersburg islands. Boronovsky, Lessner II, Erikson—smoking, throbbing engines that were driving Russia's meteoric industrial progress. Twelve per cent per annum, someone had told him—the fastest in the world.

A doctor came by and looked him over, smiled with satisfaction.

'You've made progress,' the doctor smiled. 'More than satisfactory . . .'

After that they only let him stay one more night and then in the afternoon they sent an orderly around to help him get dressed and tell him that he was discharged. They gave him his possessions in a paper bag. The salter was still in his trouser pocket, but someone had emptied it. Once he had signed himself out the orderly walked him out to the tram stop, and left him there saying that now he could go back to being who he was supposed to be.

The way he said, it sounded like some kind of reward.

The building at 17 Pushkinskaya was one of several supposedly anonymous havens for agents and functionaries of the Internal branch. It was a drab three-storey trapezoid, occupying an unevenly sloping site in a corner by the Moika Canal, the courtyard pierced by three entrances through which agents could enter and leave with sufficient discretion. Ostensibly the ground-floor offices, set back from the street and barred by a gate that could be opened electrically from inside, were the headquarters of the *Volga Metals Assurance Company*.

In reality it sheltered the fiefdom of Chief Inspector Velimir Zezulin, Ryzhkov's superior, a tired man who could pass for a shabby tradesman, judging by his perpetually uncouth appearance and the sour smell of yesterday's vodka that enveloped him. He was rarely in, or if he was in, he was not to be disturbed.

Ryzhkov entered the courtyard through a narrow door off the embankment. There was a stable there, sheltered by a huge linden tree, beside it a shop where Muta and the other drivers spent their free time.

The front room of 17 Pushkinskaya was divided by a counter to separate the waiting-room from the office. There were glass cases with dusty fragments of minerals, a tiny model of a coal mine that lit up when you pressed certain buttons on a panel in front of it. Faded photographs of men standing in front of huge machines.

He had to show his disc to a new kid, a pimply-faced secretary that he'd never seen before. The boy checked his number, looked at his photograph, and smiled. Something that wouldn't last long, Ryzhkov thought.

'Oh, you're Inspector Ryzhkov!' The boy nearly clicked his heels and bowed, then came around and opened the gate for him. Something about the gesture Ryzhkov found irritating, the sort of kindness one showed to an old man, someone grown feeble. And then he was climbing the narrow stairway to the first floor, moving from the secular fantasy of the Volga Metals Assurance Company to the sacred realm of the Internal branch of the Tsar's secret political police.

The first floor was divided into a clutch of offices, open warrens really, that filled one side of a large room on the south side of the building. Tiny, stale little cubicles separated by glassed-in partitions and counters. Izachik, their secretary, jumped up from his chair when Ryzhkov entered.

While making a fuss with Ryzhkov's coat, he explained how External agents had raided a party given by the editors of the revolutionary newspaper Pravda. In the process several Internal informants had been arrested. It was all still being sorted out.

Konstantin Hokhodiev came in, right on Ryzhkov's heels, still sweating from the summer streets.

'Is he in?' Ryzhkov pointed to the stairway that led to Zezulin's sanctum. Izachik winced.

'Yes, but, ah . . . *sleeping*, I think.'

'Perhaps I could just . . .' He sidled past the two men towards the narrow stairway to Zezulin's garret-office. They both watched him go. At the top of the stairs he rapped against the door jamb. There was no reply. From inside he thought he could hear snoring. He eased the door open a crack and peered in. Zezulin was on the couch, a pillow flung over his face, mouth open, dead to the world; snoring like a man who was being choked to death.

The room was an archive, the place documents went to die. Piled all across the carpet were mounds of files. Each might represent a terrorist cell, a conspiracy, or a suspected assassination attempt. Propped on the end of the couch was a painted gypsy guitar. When Zezulin got drunk, he forgot where he was, then he would sing. It was pathetic.

Ryzhkov sighed and went back down the stairs. 'Well, since you're fully recovered and couldn't stay away from us, you may as well surround yourself with the mountains of paper work, eh?' Hokhodiev reached out with a huge paw and guided him down the narrow corridor towards the rear of the building.

At the back there was just enough space for one cubicle and a storeroom. The storeroom had been full since the days of Alexander II and the cubicle was Ryzhkov's 'office'. The room was less than ten feet square but it had a miniature desk, a cabinet for papers, a door for privacy, and—the real treasure—a single tall window that looked onto the courtyard. He stood there for a moment at the threshold and realised that he was actually glad to be facing another day in the tiny space. Inside it he could think, he could leave word that he was not to be disturbed, and, except for those occasions when Izachik thought it important, he wouldn't be.

'I'll bring you tea, sir, or would that be too hot?' Izachik cooed behind him.

'No, they said it would help the healing to drink it, so . . .'

'Excellent, sir.' Izachik bowed. 'You might be interested in the red folder, sir.'

'The red folder?'

'The one on the girl,' Izachik said and left.

When he turned back to his desk he saw that beneath the standard Okhrana files Izachik had brought in a red folder from the Military Hospital. When he untied the seal he discovered a 3rd Spasskaya District St Petersburg Police report and a two page copy of a morgue report on the cause of death of the girl who had fallen out of the apartment on Peplovskaya Street. *Lvova, Ekatarina*

The police report told him nothing. The morgue report stated that Dr V. Bondarenko had examined the body. He had estimated the girl's age as eleven or twelve. There was no address, names of relatives, or other details. The girl Lvova died from internal injuries due to falling from a third-storey window on the south side of a building at 34 Peplovskaya Street in the 3rd Spasskaya district. The time of death was approximately three forty-five in the morning of the eighteenth of June.

Behind the cover sheet was a diagram on thick yellow paper with the girl's name and file numbers. Across the stick figure Bondarenko had drawn slashes to indicate the fracture of the skull, the broken back . . . the blood. Nothing on the neck or throat.

There was a column of boxes on one side of the paper that indicated whether the death was due to natural causes, foul play, contagion, or other. In 'Other' Bondarenko had scrawled an S.

Suicide.

He leafed through the rest of the papers that had accumulated on his desk, then piled the ones he didn't need immediately on top of the cabinet by the window. He stood there for a moment watching the drivers hitch up a troika. The Okhrana had stables and garages all over the city. Somewhere in their collection could be found a sample of nearly every form of transportation. In their armoires Okhrana drivers had uniforms sufficient to impersonate cab drivers, tradesmen, or royal postillions. Their garages housed expensive lacquered motorcars side-by-side with undistinguished one-pony *izvolchiks*.

For a moment longer he watched the swirl of men and animals crawling about below him in the courtyard, then he picked up his telephone and got Izachik to have a carriage brought around.

'Yes, sir,' Izachik said, sounding a little puzzled as Ryzhkov gave him the destination.

'Just as soon as you can,' Ryzhkov said, and hung up.

Once again he found himself across the Neva, wandering through the maze of convalescent wards of the Military Hospital, this time heading downstairs to the morgue. Bondarenko was sitting at a desk in a corner of the room, filling in forms with a younger man, presumably his assistant. Ryzhkov took off his hat as he approached.

'Doctor?' Ryzhkov flashed his disc.

'Yes, one moment, please . . .' Bondarenko said, giving it a brief glance. An irritable man who obviously had little time for police officers, less for the political police.

The room was cold, dark. Low ceilings with stone arches that supported the upper floors of the hospital. The pillars had been whitewashed. It reminded Ryzhkov of the way they had painted the palm trees he had seen in the south of France. Something to do with killing the insects. There were footsteps and he turned to see the assistant vanish through the double-doors.

'Inspector?' Bondarenko stood, held out his hand and Ryzhkov shook it. 'Have we met?'

'Perhaps. I've been here on occasion.' He didn't elaborate.

'Well, then . . . What do you need?' Bondarenko said levelly; a tall man to whom a smile came rarely, a man who'd learned to wear a hard set to his chin. Flinty eyes behind the tiny gold-rimmed spectacles. Maybe he hated his life, too, Ryzhkov thought. Maybe he just wanted to get out of the chilly room. Bondarenko was wearing an acid-burned white coat to protect his waistcoat, and on top of that a thick sweater embroidered with the crest of St Petersburg University. The sleeves were stained from chemicals.

'I wanted to ask about this girl, Lvova.' He passed Bondarenko the envelope.

The doctor looked at it, sighed, gave the briefest shake of his head. 'I don't know what else we can do . . .' He crossed the room to one of the heavy porcelain tables, reached up and flicked on a bright light, smoothed the pages out on the spotless white surface. 'Ah, yes. Fall from a height, internal injuries, spinal injuries, fractured skull . . .' Bondarenko shrugged, frowned.

'And were there any cuts, or . . . ?'

'*Cuts?* You mean like a puncture from stabbing?'

'I was thinking of glass.'

Bondarenko looked at him for a second then back to the paper. 'Hmm . . .' he said and raised his eyebrows. 'There's nothing marked here, but that doesn't mean anything in particular.' He showed Ryzhkov the paper; there was an inked slash through the spine, another across the figure. Nothing on the arms.

'Now . . . to be honest, Inspector, there may have been cuts, or other fractures that were not marked, but nothing unusual. We received the girl, they told us she was a prostitute who had thrown herself off a roof. Tragic perhaps, but it was obvious what had happened, so I . . . I didn't test her stomach contents or anything dramatic. Besides, I thought we had taken care of all this.' Bondarenko looked helplessly around the dark room.

Ryzhkov stood there for a moment. 'Well, perhaps we have, but I'm only trying to make sure of the details.'

'Yes, of course. Discretion, yes, yes. That's all very clear.' Bondarenko was still staring around the room. Uncomfortable.

There was a noise. Behind them the assistant came in pulling a wheeled stretcher. There was something wrapped in a stained bedsheet resting on it. Something waiting for Ryzhkov to leave.

'So let me very clear,' Ryzhkov said. 'You saw nothing unusual at all. That would be your position if you were to be interviewed, or if you were expected to testify—'

Bondarenko looked around at him, suddenly shocked. 'Testify?'

'I'm only speculating, Doctor. If one day you might be asked, you could say truthfully that you saw nothing unusual, no cuts, no marks—'

'What kind of *marks*?'

'Bruises. Maybe from a rope, maybe just from—' Ryzhkov put his hands up around his own neck for a moment.

Bondarenko looked at him, his frown deepening. 'Absolutely no marks. As you can see in my report, there are no *marks* indicated, Inspector. Anyone who saw such marks may have been mistaken. Sometimes in the pressure of the moment—'

'Yes . . . the *pressure*, yes . . .'

'Besides she's in Volkovo Cemetery now with two or three others on top of her. I'm sure someone could get an order to disinter, but they wouldn't find anything.'

'Well . . . I want to thank you *again* for your discretion, Doctor,' Ryzhkov said quietly, unable to take his eyes off the assistant laboriously shifting a corpse on to the porcelain table next to them. It was a woman, grey hair come undone, her large body grown stiff in death. Bondarenko looked over for a moment, saw the assistant struggling, sighed again, stubbed his cigarette out, and moved to help the assistant shift the woman on to the table. Together they did it easily.

Bondarenko straightened and turned back to Ryzhkov. 'I'm sorry, we're short on staff here and, honestly, I've done everything I could, eh? But now if you'll excuse me, please?' Behind him the assistant was stropping a curved knife. It looked like the kind of tool you'd use to clean a fish.

'Yes, well . . . Thank you for your time, Doctor,' Ryzhkov said, and headed for the door so he would be out of there before they began their work.

EIGHT

Pyotr Ryzhkov spent the next week following Rasputin from whorehouses where his sexual appetites were indulged for free, to restaurants where they would tolerate his taking over the entire room and throwing his food on the floor, to mansions of the rich and addled where they submitted to his insults and religious instruction. When Ryzhkov wasn't standing outside in the rain waiting for the Holy One to surrender to boredom, he was seconded to the ongoing effort to prevent Socialist Revolutionary terrorists from blowing up the capital or shooting its leading dignitaries.

Zezulin, acting on information from Internal agents who were certain that they had discovered a cell of SR bombmakers, had assigned Dudenko and his watchers to conduct surveillance on a suspected 'explosives factory', a bakery. He, Ryzhkov and Hokhodiev supervised the surveillance in shifts; in addition they were expected to devise a strategy for an eventual raid on the premises.

He read through all the reports, Dima's carefully noted schedules. Apparently the bombers were well along with their work. Luckily for the Okhrana, when the plotters mixed their volatile chemicals the fumes became intoxicating, and they were forced to take frequent walks in the park. They were not thinking clearly at such times, they got lazy and were easy to see. Sometimes they would try to disguise their activities by acting casually, standing around with a lit cigarette they weren't smoking. A long stroll to a newspaper kiosk, trying to look like they were normal people leading a normal life. How many newspapers can you buy in one day?

The answer was right there in Dudenko's cramped handwriting—*seven*.

The neighbourhood was grouped around a filthy little plaza, an unplanned confluence of narrow uneven streets somewhere in the Narva district. There was a brick 'fountain' in the middle of the octagonal square. It had a pedestal at its centre and the remains of a bronze statue that had gone missing or had been melted down. It was crowded. During the day people came and went constantly, the traffic falling into patterns of astonishing regularity. All of it synchronized to the steam whistles of the gigantic factories that surrounded the district; the *Putilov* armaments buildings, the *Northern Boiler* works, and the *St Petersburg Freight Carriage* factories.

There were no vacant apartments for rent, whole families were packed into two rooms; children were everywhere, running through the street like packs of dogs. The kind of place that was busy all the time, but nothing ever changed. Except that for the last few days, teams of repairmen (all Dudenko's technicians) had been climbing the recently installed telephone poles. At night they'd rope off their wagon at the end of the street. Dudenko and his boys listened from inside the cart, taking it all down in shorthand.

Ryzhkov rode through the street a little after midnight, to all appearances just a drunk in a cab heading home, singing to himself as he admired the unfamiliar neighbourhood. There was nothing happening in the bakery. No lights. Nothing. Finally the plaza vanished behind him as his carriage clattered around a corner.

Taken as a whole it was exhausting work, and he'd fallen asleep in his tiny office, when there was a discreet cough, a quick rapping and Izachik popped his head in the door.

'Sir,' he said in a stage whisper, pointing one finger toward the ceiling. 'It appears that Christ has risen, and would like to confer with you.'

He nodded, took a moment to realize where exactly in the universe he was—this is my office, this is my window, those are the leaves falling from my linden . . . 'Yes, thank you,' he said softly to no one—Izachik had already left the doorway. He stood up, stretched the soreness from his joints, washed his mouth out with tea, straightened his clothing, rubbed his eyes, and headed upstairs.

'Ah, Pyotr Mikhalovich!' As Ryzhkov knocked on the door of his office, Zezulin was just coming out of the toilet, doing up the buttons on his trousers as he paced across the room in his socks. Ryzhkov was trying to think of an excuse to open a window.

'Good afternoon, sir.'

'I'm sure you will be as thankful as the rest of us that this terrorist activity is about to be tidied up, eh?'

'Yes, sir, I will.'

'Then we can get back to something resembling normality. Not that pursuing these misguided radicals isn't of value. Yes.' Zezulin smiled, patted his pockets trying to find something he'd lost, padded around behind his desk and started opening the drawers one at a time. He seemed comparatively alert and Ryzhkov decided that he might as well take the opportunity.

'I wanted to speak to you about the Lvova case, if there's a chance. I'm convinced that there is something more to it all, sir.'

'Lvova, Lvova . . .' Like Hokhodiev, Zezulin was a big man. Strong, with bushy dark hair and almost blond moustaches. He looked like a sleepy wolverine with a pair of spectacles. 'What's that again? Perk me up.'

'The girl that was . . . defenestrated in June. When I spoke to the police I got nothing—'

'Well, those cretins couldn't find their way out of a paper bag if it had two holes.'

'And as well, the mortuary report raised some questions. I thought that perhaps further investigation was needed. Blue Shirt was there, that night, after all. And someone is attempting to call it a suicide when it wasn't—'

'Certainly, Pyotr Mikhalovich. Absolutely. You have my complete trust. Circumspect. Diligent . . .' Zezulin had forgotten about the desk drawers and their contents. He was staring out through one of the little attic windows that overlooked the canal.

'Thank you then, sir. I'll start on the paperwork.' Zezulin continued his vigil. Ryzhkov might as well have been invisible. 'Well, then. Will there be anything, else, sir?'

'Well, there's always something else, isn't there!' Zezulin laughed at his own joke. 'So! Well, good to have

you back, Inspector. And keep me up to date on that . . .
on your . . . project. Sounds suspicious, to me. Don't
like it.'

'Yes, sir. Nor do I.'

'Good, good . . . whatever you need.' Zezulin gave
him a kind of salute, a spinning motion with his hand, a
cross between a wave goodbye and a Moorish salaam.

'Very good, sir.'

At the end of that same night Ryzhkov, Dudenko and
Hokhodiev treated themselves to a visit to the Egorov
baths. At five in the morning they almost had the place
to themselves. They passed a bottle of vodka back and
forth and talked. Ryzhkov told Hokhodiev about what
he had been doing: the Lvova reports, what Bondarenko
had said and the odd way he had said it. Hokhodiev just
listened and nodded. When it was all over he spat into
the drain and sat there for a long moment. 'Big people,'
he said and shook his head. 'Real aristocrats.'

'It's an expensive place, that whorehouse,' Ryzhkov
said.

'So, you don't know what to do now? That's not like
you. What do you care anyway?'

Ryzhkov looked at his friend for a moment,
shrugged. It was a good question. 'I don't know.
Someone killed her, Kostya. Someone is lying about it,
now someone is going to get away with it . . . with
doing something like that.' He shrugged again. What
did he care? It was hard to put into words.

'Fine, fine. You have a sense of justice, I know, even
if she was a whore. It's touching and it's why you have
so many friends in the police force, but do you really
think there's the slightest chance of getting to the
bottom of it? These big shots, they have resources,

brother . . .' Hokhodiev wagged a finger and even tried to laugh, but it didn't sound happy.

'Well, I guess I'll try to see if there are any witnesses, talk to the madam—but I thought I should tell you about it at least.'

'Look, I don't give a damn if you have to slip it through the cracks, I'll help you, brother, and he will too, won't you—' Kostya turned to elbow Dudenko, but stopped. 'Look at that,' he said. Dudenko lay sleeping on the narrow bench across from them, wrapped up in a sheet, his hands pressed down between his knees, snoring. 'A babe in the woods, a sheep waiting for the wolves . . .'

'. . . teacup in an earthquake . . .'

'. . . virgin in the barracks . . . God have mercy.' The big man turned and laughed quietly. 'And, of course, Dima's the only one who'll get out of this, you know that, don't you? He's young, intelligent, he has savoir faire . . . he has a future,' Hokhodiev said and raised the bottle to his lips. The vodka was warm and almost gone.

'Oh, yes . . . Smart, educated.'

'Oh, the boy's a genius. A fucking genius, with his little earphones and things that he can screw into your telephone set. Without ones like him they'd be shitting Bolshevik bombs in Peterhof, but does he get any credit, will it do him any good?' He looked up at Ryzhkov and winked.

'I doubt it.'

'Nothing. There's no loyalty any more. The three of us here in this room are loyal, the only loyal ones left. Protect the Tsar, protect the Tsarina, protect the grand dukes, the grand duchesses . . . on and on . . .' Hokhodiev closed his eyes for a few moments as if he were falling asleep, then his lids flickered. 'No one ever asks the question, if these people are so fucking holy why do they need so much protection in the first place, eh?'

'There's always someone trying to get to the top,' Ryzhkov muttered.

'Blue Shirt . . .' Hokhodiev said, coming out of his dream, then looked over at Ryzhkov as if he were surprised to be awake.

'Yes, I know, I know,' Ryzhkov said. 'We have to protect him, too.'

'And all of it is just to keep the rich ones getting richer and the powerful ones getting more powerful. But Russia . . . poor Russia, she's just a fucking house of cards and she's just going to cave in on herself. It's all sick, a goddamned pestilence.'

'It's Rasputin.'

'All of them, they're all sick. Rotten. Like a fish rots, from the head down. Dima . . .' Hokhodiev looked over at Dudenko and started laughing quietly. 'Poor fellow, to be coming along in a world like this.'

'He should do well, he seems to know a lot about the telephone system—' Ryzhkov had started laughing, too.

They talked about women. Ryzhkov's bad luck, about Filippa and her mother, how the disease of irrational femininity seemed to somehow get passed along from mother to daughter.

After a few moments of silence Hokhodiev leaned forward, elbows propped on thick knees, one hand stroking the wispy hair on the crown of his head, and told Ryzhkov that his wife was dying. His voice sounded thick. They had drunk too much. Far, far too much. '. . . and you know, Pyotr, it's not a moment too soon, if you ask me.'

'Is she in pain?' Ryzhkov finally said, his words coming slowly, one at a time; is—she—in—pain.

'Pain . . .' Hokhodiev said, thinking it over. 'Well, who isn't?'

'I mean . . .'

'In the mornings, yes. Pain.'

'Mmm.' Ryzhkov closed his eyes.

'Listen, Pyotr. You're not like me. You're different, you're smart. You still have, you still have . . .'

'Be quiet.'

'You look around us? You see these bastards, these fucking cabinet ministers and their grandiose . . . fiefdoms? It doesn't matter about the Tsar. We have no Tsar. It's not Nicholas, it's fucking Alexandra that's running everything.'

'Kostya, Kostya—'

'And you see that poor little boy in his uniform . . . and they get Blue Shirt to pray for him and think that's going to make the difference? Where are the damn patriots, that's what I mean.'

'They're all patriots, just ask them.'

'Oh, I know . . . patriots are the worst, it's so cheap. The patriots and the fucking Church. You poke around the Narva district for awhile. Are there any blessings, any blessings at all?' He trailed off for a moment. 'That's what's killing Lena. It's all this shit around us, the impossibility of ever, of ever . . . getting out, or growing, or anything.' They had no children, Ryzhkov remembered. No, that was wrong. They had had one child. Died from typhoid fever before Ryzhkov had met him. 'And when they do finally look up, when they see how these fools, fucking Blue Shirt, and the fucking Tsarina who will give him any damn thing if he just lets her suck his cock—'

'Hey, hey . . .' Ryzhkov said gently to quieten him down. They had their own room, but the walls were thin.

'. . . And then there's your day of reckoning, right there, your Armageddon, and your fucking Sodom and Gomorrah turning into salt. You free all the damn serfs and they don't know any better. They pile into the city, heading for the bright lights, work themselves to death in some factory and they think that's heaven on earth. They just want money like anyone else. And when they wake up, you know who they'll blame? Who they'll be stoning to death in the damn square, when the whole pile of shit goes down the shitter? It won't be the damn Tsar, he'll be on his yacht, safe and sound, heading for some spa—'

'Hey, Kostya—'

'No, brother, it'll be *us* that'll be dragged through the streets. *Us*, that's who.'

Ryzhkov reached out and poured out the last inch of vodka on to the floor.

'You think I'm drunk,' Hokhodiev said, an expression somewhere between a smile and a grimace.

'Well . . . maybe just a little—' The bottle suddenly slipped from his fingers and he reflexively swiped at it and, only by chance, managed to knock it up on to the bench where it spun around harmlessly. Dudenko woke up with a jerk and looked around with a horrified expression. They both found the spasm funny, laughed and leaned back against the wall.

'You two are drunk,' Dudenko said dully.

'I am drunk,' Hokhodiev said quietly. 'But that doesn't mean I don't know whereof I speak, eh? Remember the words of your friend, the prophet.'

'All right, I will.'

'They're coming to get . . . *us* . . .'

'If we don't get them first,' he said.

'Yes. That's right. So, yes, brother. Them first. I will

help you,' Kostya said and put a hand on his shoulder. The weight of his arm felt like a log. 'I'll help you right now. And you will too, won't you Dima?'

Dudenko looked up from the floor and blinked his eyes. Without his glasses he was blind. 'What?' he asked, not having been listening. 'What? Whatever it is, yes,' he said. And then he laughed.

Exhausted, drained, and dizzy from the heat of the baths, they dressed, paid their bill, and climbed out into the yellow dawn. Stood like dimwitted beasts on the embankment, blinking and looking around for a cab. 'I think it's time to go home,' Hokhodiev said.

'Yes . . .' Ryzhkov muttered, suddenly bone-tired, staggering out on to the cobbles in the direction of the Obvodni.

'Goodnight,' he said to his friends, to the shining waters in the canal, to the impassive façades with their metalled roofs. Goodnight to the gleaming spire of the Admiralty, goodnight to the morning sun.

Only a few groggy hours later, supposedly the *start* of a new week, Izachik slipped another thin envelope across his desk. 'Here are more of the papers you requested, sir . . .'

Inside Ryzhkov found a one-page carbon-copied list of the owners of the Apollo Bindery at 34 Peplovskaya. According to the police, the Apollo Bindery had long since gone out of business; the building itself was owned by a private property trust, and on the date of the girl's defenestration the lessee had been a Monsieur T.N. Hynninen, a Finnish speculator who lived in Helsingfors. Nothing new.

Ryzhkov turned over the single page but there was nothing else. He looked more closely at the list—

investors in the numbered property consortium, twenty-four partners, all of them anonymous, sheltered behind numbered titles.

He slipped the thin sheet of nearly transparent onion-skin paper back into the envelope and filed it together with the police statement and Bondarenko's cause-of-death report. Tried not to look at the little human diagram with the wounds inked on it as he put all of it in his bottom drawer. Now, he thought, all that was left of Lvova, Ekatarina was resting undisturbed inside a green Okhrana folder, like everything else that was wrong with the world.

Another *little tail-twister* vanished? What did it matter? Some marks, some bloodstains that had spread in strange patterns, some loose ends, some details that didn't fit . . . What did he think he could do about it? Dig her up? Call in a few dozen of Petersburg's richest and most prominent men for some discussions about exactly what they had been doing and to whom?

He rubbed his hand across his forehead. He was tired, trying to do too much, too fast. He was hot, feverish perhaps. Coming down with something.

The girl was dead and someone in the Okhrana was protecting the killer, or had at least taken steps to ensure that Bondarenko would sanitize his statement. Things like that didn't just happen by coincidence, there had to be a reason for it. Rasputin?

What if he had done it? The girl had been thrown out of an upstairs window at the corner of the lane. It could have only been reached by a hallway, via a staircase. Did the building have a lift? And if Rasputin had done it, how would he have made it back downstairs to the table so quickly? Perhaps he should get inside the building . . . run up and down the stairs with a stopwatch in hand.

Certainly he should pursue the case—what if Rasputin had done it and someone was attempting to blackmail him?

Was such a thing plausible? Rasputin was untouchable, wasn't he? And the girl wasn't going to come back just because he got soft and went on some idiot's crusade. Never trust someone with an axe to grind, never trust a priest. Never trust anyone with ideals . . . with illusions, he told himself over and over again. Actually chanting the words under his breath '. . . Realism . . . realism . . . realism . . .'

But maybe Rasputin had done it after all . . .

Murder, he heard a woman scream.

NINE

'Go to sleep,' Larissa had said. 'It was just an accident, Vera . . . go to sleep now,' she'd said.

And she had. Even though it was a lie; it hadn't been an accident. No. Not an accident at all.

'Go to sleep, Vera . . . it wasn't your fault, it's over now.'

Vera, Larissa, and another girl had slept on the stage in the back room that first night after the . . . accident. Passing out from too much konyak and exhausted from fending everyone off. When they woke up the other girl was gone.

The owner was called Izov. He had got angry when he realized they were too distraught to provide him with any fun. Well, they certainly didn't have to give anything away, but he had made his understanding clear. There was going to have to be some kind of payment. He left them with a last warning that it was a cabaret, not a flophouse, no matter how many people were sleeping on the floor. Not long after that he came back and fed them, grousing about the expense. Vera drank her kvass and decided that probably it was only Larissa's smile and her smoky laugh that got them breakfast.

The club was really two shops joined into one. At one point it had been a dressmaker's, and after that, judging from the long glass counter and the greasy floors in the back room, it had served as a butcher's shop. Izov had broken through the walls and converted the bottom floor into a bistro which he named *Komet* after the famous shooting star. The 'restaurant' was outfitted with tables and chairs, the other had a stage at one end enabling Izov to extract a little more money from his customers by providing 'entertainment' to go along with the 'food'.

Izov went out for a while and the piano-player, the one they called the Professor, came over and served the customers. He talked continuously while he ladled out the soup and took their kopeks, asking her all sorts of questions about her background. Later that evening they tried to rope her into a rehearsal. Mostly it was loud argument, shouting, and strange musical clashings. She'd fallen asleep when the 'director', Khulchaev, a tall boy with a sharp dark beard and a smirk, woke her up to make them all tea. As if she were his servant.

She hadn't even got on her feet and he started straight in, 'Hey, these are the whores, right?' loudly enough for the whole room to hear him. He liked to do things loudly, she saw.

She turned away, but he reached out and pulled her around. 'Hey, don't run off, I'm going to use you,' he said to her quietly.

'Anyway,' Larissa piped, 'We're not, we're dancers.' All the men laughed. Vera tried to scratch him in the face and he let her go quickly.

'No . . .' Vera heard the Professor say behind them. 'No, Dmitri, I think they have the correct temperament for dancers.' All of them laughing.

And hiding in the lavatory and breaking down into long silent sobs, that she hid even from Larissa. 'Don't worry,' Larissa saying as she paced outside the stall. 'Don't worry, he just wants to fuck you and can't get it up. Don't worry . . .'

When she finally came out of there, with no alternative to having to walk all the way around the stage to get out, Khulchaev started in on her again.

'Here!' he whistled at her, 'Here, we really do need a dancer. Hey, Dancer, come on here—' She just kept going. They could all go fuck themselves. 'Well, I guess she's a whore after all then,' he said as she was halfway through the door.

And even when she whirled and walked back into the room and slapped him, they all laughed.

But by the end of the week she was on stage.

And by the end of the month, sitting before the mirror, listening to Larissa and Gloriana warming up in the hallway, observing herself in the reflection, she knew she was never going to sell it again. All that was gone now. She had turned a corner in her life on to an entirely new boulevard.

Her face was powdered white like a Japanese mask. She'd even smoothed her eyebrows with soap and covered them with greasepaint so that she looked like a marble bust of herself. Her terrible hair had been chopped off in angled bangs, which was just fine, she'd hated it anyway. Now, no one would recognize her. In only one week, she'd transformed completely and forever. She was a new human, an adventure unwrit. An innocent girl in a mirror.

And then the Professor poked his head around the door and said it was time to go on.

She moved through the performance playing the part of a kind of Aztec war god crossed with an Oriental nightmare. Her costume was painted with garish colours and bizarre geometric polka dots. It wasn't real dancing, of course. All she had to do was gesture and turn and watch the fabric move about her in the lights. There was a chorus of voices that chanted between the ringing bells:

'Omicron . . . Epsilon . . . Pi . . . Sigma . . .'

With each crash Vera would tremble and react to a different invisible point in space. It was easy enough, and she had been told to 'put her energy into it', so she did. After her 'dance' she was summoned by one of the Goddesses of the Seven Winds. Her ornate feathered head-dress was taken from her and a mathematical symbol was branded across her forehead—an 8 laid over on its side. Finally, when the last of the Aztec gods was destroyed by a hurricane of ribbons, there was applause, and for a moment Vera was disoriented—sweating through the make-up, all out of breath—a little lost before she came back into her new self. Applause! She bowed, smiling, with the mark of infinity across her brow.

Afterwards there was food, and she found herself crowding to the table and stuffing herself with cakes and caviar. A man came and stood beside her, saying something over the din about how much he had enjoyed her performance. She nodded and kept on eating, and a few minutes later he was there again, the only well-dressed patron in the room, holding out a rhumki he had bought for her.

'Thank you!' she shouted and then tossed the drink back quickly, and headed away from him before he could get started on selling himself.

In the corner Dmitri Khulchaev was shouting at the man from *New Art*, a young writer with bright blond curls he'd waxed down in ringlets all around his forehead in a style that he must have thought was attractive. The atmosphere in the club was intense, as if the performance had just been a fuse for the party to come afterwards.

She was alive now after the drinks. Thrilled by the performance, but relieved that it was over, she floated through the crowd, smiling at all the audience who'd stayed behind, embracing all her new friends. She had no old ones, not any more. She saw the Professor across the room, drunk and laughing himself into a coughing fit, and on impulse she went over and kissed him.

'You!' he nearly coughed in her face. 'You are very . . . very . . . You!' And then quickly she kissed him again and laughed, bouncing away before she gave him a heart attack.

Khulchaev caught her by the arm, pressed himself right up against her, held a bottle of champagne to her lips and made her drink until she nearly choked. And then he was kissing her—a quick hard insertion of his tongue—and gone almost as quickly. And she stood there, reeling in the smoky room.

At some point she realized that she was drunk, really drunk. Too drunk, and she developed a plan, a very detailed plan to make her way to the back door and into the alley and vomit somewhere where no one could see her. It was a good plan, and she began to put it into motion. Putting one foot in front of another and heading for the back.

Then she found herself on her hands and knees in the alley, coughing and wiping her face on her sleeve, slipping as she struggled to her feet, bracing herself against the masonry wall while she caught her breath. There was a hissing sound as Tika, the cat, ran beneath her feet and she looked wildly around and nearly fell into the wet mud.

It was cool out in the alley and the air was refreshing, penetrating her bones, and driving the poison out. She would never drink again, never, never, never she told herself, and she tried to feel her way along towards the door.

She didn't see the man at first, and then she stopped, because she thought he was urinating and she'd surprised him, but he held the door for her and she recognized him as the same man as before. The one who'd bought her the drink, the one with the sad eyes.

The torrent of noise crashed out of the doorway, the roar of artists arguing and debating minutiae that no one would ever understand. There was a screamed announcement about the next performance, some wild idea Khulchaev had cooked up—a mock trial of all the oppressors; for the enslavement of artists and smothering of new ideas, for the strangulation of imagination and the censorship of newspapers, the necrophilia of history, the vampirism of peasant culture . . . A trial against the Crime of Blindness. With each item in the indictment they were screaming, laughing, cheering.

The man with the sad eyes was still holding the door open for her, why? Waiting for her to make up her mind? Pretending to be a gentleman? She let her eyes slide over to him. His face seemed to float lazily in front of her. She tried to focus.

'I saw you before,' he said quietly.

'Oh? That's right . . .' Like all the rest, she thought. Did he expect her to thank him for the cheap drink that had started the whole thing off? She leaned against the frame of the doorway and tried to make her feet work.

'No, I've seen you, before tonight, I mean . . .' His voice had a tone of urgency; soon he'd be whining about his wife not understanding him. Maybe he had been a customer back in her old life, someone who'd paid his money and fallen in love. Another fool. Trying to get away she managed to take one step into the corridor. Inside they were all singing now, one of the songs in the show . . .

So what! It doesn't matter,
So what! I just don't care, So what . . .

On and on, people stamping the time on the floor.

She wanted to go back and find Dmitri, maybe he'd be nice for a change, maybe he was tired of laughing at her. They were all waiting to see who she was going to start sleeping with. They'd even applauded when he kissed her and left her spinning around there on the dance floor. So, maybe it looked like it was going to be Dmitri. So what . . . So, maybe that was how he said 'I love you', by insulting her all the time.

The man was explaining that he had never really seen anything like the theatre they'd produced this evening, it was different, he said. Unusual. He needed to talk to her, to have a conversation. Now was not the time, but perhaps in the morning?

She laughed, spun around in the alley looking for escape. But the only other person in the alley was him— smiling his droopy smile, helping her back down the corridor where she could rejoin the party, if that's what she wanted? Or perhaps she would enjoy some coffee right now?

> . . . *the consequence, the consequence,*
> . . . *the consequence of No–thing!*

Oh, yes, join the party. And she let herself sing with the others the last phrases of the Professor's anthem, raising her fist into the air at the end for the three cheers. She threw her head back with the last triumphant chorus, and found herself looking up, following the upraised arms and staring up at the patterns pressed into the metal ceiling . . .

And all of a sudden it was as if she, Vera Aliyeva, was the only person that could see, really see. It had come to her all in a haze, dreamily, but truly she could see the future, see it all speeded up, see Izov's old building crumbling, the Komet beginning to collapse all around them. She saw it in sudden images as if she were running through a gallery of hideous paintings—the collapse of the world spreading out, like a ripple in a still lake, wider, wider, wider.

Perhaps the vision was the result of a curse. Perhaps they had mocked the ancient Aztec gods during tonight's performance, and in revenge been issued an apocalyptic challenge. Perhaps a great wave was about to smash down upon them and drive them into oblivion; the Komet, her, Dmitri, the whole city, everything . . . Everything.

Oh, how far she'd come in this, the find chapter of her life on Earth! She stood in the corridor hanging on to the sad man's arm as the world disintegrated around them.

She woke late in the morning, the thunder of carriages rumbling along the embankment nudging her out of sleep. She was in a soft, wide bed . . . the heavy coverings. Ah, yes . . . She remembered.

She wrenched herself upright and swung herself to the edge of the mattress for a moment, got up and shuffled out of the bedroom—everything heavily furnished in an oriental motif, with Persian rugs hung from the walls, a lot of plants that needed watering. Yes . . . yes . . . what was his name?

His place was on the second floor and the parquet was warm from the heat of the flats below. Everything was dusty, she could feel the little pieces of dirt under her feet. Everything needed to be cleaned. The apartment looked like it needed a good shaking out.

She discovered him in the kitchen. There was a little balcony there and he was dressed, sitting in the doorway smoking and reading a copy of *Gazette*.

'If you want tea, it's on the stove,' he said without looking up.

'Yes, good,' she said, making her voice flat. She groped for the glasses and poured herself a tall glass of tea as quietly as she could.

'When you're dressed and awake I need to talk to you.'

'Um . . . I have a real *katzenjammer* . . .' She put her hand up to her forehead.

'Whenever you're ready,' he said and turned a page of the paper. She took the tea and walked back out into his front rooms without answering.

She didn't think he'd touched her during the night. Maybe he was too drunk, maybe he was scared, maybe he wanted to make love to someone who was awake. She found his writing desk and, tucked under a stack of mail, the solitary portrait of the woman. The wife, he'd admitted. Gone, he'd told her. So he was married, then. From the envelopes tucked into his blotter she learned his name—Ryzhkov. Yes, she remembered now. Pyotr, spelled the old way. She went to the lavatory and sat on the cold seat and shivered while she had a morning pee. Inspected herself in his mirror. No. He hadn't touched her.

She went back out to his sitting-room, and stood in the sunny window, rested her head against the glass and stared out at the misty Obvodni Canal below her. To the south were the working-class neighbourhoods—long identical rows of wooden houses. In the distance to the west was the cluster of smokestacks from the Putilov works. She could see the shining threads of the rails at the Tsarskoye Selo Station.

She could get enough money to leave, she thought. She could go away. Maybe the sad man would lend her the money. Italy, she thought. Somewhere warm. Somewhere where there were flowers in March instead of chunks of ice floating down the river. She could dance there in Rome, or act, or become a governess, teach Russian. Or she'd meet someone who made her laugh, someone who was a real gentleman.

'All right, why don't you sit down and talk to me for a while.' She whirled at the sound of his voice. He came in and took a pad and pencil off the desk, moved to the sofa and waited for her.

'Let's start with the basics. Your name?'

'What are you, police?'

'Kind of a policeman. I wanted to talk to you about the girl that fell out the window that night.'

She looked at him for a long moment while she went cold inside. 'Aliyeva, Vera Evgeniya,' she said angrily. 'I don't want to talk about any of that, there's nothing to talk about anyway.'

'Look, you're going to talk to me one way or the other, let's be clear about that from the start, eh? Now, what did you see?'

'No, I'm not. Go to hell—' she started to walk out, but he grabbed her wrist and spun her back into the kitchen. She hit her elbow on the counter and it hurt.

'Calm down. Do what I tell you or I'll telephone my friends and they'll pull your yellow card and you'll be waiting in jail until they throw you on a riverboat back to wherever you came from, understand?' He was standing there, close. Blocking her off in the corner of the kitchen. 'I can do whatever I want with you,' he said; his voice was low, almost a whisper. 'For now you're mine and you're going to cooperate and give me an answer for everything I ask. The quicker you get that through your head, the easier we'll get along. Now . . . tell me about how she died.'

'I don't want to talk about that . . .'

'You were screaming in the street about it.'

'I hate you people.' She had started to cry now, all of it his fault, and she flung the glass at him—it glanced off his elbow and spun across the floor.

'I heard you. You were screaming about murder,' he said. 'What did you see? Did you see anyone you recognized? Did you know Rasputin was there? Did you see him?'

'No . . . no.' She almost laughed.

'Were you acquainted with the girl?' he said quietly.

'I had met her before. There are always girls around . . . Katya was one of them.' She took a deep breath and wiped her eyes.

'Do you know who did it?' He was looking at her fixedly. He wasn't going to stop with his questions. It was as if she had run into a wall, an immovable, logical wall that was too high to climb, to wide to go around. He kept staring, a serious priest demanding a confession. She didn't have to tell him everything. Just enough to get rid of him. Give him something to make him happy, then he'd leave her alone. Like all men.

'There were two of them,' she said finally in a voice like a bedtime story. 'A little one—shorter, younger, and with a pointed nose like a mouse, and the old one . . . the one who did it.'

'Good, Vera. Go and get some more tea if you want,' he said.

'I don't want your tea, I want to leave.'

'Tell me what happened. If I like the sound of it, maybe you can go.'

'I don't know anything. I suppose it was some kind of party, some kind of special party. It was a celebration of something, an anniversary? Some kind of party in the old man's honour. Both of them were wearing funny little hats. They had a room all to themselves for a while. We weren't allowed to watch that part. No girls allowed, I guess they were shy.'

'How many?'

'Maybe a dozen at a big party at the beginning. Then they came and went, I don't know. Then we were supposed to come in and entertain them. Some of them weren't so bad. Some of them were nice. They're afraid at first. They want to talk to you, some of them. Sometimes one of them might think they've fallen in love with you.' She turned her face from the window, let her gaze fall on Ryzhkov for a long moment. Was he a fool, too? No reason to think otherwise. Being a policeman didn't give him some special immunity. She'd never met a man who wasn't a fool one way or another.

'Then what?' He held out a cigarette for her. A reward? After a moment she gave in and took it.

'After they'd all gone off to the other rooms then it

was time for us to go with the short one and his guest of honour.'

'The old one?'

She nodded. 'They had wanted a show, so Larissa and I were doing our act and in the middle of it they brought Katya in. You could see the old one perk right up then. A little while later they took her with them.' She suddenly shifted in the seat, rocked forwards. 'I don't know his name or why he was so important, who he was . . .'

'Just tell me what happened. Now you were in another room?'

'There's a hallway, and I heard the screaming when Larissa and I were going to the men in the next room. We had been drinking, of course. Champagne, champagne and more champagne . . . And I could hear this argument. Two men yelling at each other at the end of the hall, and Larissa stopped and looked at me and I thought, that . . . maybe if I went in there, maybe I could say that I just made a mistake. I don't know, I was thinking that maybe just having some other girl, an older girl come in there would be a way of making him stop but . . .'

Vera was staring at the nothingness in front of her. He let her gather herself, take her time.

'The first thing . . . The first thing I saw was the short one, he was carrying her in his arms. The old man was screaming at him, promising that he would do anything. He was on his knees, this angry old man. So old, so fat, with his white whiskers, and little thin white legs that could hardly hold him up. They must have given him something, a powder or an injection, something to make him strong. He was enraged, like a bull. Red, sweating, talking nonsense. The small man was laughing at him.

When he saw us he told us to leave, and ran into a different room. Then . . . some others from the party came into the hallway and tried to get us to leave, and that was when I heard the glass breaking.'

'All right, Vera.'

'You can tell, sometimes. The ones like that, they're different. If you look close, you can see it. I should have seen it.' She gave a sudden bitter laugh. 'They were treating him like a fucking god. He was someone's special friend. And she was so little, and he wanted to . . . It makes it better supposedly, everybody always wants to make it better.'

'Who else did you see?'

She shook her head. 'No one. The others came and took the old man away, kicked us out.'

'Could you recognize these men? I need to get names for all of them. Will you help me?' He half-expected her to break down again, but she didn't. She just fell silent for a long minute, the cigarette burned down so much now that he reached out and pried it from her fingers. 'The police are saying it was suicide, did you know?' he said. 'They say she wanted to fly.'

'I don't want to hear any bullshit. You really think she killed herself because she was a whore? She'd been doing what she did for years! She didn't suddenly realize she was in a degrading, disgusting profession, and just because she was wallowing in sin that she had to end it all.'

'All right, fine . . .'

'She was dead the moment she walked in that room! She was his gift, a sacrifice! Then while he was using his pretend cock on her, he was strangling her—that's the kind of shit they dream up.' She shook herself, trying to lose her anger. It didn't work. 'It wasn't a suicide! Christ . . .'

He looked down. She had been squeezing his hand, so hard he could feel the nails biting into the flesh of his thumb.

'His friend knew it was going to happen. He was laughing the whole time. He knew the old one's dream—some men have that fantasy, you see? That the spasms of death are . . . are . . .' Her face twisted up and she began to cry, for real this time.

Finally she stalked off to his bathroom; he could hear the water running, Vera blowing her nose once, twice. When she returned she was red-faced, clear-eyed. Done now with all that, the whole thing put away somewhere safe.

He took a deep breath, not wanting to ask, then did it quickly. 'If we looked at photographs, do you think you could identify any of them?' Nothing for a long moment, just her hard look.

'If you make me I suppose I have no choice, do I?' So many questions, she was thinking. Names she was supposed to come up with, just a few questions he wanted her to answer. 'And it's dangerous, too, I suppose? Yes? It's dangerous and if I go along and you let my name slip out, what do you think will happen to me? Nothing good, that's the real situation, yes?'

'I'll try and keep you out of it, if I can.'

'If . . .'

'If I can.'

She made a little sound, partly a laugh, partly a sob. One tear escaped from her eye and she wiped it away, her mouth got hard. She'd made up her mind not to cry any more. 'I've got a rehearsal to go to. Can I go? Do you think you're finished now?'

'For now, yes . . . What time is your rehearsal over?'

'Four,' she said quietly, without looking at him.

'I'll come by for you later, then.' She looked up, angrily. 'You and I have a date,' he said.

'Oh?'

'We're going to your friend's place, have a look around.'

'Wait a minute, you're serious?'

'Why not?'

'All those places are members only, you can't just walk in off the street.'

'But *you* can,' he said levelly.

'Christ,' she turned away. 'Irini, she hates me now. She stole all my clothing. She's not going to let me back there. You're insane,' she said, her voice alternately hissing and spitting her words.

'She'll let us in. I have the money, and you need to get back in her good graces. That's the way we'll play it.'

'Go to hell, I'm not looking to die for some lunatic proposal. I don't associate with . . . liars, with spies.' She still had traces of her theatre make-up ringing her eyes, an angry slash of lipstick barely wiped from her mouth.

'Just tell her you're sorry, you were drunk, you'll never do it again . . .'

'I don't care who you are—*Get away* . . .' she hissed, and slapped him hard across the cheek. It stung his face but must have hurt her too, she'd hit him so hard. 'You're a vulture . . . you're worse than that. You're a *rodent*—'

'Get all dressed up for a good time,' he said coldly. 'I'll wait for you out front. If anybody asks you can tell them I'm a commercial traveller.'

'Oh, that's plausible. And what exactly do you sell on your travels that brings you to the Komet?'

'Paintbrushes. I'm interested in art. The way they paint those big curtains.'

'You mean the scenery?'

'That's it. The scenery. It'll do for now,' he said.

She slipped on her shoes and headed for the door. 'Big policeman. Big ideas. Do you really think you can do anything about any of this?' she asked without turning around.

'I don't know, I doubt it. Probably not. But I'll try.'

'Yes, well . . .' and then she gave a little nod and walked out of his door.

TEN

Evdaev smiled as he gazed at little Pippa, only nineteen, and as a bride she had never been more beautiful. Blessed with porcelain skin, meaning that you could see the blue blood beneath the glaze; blessed, too, with masses of chestnut hair that in the summer was suffused with red, a strong brow and clear amber-coloured eyes that gave her a dreamy, seductive look. She was a little taller than Miki, her betrothed—Michael Pavlovich Evdaev, his late brother's youngest. Only his boots raised him to her height. Nestor, as guardian, had watched over the boy's youth, eased his rise through the ranks with some satisfaction.

Standing a pace behind the nervous pair were four young officer friends of Miki's, also members of the venerable Preobrazhensky Guards. Each pair took turns holding the heavy crowns above the heads of the couple while the priest droned on. No young man wanted to show how much effort it took to hold the crowns, but it was equally gauche to display your strength until your arm began to tremble. Evdaev was pleased to see that, if only as a mark of respect for him, the young officers did not hesitate to trade the crowns smoothly, seamlessly.

They were gathered, of course, in the great Transfiguration Cathedral, a mass of candle-lit scarlet and gold, a little chilly owing to the sudden cold spell that had descended upon the city. The building had been suitably designed in the Russian style, and was the dedicated cathedral of the guards, of which Prince Evdaev was an honorary member. He had celebrated his betrothal in this same chamber, and out of respect he was dressed in the regimental colours, scarlet with all the gold trimmings.

Little Pippa had been one of those girls on the horizon, a lovely creature that any man would like to snap up. And had it not been for the strict and morally severe education that her mother, Countess Gorchakova, had forced on the girl it would be all too easy to imagine her being betrothed to a much less worthy mate than Michael, but the arrangements had been made, dowry agreed upon, and now two great houses had come together again—for both could trace their lineage to the ancient Rurik dynasty, two great families intertwined like vines as they flourished in the sunlight of history.

The blessed ones drank from the cup three times, their wrists were bound together by a silken handkerchief, they followed the priest around the altar three times to illustrate that they would be bound together for the long journey through life. Behind Pippa the pages scurried along untangling her train, causing the couple to proceed along the journey of life in fits and starts. Everyone knew what a trial it was, there were little sighs, titters of under-standing. Even the priest could forgive, pausing with a benign smile while the boys crawled about.

And then, finally the union was solemnized and there was the disorganized rush to the great doors of the cathedral, a buzz of congratulations, the wiping away of tears of joy, a hundred different conversations, greetings exchanged between relations, friends, and strangers, the push, shove, and relinquishing of places by the stairs. Among the various guests who leaned through the crowd to congratulate him was the stunning figure of Anya Serepova, a relation of the Gorchakovs. The delightful Anya brushed her lips against his cheek, murmured in his ear that they were 'cousins' now and shouldn't they take the opportunity to become closer friends? He squeezed her hand as she backed away. One little look, a promise? A fine-looking woman, not yet forty.

He realized that when . . . the Plan . . . was finally complete that he would have to reign with Liliana, his wife. It was an absurd picture. Lily as Tsarina?

Of course, he had confided nothing to her. They rarely talked. Lily was a dutiful, barren creature who preferred to spend her time in Soroki on their Bessarabian estate. It was warm there and she fancied herself an agricultur-alist, continually pottering in her experimental green-houses and forcing beds. And Soroki on the Driester was a healthful place, much better than the fetid air of Piter in summer. He would have to tell her sometime, he supposed, for when he was Tsar they would be required to spend a significant amount of time in the city. There would be a constant round of ceremonial functions, particularly in the beginning of their reign.

He and Sergei had discussed this transitional strategy and after each session he was more impressed with the immensity of their task. It was not just a matter of bribing guards and sneaking down palace hallways. In some fundamental way they were striking a blow at the very soul of Russia, for the Romanov name was sacred, the family had ruled absolutely for three centuries. To overturn such a tradition was no simple snap of the fingers. Peasants, the merchant class, not to mention the nobility—everyone would have to be brought along slowly. There were . . . nuances, superstitions, traditions which in themselves mean nothing but must be respected and dealt with. Thank God that Sergei was well aware of this aspect of the Plan and had been shown to be sensitive to the deeper ramifications. Gulka didn't see it at all. If things were left to him everything would be managed with a knife, a bullet, or a knotted handkerchief.

Honestly, Evdaev didn't like to think about it, it was too complicated. He was a warrior, conditioned to fight, to attack, to win great victories, not to administrate. Administration was a job for beetles in tailcoats, and there was no shortage of them. The city was choked with administrators, clerks, agents, factors and petty officials. All supervised by Andrianov and other men of his ilk, men who enjoyed organizing industrial combines, managing ledgers, bookkeepers and banking houses. None of it was a fit task for a warrior Tsar. He sighed. Only God could truly decide, he thought, driving the troublesome ideas from his mind. Yes, the Hand of God would reach out and direct his steps resolutely towards the throne, therefore wouldn't the Hand of God guide Lily too?

There was a commotion at the top of the stairs beneath the monstrous columns that fronted the cathedral; cheers and witticisms shouted out towards the pair, just now reaching the top of the stairs. A squad of Michael's comrades raised their sabres to form a shelter for the happy couple as they descended, the glittering blades unable to block a cascade of flowers. A sudden crashing of gigantic bells filled the air of the boulevard, startling the gulls into wheeling, shrieking flight.

There was a command, a cheer from the crowd and simultaneously the sabres were lowered, presented, and sheathed. A rush of expensive silks and hysterical laughter as a horde of tearful young noblewomen rushed to surround Pippa. A chorus of jeering and handshakes, clapping on the back and then Miki, blushing, broke away from the boys and dived into the carriage door, aiming himself directly towards a cloud of lace and petticoats.

'Well, that's it for your young Michael, eh? Before we turn around there will be a lot of little Pippitas to trip over on the stairs, then his hair will go, he'll get fat, eh?' It was Ostrov, great friend of Tsar Nicholas since childhood, and his sometime chauffeur and motoring instructor. Ostrov was red-faced with laughter, sweating even in the cool air. Whatever possessed them to decide on an autumn wedding? In their scarlets he and Ostrov looked like different versions from the uniform-maker's pattern book. One a great pole, the other a puffball.

'Life happens this way, or so I am told. How is your boy?' Evdaev asked.

'Certainly fine and young. He grows, prowls around the river at our dacha, he is entering the Admiralty cadets.'

'The navy?'

'He wants to see the world.'

'Yes, but what a way to see it. And most of what you see is water!'

For a moment they stared at the retreating carriage as it rushed away across the square towards the Liteiny. Inanities were traded, a few moments later Countess Gorchakova made an entrance at the top of the stairs. As the most honoured woman of the day you would have thought she would be happy, but when she did finally produce a grimace, the smile looked garish and unnatural on her face. She loathed young Michael of course, something about the House of Evdaev had never been quite good enough for her, but there was no husband and a dwindling income, old Gorchakov had been dead these many years, the boy claimed to be in love, and so on balance it was hard to say which house, Evdaev or Gorchakov, had come out best in the transaction.

The reception at the Gorchakov Palace developed into a tawdry, drunken affair. No one, it seemed, could properly celebrate the union of these two perfect young people. In the midst of the confusion young Baron Rudolph Nikolsky came up to talk. He was something in the Ministry of War, a man whose closest companions were financiers and manufacturers. One of the modern ones, all dash and short hair. On Nikolsky's heels the huge Mikhail Rodzianko appeared, President of the Duma but a monarchist still, not at all a bad fellow to converse with, and so obese that he made Ostrov look thin. Sazonov, the Foreign Minister, also joined them and they clustered there watched over by huge oil portraits, all mythological in nature, since no Gorchakovs had ever participated in slaying dragons, or wrestling Napoleonic demons from the sky.

At first the conversation was casual, everyone talking about their plans to vacate the capital for the sunny south when the weather turned. Within weeks, everyone would be following in the wake of the youngsters, who would begin their honeymoon tonight within his private car, which he had kindly loaned to Miki.

The talk veered to the subject of Rasputin—there were none of his circle of sycophants gathered there under the gigantic paintings—and rumours of how interference by Rasputin was the cause of the probable replacement of Kokovtsov as Prime Minister. Everyone shrugged. The talk swerved again towards the recent negotiations over the war.

Sazonov was doing most of the talking. 'They entered the first war all brothers—Greece, the Serbs, little Montenegro . . . the Bulgars, and they all expected to eradicate the Turkish presence, drive out the heathens, and push all the way to Constantinople. Everything was going to be flowers and smiles, divide the pie together . . .'

'But it didn't work out that way,' Nikolsky put in. A tight little smile.

'Yes, too much blood, not willing to pay the price, and then when they drew up the treaty, Bulgaria—'

'Who'd bled the most, lost the most, fought the hardest—' Evdaev put in. The men smiled.

'In their minds at least—'

'Yes, well they see what Serbia gets, and they feel cheated at the negotiations and they want what they think is theirs and so, like fools . . .'

'But for Bulgaria to think they can advance their interests by attacking their Slavic brothers, that's not the way forward,' Evdaev said.

'No, it's not, Nestor. I realize that,' Sazonov sighed. 'But the Bulgarians are learning the lesson the hard way.' Rodzianko nodded wisely and stepped in, proclaiming his faith in Sazonov's diplomats and their ability to conjure a united, peaceful Europe. The men laughed.

They had been joined by Prince Meshchersky, famous homosexual and publisher of a leading newspaper that catered to the ultra-conservative Black Hundreds, an entertaining character. He and Evdaev had been kammerpages together, best friends. It was only later that he realized Meshchersky's peculiarities, but for years there had been no sign at all. Now, of course, he was dangerously flamboyant.

Meshchersky prodded Evdaev to continue with his views. 'It is simple,' he replied strongly. 'Eventually we must have Constantinople. It is in the natural order of things, just as birds need air. And we shall have it, but we could have had it all by now. Think of that, eh?' Eyebrows were raised. The opinion directly challenged Sazonov, who, it was widely reported, had consistently backed away from any confrontation with the Austrians, who were sure to react to any Russian pressure in the Balkans. 'Go on,' someone said, but Evdaev politely would say no more.

'No,' urged Nikolsky. 'Continue, please. This is a social occasion and we are among friends,' the young man said with a meaningful look towards Sazonov, who was smiling politely. Rodzianko gave him an almost invisible nod, and so Evdaev launched his torpedoes.

'I say that if we had fully supported our brothers in the first of these Balkan wars, we could have kept the alliance together, and driven our armies straight through Turkey in a single thrust. And had we been in at the start, our dreadnoughts would be moored at the entrance to the Dardanelles at this very moment, and I would be giving Miki and Pippa a villa on the Aegean for a wedding present.'

Meshchersky laughed, Rodzianko applauded. 'Continue. Nestor, please . . .' Sazonov said solemnly, polite enough to hear him out. Someone clapped him on the back to start him up again.

'And had we taken that golden opportunity, the Austrians would have backed down because we would have assured them we had no designs on their territory. That would have been the way to placate them.'

Sazonov nodded, smiled, and glanced down at his shoes. There was a chuckle of disbelief at Evdaev's directness, and to buttress his statements Evdaev turned to Rodzianko. 'Did you not urge such a course? Did you not say we should profit from the war fever?' For a moment everyone held their breath. After all, Rodzianko was a politician, and his opinions on foreign policy were only the opinions of a loud-voiced civilian who represented the vague force of the 'people', something unknown waiting in the wings.

Before Rodzianko could speak, Sazonov stepped in, trying to cut the argument short, measuring the men's discretion with a glance. 'Everyone likes an opportunity, Nestor, but I can tell you the Turkish question was carefully considered and it was rejected at the highest levels,' he said quietly, formally. The men nodded gravely. Everyone knew this meant Tsar Nicholas, there was no higher level.

Sazonov glanced at them with his sharp eyes, nodded and then turned to Evdaev. 'But, yes, Nestor, I agree. It would have been heroic, a glorious stroke, to take Constantinople.' He reached up and grasped Evdaev's forearm, one Roman to another. 'Pure heroics, pure glory, fraught with danger, of course, and only history will judge if it was not the best thing to do,' the Foreign Minister said with a small bow, and then left the little circle.

'He's ill,' Ostrov said.

'He's next,' Meshchersky shot right back, and they all laughed at Sazonov's departing figure.

By the end of the night, Evdaev found himself by the window staring out at the trees blowing in the glow of the streetlamps. It had begun to rain, a slanting downpour that discouraged one from the prospect of simply getting to one's carriage, making it easier to stay at the party. He was thinking about his own plans to leave the city, spend a bit of time at Soroki, but then he would have to return. He would be busy, Sergei had told him; everything must be ready for the turning of the weather in spring.

Weather, he thought. That was the true story of Russia: a nation held prisoner by the thermometer, hostage of the moon, the snow, the flooding river, the infinite reach of the continent. A titanic nation moulded by titanic forces, that engendered a race of titanic men.

Young Nikolsky came up again and they regarded the street, talked about the misery outside, and then fell into a conversation about money.

'You know, Nestor, I do not know about this Andrianov,' Nikolsky said. Evdaev turned, suddenly alert. He had not been paying that much attention. Money was not something he was overly interested in. Money was always just . . . there. Like water, food, servants, things assumed to be the basics of life. You reached out and it was already waiting for you. For a moment he looked at Nikolsky, before he remembered that they were all connected through a private syndicate, a pool of twenty or so investors that Sergei had set up. He'd nearly forgotten all about it.

'Well, Sergei . . . he is certainly a very smart fellow, always up on the latest developments.'

'He is modern, I'll give him that,' Nikolsky said.

'Exactly, yes. Modern.'

'Perhaps a little quick to seize on the latest toy, and you know he's happily in bed with every Jewish banker from here to London,' Nikolsky said sourly, giving him a meaningful look.

Across the room there was a little drama; Sukhomlinov, the ageing Minister of War, had collapsed in the corner with his thick head leaning against the panelling. His young wife was fanning his beet-red face. A butler hovered beside them, and from the far room he saw Dr Lemmers walking briskly, having been fetched to attend the crisis.

'I'm sure that Andrianov's arrangements, this relationship with . . .' Evdaev began.

'With the Jews?'

'Yes, I'm sure it's just temporary. These marketplaces, they are changing all the time, so I am given to understand. And he's a great one for opportunities, and you don't want to throw out the good with the bad.'

'No, no, Nestor. Money is money. Still . . .'

'In fact they say he's a genius, in that way. A financial genius, don't you agree?'

'We're all making money right now, that's sure. Perhaps he may be a genius, but I don't trust those fellows. He practically lives with that crowd at the Stock Market. He has offices in there,' Nikolsky said.

'Oh, really?' Evdaev said. In fact he had often met Andrianov there for their treasonous conversations.

'But I suppose we cannot complain,' the younger man sighed.

'No, as long as the roubles come in, the roubles come in. I get a statement every so often . . .' He shrugged.

'Yes, but after the flood, Nestor, when all this . . .'

Nikolsky made a dismissive gesture at the clot of aristo-crats bent over the ailing Sukhomlinov. 'After, when all these Romanovs and Rasputin-lovers have been cleansed away, then we can see what happens to Monsieur Andrianov, eh?' Nikolsky said, his voice fallen to a whisper. Evdaev looked around to him, but Nikolsky was looking across the room where Sukhomlinov was trying to get on his feet.

For a moment Evdaev was struck dumb. He stood there staring at Nikolsky's hard little face, the spiky ginger hair. After a moment the smaller man turned.

'Yes, after it's done then you won't need Sergei any more, will you, Nestor?' he said, still wearing that thin-lipped smile. The smile of a man who was never happy, but often amused.

Nikolsky waited for a reply, but Evdaev just gaped. Nikolsky reached up and gave him a pat on the shoulder, made only the slightest bow of his head and reached inside his breast pocket for a cigarette case. 'Now I must retreat to the balcony . . . to take a little fresh air before the ride home. It always helps me sleep,' he said quietly, and walked away.

Still paralysed, Evdaev watched Nikolsky cross the parquet. The room had grown suddenly hot, full of the perfume and powder of aging matrons, the disgusting smell of the remains of the food that had been spread out on the tables. Hollow laughter echoed through the huge empty rooms of the palace. The party was over and it was long past the time to leave. He felt a sudden trickle of cold perspiration race down his spine.

Across the room Nikolsky paused at the balcony doors, allowed a servant to light his cigarette, and stepped out into the cool air. Involuntarily a smile played across his features. He had laid the bait and it had been taken, the Prince's dismayed expression had been all the confirmation he required. There were only two real factions in Russia these days: those who derived sustenance and protection from the Romanov regime and everyone else. The pairing of Andrianov, the modern industrialist, who owed none of his success to the Tzar, and Evdaev, the ultra-traditional aristocrat with autocracy in his blood, had struck Nikolsky the moment he'd first seen them together. They were opposites, but each had what the other wanted, and now they were allies.

The Tsar couldn't hang on to his throne very much longer. Something was going to happen, and if Nikolsky was to survive the debacle he needed to keep a sharp eye on these two unusual companions. He flicked the cigarette away into the darkness of the Gorchakov gardens and made his way back to the ballroom. Across the floor Evdaev was still there, standing almost at attention. When he looked into his eyes there was the same expression—shock, confusion. Fear. Nikolsky smiled.

Evdaev did not know what kind of animal he was.

ELEVEN

The way Ryzhkov had planned it, they slipped around to Sadovaya, hired the best cab he could find so that they would arrive in front of the bindery in something approaching style.

Vera was furious at the entire scheme, keeping up a running commentary of abuse. He tried to settle her down but gave up when she started screaming at him, '. . . *this is what you wanted, right? This is what you wanted* . . .' She was grinning, her eyes narrow, teeth bared in something that wasn't quite a smile. 'I hope you've got some money, Daddy,' she said. She'd brought a half-empty bottle of champagne along, and once they'd climbed into the cab she threw herself against him and poured a long slug into his mouth. He had to drink just to keep her from knocking out his teeth. Then she kissed him, so hard their teeth knocked together.

'You say you want to go down into the belly of the beast, that's good. You want to *look around*? All right, I'll show you a few things. I'll show you what's truth

and what's lies . . . Don't look so sad,' she smiled at him.
'You're going to like it,' she said, and reached over and
grabbed him by the scrotum and gave him a hard
squeeze. 'I'll show you,' she hissed and then jerked away
from him. Then she was pulling him out of the cab and
through the gate towards the entrance of the Apollo
Bindery. 'This way . . .' she said, dragging him off the
pavement to a side-door where there was a kiosk and
she pulled the bell and kissed him again.

'Vera,' he grabbed her by the arm, pulled her close.
'We have to make this look good, understand?'

'Oh, yes. It's going to look good, don't worry,
darling,' she said. 'You want to *know*, you want to
know about poor little Katya, you feel so sorry for her,
so . . .' There was a noise as a bolt was shifted in the
door and a large man peered out.

'Hey, Yuri! We're here for the party! I've brought
someone special for Irini and I'm *dying* to see her,' Vera
squealed with delight.

Yuri was a hefty fellow who knew how to follow
orders. He frowned. 'You're not welcome here, little
bird—'

'I've got a special prize here, my friend from—' she
turned and hesitated for a moment— 'all the way from
America! Tell Irini he's loaded! He's a millionaire just
from selling paintbrushes!' She laughed again and then
threw herself back on to his arm. Ryzhkov smiled as if
he didn't know what was going on.

'Wait a minute,' Yuri said, closing the door.

'So now you have to keep quiet all night, eh?' Vera
whispered, looking up at him with a particularly evil
smile.

'Straighten up,' he said, knowing it wasn't going to
happen. The door opened and a woman was there.

Ryzhkov recognized her immediately as the redheaded madam he had first seen at the front door.

'Well, well, well . . . My little Vera,' the woman said. Close up Madame Hillé was a horror; the face was a mask of paint and powder, the hair a lacquered helmet with feathers and rhinestones.

'Oh, my darling!' Vera gushed. 'I've come to apologize and give you a present, I'd like to introduce my special friend, Mr *Smith*. He's come all the way from the land of cowboys and Indians!' The woman gave him a look, extended her hand, and Ryzhkov, left with no choice, bent to kiss it.

'And this is Irini, my . . . greatest *teacher*,' she laughed and gave his arm an affectionate squeeze, pulling him close and posing beside him. 'Oh, Irini, I do want to make up! I hope we're not late, we've come for one of your parties—' She was pleading.

'Well, my sweet-sweet, you're just in the nick of time and fortunately there are a half-dozen seats left; but *where* have you been, anyway?' Madame Hillé had successfully pried Vera away from him and they swept deeper into the building. Behind them Ryzhkov heard the side-door being fastened by the big man.

'Well, after what happened . . .' Vera said softly, with just a touch of the other woman's shoulder to apologize. 'Anyway . . . I'm out of the life now, I'm down at the corner. Dancing at the Komet, it's a theatre.'

'Dancing! That will be a change, eh? I've heard of that place. Very artistic so they say, and oh, my—you do look like you've lost a little weight!' The woman laughed and poked Vera in the ribs. The two of them suddenly squealed with laughter. Maybe it was an old joke. Now the woman grasped Vera and firmly kissed her on both cheeks. Ryzhkov stood there trying to be amiable.

'She's good, isn't she,' the woman said, addressing Ryzhkov now, grasping him by his arm. A strong grip. Bright red nails. Trying to draw him out, measure him.

'He doesn't understand a word, but he's a tycoon from American and he's loaded,' Vera said laughing.

'Oh, well, *well*! Welcome aboard!' Madame Hillé laughed, giving Ryzhkov an appraising look. 'Take off your coats, we've already started. Tonight you-are-my-special-guests!' she said loudly to Ryzhkov. He smiled and nodded which drew another embrace and a giggle between the two women.

Madame Hillé stepped back and looked at them both. 'Well, I know what you like,' she said to Vera, who once again was clutching his arm like a newlywed. 'But, *you* . . .' She fixed her eye on Ryzhkov, still trying to figure him out, shrugged and quickly gave up. 'Red or Black?' she said to Vera.

'Oh, I think Black,' she said modestly.

'Yes, of course. Yuri will take you up.'

Yuri was big. He filled the narrow side-staircase, once the servants' route to the first floor. The music was louder as they got to the landing and there were only dimmed lights. Ryzhkov put a hand out in front of him, trying to find the big man by touch. Then a curtain moved ahead of them and they entered into a large ballroom that had been converted into a kind of theatre. There was a low stage surrounded by booths that were screened for privacy. They reminded Ryzhkov of the wicker sunbathers' shelters he'd seen in France. Little places where you could hide from the wind.

'Here you are, sir,' Yuri said and guided them to their own booth. The only illumination came from a ring of candles that stood like red spikes in sconces around the room, and a shaded red light that illuminated a stage in the centre.

The stage was really a low bed upon which two women were making love to a third who had been bound to the corner posts. She was groaning enthusiastically, her back arching each time the woman between her legs inserted a black dildo that Ryzhkov thought was improbably large. Every few strokes the woman at her head moved so that the bound woman would have to put her mouth to her vulva, then the two tormentors would kiss.

He felt Vera's hands unbuttoning the fly of his trousers. 'We have to make this look good,' she said.

'Look . . .'

'No, you *look*—' and she pushed him out in the booth so that he could see his neighbours. 'That's what being Black is; you sit in the shadows and you get to watch . . . you can watch them—' In the booth beside them an older man was being serviced by a woman whose head was bobbing up and down between his legs. He looked over and took his hand out of her hair and gave a desultory wave to Ryzhkov. Momentarily distracted, the woman looked up from her work and smiled briefly.

'Or you can look at our other distinguished neighbours—' She pulled him now so that he was nearly on top of her, leaning out of the booth so that he could see into the booth on the other side. Two women this time, who sat impassively, watching the show.

'Well, maybe not them . . .' Vera laughed and turned back to the stage. 'I used to do . . . something like that,' she said quietly, and then turned to Ryzhkov. Her face, he thought, had become unbelievably cold. He couldn't understand it, how someone with such a smile, someone so beautiful could be . . . so hard. With eyes like granite. She had poured him a glass of champagne. It was from a good bottle, white stripe with ice crystals, the same as the girls onstage were drinking when they got thirsty.

'So, let's drink to *art*,' Vera said and forced his glass to his mouth. He obeyed. 'This is what ballerinas do when they can't get work at the Marinsky.'

'I want to get out of here, have a look around.'

'Not so fast, we're play-acting now. You're here for a good time, remember. Besides neither of them would come back here. If you want the old one there are other places to go.'

'What other places?'

'The children don't live here, they're all hired in. The old one would be a regular somewhere, some place that caters to . . . gentlemen of particular tastes.' She was right against him again. He heaved a great sigh, tried to move away from her but her hand was inside his trousers. 'Don't think I'm doing this for you,' she said. Her voice was angry, challenging. 'You could drop dead right now and I'd laugh about it.'

A sudden screaming caused both of them to look back to the stage, the girls gyrating to a prolonged triple orgasm. There was a smattering of applause from the booths around the room. The women got up, began to untie their companion.

'Skol,' Vera said very quietly, lifting her glass to the women stretching their tired bodies.

'All right, let's go,' Ryzhkov said to her. This was crazy, he thought.

'Oh, no,' she said, and now she was on top of him, her legs straddling him, holding him down on the couch, her fingers gripping him tightly, dangerously. 'We're not going. You paid a lot of money for this, right? We're not going anywhere until you get what you came for, right?'

'We're going.' Ryzhkov pushed her off, stood up and hit his head on the top of the booth. He saw that Vera was crying now. The kohl had run down her cheeks in two great black streaks.

'You don't know what you're missing.' Suddenly she was sobbing.

'Get up. Tell them I'm disgusted, tell them we need a room, tell them anything, make something up,' he growled and pulled her to her feet.

'You don't own me,' she slipped out of his grip and struck at him, but he only took the blow and grabbed her arm and twisted it behind her and jerked her away from the booth. They stumbled up the aisle, knocking over the little table and the bucket of champagne. The two women were still sitting there, they didn't even look up.

'Didn't you like it? Didn't you have a good time?' Vera was saying behind him as he tugged her around the booths. The next act was taking the stage, men with overdeveloped muscles dressed in leather. 'Don't mind him . . . he always gets this way . . .' she was apologizing to the couples as they staggered down the aisle. He jerked her closer to him and they reached the curtains. He pulled them aside, there was a locked door there and he pounded on it.

'Now, you've spoiled everything,' she was muttering behind him. 'You've been a very impolite audience member.'

'Shut up,' he said, angry now, his face grown cold and hot all at the same time.

The door was suddenly flung open and Yuri stood there glaring at them in the red light. 'What's the bother in here—'

'He wants to show me what a stud he is, we need to go upstairs, and he's ready right now, so . . .'

'You're supposed to reserve for those, you know that.'

'It's not going to take that long. We'll take the Iron Room.'

'Hurry up then, I don't know if there's anyone up there or not.'

Yuri took them along a corridor towards the wing of the building. Even the windows on the stairs were all painted over and he could still see traces of the old Apollo Bindery, warnings against smoking painted on the wall.

At the top of the landing they went through a door and he saw that the end of the corridor had been blocked off with a stage flat with a false door to hide it. There was an electric lift opposite them and a kiosk. The lights were low and red.

'Anything open? Doesn't have to be for long,' Yuri growled at the girl sitting there.

'Iron Room?' Vera giggled.

'I've got a two-o'clock, that's only fifteen minutes.'

'Plenty of time,' Yuri said, giving Ryzhkov a look. 'And tell him to be a nice boy, eh?'

'He's under a lot of stress. It's the competition in his industry, after all one brush is much like any other—' But the big man was already gone, headed back to his post at the theatre.

'The Iron Room, it is,' the girl said, and they turned and headed down the hall.

Ryzhkov tried to match up the doorways with the windows as he remembered them from the map he'd had Vera draw and from his memory of the view from the lane. The Iron Room was at the end of the hallway.

It was where Lvova had begun her last night. 'I've seen you before, yes?' Vera said to the girl.

'Nikki. I thought I'd seen you too.'

'I worked here sometimes.'

'That's right, now I—'

'Hey, what about the Blue Room, anyone in here?' Vera interrupted. They had stopped halfway down the hall. The door was painted with blue clouds and little rays of sunshine. Down by the floor there was a landscape with ponies.

'They just got in there and they've got it all night, I think.'

'Oh, too bad. He'd love that,' Vera said, pouting.

'Here we are . . .' The girl stopped before a door that was clad in metal plates. She had to lean against it to push it open.

'Wonderful, you've been so sweet,' Vera said and touched her fingers to the girl's cheek.

The room was long and wide. At one time it must have been a rather pleasant office. Now the windows were curtained with gauze and heavy blinds. The opposite wall had been decorated with implements of torture; everything was leather, metal, and curtained in black velvet.

There was a series of chairs and trapezes that were suspended from the ceiling, and a leather-covered table with stirrups that looked like something one might find in a hospital. The carpet had been replaced with rubber matting in a circle extending six feet around the base of the table.

'Do we have to make this look good too?' Ryzhkov said dryly.

'You're the detective,' she said, walking past him towards the table.

'So this is where she was?'

Vera only nodded. Ryzhkov looked around. There were a hundred ways someone could die in that room.

'The small man was watching, I think. There's always somewhere . . . back here.' She reached down and pulled on a fitting in the wall. 'Yes . . . In here.'

Ryzhkov walked into what he imagined used to be a manager's private washroom and closet. He felt on the wall for a switch and a dim red light came on. Halfway down the inside wall was a curtain and a high stool. A sliding window had been built into the wall. Ryzhkov sat in the seat and slid back the window. It gave him a perfect view of the table. Vera came into view, turned and looked at him. 'You can hear everything too, right?'

He looked up and saw that there was a fabric covered hole cut in the wall.

'Yes,' he said. He sat there for a few moments more watching her standing there beside the table. The red light shone harshly on her cheekbones and the curve of her mouth. He knew that she was only looking at a mark on the wall, that she couldn't see his face. She reached out and put one hand on the cold metal of the stirrup. 'Time's running out,' she said.

He felt his way out of the dimly-lit closet and back out into the centre of the Iron Room. 'Any other special features?'

'There's a balcony. The small one could have been waiting out there. Or maybe they could have been doing it together, but . . . I don't think so.'

'She was killed in here, then.'

'Yes.'

'So . . . then you saw the small one . . .'

'. . . take her out and they went into the Blue Room . . . that's why I stopped there.'

'All right, let's go.'

'There's someone in there now.'

'That's their problem.'

'Hey—' But Ryzhkov was already out the door and into the hallway, knocking on doors and calling out 'Fire!' in a panicky voice abandoning his American persona. Down at the lift he saw the hostess turn and look at him.

'Fire!' he screamed at the girl, and simultaneously threw his weight against the door to the Blue Room. He stepped back across the hall and ran against the door a second time and it exploded off its hinges. The room had been decorated like the inside of a cloud; a mattress had been sculpted like a giant puffy pillow, and stars and sunrays beamed down from lights that were concealed behind the draperies. On the cloud-bed a naked woman was reading to an elderly man who was masturbating. They both jumped up as Ryzhkov tumbled in to their room. 'Get out,' he said to the woman who dashed past him and collided with Vera. The old man shrank back against the headboard and cupped his hands over his genitals. Ryzhkov grabbed him by the shoulder and pushed him across the room. 'This whole place is burning down! Run!' he screamed, and watched the man scrabble around for his clothing and make a dash into the hallway.

The window was in front of him. He could see where it had been repaired. Painted clouds covered all of the window frame except where the new wood had been inserted. Slowly, as if in a dream he walked towards the window and undid the latch. He pushed the window open and leaned out. On the ledge there were glass fragments, a sprinkle of sawdust the glaziers had left behind. No blood. No marks on the sill. No fingernail scratches on the wall. No traces of a struggle. Almost no traces of the crime, just a window that had been repaired before the weather changed.

And now he saw, halfway up the wall, a smudged, nearly invisible palm-print, left on the glossy paint when someone must have braced themselves against the wall, leaning out to see what was happening in the street below.

He felt his throat tighten, almost as if he were choking. Managed to control it, looked at the hand-print and finally held up his own hand to blot it out. He couldn't, not quite.

'You're really running out of time, now,' Vera said.

She was standing there at the threshold; from somewhere she had found another bottle of champagne and was cradling it against her chest. She turned and looked at someone Ryzhkov couldn't see coming down the hall. 'I think he must have had a little too much to drink—' she said just as Yuri came through the doorway.

'Madame Hillé likes her clients to have some manners—'

The Blue Room wasn't very big and the floor was soft and lumpy. He met Yuri as he rushed forward, colliding in the centre of the room with a knee that missed and an uppercut that just bounced off. Then he was suddenly spinning around with Yuri's heavy hand on his shoulder. He tried reaching for his knife before he remembered that he hadn't brought it along in his formal clothes, and then something flashed beside his ear and there was a high-pitched ringing that came from everywhere and nowhere.

He was in and out of consciousness after that. The hallway was a red and black blur. He found himself seizing on the details, as if noticing the seams in the carpet, the filigree on the lampshades, would help him regain his balance. An old naked man was cursing him, and the first thing he saw closely enough to appreciate was the heavy newel post at the bottom of the stairs. How did he ever get down so quickly, he wondered. And from a long distance away he could hear Vera's voice— 'Yes, these Americans are very direct, but as far as imagination goes . . .'

And then they were outside, stumbling on the courtyard stones. He kept trying to find his non-existent knife, and through it all came the sound of Vera laughing at him.

'*And don't come back*,' he heard Yuri calling from a great distance.

Out on the street it was suddenly too complicated to figure out the history of their escape. He sat there on the limestone and looked up; Vera was walking along the kerbing, in a kind of dancing, skipping pattern. Balancing on one foot and then hopping to another, singing to herself. She had the champagne in both hands and when she got to where he was sitting in the gutter she slowly poured it over his head.

'I'm anointing you, I'm washing your sins away . . .'

He tried to stand up, spin around and find Yuri again, but his feet slipped and he fell back down to the cobbles. His face was stinging and he shook his head so that he could see more clearly. There wasn't much to look at, the empty street and Vera as she tipped the bottle up, took the last drops on her tongue, and then flung the bottle high over her head into the night.

'Now, you're all grown up,' she said and reached down and touched his bloody cheek with her light fingers. She was a silhouette against the lights, behind her the street stretched unbroken in the distance. There might be no one else on earth but the two of them. The reflections in the street cast an eerie watery light on her. She was smiling at him, beautiful. Somehow beautiful and terrible all at once. He was suddenly afraid of her, afraid and chilled to the bone. She looked like death come alive, like an avenging wraith, like a woman capable of anything he might imagine.

'So, now you've seen what they do with little lost girls in Petersburg. Now you know the rules of the game, eh? Who comes out on top, who gets to sleep in the wet spot.' She laughed suddenly. 'Think how much you've learned!'

Vera seemed genuinely happy at his progress, like she'd discovered a puppy that had finally figured out the purpose of a newspaper. She was looking around at the deserted street.

'Yes, now you know, Mr Paintbrush . . . Now you know about everything.'

TWELVE

Mina Pohnlinskya rehearses in her dreams. Well, she has always made good use of her extra time. A fanatic, a perfectionist, her teachers said. It was the mask that hid the frustrated girl; frustrated at her inability to perform the combinations, all the many steps, leaps and poses that made up the complex choreography. Angry and ashamed at her own weakness, at her awkwardness, her lack of endurance. To advance, to get ahead, to get a solo, she had always been the one who worked harder. She had rehearsed even after her body had succumbed to fatigue. In her sleep, dreaming until things came out right.

Always it has been so.

She rehearses now for her reunion with Sergei, to make it perfect. No—to make it beyond perfect—*divine*. For three days now the telephones have been ringing; people begging for appointments. Invitations, telegrams, Sergei from Vienna, Sergei from Warsaw, Sergei from Riga. Boys delivering special sealed letters, pouches that are constantly arriving. Porters waiting on stand-by. The maids have dusted the library—she never uses it. There are fresh flowers. The cook has gone out early to order necessary provisions. A week he has promised her. An entire, glorious week.

She rehearses what she will say to him, what he will say to her. The first kiss after being apart for far too long. What they will eat, what they will do.

She has bathed again, gone to Basia's and been coiffed, plucked, waxed and scoured. All in the service of beauty. Beauty eternal, always fragile and ephemeral, always the loser in the battle against time and gravity.

Well, she hardly needs to worry, she is not yet thirty and still radiant as a virgin. Everywhere she goes she is Pohnlinskya, the Lilac Soap Goddess. Often simply *Lilac*. Men, soldiers, boys and grandfathers, women and even their infants recognize her.

She did it on the cusp of meeting Sergei. Took the soap money. A fortune, and alone it would have been enough for her to retire. Thus, when they met she was able to face him as something like an equal. Perhaps it was the challenge that attracted him, to take a famous woman, a woman of means, and bring her into his stable. Perhaps he saw her as a great trophy, merely one more superb jewel to add to his crown. In those years every girl wanted to land Sergei. Every girl wants him still.

Once, when she'd got tired of one more gawker tripping over themselves trying to back out of her way, interrupting their shopping in the Passage arcade, he whisked her out of the building and the next day bought the Lilac brand from Zhukov and took her face off the packages. That was when she knew he loved her.

But often times, if she were going to be truthful, she misses all that attention. Of course it was a famous

image, Pohnlinskya and her little fairy fan in a clean
sunlit glow, dressed in the whitest of white. An indelible
portrait and yes, there are plenty who still remember,
when she goes out to shop or to see the circus.
Everywhere, really.

At Basia's all the women know what's coming. You
can only keep a secret so long. Maybe tonight it's a
special occasion, a birthday, a party at Countess
Sophie's. Tomorrow it's something even more splendid,
a christening, a recital, a theatrical opening. She attends
Basia's salon and the atmosphere is heavenly. Right
away the girls there notice her exhilaration—she could
not conceal it if she tried. An afternoon in the salon is
an afternoon of cosseted luxury. A triumph of maternal
understanding and unspoken conspiracy, a secret realm
for women only and the occasional homosexual
couturier—the only kind of man capable of understanding the minutiae of feminine allure. All of Basia's
staff are endlessly supportive and, for something that,
let's face it, can engender such anxiety—the adjustment
of fashion and cosmetics—they are remarkably carefree.
Everyone is smiling, with little thimbles of konyak
delivered to your room on a pink tray.

He will be here on the Tuesday, he has telegraphed.

In the morning arrives a fresh batch of cables. Some
are for his eyes only and they are taken upstairs to a
table in the library. The others—for her—are brought by
Anna to wherever she might be in the great house. She
rips them open and follows his progress across Europe.
Sergei busy with this, busy with that. Sergei dashing
quickly to Berlin; in Paris for an extra day.

Oh, Paris! How lucky he is, the bastard. She is
jealous, she will make him pay. But he does, he pays for
it all. Even though she has her money, which she has

carefully hoarded for . . . for some undreamed disaster, he has paid for this fantastic residence, *Luxe*, on the Morskaya, and he has given it to her! It's a love-present for her, his big bouquet on the finest street in the city. Yes, he was a little disappointed that she hadn't taken number thirty-two right across the street, but she had wanted the sunny courtyard and the cold façade. Just like a ballerina, he'd laughed. Oh, his laugh!

Then on Tuesday he arrives. First, there is the commotion at the foyer, the doors are thrown open, his gay hello! She calls out and . . . flies, floats down the staircase into his arms. The kiss, not at all what she had rehearsed. A quick wet, hard, pressure on her mouth, modestly restrained because behind him comes a stream of porters, sent by the brokers at the station who manage his trunks. The remaining baggage will be coming in all week long, since some of it is on different trains following him around Europe, some of it still waiting in his private car.

While the minions go about their chores she joins him in the parlour. He notices a few things, the new fabric on the chairs, the flowers. And his smile!

His packets, his correspondence and telegrams are stacked exactly where he likes them. He leafs through the pile while she has some refreshments brought up to her bedroom.

The boudoir is gigantic, designed for lavish recreation followed by sound sleep. Large windows on the southern side that open on to the courtyard, heavy drapes to keep out the white nights, a fringe of trees that soften the high wall that separates the courtyard from the block of residences on the corner. An ornate back gate off the lane so that piles of firewood can be delivered. The firewood is only for the servants or a particularly chill autumn day like this one, because Mina always goes to France in the winter. A month from now she'll have closed up the house.

The servants potter continuously. She waits. They circle each other. How was Sofia? How was Wien? What about Oslo? And Paris . . . I'm so jealous. She pretends to slap him, it ends in a little kiss.

While they wait for their own special time, he goes about his business. There are telephone calls to make, but he has arrived in the afternoon, and therefore can return only two or three. Some urgent problem at his Saratov plant; a senior manager has died during his tour. The man was valuable to his entire operation. One of those rare finds; a self-taught engineer a veteran from his father's years at the helm. He tells her about him with genuine grief—oh, the old fellow was too kind to the workers by half, not really one for maximizing efficiency, but what she may not realize is that it was this old fellow's improvements to the basic design which enabled the Saratov valve model number four to take over the market for high-pressure fixed piping! Of course recruiting a replacement for this unique individual must become a priority. Sadly the funeral was nearly two weeks ago.

The food has come up, some cakes and a bottle of white stripe champagne. Mina has arrayed herself seductively on the chaise and awaits his presence. Thank God she is not a woman who hovers.

They talk about things, it comes out in disorganized snatches. Fragments gathered from their time apart—the relative conditions of his trip, unforeseen encounters, the status of old friends. Much of what he was doing he cannot talk about. She knows this, she has long ago accepted that she does not know everything.

What Andrianov talks about is his cover, his excuses. He says nothing of the artillery that he diverted to Serbia, nothing about his meeting with Fox in Vienna, *Apis* in Belgrade, nothing about the Plan. He watches her as she laughs at his witticisms. She can see he is tired and pouts sympathetically as he puts the telephone down with unconcealed relief. Tired, yes, but not too tired. He smiles at her direct gaze; soon now, a night with the delightful Mina.

He has given her everything but marriage. There is no wife, and she does not even have the semi-official status of mistress to a great man. She is something else; a kept woman, a girlfriend, an unmarried wife, a lover. Something modern and vague. It has been that way for five years now. An eternity. What hurts most is the time apart, the lure of motherhood, and having to manage the awkward architecture of her life as a single, yet very much attached woman, which for a girl as attractive as Mina is . . . difficult.

People expect things of her, people expect things of a genuine star as she was until Sergei plucked her off the stage and erased her from the soap cartons. It wasn't so bad—well, by then Nijinsky and that crowd were all the rage. You had to be able to jump over mountains and bend your body into the kind of poses you might find on an Egyptian wall, there was no classicism and very little beauty, and she'd had enough before it all started. Enough frustration and enough perfection.

She saw the same relentless drive in Sergei when they met. It was like two dynamos who are finally linked to the same wires. He never tried to pretend that he was not obsessively concerned with riches, with success, with . . . whatever he was obsessed about at the time. Yes, to his credit, at least he was honest about it, and she has always assumed that soon, one day next week, next month, or sometime maybe in spring, that he will mellow; lose at least some portion of his all-consuming drive to be . . . to be whatever he is trying to be . . . and then he will finally ask her.

Of course she will agree.

But, while she waits, he has been generous; the villa in Antibes on the Riviera is absolute paradise and the one place on earth that she feels truly alive. If all else falls away she is determined to hold on to the villa. The winters are glorious there, every now and then a draught, or one of those pelting rains that send floods coursing down the mountain rills, washing out the road to Cannes.

The servants are gone. The doors are closed and she slips on to the floor at his knees and allows herself to be kissed. These times she floats away, these times it is easy. For these times she is prepared; more awake than he is, more energetic, his dominatrix and now is her time. She has him in these hours and she will not let him go.

She has him again. And he sleeps and she watches him, watches and tries to imagine him as a boy . . . Naturally she has perused family photographs, but she never can quite see the transformation when the boy is lost to the man; something about the strength of the nose, the darkness around his eyes; the way he frowns as he sleeps. The way his mouth can fall open in sleep, as if he is trying to suck up all the air in the sky.

And she puts out the last candle, throws off her negligée and stands shivering in front of the great window. A nightscape of the trees, the leaves beginning to yellow, and the clouds coming in to erase the stars; infringing on the trees are the lead roofs and the tiled pediments of the Shugalov Palace. Over there all the lights are on, if she opened the window she might hear the strains of music—that's right, Betsy is giving a party tonight for her circle of all the liberals, journalists, and representatives of the Duma. Princes Trubetskoy and Cantacuzène of course, a mob of high-borns who think they understand the workers, tedious dreamers with foreign ideas that they keep pushing on everyone they meet. She was not invited. Of course. Betsy and that fool husband of hers.

She stands there naked, the sweat turning cold on her skin, her nipples hard, the gooseflesh spreading up her arms and across her strong thighs to her belly. Would they have a girl or a boy, she wonders. She will have it out with him, she will strike a bargain with him, have the child. Bastards, everyone has bastards, it's no shame any more, this is a modern age. She considers the matter as she stretches there in the night-light. She'll take the girl away and raise her in France, bring her back to Petersburg occasionally. What can he do about it? Nothing. She has her own money. Safe.

She returns to the huge bed, slips under the sheets, and he wakes a little, rolls over to meet her, pressing his face into the hollow of her neck, one arm thrown around her, latched together there in the great bed like two perfect beings finally made one. As close to heaven, or closer even, than most poor souls will ever get.

In the night she wakes . . . there is light pouring from the doorway of his den. His special room, not much bigger than a cupboard off the library, the door to which he always keeps locked. Inside he has installed a machine for receiving cable traffic. It is a large glass-enclosed machine hooked to a typewriter that fills the space and clatters and snaps at all hours of the night.

She always thinks it will catch fire. Even through the soundproofing she can hear it and whenever she is sleeping it wakes her up immediately.

In that little room he has things that are too secret for her to know. Business that is too private to be carried out at his offices. Clandestine matters. No one must ever go inside, he says.

The door has been constructed behind a bookcase, built on swivels so that he can push it out of the way. It is heavy because the books are real ones, and unless you knew where to put the key you would never find it. There is a telephone in the room that he sometimes uses. She has been allowed to look inside, but never enters. She would not presume. An ashtray. An extra leather chair that, as far as she knows, no one has ever sat upon.

Well, of course he sometimes uses the Morskaya house when she is in France, he could have someone in the bedroom then. But surely Anna would tell her. Is he unfaithful, is that why he spends time in the little room? Does he have a lover in Warsaw? Or, where else did he go, in Belgrade, or Berlin. He's always been so impressed with the Germans. Some girl in Germany. As she curls there in half-sleep, images of German ballerinas she has known flash through her imagination like bejewelled sheep leaping a turnstile. It makes her laugh, these girls. He doesn't like women like that. He likes the thin ones. The skeletal ones. So, some German wraith then, some ghoul that he brings to Petersburg while she is sunning herself in Antibes and cooking squid on the rocks. Well, there are men in France, too. Plenty of them who come for the sun in the winter, so he'd better watch out. Two can play that game, after all.

She rolls over. There is a little noise and she realizes he is pulling the bookcase closed for silence, and then a few moments later, as she falls asleep, she hears him composing a message, the little taps taking her down into slumber.

Over breakfast he is angry. At her, at the cook, at the newspapers, and without finishing his food, he telephones an attaché at some embassy. She looks at the headlines and finds that peace has broken out in the Balkans. But he is angry? Yes, angry at the peace. Angry at the diplomats and the negotiators. Angry that they have backed down at some conference in Bucharest. By they he means Bulgaria, who have surrendered to the Turks, not to mention Serbia, who he says could have won it all; he spits his words, little flakes of egg and pastry fly across the table. Peace! It is like an obscene curse. It throws everything off schedule, he complains. Everything? What everything? He is too busy to explain. She had wanted them both to go to the botanical gardens. It is getting colder outside and in there are the most amazing flowers and beneath the glass it is like spring. He had already agreed and now he is angry about peace?

They go. He sulks the entire time. It is the kind of place he hates, but he still goes. This is how she knows he loves her still.

At the entrance there is a courier waiting for him. A reply from an embassy. He walks away from her to the kiosk at the front. He'll only be a few moments.

She looks at the plants and thinks about how she's going to get even, how he doesn't deserve her. Watches him through the glass, pretending to look at the curious cacti, the rare orchids. Now he's smoking, pacing along the gravel path dictating a telegram with another in his hands. Throws the cigarillo stub away with an angry gesture. Well, for someone who sells guns she can understand why the onset of peace might be vexing.

She has worked her way to the strange little tortured Japanese trees by the time he comes in to join her. An apology, but he has to see Nestor tonight. Nestor and some others, business associates.

She cannot understand what he sees in Nestor. An oversexed oaf. A man with the brain of a boar. It cannot be business, or any business that she can imagine. Nestor can barely count. It is more than business, it is . . . politics.

He loves his country, she thinks. He loves his country more than he loves her.

It is so touching, so boyish of him. It causes a little tear to spring from her eye. Another telegram, another excursion outside, something quick this time, a yes or a no.

Now she can hear his heels on the tiles, and he is there, happier, energized. Whatever he has been doing she can see that he believes it will work.

And standing there in front of the little crippled trees, with his arm around her, she is filled with warmth.

THIRTEEN

Hand-wringers and old women! Weak sisters and dilettantes! Andrianov was beside himself. He managed to keep his voice down, pushed his chair back from the table, started for the toilets and then returned, turned his withering fire on Gulka. Gulka! Who was supposed to be in charge of security, who was supposed to take care of the . . . troublesome cases.

'Yes, but as a high official, my hands are tied, Sergei. There's a procedure, even for me, rules and regulations. In the past too much corruption and various temptations put in front of various parties have muddied the waters,' he whined. That was it. That was when Andrianov whirled on him.

'Don't you understand, Alexandr Ivanovich? This is not a game, this is not a theory, this is a war. Can't you understand that? I wanted *Gosling* protected and you said that was something you could do. And did you protect him, *General*?'

'Well, in a manner of speaking . . .' Gulka made his jelly face, double, triple chins waggling in equivocation.

'Well, what's all this about someone in your own department starting an investigation? Why am I hearing about this? Aren't you in charge of these people?'

'I only mentioned the investigation, I only reported this because I wanted to *emphasize* that it's nothing. It's routine.' Gulka shrugged but only managed a half-smile.

'You'll have to explain that to me, Alexandr. I wanted *Gosling* to be invisible. No one should notice him or be able to discover what he is doing for us. That's why covering up his mistake was important. And you said you could take care of that. If you *have*, if you are *taking steps*, everything is fine, there is no reason for us to talk. If you did it, wonderful. Perhaps something can be salvaged.'

'Something can probably be salvaged . . .'

For a moment Andrianov just stared at him, a thousand invisible bullets smashed into the fat man's skull. He fought for control, fought to keep his voice calm, refusing to shout, to scream curses. 'All right, Alexandr,' he managed to say. 'Why can't this all be hushed up? Why can't you stop an investigation in your own department? Why can't these people be transferred, or fired, or simply reassigned. Don't you have any power at all in Okhrana? Aren't you supposed to be in command?'

'You'd best answer him,' Evdaev glowered across the table. They had finished the dinner, except for Gulka who was lingering over his dessert.

'I am trying to explain! Good God, Sergei! Try to understand!' Gulka exploded. He looked like he was arguing with his mother over having to do his homework. Perhaps he was going to cry?

'I'm sorry, Alexandr Ivanovich . . . please.'

'We're both sorry, Alexei,' Evdaev put in.

'You say you wanted him protected and we did it, the St Petersburg police know nothing at all, but, yes . . . *unaccountably* an investigation has been started, files have been opened by a low-level section chief here in the city. It's purely routine, they've requested all the reports and probably they've started a search for witnesses—'

'You said there were no witnesses!'

'No one in the room, that's correct. Ivo told me—'

'*Heron*,' Evdaev prompted.

'Yes, all right, *Heron*, then. *Heron* told me there was no one in the room. But there were people around that night. The photographer has been taken care of, but there were all our guests, various whores, servants, assorted persons who may have seen him arrive, those kind of witnesses . . .'

Andrianov stood there watching him, the strength of his focus driving Gulka into silence. 'What?' the fat man asked, nervously.

'Fine, fine. I see,' Andrianov said quietly. Evdaev looked up at him, a little surprised at the calm that had suddenly dispersed the storm. 'I think I understand, Alexandr. You're saying that if you were to attempt to stifle this investigation you would betray your interest.'

'Exactly,' Gulka said, relieved that he had broken through. 'It might cause even more damage. It would look too curious, Sergei. Someone like me, someone from on high who's suddenly interested. You know, excite their scrutiny, provoke them, raise a flag of warning. We'll do our utmost of course.'

'Of course,' he said quietly. He returned to the table and sat for a long moment. Gulka relaxed and went back to the dessert.

Evdaev looked at the pair of them, nodded in agreement, then twisted in his seat and cleared his throat. 'Also, I'm somewhat concerned about the winter, Sergei. Perhaps this delay isn't so terrible after all. Fighting in the mountains in winter . . . awfully difficult. Not good for the horses at all.' His brow was furrowed in concentration. 'I know we were winning. Three cheers for those Rumanians, eh? Seize the day, attack the rear. First principles right out of the book. I can't for the life of me understand why Serbia knuckled under like that. All we need is a spark, as you've said many times. I've spoken to . . . ah . . . all the relevant parties and we've moved men up to the border. Quietly, of course—'

Andrianov cut him off. 'No, the delay is simply what it is, a delay, nothing more, Nestor. And, yes, we can use the delay they've given us to our own advantage. Never mind. Here, Alexandr Ivanovich, this is what I want you to do next.' Gulka sat there, licking his spoon, placed it carefully on the edge of the dish, detached his napkin, waited for instructions.

'*Very* discreetly take whatever steps you must to impede the investigation. Don't get involved personally, don't tip your hand, but find other business for them to do. Keep them busy. If they are going to discover anything, at least they will have to work for it, eh?'

'Yes,' said Gulka. 'Grind away.'

'Exactly,' Andrianov said. 'Grind away. For now that's enough.'

'And there'll be no war in the winter?' Evdaev was smiling.

'Oh, make no mistake, Nestor, even now we are at war, but your horses will be warm.'

And not a half-hour later he was in his car being driven back to Mina's *Luxe* on the Morskaya. Once there he climbed the stairs to his secret room, and pulled the bookcase-door closed behind him. He turned on the ticker and took a few moments to compose the message. The encryption took longer because the code was his most secure. It had only one receiver, Apis. And in one sentence he phrased his request.

He would require four men from Serbia to do a better job.

Gosling is going to fly.

FOURTEEN

Ryzhkov and Hokhodiev met Inspector Iosif Schliff at the crowded entrance to the Gostiny Dvor market on the Nevsky and went from there to the Central Police Department at the head of Gorokhovaya. Schliff was an officer in the St Petersburg police but you would never suspect it; a diminutive man, well fed within his shabby clothes laced with the sharp tang of body odour. He went about in a raincoat that was even more tattered than a typical police detective's, and he seemed always to have a cigar stub clamped between his lips. He was one half of the St Petersburg Police Department's 'Morality Detachment'; the other officer was on sick leave. The Morality Detachment's fortunes drifted as politics drifted it into or out of the spotlight. If the newspapers reported a particularly hideous sex crime then there was a sudden call for additional resources for the detachment's eternal battle against perversion. Instant largess that would cause procedures to be improved, new equipment to be purchased, new recruits trained, and even rumours of upgraded offices. Then the excitement would die, gradually the new officers would be required elsewhere, the detachment would begin to wither away. Schliff didn't seem to mind. 'Frankly I like it out of the public eye. I can make my own hours, there are relatively few reports to write. I can take my time and get to know all the significant personalities.'

They had asked about violent paedophiles and were met at first with a long pause of assessment, followed by a nod and Schliff's wordless tour through the bowels of the Central Police Department until they discovered a small conference room. The walls were stone and cold, the paint was flaking off due to the moisture that seeped through from the embankment. The best you could say for the atmosphere was that it was mouldy; it looked to Ryzhkov like a good place to grow mushrooms. Schliff left them and a few minutes later tea was brought around. After about fifteen minutes he returned with a trolley stacked with boxes of files.

'If I am correct you're looking for someone in here,' Schliff gestured to the overladen cart.

'Oh God,' moaned Kostya.

Ryzhkov looked so aghast that Schliff suddenly said, 'But I think I might have a way of narrowing this down. It will mean going about the city.'

'Anything you can suggest, anything at all,' Ryzhkov said.

As Schliff explained it, the killer of Ekaterina Lvova was most likely a habitual violent sex criminal. 'And it is highly likely that he had flown off the handle before. If so, he is almost certainly a regular patron of any one of several . . . houses of special interest, where he can indulge himself in his particular form of debasement. If he has lost control he would be known, barred from such establishments, and we might be able to track him that way. Paedophile? It shouldn't be that difficult, a lot easier than if we were trying to find an opium-seller.' Schliff smiled. 'Let's go.'

'Now?' Ryzhkov said. It was only ten in the morning.

'Oh, yes. If we leave now we have a chance to catch some of the children before they start to work. That way we don't interrupt anyone's business, it will be much easier to talk. I've got a list of six places, all within the central districts where we can start.'

Accordingly the three of them crowded into a police droshky and headed across the city. Schliff had decided to work his way through the richer neighbourhoods, on the supposition that the killer was from the upper classes, which would have fitted with Ryzhkov's description of the clientele at the bindery. The first place they stopped was an ornate town house across the street from the Italian embassy, an old structure with high windows and sculptural touches beneath the eaves, the whole of it surrounded by a wall. There were children's toys littered across a wide lawn, which itself was ragged with pathways, treasure-holes and play-fortresses that were in various states of assembly or destruction.

'What is this? A school?' Hokhodiev asked.

'A type of orphanage,' Schliff replied, shrugging.

Inside they met with a Madame Khory who obviously knew Schliff well. She invited them into the parlour to talk, asked if they desired tea, had some brought in anyway. Ryzhkov put the case to her, watched her frown grow as he described the type of man they were looking for, watched her look nervously to Schliff.

'We would never send one of ours to a client like that. We only cater to the most exclusive of tastes. Men and women of culture.' Madame Khory shook her head in evident distress.

'All of your customers come recommended, isn't that right?' Schliff added helpfully.

'Of course. We're all too aware of the dangers that our little ones face when we send them off.'

'Perhaps we could talk to some of the children, the girls? Perhaps some of them have had experiences—' Ryzhkov started.

'No, we always talk afterwards. They never handle the money so they can't be cheated or intimidated in any way. We know when to expect them back. I can't remember the last incident we've had . . . well, sometimes you have one person who wants to add a friend at the last moment, things like that.'

'Ah, well . . .' Schliff said and got up to go. Madame Khory stood to meet him, plainly relieved, offered her cheek to be kissed, once, twice, three times, and then they were shown the door.

Hokhodiev, seeing Ryzhkov's dark mood, turned on the little city detective. 'Look here, how do you know she's not lying?'

Schliff thought for a moment, then faced Hokhodiev with a smile. 'Strictly speaking I don't, but she knows I'm not going to pressure her and if she learns something she'll tell us. Moreover, she knows that if I do catch her in a lie, well . . .' He waggled his hand to indicate an entire range of consequences.

'You didn't grill her very hard in there. It all looked light to me,' Hokhodiev protested.

'Don't worry, gentlemen. This is a different world, eh? A different type of investigation.'

If Madame Khory's billed itself as an orphanage, the next establishment called itself a school. At the door they could hear the children inside. Apparently they had arrived at breakfast. It was a noisy house, presided over by a husband and wife team. They were both in aprons. No servants. It looked like catering to the paedophile market was a poor way to make ends meet.

'Oh, hello, Iosif. What's the matter?' The woman of the house hovered nervously in the foyer.

'Good afternoon, Tanya. We're just here for some questions. We're searching for a bad case, someone who enjoys hurting the girls a little too much,' Schliff said, pleasantly.

'Someone who enjoys killing them a little too much,' Ryzhkov put in, growing impatient. Schliff turned to him, smiled tightly. The husband appeared at the door, saw Schliff and visibly relaxed.

'Oh, dear,' said the woman. 'Well, come in, then. We're all just at breakfast.' It wasn't that late for breakfast considering the hours the children had to work.

Inside was a large room with perhaps a half-dozen children, mostly girls, but with a couple of boys sitting around a long table with all its leaves added, causing it to project out of the dining area and into the front room of the dwelling. It was warm in the 'school'; the whole place smelled of food and sour milk, Ryzhkov thought.

'Listen, everyone,' the woman announced. 'Mr Schliff wants to ask you some questions. Think hard about what he says and then tell him anything that might be helpful, please?'

Schliff held his hat in his hand and took the centre of the room. As he talked he looked at each of the children in turn. 'We're trying to find someone, a man, an old man with white whiskers, but not like Père Christmas . . .' The children laughed. 'No, he's got a beard here on the side and he divides it into halves sometimes. And not much hair on his head. And we're trying to find him because sometimes he . . . gets a little . . . carried away, you know?' There was a murmur of understanding from the children. A couple of titters. 'Can anyone remember meeting anyone like that?' Schliff looked around hopefully.

'Does he like boys or girls?' a boy asked from the corner of the table.

'Girls,' Schliff said. 'Just girls. Has anyone met someone like that? We want you to think about it, try to remember.'

'There's a lot of them,' a little girl said. She was sitting on the floor and playing with a dolly that someone had made from knotted rags. A younger version of Lvova. 'We can't be expected to remember everyone, you know?' she said, ladylike and a little piqued at the whole thing.

'But you would remember him if he had hurt you, yes? He likes to squeeze—' Schliff put his hands out to choke an invisible child. 'Like this. Have any of you met anyone of that sort?' There was a moment when the children began to murmur together. The man and woman looked around and shrugged.

'I met someone like that, but you said he liked girls, so . . .' another one of the boys said.

'Was he old, with white whiskers?'

The boy searched his memory for a moment. 'Not then but he could have dyed his hair!' The children laughed. Now they were playing detective.

'When was it?'

'Last year. He liked to squeeze, but he wanted me to squeeze him too.' There was more laughter at the word-play. Schliff smiled.

'Thank you, but we don't think he'd dye his hair. If anyone does see him . . . any of you girls, make sure to tell Tanya or Georg, eh? If you find him, Inspector Ryzhkov here will bring you all a big package of sweets.' A cheer from the children. The little girl stood up and hugged his leg before they left.

'My God,' said Hokhodiev as they got in the carriage. Schliff was still making conversation at the door with the patrons. 'Sometimes I feel like I've slipped into a dream . . . a nightmare. Something where up is down and nothing makes sense.'

'He's obvious being paid off by all these people,' Ryzhkov said. He was frustrated. They were going nowhere. It reminded him of the kind of visits you made after Christmas to see the relatives and parade your latest pair of shoes. Talking about nothing, niceties and gossip. All that was missing was the tea and cakes.

'Oh, I don't doubt it. All these boys who till the fields at the bottom, they're always on the take. If they weren't, you'd suspect them of something,' Hokhodiev said sourly.

Schliff was coming back from the door. He seemed pleased. 'Only four more to go, gentlemen,' he said.

'Look, are you sure this is getting us somewhere?' Ryzhkov said, harder than he meant to. He was trying to be patient, but . . .

'Certainly, as I said, before, it's a different type of investigation.' He smiled and reached out to tap their driver on the back. 'We're going to Nevsky Prospekt. All the way to the end, a little place behind the monastery.'

The rest of the day was like that, a series of 'schools', 'foundlings rescue societies' and 'boarding hostels' all of which were, in reality, dispatching agencies for child prostitutes. As the hours passed, the owners they dropped in on had grown increasingly irritable and it was obvious that the children were being bathed, dressed and coached for their nightly chores. Little cheeks were being rouged, little nails clipped, little teeth brushed. Everyone was too busy to talk to them. They called it a day and agreed to meet in another two days when Schliff would have had time to draw up a fresh list of establishments they could investigate. When they returned to headquarters one of the St Petersburg police clerks handed them a buff folder. Schliff waved goodbye. It was almost the dinner hour, the start of his normal workday.

In the droshky on the way back to 17 Pushkinskaya Ryzhkov looked through the dossier. It was a series of single-spaced typewritten pages—a master list of children who had either been found murdered, or had simply disappeared within Petersburg over the last three years.

There were fourteen pages in the file.

FIFTEEN

The bomb exploded before dawn, and by the time Ryzhkov dragged himself out of bed and got to the little house off Baltiskaya Street, it was all over but the cleaning up.

It had detonated by accident just as a terrorist had been ascending the steps from a second bomb factory, only a few streets away from the one the Okhrana had been watching. The terrorist, or terrorists (no one knew exactly) had been blown into a fine spray of flesh that had spattered the walls of surrounding buildings; a few dozen windows had been shattered by the blast. The front of a little rooming-house had been knocked off its foundations, collapsed, and immediately caught fire.

No one knew if this second bomb factory had any connection with the group that were now being arrested by the St Petersburg gendarmes, the anarchists taken by surprise, caught asleep in their various boltholes, enfeebled by the noxious fumes in their 'laboratory'.

Now Ryzhkov and Hokhodiev stood in the background, trying not to gag as Baron Colonel Tuitchevsky, commander of the local Okhrana bureau, strode through the devastation, with a grave and embarrassed expression on his face, angry and worried that he would be blamed for overlooking the second set of terrorists. Clearly he was looking for any excuse he could find; a way to treat the explosion as a great victory would be best, but failing that, someone else's career was going to have to go. Eventually Tuitchevsky came around to Ryzhkov, shook his hand, but completely ignored Hokhodiev, who just stood there calmly, having seen it all before a million times.

It could have been much, much worse; only one bystander had been killed, no one important, only a newsboy who had the misfortune to be standing outside on the corner in the early hours waiting to pick up his papers for the day. He was blown into the street and died quickly from the concussion. There were fragments of Russian Word floating about the street, or turning into soggy mush from the water the firemen had soaked everything with. Now they were rolling up their hoses and smoking cigarettes.

'Oh, God . . .' Ryzhkov heard Hokhodiev mutter behind him, and he turned to see a thickset woman running up. She went from gendarme to gendarme tugging on their lapels trying to find her son, but no one knew where he was, perhaps they had already taken him away.

From the neighbours Ryzhkov learned something of the ownership of the building. It was a property managed by a banking firm as it turned out, undoubtedly purchased for speculative purposes by a rich investor. Hokhodiev telephoned and informed a bank clerk and they promised they would send someone out right away; the basement was leased to a family named Popov the clerk said. They had only rented a few days before and had paid up to the end of the month.

Ryzhkov walked around in the soggy embers and peered down the stone stairwell into the flooded basement. 'Popov' would undoubtedly prove to be an alias. He wondered if there were any other bodies down there and how long it would take the police to sift through the wreckage.

'What I cannot fathom—' Colonel Tuitchevsky was complaining behind him, '—is why we had no indication, no indication at all. We followed them, your people were listening to the others, yes? But you say you didn't hear anything did you?' His eyes were narrowed and he had focused on Ryzhkov. 'Where's Zezulin? I thought he was in charge of this entire case? Why isn't he here?'

'I don't know, Colonel. We were all called from our station, so . . . Perhaps he is en route,' Ryzhkov said. In reality Zezulin had probably slept through any telephone call he would have received in the early morning.

'Well, we were told about the *one* set of bombers, now it turns out there were *two*. I suppose Zezulin simply missed it entirely, eh?'

'I really couldn't say, Colonel. There were several telephone calls from the other site, from the bakery. Perhaps some were made to this group. We really have no way of knowing.'

'Hmmph . . .' Tuitchevsky looked at him for a moment, the trace of a smile. He could see as well as anyone when someone was protecting his boss. 'Well, don't worry. I'll get to the bottom of things,' he said. Tuitchevsky kicked a charred window frame with his shiny boot. In fact no one would ever know what had happened. The explanation had gone up in smoke. 'What is that?' The window frame had slid down a hill of debris and Tuitchevsky was bending down to look at something gleaming in the cinders.

'It's a hand.'

'Good God!' Tuitchevsky abruptly took a step back.

'There's a ring,' said Ryzhkov bending closer, taking out his handkerchief. 'See the corrosion? That's probably from the chemicals.'

'The hand of the bomber?' Tuitchevsky's eyebrows had shot up.

'Perhaps.'

Now the colonel came closer and squatted down over the relic. From the dark hairs and blunt nails, the hand had once belonged to a man. There was a thick band around the ring finger, too tarnished to tell if it was gold or silver. '*The hand of the bomber* . . .' Tuitchevsky breathed wonderingly. And when Ryzhkov turned he saw that Tuitchevsky was smiling.

'I *want* this,' Tuitchevsky said in a hushed voice, almost amazed at himself. 'I want this for my *collection*. There ought to be a way to preserve it, don't you think?'

'I . . . I really don't know. I suppose . . . but we need it first.'

'Yes,' Tuitchevsky said reaching out and touching the hand for the first time, turning it over to examine the calloused palm, the shredded flesh at the wrist. 'It's beautiful, in a way. I mean, it is beautiful, you can't deny that, eh?'

Ryzhkov shook his head. For a moment he thought he was going to faint. Dizzy, knocked out from lack of sleep, from an overdose of absurdity.

'If you say so.'

'I do,' Tuitchevsky said quietly. 'I *do* say so.'

When they finally got in their carriage they passed the woman again. She was sitting on the kerb, rocking back and forth, clutching a blue cloth cap in her hand. Another child was standing beside her, too young to understand, one hand on her mother's shoulder. It only took a few moments to drive past her and neither of them said anything about it.

Ryzhkov dropped Hokhodiev off and continued on with Tuitchevsky's hand to the Military Hospital so that the ring could be removed and cleaned. It turned out to be a common silver band. An assistant took fingerprints from the hand so that Ryzhkov could take them back to the External branch's Records Division.

Bondarenko came in right at the end of it. The grisly nature of the project seemed to catch his interest. 'Well . . . it's a wedding band, or perhaps an engagement present. Not of great quality, I'd say. There is a jeweller's mark beside the inscription. It's somewhat worn. You might be able to find something via the fingerprints, and at the Records Division there is an extensive library of jeweller's marks.' He used a pair of tweezers to put the ring back in its envelope.

'Thank you, Doctor. Ah . . . Colonel Tuitchevsky wants, for some reason . . . well, he's asked me to enquire if the hand itself could be preserved somehow? Is that possible?' Bondarenko had suddenly lost his good humour. He frowned.

'Preserved?'

'Yes . . . I don't know . . .'

'I'm not a taxidermist,' Bondarenko said, offended. 'Tell him it's absolutely out of the question.' Bondarenko abruptly turned away and retreated into his labyrinth, shaking his head and muttering curses under his breath.

Upstairs in the lobby Ryzhkov borrowed a telephone to check in with 17 Pushkinskaya and got an excited Izachik on the line. 'Monsieur Zezulin has found out about this morning's events and wishes everyone to come in, sir, and also for you there is a message from'— a pause—'an Inspector Schliff.'

'Oh?'

'Yes, sir. He asks you to meet him at the front of the Haymarket, sir.'

'Really?'

'Yes sir. He seemed to think it was important.'

The boy sat across the room. It was a large dusty open space, where rows of seamstresses had once worked. The fine wood floor had holes drilled through it that had been puttied over when they removed the machines but never repaired.

'He says he only wants to speak to you.'

'How did he know about me?' Ryzhkov asked.

'I've been passing the word around. He heard somehow, went out and telephoned in. He's scared that he's in trouble,' Schliff said quietly, not quite whispering.

'I can't imagine he could get in worse trouble than in this place.'

'He's not worried about trouble with us, just with the old man that owns him,' Schliff said. 'See, if you go investigating in places like this, if you want to get anywhere, you have to stand between the pimp and the bird. I spent a little on him, just so you know.'

'How much?'

'A twenty.'

'All right,' Ryzhkov said. He had no way to tell if Schliff was just lining his own pockets. It didn't matter. It was the price of doing business; he would put in a request when Zezulin was asleep.

They walked across the open room. The boy looked up at them. He was about twelve years of age—or maybe he was older and just looked younger. Schliff had already told him that the boys were forced to move on when they got older. Either sold to individuals, or the homosexual brothels, or, if they were very handsome, to more luxurious establishments that catered to wealthy female clients. Any one of those choices was considered lucky. If they failed to land a position in one of the bordellos a life on the street was the only other possibility. It was the great dividing line in the life of a prostitute. The boy looked at him steadily.

'This is Teodor,' said Schliff. 'Teodor, this is Inspector Ryzhkov. He's investigating the murder of a *vertika* that happened recently. Tell him about your friend.'

'First I tell you, then I have to tell him,' the boy complained.

'Fine, stop whenever you want to.'

'You're looking for an old man. White hair, big side-whiskers like that?' The boy put his hands up to show them.

'Yes.'

'He likes to squeeze girls?'

'We think so, yes.'

'He killed this other girl?'

'That's right.'

The boy looked at both of them for a moment. Making up his mind. He was older than twelve, Ryzhkov decided. Or maybe just old before his time.

'There was a guy that killed my wife,' Teodor said quietly.

'Your wi—' Ryzhkov started but Schliff put his hand on his arm. 'Keep going,' he told the boy.

'She went to this place and was with a grandfather, an old one like you said. She came back, they brought her back, she was sick when she came back, and then she died that night. She had something break up here from when he squeezed her.'

'Can you tell us where she was that night, who sent for her?' Ryzhkov asked quietly. The boy gave a tight smile, shook his head, then looked up at Schliff.

'No, no. Fine, Teo. You can stop. We don't want you to get in any trouble.'

The boy looked back across to the door. 'Don't worry,' he said.

'Anything you can tell us, Teodor . . .'

'Sure,' he said. 'Go and look in that cupboard.' The boy pointed across to the end of the big garret room where cupboards and open shelving had been built-in to store bolts of fabric. 'Not that one, the one over against the roof.'

Ryzhkov opened the little cupboard. There was a box of wooden bobbins, some scraps of paper. Everything was covered in dust and mouse shit.

'Reach back in the corner up at the top and there's a nail that sticks out.'

'All right.' He felt back into the cupboard where the shelving joined the rafters.

'If you pulled on that nail you might find something. It wouldn't be my fault.'

Ryzhkov tugged on the little nail and the board that formed the back wall of the cupboard teetered out and pivoted so that he could slide it away. Inside there was a tin box, about the size of a tea-box, and a black velvet handbag of high quality.

'Just take the bag, leave the other, and put it back, eh?' the boy said. Schliff had taken a few steps across the floor but the boy stopped him. 'You stay and watch the door. Everything I've got is in there.'

In the purse was a cheap gold-plated bracelet, a man's tie clip with some sort of stone set in its centre, several postcards, a photograph of a woman in a rather ordinary dress, and a man's empty leather wallet.

'That's all her things she left me.'

'She had light fingers, your wife did?' Schliff was smiling at the boy.

'We were saving up to go away,' the boy said flatly. Ryzhkov looked at him for a moment and then opened the wallet.

Schliff took the bag, walked over and examined it under the light from the window. Looked at the portrait of the woman. 'That her mother?' he asked, but the boy didn't say anything.

Inside the wallet Ryzhkov saw a small pocket for business cards, a worn yellow slip that indicated a St Petersburg residency permit. It was one of the old permits, all the newer ones had photographs and were supposed to be stamped . . . a name written across the top line in steel-pointed cursive script: *Lavrik, Oleg Karlovich*. With an address on Liteiny Prospekt. Not big money, but enough, he thought.

The boy was watching him. 'Got what you want?'

'Yes, thank you.'

'You can keep it. I only held on to it hoping that one day I might run into him, you know?' The boy's eyes were steady as a knife's edge.

'You might be able to get something for the bracelet.'
Schliff said, closing the catch on the bag.

'I don't think so. It's something she found when she
was little,' he said.

'Do you want a smoke?' Schliff asked.

'I'm not supposed to unless they offer,' he said flatly.
'She had a box, with some clothes. I gave those to some
of the girls. Eva wanted the combs and her ribbons.
There is a letter inside from her mother maybe, but I
don't know. It might be someone else's mother.'

Ryzhkov tucked the bag with its souvenirs back
inside the rafters, fumbled in his pocket and came out
with a ten-rouble note. A lot. 'Here . . . this is something
for your savings.' He held the note out for the boy.
Schliff reached out first and took it away, dug in his
pocket and came up with a five and some coins. 'Your
boss, the old man will ask you if we paid, won't he?'
Schliff said, looking at Ryzhkov.

'Yeah, I'll have to give him something. He'll want to
know everything. I don't care about the money. If you
can get him, that will be enough.' Steady eyes looking at
him.

Ryzhkov nodded. 'Take it anyway. If he gives you any
trouble, get in touch with me through Inspector Schliff
here, and I'll protect you,' Ryzhkov said. He took out
his Okhrana disc and showed it to the boy. 'Do you
know what this means?' he asked.

The boy looked at the flat circle of metal, with its
worn double-eagle and the engraved numerals, and then
up to Ryzhkov.

'It means you think you can protect me,' he said.

By midnight Ryzhkov was sitting in an *izvolchik* with
the canopy raised so that he could watch the front of

Baron Oleg Karlovich Lavrik's city house. The files had not come over from the General Staff building, that would have to wait for morning, but he had looked up the address in the Petersburg directory, and verified that he still lived there.

The Liteiny house was high and narrow. Probably six or seven bedrooms. No stables or courtyard. They must travel everywhere by hired carriage. No one had come or gone from the time he had arrived, just after six in the evening. Lights came on and went off. There was a tail of smoke from the chimneys. He moved around the building and watched from different angles, but no one raised the corner of a curtain. Lamps were on in the upper bedrooms until after ten and then one after the other were snapped off. Two people were living there, he thought. Two people in two different bedrooms; if there were servants they would have rooms at the back.

He watched the darkened house for a half-hour more. The street was quiet. An ordinary Thursday evening with the air getting colder and colder. A little sheen of ice in the wet gutters. A crispness to the air. He decided there was no point in spending the night watching. He would turn up a photograph of Baron Lavrik, take it to Vera and her friend and if they could put Lavrik in the Iron Room, then he'd request a protocol to formally investigate the man, find his accomplice, and hopefully send them both to jail.

He was suddenly tired. Tired, as if he had finished a great test or examination of some kind. His mind wandered, playing games. He would bring in Madame Hillé once he had the protocols. She'd give up Lavrik if it meant losing her residency permit and her yellow card or jail; he'd withhold her passport so she couldn't run, get a case together that could go before a court. Maybe he could make things right, or at least a little better.

It was cold now and he decided to go home. The air was thick with the moisture that had risen from the canals and the river.

The weather was changing.

There would be a chilly fog in the morning. A stinking yellow blanket that would greet Petersburg's citizens when they woke; a poisonous veil that would hover over the pavements, making it impossible to read the street signs, and concealing everything from view.

SIXTEEN

Andrianov sat in the ornate foyer of Mendrochovich and Lubensky, one of the empire's great financial houses; impressive offices, with splendid furnishings and arched windows above the Nevsky, spanning the front of the building and around the corner of the Fontanka embankment. It was a clear day and the sun burned through the windows, bringing out the smells of the woollen carpet, the wax on the furniture and walls, the rich leather of the furniture, the pungency of cigar smoke. Across the wide foyer were a handful of other men, heads together discussing their business, shuffling papers, waiting for appointments, some of them anonymous, some known to him by name. Clients who visited Mendrochovich and Lubensky were able to conduct business within a cocoon of complete discretion, indeed individuals, partnerships, companies or entire families could, if it was required, be identified only by secret number. Anonymity was guaranteed absolutely. Naturally there was the full panoply of investment services for ordinary clients, even simple banking accounts and safe boxes available within vaults on the top floor.

'It's such a pleasure to meet you Monsieur Andrianov, a man of your reputation. We're most happy indeed, and I am certain that you will be satisfied with our services.'

'My pleasure. You are Dr Rody?'

'Yes, sir. And I must say that you have been quite highly recommended by one of our most distinguished clients, Monsieur Brogdanovitch. Everything appears to be in order. Shall we remove to my office?'

Andrianov followed the man down a hallway. There were frosted-glass windows to hide the business of each of the factors from his neighbour. Altogether he estimated that several dozen clerks, administrators and agents inhabited the offices. There were facilities for the transfer of monies, an international division, the ability to perform any transaction you could imagine. They settled for a moment in Rody's office.

'I understand you wished to set up an anonymous account, and we have put through all the necessary papers. You have only to sign these documents. They are matched with a number and then this number is kept in another location. It is for our records only; also, in case of death, we require the name of a representative who would contact us in accordance with your estate. May I suggest a family member or some other trusted representative, a lawyer perhaps? So, if you could give us that information, then seal the envelope, take your key, and I'll return in a few moments, sir.'

Andrianov nodded his assent, the man slipped out into the hallway and left him to review the papers. He filled in a pseudonym at the bottom of the pages, sealed the papers, and pocketed the key; he had no intention of ever actually using the account. He waited in the office for a few moments longer and then went to the door. Rody was hovering a few doors away, chatting with an associate. He straightened and came back to the little office, took the envelope.

'Now, I understand you have been referred to Baron Lavrik, and that he is to be your representative at our house?'

'Yes, he comes highly recommended, himself,' Andrianov smiled.

'An excellent choice, sir. A very distinguished man of wide experience. I will introduce you.' They walked deeper into the building. There was a sort of inner foyer, with a large pyramidal skylight that allowed sufficient light for several palms to flourish in an ornate marble planter in the centre of the room. A series of offices ringed the space, all windowed in frosted glass. They crossed the thick carpet and Rody knocked on one door. 'Baron?'

'Come . . . yes?'

'Our new client,' Rody said, as he opened the door. Andrianov came in, smiling. The baron stood. He was somewhat older than his photographs, a man grown prosperous and of comfortable girth, deep into his sixties. A large beard that was carefully cultivated so that it gave him the appearance of a grandfatherly walrus. He wore a pince-nez that he tucked in his waistcoat pocket as he stood, simultaneously sweeping some papers into a folder, sealing it, extending his hand.

'Gentlemen,' Rody said, as he closed the door behind him. Andrianov took a seat in yet another of the plush leather armchairs. Lavrik offered him a cigar, but Andrianov declined. For a moment the two men sat there smiling at each other.

'Well, sir. As I am sure Dr Rody has advised you, we offer a full range of financial services here, investment advice, brokerage, international transfers and legal services throughout Europe. We also have relationships with sister houses, particularly in Paris, but also in Britain and lately in the United States . . .'

Andrianov waved him off, still smiling. 'No, it's not about anything like that. My business affairs are quite in order, thank you.'

'Ahh . . . Well, then, sir . . . how may I be of service?' Lavrik sat back in his seat, crossed his hands across his belly, preparing to dispense as much financial advice as was required. Still the smile.

'I have come here to help you,' Andrianov said, in somewhat quieter tones. Lavrik's brow furrowed. 'Indeed, I have been sent here by *Heron*.'

Lavrik's mouth opened, the eyebrows shot up. Andrianov raised a finger to warn him into silence.

'I should tell you that I am simply a messenger, sir. I know nothing of your confidential business, I am a courier with only a single piece of information.' And he smiled again at the old man.

'From . . . a *Heron* . . . you say?' Lavrik muttered, trying to assemble his features in an expression of innocent confusion.

Andrianov smiled. 'I'm sorry, sir. This is no ruse. I am to give you the message, nothing more. What you make of it, what action you decide upon is your own business.'

Lavrik looked at him for a long moment, his frown growing. 'Please, help me, sir. Have we met?'

'If we have sir, I suggest it is to our mutual advantage to forget all about it.'

Another long pause.

'Fine. Fine then.' The old man was waiting, trembling. The colour had drained from his cheeks. He looked nearer to death than ever. 'He told me there was . . . an investigation, but I thought all that had been taken care of.' His hands were wiping the surface of his desk, as if trying to divine the future hidden deep within the grain of the walnut.

'Honestly sir, I could not say.'

Lavrik nodded, sighed. His eyes were filling up, he fumbled for a handkerchief and dabbed at the corners.

'The message is this,' Andrianov said. 'On Sunday next you are to be prepared for a carriage to arrive at your residence, this to occur at nine o'clock sharp in the evening. You will be taken the Niva Club where you have a reservation for dinner. At some point in the meal you will be asked to join a Mr Petrov from Odessa. There is no such person, it is simply a coded phrase. If you do not hear those exact words, you are to refuse, finish your meal and return home. But when you do hear the invitation, you are to go with whoever gives it to you—'

'Mr Petrov? Odessa?' Lavrik repeated.

'From the Niva you will be led through the kitchens to a second carriage and from there to a boat which is waiting to take you first to Finland, and from there to Berlin. Accommodations are already arranged for you in Berlin. Where you go from there is entirely your business.'

Now Lavrik's mouth had fallen open, 'Is that it? I'm to simply . . . *leave*?'

Andrianov smiled most sympathetically. 'As I said sir, I am merely the bearer of the message, but apparently there is some imminent danger. Mortal danger? Legal danger? Really, excellency, I know nothing of these affairs. I am in no position to say.' He shrugged. 'If I may suggest, it might be best if tomorrow morning you have your man telephone that you have suddenly been taken ill and use the intervening days to put your affairs in order, draft whatever documents you require in order to access your holdings while you are abroad. I'm certain that here your firm can perform all the necessary—'

'I'm to leave?' Lavrik said again, helplessly.

'That is the message from *Heron*, sir.' Andrianov stood up, preparing to exit.

'Just a moment.' Lavrik's voice had risen in panic. 'Please . . . my daughter. She has to go with me, she can't be alone. We have to go together. Can you ask . . . *Heron* if we can go together?' The old man had come around the desk now, his fingers had reached out to pluck at Andrianov's sleeve. Desperate.

Andrianov smiled, grasped the man by the shoulders to steady him. 'I'm sure that would be acceptable, excellency.' And then leaning closer to the old man, so his words were only a whisper, something like a brotherly intimacy, shared between comrades at war, a parting prayer for encouragement, 'Remember, Baron. We are brothers of the Sacred Guard. We always take care of our own.'

As he left through the foyer he saw Rody again. He bowed to Andrianov, smiled. 'I trust everything has been concluded to your satisfaction, sir?'

'Yes,' Andrianov said, taking the man's hand in a hearty handshake. 'I could not have put it better myself.'

SEVENTEEN

. . . given us a supreme truth of vision that rubs our nose in the verities of this modern age!

'Ha!' laughed Dmitri, showing off the newspaper. Izov was so impressed he snipped it out and put it up on the door as if it were an ikon. That was the kind of thing they were saying about 'Khulchaev's Theatre'. It didn't matter that it was only in the pages of the *Gazette*.

Scandalously appropriate . . . more shocking than a tour of the lowest depths of our city, this insane pastiche mirrors exactly the nausea of modern life . . . Engulfed by flowered dancers made-up to resemble aborigines from some distant planet, hypnotically abused, the audience discovers the bliss that can only come through a protracted flagellation . . .

And there was more, much more in this vein. From the pages of Russian Standard, usually a respected paper:

Not pleasant, but necessary . . .

Unaccountably, Vera thought, Dmitri Khulchaev's shows had become wildly popular. People with real money were starting to show up; he'd bought himself an entire new wardrobe. He walked around in a red waistcoat and the tightest trousers she'd ever seen on a man who wasn't a hussar or a ballet dancer. Now that he was successful and starting to take credit for everything that was done at the Komet, all he really wanted was for people to owe him, to be in awe of his genius.

Their newest show was entitled *Long Nightmare*. The Komet girls rehearsed their steps, a slow processional in waltz time—the devil's dance—that wandered among the tables. For the performances Kushner, their designer said they would be painted up as skeletons.

She thought the music was good but *Nightmare* was proving to be a supremely pessimistic event since Bulgaria had recently gone down to defeat in her idiotic war against Greece, Serbia, and finally Rumania. Thousands of young men, not to mention innocent women and children, had been dying like flies even as the idea for the play had been hatched and the girls assigned their steps—chests out and arms held just so, one-two-three, one-two-three.

Misha Kushner, a wild man who worked through the night, stopping only to sleep with Larissa who was mad for him, Jew or not. Unshaven, unwashed, she didn't care. He was her little dose of reality, Vera supposed.

She'd tried to warn Larissa about Kushner, that he was crazy, that he was dangerous, but the girl was blind, a fool for her new lover. What made it worse was that he was the very worst kind of Bolshevik, authentically sprung from the land, raised in a seamy ghetto somewhere in the

Ukraine. Overeducated and burning with his commitment to art and truth. Fine, fine, but where was the future in that, even if he was right? Being right didn't have anything to do with it; St Petersburg was built on the corpses of thousands of people who had been *right*.

'Louder!' the Professor was calling to them and she arched her back even more and sang out:

> *Do you want to die before*
> *You know what it is to live?*
> *How much we are all missing*
> *What lies beyond so deep?*
> *Down here my love, so deep—*

At that point they were supposed to find an audience member and, grabbing their hands, encourage them to grope. When she and Gloriana objected, Khulchaev, like a hurt little boy, argued that it would get a great effect out of the audience. 'Pick somebody pretty,' he whined, 'pick somebody you like—' and of course, they all laughed.

Well, they were getting paid, so . . . And of course it *would* get an effect. Maybe she'd be lucky enough to be standing next to a great producer when the bridge came around.

She and Larissa had started to lie for each other. Contradicting themselves within minutes. The men that bought them drinks after the show seemed to like it too. They'd each tell bigger and bigger lies and then try to sustain it through the evening. They'd take on each other's names, lure the men on with fables about the other one.

Larissa had begun telling everyone that her friend Vera was a secret princess. An exiled princess, Vera decided. Dethroned because she'd had an affair with a village boy, a merchant boy. He was beneath her and her parents were enraged.

A princess. Why not? It was better than saying what really happened, that she'd found herself pregnant and alone. The real prince had been a boy named Kliment. A timid prince with beautiful eyes whose father owned things; distilleries, blast furnaces, farms. And owned his son's heart and soul as it turned out. Sent his men to intimidate her Aunt Varvara. Since the woman was a natural coward, it wasn't all that hard.

In the end his father had sent their driver to give her the news and, the price of clearing his conscience, forty roubles. The next morning she'd taken the train to Petersburg. The old driver couldn't bear to look at her when they got to the station. And he had been the one who used to laugh at them, leave them in the bushes and go off and have a smoke by the lake. Now he couldn't bring himself to look her in the eye.

So she took the forty roubles and got rid of his baby in Moscow.

Saying that she was a princess was better than saying that. So she let it stick. In the last production she had been singled out since, as the Queen of the Martians, she had been prominently featured. And now that the Komet was the latest discovery of the fast set, all the girls were being sought to grace the salons of the city's elite. She had met Zinadia Grippius, and Blok, who looked at her like he was interested in maybe a little more than talk, and Anna Akhmatova, who had sat there all night with her legs crossed. Then there was the big night, when Diaghilev dropped in and made a beeline for Khulchaev, plied him with drinks, and soon they all piled off in his red-lacquered Renault en route to a more artistic rendezvous.

Such was life in the theatre.

She turned, rolled her head around and, as they tapped their feet through the bridge, took a sip of her steaming tea.

She saw that Pyotr Ryzhkov had come in. Standing in the door talking to Izov. He'd vanish for days and then come around again. Now he was there with a package of brushes for Kushner. Free. They were samples, he said. Larissa made a face and pointed at Gloriana blowing her nose and waved him away, they were sounding so bad.

. . . my heart is a post, a stable for my hunger . . .
. . . I'm grazing, grazing, I'm just a cow, just a beautiful
cow . . .

She watched him as he went back into the bar and opened himself to the intense discussions of high finance that were overwhelming Izov, who, not knowing anyone he could trust, confided to Ryzhkov the fine print details of the great scheme. Izov's 'angels' were plotting a complete renovation. There would be a new entrance; a portico with a ticket window, and dozens of new tables, custom-designed cups, plates, saucers and silverware. It went on and on, imaginary roubles mounting to the sky.

When the girls asked about the dressing-rooms, the angels just looked up blankly. Khulchaev winced, he wanted the money for a spotlight, the Professor had asked for a better piano. There were so many priorities.

'We don't even have *water* back there.' Larissa was so irritated at them that she had come up to their table, her fingers involuntarily adopting the cat-claw pose she had taught them all.

'You can keep on taking water from the kitchen, what's the problem with that?'

'Why do you think people are coming to this hole? Could it have anything to do with the fact that the Martians are all naked women in red paint, or what?' But they couldn't figure it out, ha, ha, ha.

Pyotr came back and she looked away again. Looked down and tapped her feet to the music and then afterwards, thinking she couldn't stare at the floor for the rest of her life, looked up and met his eyes until he left the room. Probably wanting to talk again, to ask more questions. Wanting to get her to go along with some big plan to cure all the ills of the Earth. And then afterwards, knowing he was out there waiting for her, she took her good time about putting on her boots. It made her furious. She started for the door but he was standing right there. She tried to make her eyes hard. 'Good evening,' was all she could manage.

'Yes . . .'

She settled there on one hip, staring at him, assessing him like she was trying to decide if he was the right colour to hang on the wall. Her princess look.

'I thought, by way of apology, that—' he started.

'Apology?'

'Well . . . yes . . .'

'What do you have to apologize for?'

'For putting you through—'

'For making me think you knew what you were doing, you mean? For opening old wounds, for not being the friend you pretended to be? For all that, now you're sorry?'

'Let's go outside.'

'I'm not going outside with you. God knows where I might end up.'

'Honestly, Vera. Really. Apologize. For all of it. Yes. And to tell you what's happened. We've found him, the old one.' He looked like he wanted to smile, but it manifested itself as a shrug.

She stood there staring a hole right through his forehead. 'What are you going to do?' Her voice sounded shaky and distant, like it belonged to someone else.

'We'll watch him, follow him. Try to find the other one. Get more witnesses, make a case. Take it to the prosecutor. Finally we'll arrest him. By that time it will be long out of my hands.'

'Out of your hands.'

That shrug again.

'Well . . . so you've come to me to confess, then? You've discovered your errors and you know who you are at last, although you also say you are not in control of events? Your hands are too little? Not strong enough?'

Ryzhkov looked at her, maybe buried somewhere under there was the hint of a smile, just a flicker, like a candle that could blow out any second. 'I'm sorry.' He tried not to shrug.

'Yes, that was what you almost said . . .'

'I thought that . . . I don't know what I thought.'

'Do you know what Irini will do when she sees me again? Do you think I feel happy about that? Do you think I want Yuri and his friends to come down here and break the place up because of me? Maybe break me up too?' She let her eyes travel over his shabby suit. Not really up to the level of the embassy crowd she'd been seeing lately.

'Yes, yes.' Ryzhkov nodded to her. 'I'm . . .' He started to apologize yet again and then just trailed off.

'I know,' she said, looking at him for a long moment.

Ryzhkov put the empty glass back on Izov's new bar. 'Look . . .' He was lost for words. He suddenly saw himself, standing there like some clown, clutching his hat in his hand. A profoundly foolish man, in his out-of-fashion suit, in need of a good haircut, his shoes scuffed and stained from standing on too many street corners for too many hours. Making himself into an idiot over a woman, a prostitute he'd first seen in the gutter, a crazy woman who associated with anarchists and addicts. He nearly laughed because he was the same, the same as her. A rat crawling through the same gutters, wasn't he? He nearly laughed right in her face; a clown, a fool. Just get out.

'So, where are you off to in such a hurry?' she asked, but he was already going out of the doors. She followed him into the blustery street, trying to catch him. A real terrier. 'All right, fine. I accept!' she called out as he stalked down the rainy pavement. It stopped him and he turned to face her.

'Yes. I accept. You've made your confession, although it's a little short on information. Your motivation is not exactly clear. Nevertheless, we hereby . . . forgive *you*, Pyotr Mikhalovich Ryzhkov, alleged seller of brushes.' She made the sign of the cross, blessing him.

'"Verily, he has risen . . ."' he bowed, surprised at the way he felt—lighter by a hundredweight, swollen with a swirling confusion that nearly made him choke. Smiling maniacally at her and at the same time, full of dread, because soon he would have to betray her all over again.

'So, finally having been revealed as a poor sinner, you must now do a great penance,' Vera declaimed and came forward to take his arm. 'I am a hungry woman. I am very, very hungry and I have to eat right now so that I won't be full for our opening night. Have you prudently reserved your tickets?'

'Oh, yes,' he said.

'We could get something and walk over there to your place on—' she said suddenly.

'On Glasovskaya, the corner by the race track.'

'All right, then,' she said, smiling.

He looked over at her, surprised. 'All right?'

'Or we can take a cab . . . if you'd rather take your time.'

EIGHTEEN

The evening is perfect. Well, not perfect, but almost. Well, yes, cold. Too cold by far. Dank outside, with a chill fog that coats everything with a layer of ice, suspending the grime of the city inside fragile transparency. As if they all have been dipped in glass for an instant; little glass houses, little glass people, automobiles, trams. The foggy breath of the ponies in their harness, the filthy smoke that is held close to the ground by the still frigid air. All of it mysterious, fearful, but entrancing and magical too, somehow.

But all that is outside; inside is paradise: the first floor of the excellent Restaurant Mandusa, with high windows, candles, comfortable furniture and thick draperies to guard against the gloom beyond the walls.

Sergei is in an expansive, triumphal mood. Something has gone very well indeed judging from his demeanour. He has been flirtatious, complimentary, even humorous. He is talking, talking, talking. It must mean money, she

thinks. When he is like this it always means money.
Perhaps peace hasn't been so bad for business after all.
She wonders if she should tease him, probe a little. But
you can never really tell with Sergei. He can turn
instantly, become a changeling—peeling away a layer of
his personality like a dancer shedding a fan. Instead she
smiles and listens to him run on about the exciting possibilities of electrification. Did she know that soon there
will be ocean cruising vessels that run on electricity?
There are already submarines, he says, quietly, as if this
is privileged information that she is not supposed to
know. As if this is a great military secret. All the great
empires are at each other's throats. It is a particularly
good time to be in the munitions business. Boys must
have their toys.

'Oh, I know you don't care for any of this, dear . . .'
Dear! She cannot help but giggle. And the whole
evening is the same. He has overthrown her defences
and reduced her to schoolgirl age. She is, frankly,
amazed. For their evening he has reserved the best table.
Kasimir and his most experienced waiters hover around
them like expensively dressed crows. Sergei is so happy
he even teases Kasimir about his daughter. How does he
know Kasimir's daughter, she instantly thinks. But it
develops that it is only a child, born late to the old man
and his younger second wife. Do all men attempt to
have a second, younger wife? Yes, she supposes and
smiles at their banter, secure in knowing, if not everything about electric boats, at least the most important
things of all.

The dishes will be prepared especially for them,
Kasimir explains. In the kitchen they have already
ordered anything you can imagine. Apricots from

Greece, oranges from Spain, unpronounceable fish from Sweden. Everything freshly harvested and rushed to Mandusa via refrigerated express.

Kasimir and the waiters vanish, except for one immaculately groomed Tartar who tops up her champagne after every second sip. While they wait Sergei spots someone he knows across the room, a smile, a nod, a wave. In a few moments the man comes over. Another industrialist, a German, something to do with wire. Her gloved hand is kissed, her bosom appraised. Sergei claps the man on the back. It all goes by her in a fog. His business, not hers.

Tiny dishes are brought out. Exotic foods, snails, garnished with leaves from magical plants that are grown only in the Orient. She pushes the morsels around, smiles appreciatively, laughs. She spots Valina Chrasnova on the arm of her husband. They are having trouble, fighting these days, and Valina has been seeing a young major in the Life Guards. She has even hired detectives to follow her husband to and from his new mistress's, but it might end well because the mistress is a silly fool and keeps asking for more and Chrasnov has no money to speak of, although he puts up a good show. But when Valina detours through the room to kiss her— a smell of roses, a touch against her powdered cheek— even then Sergei is glad to meet Chrasnov, a complete stranger with no business connections whatever. They have nothing in common, really, but Sergei even takes out his card to give the man. They stop for a while at the table, linger a little too long, not the best manners, but Valina is famished for a friendly ear, even if she can't divulge anything there at the table. The plan is to meet for lunch on Tuesday. Another little kiss goodbye, and seamlessly another dish arrives. This is fish, splendid and tart, with lime and caviar dotted in some sauce they've dreamed up between absinthes in the back.

Sergei rejoices in the food. He has plans, and he wants to share them with her. *Plans!* Beyond all that, beyond the plans and the schemes, he is thinking of spending more time abroad, but he wants her to come along. Move out of Petersburg altogether? Oh no, nothing so drastic. Petersburg will always be home, but . . . sell the little apartments in Paris, get something bigger? Would she like that?

Well who wouldn't? Move into something bigger in Paris? To be closer to Antibes would be one great advantage. Away from the endless court politics and the gossip of the capital would be another, she couldn't care less for Rasputin and Alexandra and all that. It's a world that is closed to her anyway, no royal blood in this soap queen. The Parisians are a better crowd on the whole, and besides anyone who is anyone interesting visits there for at least part of the year.

'What about Vienna?' he muses between bites.

Her mouth falls open, it is clear that this is all a dream. Vienna is nice, she says. Indeed, a beautiful, civilized city. But she thought he didn't like the Austrians? For a moment she thinks she's gone too far.

'I like everyone, you know that.' His smile is tight. Yes, he likes anyone who can get him a little further down whatever road he's decided to travel, that's really what he means.

'If you would enjoy Vienna, Sergei, I'm sure I could find something to do there,' she breathes sweetly. In fact she knows no one in Vienna. And they never sold *Lilac* soap there. But he smiles tenderly, takes her hand and for a moment his gaze travels around the room. Two of Kasimir's boys take the plates away. The pheasant arrives.

She once more gives a master class in how to pretend to eat while actually consuming nothing. Sergei doesn't mind, or even notice. Once more he is off on the electric theme again, electric ships, electric aero craft, he says, eyes wide. The future is limitless. It is an opportunity, ripe for the picking. It is like a golden apple hanging from a golden branch. It will go to whomever reaches for it first. She laughs, not having any idea what he is talking about. Maybe he has a speech to give soon, maybe he's using her to polish up his personal philosophy.

There is a chamber orchestra on a low stage at the centre of the room and Sergei asks one of the boys to take a request—the *Fairy Dance*, the theme from her triumph. Everyone brightens at the famous melody. Those closest to them turn to her and nod. No, they have not forgotten, perhaps they never will forget. At the end the maestro bows to them and she gives a discreet nod. There is applause. Everyone is looking at them. Sergei kisses her hand. Looks deeply into her eyes.

Dessert is shaved chocolate over a lemon torte that Kasimir orders from Krafft's. She cannot help but eat it. Afterwards there is dancing in the ballroom, and they turn about the floor. Her head is a little light from the champagne and the bliss of it all. Yes, a perfect evening. With Sergei's lips against her cheek, his assured steps leading her as she glides, like a beautiful flower spinning on smooth water, round and round, laughter and diamonds.

She finds herself in his Renault, freshly back from the garage and brought out for the evening, warmed by a little heater that is cleverly built into the passenger compartment. His lips against hers, they float up the steps and directly upstairs.

He has her before they even reach the bed, and she is on fire and together they twist there like two wrestlers straining against each other, a tangled, stumbling, love-dance, that ends with him gasping and laughing— '. . . wanted to do that all night . . .' With his teeth against her collarbone, and her fingers clawing at his shoulders. She'll have his child. They'll send their daughter to school in Vienna, or Paris, or . . . it doesn't matter. She'll be a good dancer like her parents. The music is still swirling around in her head. Her hair has come undone, sheltering their faces in a shimmering private garden, and she falls apart, kissing him like a starving woman.

And he is laughing, laughing.

Waking the next morning, Vera turned at the sound of Pyotr's breathing, his face only inches away.

He looked frightened, she thought. Lost in some worried dream. But she thought his face . . . kind. So kind she wanted to kiss him. A little wave of tenderness that almost made her angry. Fine, so maybe he was a good man, one of the rare ones. A man who might be able to . . . A man who might turn out to be different from the rest. And if he wasn't? If he was as big a fool as any of them, well, what did it matter, he'd be gone soon, or she would. So what, who cares . . .

Maybe he was the kind who thought he was going to take care of her, be a new father for her. First he'd want to pull her out of the club, to stop her dancing, then it would be a whole series of little things; disapproval of how she cut her hair, the clothing she wore, her choice of fragrance. Then he'd forbid her drinking or smoking, or seeing any of her friends.

He probably thought she was damaged. Well . . . she could understand how he might. He probably thought he could just give her a little polish and then she'd come to him out of gratitude. First he'd try and transform her into someone who was worthy of his attention, and once she was all repaired into an acceptable version of a bourgeois frau, he would ask her to be wife number two. From then on it would be a slow calcification; because he'd picked her up in a bar, he'd always look down on her. See her as something to be cleaned up and transformed, and then used. Something to feel grateful to its maker.

Her big reward? She could be *Ryzhkova*. Then he could live out his remaining years sitting back and watching her enjoying the heaven he'd created for her. Maybe he'd want a few children in his old age, one after another. Little perfect boys, probably. Wouldn't that be lovely?

She slipped out of bed, gave the mirror a hard look, sniffed and started back through the rooms to get her clothes and leave. She had decided to get dressed without waking him, get out without any words or conversations.

The telephone interrupted her as she padded through the cold front room looking for her shoes. She answered it in one lunge to stop the ringing.

'*Hello, who's this? Is Pyotr Mikhalovich there?*' It was the gravelly voice of a big man, she could tell just from hearing it. The big man sounded surprised at getting anyone else on the line.

'Yes . . . He's sleeping'

'*Oh. Well, wake him up, eh?*' A big man in a hurry.

'Is it important?'

'*Important? Well, it all depends on how you look at it,*' the voice explained. Maybe she could just take a message and get out of there before he woke up and decided he was ready for some amorous adventures prior to breakfast.

But it was too late, Pyotr had pushed his head under the pillow and flung out one arm across the covers. Probably crawling around looking for her, she thought. Was he sad to find all that empty space in the bed? Did he mind if she answered his calls?

'It's someone called Konstantin,' she said, and watched him blink himself awake, watched him frown, watched him remember. She grabbed her clothes and was already moving out of his bedroom before he sat up.

'He said something happened and somebody got to Baron somebody-or-other—I guess they need some paintbrushes.'

NINETEEN

Galleyhaven was one of the lesser quarters of the city. On the western low ground of Vasilevsky Island, way out past the 27th Line Street, a long way from the university. It was a neighbourhood of lofts and fishermen's lodgings, where sailors too desperate to make it into the city spent their port-time in brothels that were phantasmagoric in their squalor. Galleyhaven had grown up at the edge of the docks, a perpetually shifting neighbourhood that served the demands of its particular slice of Petersburg's maritime industry. The 'streets' that divided the quarter vanished into the mud of the Gulf of Finland. When the wind shifted and the Baltic tides combined with the spring thaws, there were floods that regularly drowned the quarter. Less than a hundred years before, all of Galleyhaven had been submerged to a depth of twenty-four feet, and when the waters subsided, rebuilt.

His driver had to search for the address. It was on a point of boggy land at the end of Chose Line. Two sleepy gendarmes were waiting by a woodpile. They stiffened when they saw the Okhrana carriage heading towards them, and moved aside so it could pull up. Except for a dog barking in the distance everything was quiet. Ryzhkov saw Hokhodiev walking over to report. There was no reason to run.

'It's just in here.'

They walked along the stinking treacherous ground to a long low building that was built on piles over a mud bank. The building looked like it had been built of salvaged materials. There were planks and logs of different dimensions and a variety of colours. On a square sign over the wide door was a large picture of a fish for illiterates who couldn't read the name written under it in old-style characters: *Baltic Prospector*.

By the door he saw Dudenko and more gendarmes waiting for him. He could tell just by looking at them that something had gone wrong.

'At roughly nine o'clock last night the baron went out to dinner, all the way across town. He had his daughter with him—

'His daughter?'

'We think that's who it was. Personally, I've never seen her before.'

'All right, go on.' Ryzhkov was starting to grow worried.

'The two of them ended up at a restaurant on the Kamenoovstrovsky Prospekt, the Niva, you know it?'

'Not my type of food.'

'Nor mine, brother. They got there, then they vanished. We had Diakun and Hrothgar waiting out front, but they got out the back. I had a man on it, but I don't know. They got out somehow and we didn't find out about it until after midnight.'

'Oh, no . . . and?'

'It turns out they got in a hired cab. I guess we're lucky the daughter was there because one of the stewards in the cellars was just coming up and nearly ran into her, remembered them going through to a carriage in the back lane, and he got the number. Maybe he thought they were running out on their bill, I don't know. It was just sheer caprice. He told us, we went around to the company and got the destination. So, Dima came out here and then called me . . .' Hokhodiev turned aside to let Dudenko carry the story on from there.

'Well, the driver says he was called to deliver them over here to the island. They came by themselves, straight down the Bolshoi Prospekt, heading towards the water, and on to Kosaya, and then he helped them inside this place with their bags. He said there was no other carriage waiting for them.'

'Bags, what bags?'

'Bags. That's what he said.'

'Right . . .' So Lavrik had decided to make a break for it. 'They must have been planning to get out on a boat. Have you been around by the water?'

'Oh yes.' Dudenko looked down at his trousers which were ruined from crawling about in the mud under the pilings. 'I don't know what they were thinking. It's too shallow for a boat. A dinghy could get in, pick them up and take them out, still . . .'

Ryzhkov stood quietly for a moment, a growing hollowness spreading through his insides. Yes, it had all gone wrong, it was all over. 'Let's go,' he said and they headed for the door.

Inside *Baltic Prospector* it was warmer but the smell was worse.

The building had been wired for electric lights but the power was off. His men moved slowly across the large open room ahead of him. In the lantern glow he saw three rows of wooden tables where they cut up the fish, a cluster of tin buckets where they dumped the entrails. It looked like it hadn't been used for at least a few years. There was a thick film of grime and gull droppings on the tables. All the tools had been taken away.

There was a small office with no typewriter, a spray of mouldering papers spread across the floor. Abandoned.

In the corner there was a room for the watchman where the heat was coming from and they saw right away that the man was drunk, passed out and cradling a nearly empty bottle of vodka. Holding it close to his heart, like a Madonna with her baby from hell. The heat was coming from a bundle of rags burning in the furnace. The room smelled like someone had been too lazy to go outside and had decided to do their shitting in the corner.

'Hey.' Hokhodiev reached down and slapped the man by his foot. There was only a brief interruption in the snoring.

'He's dead to the world,' Dudenko said.

'Get him up. What's burning in there?' Ryzhkov went to the furnace and opened the vent. The room was suffused with a smell of wool burning.

'It's some clothes that are jammed up in here, just a second—' He yanked the bundle out of the grate and kicked the smoking rags out on the floor. The cloth looked shiny and expensive, and after a moment he saw that part of it was what was left of a woman's dress.

'Well . . .' Dima said, watching Ryzhkov separate the rags with the point of his shoe. A pair of woollen trousers with the remains of a charred pair of braces. Too wet from all the blood to catch fire; some silky material, white underclothing worked with lace— something that had belonged to the daughter Lavrik had cared for enough to take with him. He stamped out the flames on the burning lace, wondered what kind of thrilling childhood Lavrik's daughter had. And after all of it she had still trusted him enough to go with him tonight. To get out. It had been a good idea that hadn't worked, Ryzhkov thought.

'Well, let's get some light and find them,' he said quietly.

It didn't take much longer. The gendarmes walked around with lanterns and torches until they discovered new bloodstains on the floor over by the farthest of the fish tables. Marks on the floor where things had been moved about. The loading door was open.

Ryzhkov went outside and stood on the pier and lit a cigarette and before he was finished they had found the casks in the barge. Hokhodiev was the one who came and told him. He walked down the pier to the corner of the building. There was a gangway there, slippery with frozen algae and moss that had grown all over the boards. He carefully went down to a rotten barge that had been tied up there for so long that it was half-submerged in frozen mud. It was the kind of place where people piled their rubbish, where any shells or fish guts got flung. The domain of rats and gulls.

There were two herring casks in there, right on top of the muck. They had just been tossed over the railing from above, no attempt to hide them. Nothing growing on them at all.

'Be careful, Kostya,' Dima said as Hokhodiev climbed over. He'd found a pair of wading boots and tucked his trousers into the tops of them; he reached out with a gaff to try and tease the first cask around where he could reach it.

'It's too heavy,' Hokhodiev said, his breath making clouds of steam in the cold air. He stopped after a moment, shook his head, not wanting to walk further out into the barge because he was sinking in too deep.

'Christ,' said Ryzhkov under his breath. 'Go and get the watchman,' he said angrily, and went back up the gangplank. The gendarmes rushed ahead of him and went inside and pulled the man out of bed. When they hauled him out to the loading door he was just awake, smiling at the men who'd led him out on to the pier.

'Wake up, you've got some work to do,' Ryzhkov said and grabbed the man by his greasy collar. The fabric was rotten and the collar tore off in his hands. It made him so angry that he reached out and pulled the watchman away from the gendarmes and threw him down on the pier. The man started groaning like a sow giving birth. It was everything Ryzhkov could do to not kick him. He thought if he did actually kick him it would probably kill him.

'Get him up.' Two young gendarmes bent to do it.

'I'm sorry . . . y'reckency . . . sorry . . .' When they had pulled the watchman up to his feet, Ryzhkov slapped him hard across the face twice. It couldn't have hurt that much because the man had a thick matted beard that cushioned the shock of the blows. Maybe it woke him up to the fact that he was in trouble.

'Who was it that came here last night? Who?' The watchman didn't say anything and Ryzhkov hit him another two times. 'Who came here!'

'I . . . I . . .'

'Did they give you the bottle? They gave you the bottle, right?' The watchman looked back towards the door; somewhere back there was his happy memory of the bottle, so he nodded.

'Do you know them? Do you know their names? How many of them came here tonight?' All of it was too complicated for the man, he bowed his head.

'Srry . . . r'excence.' Ryzhkov felt his fist draw back to strike the man directly on the nose. But instead he made himself take a step backwards to the railing of the pier.

'Get him down there, put him to work getting those casks where we can reach them, then come and get me.'

'Yes sir.'

He moved to the other end of the pier, as far away as he could get from the barge and the policemen watching the drunken watchman go about his labours.

Lavrik must have gone to someone he trusted, someone he felt could organize an escape. He must have been desperate, spilled everything to his friend. Sure, the friend had said, I'll do everything in my power to help you and your daughter get away. Here's a simple plan; a boat to Finland in the middle of the night, slip past the forts at the Kronstadt in the cosy cabin of a little fishing boat I know . . . and freedom, eh? No more worries. I'll take care of everything, leave it to me, Oleg.

And Oleg had.

And there had been somebody waiting to meet them, they would have already taken care of the watchman, sent the carriage away, and then, after it was done, the only way to get away would have been in a small boat. Three or four men at the most. They had assumed that Lavrik would be watched, suspected that he might be followed.

It meant that they knew about the investigation he'd started under Zezulin's signature. They had been informed somehow.

Not good.

He looked out at the Gulf. The light was growing now into a dark mustard-coloured morning, washed in the sound of foghorns as the boats began their day. Across the mouth of the Neva were the big docks at Gutuevskaya, in the Narva district, and only a little further upriver an entrance where the mouth of the Fontanka met a canal that ran past the Yekaterinhof Park. There was a little island there, Podzorni it was named.

He tossed the cigarette stub over the railing and walked along the pier even further so that he was all the way around the corner of the cannery, with a view across to Podzorni, where the river was narrower.

To get to Galleyhaven they would have had to row their boat directly across and tie up to the pilings just below him. After it was all over, they would have re-crossed south to the Narva side. A carriage would have been waiting, they'd be home and celebrating right now, he thought. Drinking away the chill of it all.

He went back and pulled Kostya away from the group of gendarmes. They were standing there watching the tearful watchman as he slopped about trying to push the heavy casks through the icy muck to where they could reach over and haul them out. They were cursing and laughing at him; he was covered in sludge now, complaining that he had cut one of his hands which made it difficult to get a grip on the barrels.

'Let's put a call into the police stations at Kolomenskaya two and Narva three, see if any of their constables saw three or four men tie up in a small boat, near the little island, there—'

'There at the canal?'

'Somewhere near Podzorni there, I think. Perhaps at Galerni where the canal enters the river, somewhere around there. They would have left the boat and taken a carriage. Someone might have noticed something in the early hours this morning.'

'Yes, maybe,' Kostya said, and actually smiled, and headed out to find the nearest call box. Probably glad to get a chance to get away from the stench.

'We're ready now, Pyotr.' Dima came up behind him.

'Yes, fine.' He walked back to the barge where the casks were being lifted out on to the dock. The watchman was too weak to get out of the barge. He had collapsed at the edge and was methodically beating his head against the soggy wooden gunwale.

'Take him, throw him in the water to clean him off, then carry him to the Vasilevskaya lock-up and hold him for questioning,' Ryzhkov told the gendarmes.

The casks were standing upright at the top of the pier now, and the men paused there waiting for his permission to open them. There was nothing to distinguish one from the other, but he picked one and one of the gendarmes set about knocking in the top and prying out the boards so they could get a look inside. The men lifted their lanterns higher.

All he could see at first were the feet.

Toes, cruelly bent back and squashed against the side of the wood; it looked all wrong and then he saw that the legs had been broken so that they could be wedged in.

'More light . . .' he said and someone shone a torch down into the cask and he was able to see it was a man they'd pushed down there. Naked. Lavrik.

'Christ . . .' he breathed. Lavrik's face peered up at him, one eye half-open staring up from the bottom of the barrel. Locked away like a genie in a bottle. He tried to make himself feel happy about it but instead all he felt was cheated, as if something good had been stolen from him in the night. The monster was dead, but he'd wanted it for himself, he realized. He had wanted him very, very badly.

'Christ . . .' he heard himself say again. One of the gendarmes was staring at him. He stepped away so they could keep working.

The top of the second cask came off and they had done this one differently. A woman, her brown hair spread out across her face, a slash across the neck where they'd cut her throat. Still a lot of blood smeared across her torso. The cut had opened up wide, like an extra smile under her chin, when they'd bent her head over to hammer the lid down.

'Is that his daughter?' Dima asked.

'I don't know. Probably.' None of them had ever seen her before. Lavrik must have kept her in the house all the time. She was in her thirties now and still daddy's girl. They all stood around regarding the barrels for a little longer. The men were silent. There was very little to say and nowhere else to look.

'Well . . .' He thought he'd make it easy on them. 'Dima, have them get a wagon around and take them to the morgue at the Military Hospital. Maybe there's something down in there inside, so be careful.'

Back inside the cannery one of the gendarmes had found Lavrik's trunk behind the door, pushed back into the shadows. They had started to change clothes for some reason, the trunk was opened and clothing bulged out, then there had been an interruption and it had been pushed to one side and ignored. Beyond it, deeper in the shadows, a wide pool of blood had spread out beneath a locker.

Ryzhkov squatted beside the trunk and pulled the clothing out. Down underneath everything was a jewel case which had been emptied, and beneath that a wallet which the killers had missed. It had their passports and a packet of roubles. Beneath that was a stuffed envelope in which he discovered a thick wad of stock certificates.

'My God . . .' said the young constable behind him. 'It's a fortune in there, sir.'

'By our standards a fortune indeed.' Ryzhkov took the wallet and the envelope, reminded the young gendarme not to let anyone open the locker or trample over the floor until the technician arrived, then went out and made sure that all the arrangements had been made.

Outside the horses were shifting from foot to foot, hungry, cold and ready to loose their harness.

'I'll take it in myself,' he told Dima, and climbed into a carriage.

He told the driver to go all the way across to the mouth of the Fontanka where the St Petersburg police would already be looking for the boat, rejected the idea, and instead changed their route, driving slowly along the university embankment as a muddy yellow sun fought a losing battle against the fog that clung to the freezing surface of the river.

Did Lavrik love his daughter? Did he think that he would cash in his chips, pull a fast one and save her? How could someone do the kinds of things he'd done to Katya Lvova and then claim that it was love he felt for his daughter, that he cared for her, gave her presents, wished for grandchildren?

He half-expected to see angels descending from the snowy skies, the pavements splitting open and tongues of fire erupting to swallow the city. But the only indication that God was watching over Petersburg was the dull ringing of the church bells just as he turned on the Nicholas Bridge to let the irritated horses carry him over the Neva.

TWENTY

He didn't feel like much of a heroic investigator, not very much of a man, and that's the way they meant it to be.

They took him awkwardly, at the end of a long day, meeting him in the foyer of his building as he stumbled back home in a blizzard; the wind blowing raw out of the Gulf, the absolute of winter sweeping him along the street, all too eager for his warm bed. While it was happening he was thinking they were lucky because he was exhausted.

Still, they took him.

He knew they were amateurs by the way they talked. They had a man inside waiting, another behind him to make sure they could get him out of the door, one in the carriage to help pull him in. And the driver, of course, a big rascal named Jekes. But then—too quickly, he was inside the carriage with the two other men pinning him back into the seat, the hard barrel of a pistol in his side for emphasis. The one who'd been waiting inside was huge, taking up one side of the covered carriage; his name was Tomlinovich. They started along the embankment of the Obvodni Canal. If he tried to push his way out of the carriage door they'd either kill him or be able to drag him back in before anyone came to his aid.

'Well?' he asked the big man across from him. They'd fallen silent. The carriage was so small their knees were knocking together.

'Monsieur Ryzhkov?' Tomlinovich asked.

Yes, yes, of course, he thought. Who else are you planning to abduct tonight?

'Please . . . just a short ride and a little conversation.'

A moment of panic seized him. They had turned off the Obvodni, along an almost deserted street that ran behind the race track. No one around. A fence closed him off from running into the back lanes. Sharp wooden poles that he would have to *try* to vault. Ahead of him was the high wall of a school dissolving into a white blur. Everything would be icy, equally slippery for all of them, but still . . . too far, he thought. Too far to run.

Amazingly they hadn't taken his knife, and he had the beginnings of a plan, to make a slash at the gunman, bull his way through the door, go after the horses and then . . . well, run through the snow, hide. Fool, he thought, fool.

Tomlinovich was a big man. Very big. Obese, dressed in the flamboyant style of an embassy functionary. His face puffy, the flesh exploding over the rim of his shirt collar.

Trying to get away was insane, crazy. But if they were going to kill him they could have just done it in his doorway. 'All right,' he said.

'Good.' Tomlinovich reached inside his coat and came out with a silver case.

'You've got what you wanted. I'm here now,' Ryzhkov said firmly. The fear had made him angry. Angry that they would be toying with him in this way, angry that he'd let them surprise him with the phantom carriage.

Tomlinovich had his hands up, like a frightened actor in a film at the cinema, eyes wide as frying eggs. 'You have my sincere apologies, sir.' The little man with the gun started laughing.

'We're going to a meeting. Really, it won't be a problem. How long it takes is up to you, of course.' A bribe, Ryzhkov thought. The carriage, the expensive clothes. The amateur theatrics. A bribe. He nodded. Keep it going, he was thinking. But then Tomlinovich stopped, his expression changing, suddenly grown harder beneath the fat. Maybe he was peeved for some reason, as if somehow he was the one being inconvenienced, as if it was all Ryzhkov's fault.

And now Ryzhkov was realizing; too late, that they had taken him like amateurs and they were going to kill him that way too.

'Shall I give it to him?' the little man with the pistol in his ribs asked.

And—he did go for his knife then, actually had his hand in his pocket before the little man pulled the trigger and everything went black.

Voices.

Voices blurring through his dream. Murmuring, laughing. Recollecting, admonishing. The first clear thought that made it through was 'alive', and then he wondered if his dentist had taken his tooth out, and then he remembered that he'd already done all that.

'Is he awake?'

Someone shook him.

'Hey, are you awake?' Followed by a series of little slaps on his cheeks. He opened his eyes and everything was a silvery blur. Maybe I am dead, he thought. Maybe this is some kind of test to see if I get into paradise or not.

Something cold washed across his forehead, he smelled mint. There was a scraping from somewhere and he saw the bare branches of a tree brushing against an old cracked attic window. There were other voices from what he somehow knew was downstairs, a woman's squawking laugh, the clatter of crockery from a kitchen.

A tall, thin man hovered in the background. He had cadaverous cheeks only partially covered by dark side-whiskers and carried a bowl and a cloth in his hand.

'Hey, he's awake now.' The sound of his feet as he went down the stairs.

The branches scraped against the window again. He was on one of the islands, Ryzhkov decided, in some dacha out on Yelagin Island or Krestovsky. Out on the north side of the city surrounded by nature, out where the rich people spent their summers and watched the leaves change colour and the squirrels run about. In winter there was no one there. No one to hear, no one to witness. There were heavy footsteps on the stairs and Tomlinovich came in.

'We'll save a lot of time if you follow instructions,' he said. 'How is your thinking? Is your mind clear, eh?'

Ryzhkov looked up at him, a little insulted. Nodded.

'I only ask because, well . . . unfortunately we had to use this.' Tomlinovich held up what looked like a fountain pen—an aluminium cylinder with a catch at one end. 'It's a *morphia pistol*. Luckily the dose travelled through the cloth of your jacket, unluckily you seem to be quite susceptible to opiates,' he said, standing there with one hand in his pocket, rocking back and forth.

'Now—you're going to tell us all about the baron, you're going to tell us all about the ones you work for, and you're going to fill us in on the entire petroleum scheme, yes?'

Ryzhkov sighed. 'Fine, but look . . . I don't know—' he said. His voice was slurred and cracked like someone who was dying of thirst. He really didn't know what he had planned to say. Something witty to talk himself out of a bad situation. Petroleum? The best he could do was to stare up at the man for a long moment. 'I don't know . . .' he repeated.

'Now, you see, that is just what I mean.' Tomlinovich stepped over to the bed, gave him a quick kick to the ribs. Just a little warning that knocked the wind out of him and brought tears to his eyes.

'So . . .' Ryzhkov said. His voice rasped. It sounded pathetic and weak, like a feverish child in the night.

'So, Ryzhkov, you're going to talk to me, yes?'

'There must be some mis—' he started.

'Let's be *very* clear.' Tomlinovich was jabbing him in the chest with one blunt finger. A deep well of resignation began to overtake Ryzhkov. Maybe he could incite Tomlinovich, get him angry enough to explode, get it over with quickly. 'From now on you're going to follow my instructions. You're going to be good and answer questions, eh? Good, we have an understanding.' He reached inside his jacket and took out a typewritten sheet of paper. 'When did you first meet the baron?'

'I don't know—'

'They're not expecting you at work, did you know that?'

'Ah . . . no, ahh . . .'

'They're not expecting you because there's a note from your doctor. We fixed it up.' Tomlinovich smiled, shook his head sadly. 'Now look, I thought we had an agreement? You said you were going to talk, eh? So, tell me all about how, when, and where you first met the baron.'

'I don't—'

'Ah-ah-ah . . .' Tomlinovich said, and then he hit him, hard this time in the centre of his chest. It knocked him out and when he came back the air was still crackling and Tomlinovich was in mid-lecture. '. . . so there's no escape. You should be forthcoming. That's the sensible thing, obviously. If you help us perhaps we can work together. Was it about the money? How much did he give you? We know he put through the Gagental contracts for you? For your bosses? We want their names. He was holding out, wasn't he. Was he after more?'

'Wait . . . money? What?' Ryzhkov asked, involuntarily. For a moment he wondered if he was dreaming the whole thing.

'So . . .' Tomlinovich nodded. 'You maintain that you knew nothing about the baron, you are not an associate of his, you are not part of the cabal, you know nothing of the contracts, you're involved in none of it? This is your side of the story?' He was frowning, his wide mouth was turned down at the corners. He looked like an immeasurably sad circus bear tricked out in expensive clothing. He came over to the bed again, was about to raise his foot. 'We can make you talk, boy.'

'Well, then . . .' Ryzhkov did his best to smile and shrug but his wrists were handcuffed to the bedstead.

'Hard-headed,' someone said from the shadows; the fellow who'd shot him it sounded like. For a moment they just looked at each other. The tree scraped along the glass, a faint shrieking noise. Tomlinovich heaved a great sigh. 'Last chance,' he said quietly. And Ryzhkov could tell that he meant it.

'I don't know anything about this petroleum scheme or contracts or whatever it is.'

'No?'

'I was following him because . . . because of what he did to the girl. Trying to bring a case against him, so . . . There were two of them. I'm looking for the other one now, the one that threw her out of the window.' He said it flatly, not even looking at them. It came out sounding like an admission of failure; he was a policeman who had tried to play by the book, but sometimes, you couldn't. Sometimes you didn't, sometimes, *many* times, it wasn't possible to fix things. And he hadn't. And now he'd been caught.

Tomlinovich came back into the light; his face was twisted in frustration. 'What *girl*? What in hell are you talking about?' He stepped over to the bed and grabbed Ryzhkov by the shirt collar, pulled him up off the bed, the handcuffs riding up the rods so that his arms were pulled back behind him.

'Start at the beginning, boy. One step at a time,' he said and then dropped him back on to the bed.

And so he told them. All of it. About stumbling on to the murder, about Lvova, Ekaterina, about Bondarenko, and his visit to the Iron Room, about the boy and his wife. He listened to himself as he told them, almost amazed at how detached he was. His voice oddly controlled, sounding like a priest reading from some ghastly scriptural passage. Thousands died, cities were

burned, pestilence, famine and burning sulphur, all of it
ending up as dry facts, like a laundry list. So detached
that the horror was all burned away. And so, he told it
all, as objectively as he could make the sounds come out
of his mouth. The only thing he managed to do was
leave Vera out of it entirely. At least he could do that
much, he told himself. At least that.

When it was all over Tomlinovich sat there for a long
moment, nodded and then stood up. He stood there
staring at the floorboards for a moment, then put one
hand on Ryzhkov's shoulder like a father consoling a
son over some sporting defeat.

'You better start praying,' he said, as he left the attic.

It took them all that day, through the night until the
next morning to check on what he'd told them. They
came and went grim-faced, saying nothing; gave him
food and unhooked one wrist. He slept. The smallest of
them, and probably the most dangerous, was Dziga. He
uncuffed him so he could shit in a bucket they'd brought
up and then stood there watching and making jokes. He
had bad teeth and a big smile and a brown, nearly bald
head that had scars with little twisted stumps of black
hair growing out of it. He looked like an acrobat who
had escaped the circus to become a dishwasher. When he
finished Dziga took the bucket away. 'Don't spill any,'
Ryzhkov called after him as he went, and drew one of
his sharp little laughs.

They brought him a big plate of soup and a loaf of
bread and after he'd got started Tomlinovich came in
and took a seat. He had more paper to read from and a
new man—a shorthand typist to take down all the
answers. Basically Ryzhkov recounted his connection
with Lavrik, the details of the surveillance, the progress

of his attempt to bring charges in court. He didn't say anything about petroleum or cartels. After he'd finished the list of questions, Tomlinovich tipped back his hat and settled down in the chair.

'Do you want some wine with that, eh?'

'Why not,' Ryzhkov said between bites. He had to lean over to use the spoon. 'That's no good,' Tomlinovich said as he watched him eat. 'Dziga, put the shackles only on his feet. We'll catch him if he tries to shuffle away from us . . . You're not going to try to run away are you, boy?' Tomlinovich laughed. It came out as a series of wheezes.

They let him eat at the table and the one they called 'Doctor' brought up a tray with two glasses of wine. When he finished the soup they brought him another plate. Tomlinovich took the time to go fishing. The tall secretary took it all down.

'Have you ever visited Lavrik's firm, or spoken to members of his staff?'

'You mean the banking place?'

'Mendrochovich and Lubensky, 112 Nevsky. Ever been there?'

'Walked past it, maybe.'

'We were following Lavrik, that's how we saw you.'

'Mmm.'

'But now we don't know who to follow, you see? You shat in our eggs, boy.'

Ryzhkov shrugged and finished his second plate of soup. 'Who are *you* anyway?' he said, standing and taking the glass of wine with him to the bed, exhausted from the meal and eager to fall asleep as soon as they decided to leave him alone.

Tomlinovich didn't quite answer the question. 'I admit we were surprised to learn you were a *gorokhovnik.* Yes . . . And you're sure you don't have anything to add to that, eh?'

'No.' Ryzhkov burrowed in the sheets and held his arm up for Dziga to chain it to the rail.

'Yes, well you shat in our eggs, boy, and now you're going to eat them.'

'Whatever you say.'

'Everything has changed. We're thrown off the track. So now, things have stepped up, we have to move. We don't have time to coddle you, eh?'

Ryzhkov stared at the ceiling, almost at peace. He was trying to conjure up a picture of Vera. He could almost animate her, see her dancing in one of the Komet extravaganzas, her smile . . . genuine or not, it didn't matter. He wondered if they had put something in the wine. 'Has it occurred to you that perhaps he *deserved* to die,' he said dreamily.

'Undoubtedly he did,' Tomlinovich said softly. 'But then again, who among us doesn't?'

Ryzhkov shook his head. Now he was dreaming of Vera dancing up on an orange-lit stage. Dancing just for him, watching him watching her. There were voices in the stairwell. Tomlinovich stood up, and so did the secretary. Vera made her exit and Ryzhkov opened his eyes to see a new fellow. Someone important. He looked like he had just come from an evening at the theatre. He smelled of women's perfume and cigar smoke and he was dressed in tails and decorations. Sleek. He took a chair beside Ryzhkov's bed and looked at him for a long moment.

'We've been investigating your story, of course,' the sleek fellow said. The voice sounded like a mother giving her child the background to a lullaby she was about to sing.

'The newspapers are describing the baron's death as the result of a "crime of passion" perpetrated by a jealous lover. This is plausible since the baron was known to have a series of liaisons, not only with children—although he did meet frequently with children, some of them the children of his friends and associates. Did you know that?' The new man could not keep the disgust out of his voice. 'In some circles this is considered fashionable. Do you want a cigar?'

'Who are you?' Ryzhkov said.

'I'm Boris Fauré, Deputy Minister of Justice.' He opened his jacket and removed a wallet, held it open for Ryzhkov's inspection. It all looked official enough. A passport, *Fauré, Boris Grigorovich*, behind a leather flap, an engraved card with an address and telephone number that placed him somewhere deep within the warrens of the Ministry of Justice. The best part of town if you actually had to work—just off the Nevsky with easy access to the Passage market.

Fauré clipped a small cigar and lit it for Ryzhkov. 'As a story . . . for me it doesn't quite ring true. At any rate, we can thank God that the public is as stupid as it is,' he said. He tapped his ash on the floor and loosened his white tie. 'You see, we were on the track of a financial scandal, before you—'

'Shat in your eggs? Yes I know.'

'I'll accept your apology, but it doesn't change things. It only makes things a great deal more difficult. For example we don't quite know what to do with you, Inspector.'

'Ahh . . .' Maybe the soup was going to be his last meal after all.

'We were following Baron Lavrik because we were trying to find his associate. One in particular and for now we will simply call him Mr X. It's this Mr X we want, he meets people, he puts combinations together. Sometimes legal, sometimes not so legal. This time he was working something up that broke so many laws he needed a veil of secrecy. It was Lavrik who provided the legal subterfuge, but it is Mr X who is the paymaster. We don't know who he is and we don't know where he gets his money. We were using Lavrik to find him, so . . .'

'Ahh.'

'Therefore, while you paint a convincing picture of a white knight consumed with the need to avenge the spirit of a murdered vertika, somehow we wish to take a more prudent course, you understand? We want to exercise caution. You could be a great actor, or a simple pawn. Maybe only something tossed our way to throw us off the track. I'm sure you understand this need for suspicion, given the sort of things you do in the Internal branch.'

'Oh, yes. I understand,' he said quietly, watching the smoke curl towards the ceiling.

'Splendid then. So . . .' There was a rustle of papers as Fauré pulled a letter from his pocket. It was a document typed on a single sheet of paper with a seal at the bottom. Fauré cleared his throat and began reading in his motherly way.

'On this date and hour, I, by my authority as an officer of the Ministry of Justice, an officer of the Duma, and representative of the infallible will of his supreme majesty, Nicholas Romanov, hereby declare a charge against you, Pyotr Mikhalovich Ryzhkov, of murder.'

TWENTY-ONE

The suite of rooms at 40 Furshtatskaya, at the very end of one of the lower corridors, had taken a month to prepare. Entry to the corridors, guarded by custodians at the landings in each stairway, was controlled by numbered and coloured discs that one wore around the neck, like decorations for valour. To protect against theft the discs were signed in and out. To guard against counterfeit the shapes and colours changed every day.

The Third Branch's offices were at the fashionable headquarters at 16 Fontanka, but the Okhrana utilized several other buildings around the capital, including External's archives within the gargantuan General Staff building. All of them were cordoned off and guarded, but this suite was uniquely secure, for access to these rooms was restricted to *one*—General A.I. Gulka, the man who knew everything, the eyes and ears of the empire.

Tonight he was tired, dressed in formal clothing which had grown too tight, and as he walked down the corridor he jerked his collar open and heaved a great sigh. It was ironic. Now, when everyone who obligated themselves to him was comfortably asleep, secure with full bellies, he was only beginning to work. All through the holidays his family had been making demands, his mistress had run away to her ancestral home in Athens, and all his other political and social contacts had been pushed to the margins, and of course, the business of guarding Mother Russia from revolutionaries hadn't simply stopped because he'd been forced to play Father Christmas. But now, he was almost happy to be back on the job. As he turned the combination which would allow him to use his key in the special electric lock, he allowed himself a smile that on anyone else would have looked like a grimace of pain.

The first chamber was code named *Red* and he had appointed a single pair of Red Assistants who entered the room solely to pick up or drop off sealed bags into a metal box that was affixed to the connecting wall.

Gulka used another key to move deeper into the second room, into the *Blue* chamber. He switched on the lamps and re-locked the door behind him. The inner walls had been covered in cork panels, and held a series of photographs, maps, columns of paper that had been glued together, all of it representing Gulka's translation of Sergei Andrianov's great Plan.

Now he simply sat in a chair and stared at the wall for a few moments before beginning to sift through the two bags that had been dropped off in the day.

The first sealed bag was the evening report; it bore the serial numbers of the bags, including the one containing it, and the time and sub-department from which they had been received, the signatures of the officers concerned, and the time the Red Assistant had dropped them off. Gulka put the receipt in a drawer containing hundreds of others, and turned himself to the second bag. It was a report from the investigator responsible for his surveillance of Count Ivo Smyrba, or, in Andrianov's universe—Heron.

It was a ridiculous designation, the man looked nothing like a heron, nothing like a bird in fact. He looked more like some pathetic urban rodent . . . like a squirrel polluted by contact with the filth of the streets, become threadbare with vermin and infection. Smyrba could wear the smartest wardrobe in Europe, but he would still be a target of Gulka's disgust. Gulka scanned the report of *Heron*'s movements; it contained nothing informative; a list of the man's traffic about the city over the last twenty-four hours, a series of vain, self-serving flailings across the capital. Either fawning to superiors or those from whom he anticipated some favour, his sudden impulses—a fine luncheon at the Klava, a dalliance with the Sakhazinskaya twins, both of them failed sopranos. Passing time over tea with an expensive harlot from whom he bought his narcotics.

Gulka took the report and placed it on the board under the column marked *Heron* and returned to his chair. He had built up nine columns on the two cork panels that spanned the corner of the inner chamber, nine animalistic coded designations.

The panel for *Gosling* had been marked with a black ribbon running down its centre. An effete gesture, the General thought. Almost sentimental, but after all, he admitted, he sometimes felt that way; he prided himself on his charitable Russian heart, his generous and empathetic nature.

Prior to Andrianov's scheme, he had known Baron Lavrik, but only peripherally. He had first known him by his signature connected to bids that were continually issued for all manner of government procurement. In the course of routine activities, they had met once or twice; well, perhaps more, but not that Gulka could recall. He had only a dim memory of the man—an older, stooped sort of fellow, almost invisible really, except for his bizarre forked beard.

Now, the photographs had begun to replace the man.

Of course, he knew that Andrianov had ordered Lavrik's murder without consulting with him, or even informing him of the details afterwards. When they had eventually discussed the matter, Gulka had professed to agree with Andrianov's decision—obviously it was better for the Plan for him not to have been in on it. And he had smiled. Gone into his act, pretended that he had no interest, no cares in the world.

It was always better to be underestimated, Gulka believed. The drunken, dissolute, great, happy *Bear*. The only one of Andrianov's juvenile code names that was appropriate.

Of course it was all about Serbia, and the setting of the spark. He knew that Andrianov was frequently travelling to Belgrade; at least three times within the year, even managing to cross the borders during wartime. There had been veiled and not so veiled references to arms sales or promises of arms to be delivered in the future, all manipulations designed to push the Balkans over the boiling point. And all very profitable.

That was Lavrik's part in the scheme. He was the banker. All the money flowed through him in one way or another, and all of it through numbered or anonymous accounts that Lavrik oversaw. Lavrik was their cut-out. But then when suddenly Lavrik had . . . embarrassed himself, he'd become a liability. Andrianov had wanted Lavrik out of the focus; having made that decision, and no longer having any confidence in Gulka's methods, he'd been forced to go outside for his hired killers. He'd undoubtedly assembled them through his Serbian connections.

They were amateurs, little more than thugs who had operated, as near as he could tell, with a knife and something heavy, like a hammer, to break up the bodies of the baron and his daughter and force them into the casks. There had been no strategy to it, an arrangement made, a slippery walk on the ice, a frigid ride in a rowing boat, a bottle for the *dvornik*. It had been ugly, efficient, and . . .

And . . . it hadn't really worked.

The Serbs would have stuck out like rude cousins in the city for the first time in their lives. Therefore, somewhere along the line they had been seen and noticed. There was still a trail, even though they had left the next morning and effectively vanished into the vastness of Europe, gone from his view. But eventually they would return to his sight. And in the world of secrets, the hand of the Okhrana could stretch across continents and time to work its revenge.

Yes, Andrianov had kept a secret from him, Gulka thought. The idea was tinged with bitterness. Gulka had risen to a position in the realms of power where any betrayal, the keeping of a secret, the utterance of a slur, even a duplicitous look, would earn the guilty party an 'accidental' death. But in this case one had to weigh the consequences. One had to take things into account. It was like a game where you were either being used, or using. Betrayal was certain, but you never knew when it would come. Sergei Andrianov's foolishness had slowed him down and shifted the advantage; he'd only been able to pursue the Serbs *after* the murders were reported to the St Petersburg police. It had cost him eight hours. And he was hampered because even he had to be discreet in his pursuit.

He knew what Andrianov had told him, the general outline of the Plan, the identity of *Eagle*, and the desired solution to Russia's problems. In theory the organizers were a troika, combining their talents and resources, but Sergei was the creator and had always been the principal financier—the first among equals. In the last months Gulka had constantly researched Andrianov's activities. He took his clues from things Andrianov had told him directly and from other leads that he had been able to ferret out using his own resources—and he had discovered more. Much more. In addition to his legitimate businesses Andrianov had a plethora of schemes going, deals on the side and various speculative affairs. Gulka harvested every scrap of information; it was like trying to draw a detailed map of a cloud.

Ultimately Sergei would fail because ultimately Sergei was a braggart. A quiet braggart, a very composed man. Dignified until the point where he felt safe. Then he'd suddenly erupt and describe for you how smart and vicious he was. Who better to listen than the big dumb bear. Yes, Sergei, no Sergei, what a wonderful idea, Sergei.

But . . . behind his subservient pose Gulka knew more.

He knew where the money was going, because he could follow it through the banking system via his agents in the Ministry of Finance. His control of the St Petersburg police was absolute, and, of course, there were the daily reports of the thousands of Okhrana agents, from the Internal, External, and Foreign branches that were available for his perusal. He could direct all these resources as he wished, and indeed this was his function within Sergei's plan. So . . . for now he would play along, enjoy the food, count the money, and be the big, dumb bear, smiling dumbly up at his master.

A buzzer sounded, and he unlocked the door, moved through the little *Red* room, checked the peephole, unlocked the door and rolled in the tea cart that had been left in the corridor, then re-locked everything behind himself, until he could pour a glass of strong tea and settle back into the comfort of his chair.

Andrianov must be feeling quite comfortable, quite satisfied with himself. He had eliminated the pervert, Lavrik, thus repairing what had been a mistake that had threatened to ruin everything. Moreover, Andrianov had done it in a way that insulated him and the rest of the Guard against discovery. Now he would be turning his attention to other details of the Plan.

It would come in the summer, Gulka thought. Perhaps as early as the spring, as soon as the roads were judged good enough to travel. Knowing the exact nature of the spark, its timing and location, was crucial. Andrianov had showed the limits of his trust, and Gulka was certain that the moment Andrianov thought he wasn't needed that he would try and jettison him. Perhaps Evdaev was in on it, too. Once he was on the throne, and all powerful, then Gulka would be *his* chained bear. Either of the two men might turn on him, he thought. Was Evdaev capable of action independent from Sergei? It was hard to imagine.

Spring would be precarious. As the weather began to change, that's when he would monitor Andrianov's movements most carefully, how his money changed hands, his travelling arrangements. He wouldn't go down for Sergei Andrianov, Gulka knew that much. If anyone swung at the end of a rope, it wasn't going to be him. He would learn the identity of the Serbian killers soon enough. He had his own connections in Belgrade, he had money and a bolthole set up in Stockholm, and he would have a fast car warmed up on the big day, and another to change to on the road to the border.

Alternatively he would use the identity of the Serbian killers to lever Andrianov into submission. When it became practical he'd have them picked up one by one and bribe or torture them into informing on each other, then he'd run them back to their paymaster, until he had evidence to arrest Andrianov for instigation of murder, and even, if it came to that, to include him in plotting with Evdaev to topple the Tsar. And if someone should strike at him, he could make sure that the evidence would come out and bring down his attackers. He would strike back, yes . . . even from the grave. A slow smile crept across his face.

He would be ready.

Through any frustration that they could throw at him, he'd be ready. Oh, it was bad enough to be having a failure like Lavrik jeopardize the entire scheme, but what was more troubling was that, even after his precautions and everything he had done to quash enquiries, one rogue Okhrana investigator had somehow attached himself to the case.

He had devoted an entire cork-panelled wall to the activities of this low-level man from the Internal Agency. He had retraced his movements through sheaves of daily, weekly and monthly reports that the more-than-thorough officer had penned and submitted. He had followed his requests for actions, approvals, for equipment and additional funds to pursue the investigation, and Gulka, while giving the man enough rope, had quietly done all he could to delay, obfuscate and otherwise thwart his pursuit.

He had told Andrianov only the minimum, purposely keeping the man blissfully unaware, allowing him to enjoy his vacation with his mistress in France, even as the sewage was starting to seep through the flooring. Sergei was turning berry-brown in the French sunshine, secure that Lavrik's murder had ended any danger. Dead, he was no longer vulnerable should anyone come looking. The cut-out had worked, just as Sergei had known.

But in reality, he knew nothing.

All of Andrianov's cunning, his savagery, and his hired killers hadn't stopped the activities of a single officer. Oh, it was nothing dramatic, nothing but a string of routine requests—for information, legal permissions, search and seizure protocols—all of it coming from the station at 17 Pushkinskaya.

The investigating officer must have an unusually ethical nature, Gulka thought. Or maybe he too had sensed an opportunity, maybe he had been blackmailing Lavrik as well, and now his personal money tree had been chopped down? Anything was possible.

But it didn't feel like that . . . Not from the formal paper requests, or the subsequent reports that had been filed.

He rubbed his heavy hands over his stubbly hair, trying to concentrate. Perhaps he should get out and meet this very special man, this unique Okhrana agent. Take the measure of the enemy, then, at the right moment he could simply be re-assigned. Or, even better, promoted to a position where he would be out of the way.

That would end things.

Gulka stood, the fatigue coming on him suddenly now that he was ready to make a decision. He walked over to the cork panel and looked at the photographs of the rogue Okhrana investigator—a man who was now fast becoming his worst threat. Someone to either be finessed or killed before the summer was out.

He smiled.

In a way he was proud. He couldn't help being proud . . . yes, here was a real hero of the Third Branch, actually the kind of agent the service needed. A man of quality and persistence. Perhaps after everything cleared, after the dust had settled from the collapse of the House of Romanov, this rare man could be brought back into the service. It would be tricky. He might not be able to spare the man's life. But perhaps if he could be shuffled far enough from the centre of things, he'd always remain in the dark, never knowing how close he had come to uncovering the plans of the Sacred Guard.

Gulka stared more intently at the images: the first was a standard service identity photograph, updated every three years. It was a stiff portrait, a man staring simply ahead, eyes and expression neutral, neck unnaturally stiff. Neither innocent nor guilty.

Beside it was a series of photographs, taken by a camera with a special lens, looking down from an upstairs window in a rented apartment across the street from 17 Pushkinskaya Street, the front from which the man's section operated. These showed a different side of his enemy—a shabbily dressed man, neglectful of his appearance, yet perfectly achieving a mask of anonymity—all of it provided by his simple overcoat, a fedora jammed down over his ears, a scarf wrapped tightly around his neck. A cigar raised halfway to his lips . . . blurred with motion as he waited to cross the icy street.

A great investigator, Gulka nodded with an almost invisible smile. A very special man, whose life, death, or salvation was his to command: a pathetic policeman who had unknowingly elevated himself to become the most dangerous man in all of Russia: Chief Inspector Velimir Antonovich Zezulin.

TWENTY-TWO

'We must have surprised them.' The manager looked as if he were going to collapse from the excitement. 'I thought I heard noises, as I was unlocking the door. At first I thought, well, frankly I thought it was birds, *pigeons* outside the doors, but then, you see, I realized, once inside . . . from the smell.'

The St Petersburg Police Commander glanced around the large showroom. There was, indeed, a low cloud of smoke, a smell of burned metal that still lingered, caused by the thieves when they had attempted to cut their way through the thick door of the safe that was walled into the back of Khrisloff's, the famously exclusive house of jewellers. During the night there had been a robbery, and upon arriving, the commander had immediately been presented with a list of the stolen items.

'And you say they gained entrance to your shop?'

'Through the roof. Well, not through our roof, our roof is especially constructed, for protection against just this type of thing. They entered through the roof of the building next door, then came through the wall.' The commander looked to the top of the stairs where one of the younger officers was inspecting a neat hole that had been cut through the plaster at the top of the landing.

'Very serious . . . very serious,' said the gendarme commander as he ignored the list and crossed the room to climb the stairway. On the first floor was a much plainer workshop, divided into long tables, individual kiosks, and tiny furnaces where craftsmen created the exquisite necklaces and the tiny 'hares' which Khrisloff's had designed to compete with the famous eggs by Fabergé, just up the street.

'And they even knew to come through the upper stories, because the lower floor of the building has iron bars set into the walls, for protection against exactly this sort of thing.' The manager was going on behind him as they climbed to the landing where the thieves had penetrated the wall to make their entrance. The commander bent over and looked through it into the next-door building.

'Mmm, yes . . . if you will excuse me, monsieur?'

The commander crawled through the hole and found himself in the upper offices of a rather ornately furnished securities investment firm. All around was a clear trail left by the departing jewel thieves; the bricks piled neatly beside the hole in the wall between the investment house and Khrisloff's, the marks where they had retracted their hoses and cutting torches when they had fled. He felt a cold draught and took a few steps into the central waiting-room; above him a ragged hatch had been sawn through the ceiling and roof, a wet patch on the floor where they'd wiped up the snow that had fallen through the hole.

Several nearly identical middle-aged men, clad in sober black suits, white shirts and gleaming spectacles, watched his progress. The commander turned to the nearest, a rather gruff and portly gentleman. 'What sort of things go on here?'

'Ah . . . this is the firm of Mendrochovich and Lubensky, excellency,' said the man with an almost imperceptible bow, as if that explained everything. 'We are a financial house, monsieur.'

'Stocks, bonds, legal services, that sort of thing?' the commander said. He thought he had heard of the firm before.

'Most certainly, sir. Financial transactions of all types.'

'Ah, well . . . but there is no money, nothing missing in here, I take it?' the commander asked as he reached down to brushing the brick dust off his trousers.

'Nothing whatsoever,' the elder man said, looking around his destroyed offices, and, with the work it needed to put things right, his holidays spoilt. 'There's a safety deposit box vault on this floor, and another in the basement, but evidently they didn't know about it. We just deal with documents up here, nothing of value in any case.'

Which, of course, was inaccurate.

TWENTY-THREE

After the burglary they let him go home. They'd be watching they said, but Ryzhkov doubted it; Tomlinovich's resources were limited, it was obvious. He slept like a dead man all that day, the window cracked to let the cold air blow the mustiness out of his bedroom. He woke to a momentary illusion of freedom. But only one test was completed, Tomlinovich had emphasized; the murder charge still hung over Ryzhkov's head and his services might be required at a moment's notice. Moreover, his next task was to subvert his own section: to recruit Hokhodiev and Dima into the deputy minister's service.

It wouldn't be hard to do, since they'd already agreed to help him track down Lavrik in the first place and because, after less than a month's association with the case, Ryzhkov found Fauré to be one of the few honest men in the empire. In the unlikely event that some form of 'democratikos' ever broke out in Russia, a sharp politician like Boris Fauré might be able to make a real difference—an aristocrat with his own money, so he wouldn't be on the take.

All the leaves were stripped from the linden tree outside his window at 17 Pushkinskaya and relentless snows crusted around the mullions. Zezulin was sick and had not come into the office, Izachik said. Everyone was preparing for the New Year's holidays.

Later, when they came in, he took Kostya and Dima for a lunch at the *Bell* and explained that he had been attached to the Ministry of Justice case and asked if he could prevail upon each of them for assistance. Hokhodiev sat there, eyeing his empty beer glass and rubbing his nose. Dima lounged in the corner of the booth, his head resting against the cushions, saying 'Yeah-yeah' to each of Ryzhkov's points.

Ryzhkov explained that he was limited in what he could tell them, and that there were many things he did not know himself. The only real certainty was that their discovery of Lavrik's murder had led to other, greater things. 'So . . . I need your help. Or I'll try to keep you out of it, if that's what you want, but—'

'And we don't know them, they are supposedly Ministry people, but they know us?'

'Yes,' Ryzhkov said, unable to keep the defeat out of his voice.

'Not much to bargain with,' Dudenko said. He had pulled a tiny screwdriver out of his jacket pocket and was picking his nails. 'Not much of a lever there . . .'

'Well, shit. Well, why not? You say you trust this fellow?' Hokhodiev sighed.

'Trust. What is trust? I don't know, Kostya. There's not a lot of choice, but, so far, yes,' Ryzhkov said flatly. He was being made to bring them along, but he wasn't going to try and turn them into believers.

Dima unfolded from the corner and arched himself over the table, began to peck at the wooden surface of their table with the screwdriver, as if to test its hardness 'Why not?' he said. 'You have to take the point of view that if he's against a scum like the baron then, you know . . .' He looked over at Hokhodiev, who was still thinking about it.

'How dangerous do you think this might be getting, brother?' Hokhodiev said quietly.

'You saw what they did to the baron and his daughter. They were involved in something, that much is obvious. But for us, it's not bad now. Just a mountain of paper at the moment.' It was true enough. Fauré's team had been poring through the stacks of photographs they'd been able to make of the contents of Lavrik's shelves in the Mendrochovich and Lubensky vault, a trove of documents, contracts, proposals for business ventures, and internal memoranda.

'I am getting too old for this, you know?' Hokhodiev looked up, but his smile didn't seem that happy.

'If you don't want to, I can't make you,' he said. 'They don't tell me much, and I'm just on call. We'll have to work with them, do whatever they say.'

'And they can fix this up . . .' Hokhodiev waggled a finger in the direction of 17 Pushkinskaya.

'I guess a deputy minister has a lot of weight.'

'Things are getting exotic,' Dima said quietly.

'Oh, I'm coming along, don't worry about that,' Hokhodiev said. 'It's just that I had the idea that if we could just nurse Zezulin along, in a few years Lena and I might be able to retire.' They started laughing at the idea of retirement on an Okhrana pension.

'Retirement is a wonderful idea, so yes, let's hold on to Brother Zezulin.' Ryzhkov raised his glass. 'Besides, if they find out what a slug he is, they'll only replace him and make our lives hell.'

'Yes, and that would make it impossible for us to have fun with you on your various fruitless crusades, eh?' Hokhodiev smiled.

'By all means. Whatever happens we'll have to keep our heads down and look busy,' Dima said, and they all laughed again.

Over the next few days he went through his backlog of work at 17 Pushkinskaya and attended morning briefings at Tomlinovich's new headquarters. The Ministry of Justice team was billeted on the second floor of an old building on Kryukov Street, a large open room that had recently been occupied by a shoe manufacturer.

The entire floor was empty, all the furniture gone except for some exceedingly uncomfortable bent-wood chairs that had been found at the last minute. Each day there would be something new delivered up the stairs and placed discreetly on the landing. One morning two desks arrived. Then a trunk full of battered electric lamps. The only things new about the place were the locks on the doors.

The name of the secretary was Sinazyorksy. He slept beside the telephones in a corner of the shoe factory. Ryzhkov spent the mornings locked in a completely vacant office waiting while Tomlinovich came and went with Fauré's latest questions, all of them relayed by telephone. It was all small-scale and careless. He came to know the entire group: Dziga, the little one who'd shot him, and Jekes, their gigantic driver.

Now they were sifting through the results, trying names and faces out on him. By virtue of the sham burglary they'd managed to photograph a good deal of Baron Oleg Lavrik's business correspondence. But from the questions they asked him, Ryzhkov could form only an incomplete idea of the direction of Fauré's investigation.

Tomlinovich came in at the tail-end of one of the morning meetings, carrying a large envelope. He took out a notebook and what looked like a journal, splayed them on the table across from Ryzhkov.

'Well, we've found out that it was blackmail,' Tomlinovich said. 'Lavrik had a lifeboat prepared, monies set aside for him and his daughter. Tickets for Stockholm. Take a look.' The notebook was small, about the size of a playing card. It was new and completely blank except for the first page which had four telephone numbers, all of them written at the same time. Numbers only, no names. The journal was older and most of it had been ripped or razored out. The back third was intact and consisted of what looked like a series of notations. It was a kind of crude code the baron must have used.

'Stock tips?' Ryzhkov mused as he thumbed through the book.

'No, there's not enough of them,' Tomlinovich said quietly. 'Appointments, perhaps.' Tomlinovich reached into the envelope and took out a sheaf of photographs, spread them across the table in front of him.

Six photographs. All of them taken in dim light with long exposure times. Just for an instant Ryzhkov thought they had been spoiled in the darkroom; they were a confusion of whorls and wispy shapes, as if someone had decided to make an artistic interpretation of the rushing waters of a stream, or leaves falling in a stiff breeze. Then he recognized Lavrik.

The girl's head was nearly below the frame, her face pressed into Lavrik's groin, her hand holding something that he could not see. Lavrik looked down on her with his pouchy eyes; his face seemed slack, devoid of emotion, as if he were mesmerized by the traffic on the Nevsky and not by Ekatarina Lvova. Ryzhkov let out a long sigh, looked up to see Tomlinovich looking at him. One by one he made himself inspect the other photographs.

Here there had been much movement—the girl was a white smear spread out in front of him, only her hands were still, where they gripped the edge of something, a table, a headboard. Then he realized he was looking at the table in the Iron Room.

In the blurring Ryzhkov saw the fury of the event, saw the frenzied rape, saw something in the baron's hands; something like reins, or a kind of scarf that he must have wrapped around her neck. Lavrik held the reins in both hands, the force of his passion causing her to be arched backwards; her blonde hair had come undone and whipped like flames.

Now Lavrik's distorted face looked like an abstract painter's version of a beast from hell; his mouth was open, the whites of his eyes bulged out, his false teeth were a bright slash across his face.

'He kept these,' Tomlinovich said. 'It's pretty damning, eh? First he paid for them, probably one at a time, and then he *kept* them . . .'

'Yes. I suppose there is no limit to stupidity,' Ryzhkov said. He couldn't take his eyes off the photographs. He tried to rearrange them into what he thought was the correct sequence; from the comparative calm of fellatio, to the hurricane of strangulation that had engulfed the girl. He was surprised at how composed he was. He had imagined the scene for months, now that he had a *version* of it in front of his eyes, it was not nearly as shocking as he had anticipated. He found that he could look at the photographs objectively, as evidence—just some confused marks on photographic paper, a swirling record of something hideous and untranslatable. He could be detached about it all.

'And then there is this one . . .' Tomlinovich pointed to the last photograph. The door to the Iron Room had been thrown open and a portion of the hallway was revealed. A second person was silhouetted in the doorway. The light revealed Lavrik, his body a huge white blob, cringing in the blast of light, one of the damned looking for a hiding place. He and a second man were struggling over something hidden between them. Ryzhkov thought that one long pale mark was Ekatarina's arm, but it might only be a trick of the light.

'Is that one there the little one, do you think?' Tomlinovich said.

'Yes,' Ryzhkov said, staring at the twisted shape of the second man in the doorway. 'It must be.'

'We thought so, too. But look, here's something good, here's something we can use. Just who is this, right at the back here?' Tomlinovich held a magnifying glass out for him to use. 'See? Right here, reflected in this mirror in the hall? One of the prostitutes, yes? Isn't this one of the girls that you talked to that night, perhaps? This woman here, whoever she is, if we track her down, she could identify the second man. What do you think about that, eh?' Tomlinovich was looking at him steadily.

In the glass he saw . . .

Vera. Frightened, trying to run, naked . . . or near enough. The dark nipples, the hair come awry, the V between her legs. The open mouth screaming.

'Hey, Ryzhkov . . . here . . . Come on . . .' Someone was holding him by the shoulder. He turned to look at the man, someone young, rancid tobacco breath, wearing spectacles. Oh, yes. Sinazyorksy, yes . . .

'I'm fine,' he said. 'What's the matter?'

'It's all right. Just sit for a bit and relax for Christ's sake. We're all under a strain,' Tomlinovich was saying, and Sinazyorksy's grip tightened on his shoulder.

'It's simple, Ryzhkov. You just go back through your notes, find the whores and track them down. We bring them in and put it gently, eh? Help us, girls, or there'll be hell to pay. It's a good enough plan. You can get started right away, yes? What's wrong?'

He sat there looking up at Tomlinovich's pouchy face, trying to come up with some excuse. His mind was a fog, the photographs danced through his imagination. A gust of wind rattled the high factory windows.

'There's nothing wrong, what's wrong? Is there anything wrong?' he heard himself saying, as the younger man held him down in the chair. But everything was wrong. Now they knew about Vera.

'For Christ's sake, get him a drink,' Tomlinovich said, a smile creasing his face like a long bloodless gash.

TWENTY-FOUR

Flakes of snow following a week of boredom. The holiday stopping everything in its tracks, even the pursuit of justice. For Ryzhkov there was no summons from Tomlinovich; he moved through a slow charade at 17 Pushkinskaya for the benefit of Zezulin who hadn't noticed a thing. If he'd believed the newspapers, Russia was heading into the abyss; the society pages were the proof of the coming apocalypse—the ornate parties, the benefactions, the orations, the acceptance of awards for philanthropy, the carefully stated opinions of the rich and high-born.

And there was the bad, dark weather, the freezing air off the river and canals that penetrated the thickest cloak, the snow and icy rain that swept along the prospekts, the grimy fog that froze to every surface, the multiplying barges of firewood crowding the canals. The putrid smell of smoke in the air, and the desperate cries of men selling warmth.

Ryzhkov wandered through the bitterly cold streets of Petersburg, hands thrust into pockets, chin jammed down into his collar, running from doorway to doorway to get out of the icy rain. Would he ever get used to the strange configuration of numbers? The calligraphy of a brave new age, a year that sounded so modern that he could have never imagined writing it: *1914.*

'Let me get this straight,' Vera said after she had let all the smoke out. 'You say that all through the holidays, people have been walking along watching us, tracking our movements, reading our mail . . .'

He had taken a long pull himself from the little hookah she had brought along, and he held the hashish smoke in as long as his lungs would allow, then let it out in a great long stream towards the ceiling, coughed experimentally, and was careful to remember to put his thumb over his end of pipe so that she could take her turn.

'Yes, or almost two weeks now. I haven't done anything about it. I don't know who they are.' He hoped it was someone from Tomlinovich's gang, someone who might protect them.

She held the smoke in and put the top over the bowl, took the pipe out of his grasp as he nodded that yes, it was enough. She got to her feet and vanished in the darkness toward the kitchen. Ryzhkov let his eyes slip towards the grate, pulled the quilt up to his chin. All in all, considering the chill of the room he was very comfortable.

He had never taken hashish before. But among Vera's crowd it was all the rage, sometimes mixed with opium as a way to enhance the effect, she had told him. He didn't notice any change at all apart from the rawness in his throat, the curious sweet smell that permeated everything in his apartment, perhaps a feeling of lethargy if anything.

She returned with a little bowl-shaped glass tumbler of hot Georgian plum brandy and passed it to him so that he'd stop coughing. Now a whole different family of smells filled his head, and the brandy warmed a long column down his centre as he sipped.

'That's better, isn't it.'

'Mmmm . . .'

'So, these people that you think you see—'

'I don't *think* I see them. They're there.'

'Fine, fine. These people who are there, they just follow you around, they don't do anything else? They don't try and knock you on the head, steal your wallet?'

'Not yet, no.'

'You don't think this is a little fanciful, perhaps a way of making your own trials and tribulations greater than they really are so that you can feel pity for yourself? You're sure you're not just imagining—'

'Vera,' he said firmly. 'I work in this business, they're out there, I assure you.'

'Well, as long as they're not hurting you?' She shrugged. 'So what?'

'Have you noticed anybody, anybody strange or different hanging around the club?'

She laughed. 'We're the centre of strangeness, if you were going to buy a cartload of strangeness, the Komet is where you'd begin your shopping.'

'Mmmm . . .'

In the lead-up to Christmas there had been a spate of men dressed as women, and vice-versa, all lured in by Khulchaev's extravagant *Song of the Sandwich*, which cleverly managed to combine traditional Russian folk melodies with the rhythms of the South Seas. Vera had played the High Princess of Tahoo, a rather naive young thing who ended up being cannibalized by the other temple virgins for the sin of being seduced by a young Russian merchant seaman. She had dyed her hair jet-black and caked herself in dusky body make-up for the part. Pyotr had stared at her the whole time, hypnotized, unable to take his eyes off her. She liked it, liked having him there. It was flattering.

'I don't know,' she said, frowning. 'Two people like us. I think that's the real strangeness,' she said looking up at him now. Serious. 'You know? Maybe we've made a mistake. Or two. Or lots of mistakes.'

He looked at her. Wanted to say something, but all he did was shrug.

'I know what I did, Pyotr. I know my mistakes and my crimes,' she said, straightening up, looking at him levelly. 'And if I hurt someone . . . I'll pay, I don't mind paying. I'll make it up to them if I can.'

'Yes.'

'But maybe it's not me that has to make the penance, maybe it's you. Maybe you're the guilty one, the one that's going to have to die for everybody else's sinning? Did you ever think of that?'

'No. I'm not that important. And I only want to save a very small number of people,' he said, reached up and touched her cheek. 'But everything I do is dangerous. Everywhere I go has bad consequences and I don't think it's fair for you to follow me around—'

'Oh! I'm following you, now, is that it? I'm suddenly a clinging vine?'

'I didn't say that—'

'I wonder,' she said, her head tilted over and assessing him.

'What?'

'We might not have a future, you and I.'

'That's what I'm talking about.'

'All right then . . .' She left and went into the kitchen. He heard her fiddling with things, a kettle being filled, drawers being opened. A moment later she was back.

'We're going forward in time.' Beside them she'd placed a little table for the hookah and the brandy. Close enough to be handy from the little bed they had made there in front of the furnace. She did things like this, he thought. She would jump the rails and avoid talking about whatever subject you were on. Slippery. Maybe she was the kind that thought that if only she kept moving nothing could hurt her.

'Relax, let your body slumber . . .' She reached over and with her fingertips massaged his face, closing his eyes, her touch somehow eerily blending with the bones in his skull.

'Are you warm enough?'

'Mmm . . .' He was warm enough, he was hot even.

'Good.' She had climbed astride him so that she could massage him better, her fingers dipped in a fragrant oil that filled his nose with the scent of flowers and mint. She was wearing the jade pendant he had given her, a simple hoop carved to represent a snake biting its own tail. It hung on a thin satin ribbon she'd found, nestled precisely between her breasts, sending off a series of hypnotic green glints in the candlelight.

'Just let yourself be open, and leave the physical plane, and be open to the influences, to the Sun and the Moon and Water and Fire . . . and you are free of all earthly desires . . .' she intoned.

'Mmm . . .'

'Concentrate.' She rose slightly and he heard her reaching for things. His eyes opened and the room was full of halos. She had brought around a bucket of melted snow she had taken from the window ledge and a little ladle of melted wax.

'Are you ready to learn your future?'

'Um . . . I think so, yes.'

'Say the magic word, *Abara-Kadabra*!'

'Abara-Kadabra!' he said importantly, trying to copy her theatrical inflections.

'Good. Now take my hand; careful, the ladle is hot—and pour in *half* the wax—' He reached out and together they poured a stream of wax into the centre of the bucket of freezing water.

'Now . . . for me, too. Since you're seeing threats everywhere, and so concerned about my welfare, and worried because I'm such a burden . . . *Abara-Kadabra*!' she said and poured in the last portion of wax. Together they peered in the bucket.

On the surface of the water two twisted, yellow shapes spun like twin galaxies. Carefully she took one of the sculptures out of the cold water, held it between them.

'It looks like . . .' He studied it as she turned it over on her palm, peered at it, frowning. It looked like a fungus or a yellowish root.

'This is a lion . . . a *puma*. This is your animal nature coming to the fore,' she said quietly.

'I'm going to be a lion in the future?'

She gave him a look that could put out a candle. 'You may become meat for the lion, you may become the hunter of a lion. Let's see, it may even be a lioness.' She turned the wax over and looked on the other side. 'No, it's a boy lion, see? It has a prick. Do you think that's funny?'

He shrugged and tried not to smile.

'Maybe you're being followed by the lion, have you thought of that? You may have to kill the lion, you may have to climb a tree to escape the lion. Maybe you won't escape, maybe that's your future. Since you're a scoffer you probably won't take the necessary precautions.'

'What precautions?'

Now it was her turn to shrug. 'Stay off the savannah, maybe. How should I know? It's your future, after all.'

'Fine, then, what's this one all about?' He had pulled her wax future out of the cold water. When it had hit the water, it had flattened and spread suddenly like a spiny sea creature. 'It looks like a starfish,' he said.

'No, that cannot be, Gloriana told me I am not a water creature. I am of the air, I am ether.'

'What does ether look like?'

'Ether has no *appearance*. Ether has a quality, ether has an effect. It makes you see visions, makes your consciousness evaporate. It kills your pain. But this . . .' She took the odd little figure from his hand, turned it over and over and inspected it from all angles.

'I know,' she said, finally. 'It is the Sun. It is the gift of life.' She turned and fastened her eyes on his. Her royal look.

'So, are you pregnant?'

'I may be. What's it to you?'

He could not keep looking at her, let his eyes fall to the little sun in her hand. She was right, he thought; it even had a closed-up little face on one side, like a sleeping newborn. 'I don't know . . . maybe you are going to create life . . . at some point in your future.'

'Perhaps I am.' She looked down at her belly, put one hand across her navel as if to comfort something that might be growing inside. 'But I don't see any children in my future,' she finally said. Her voice was grave.

'No?' She still hadn't looked up at him but had begun rubbing her belly in little slow circles.

'Do you think it would be a good thing for me to have a child?' She finally raised her eyes.

'If you wished, yes.' And when she didn't answer, he went on with a little more certainty. 'I think so, yes. I think you would be a good mother, Vera.' Her eyebrows arched at that.

'Oh, really? Why is that? Am I especially qualified?'

'I think you are a good person,' he said to her, meaning it. Meaning every word of it.

'There would be no father.' She turned her head away, maybe she was laughing at him.

'There has to be a father.'

'No. I may be the new Virgin Mary. After all, this is still Christmas. It may have just happened, just now.'

'About an hour ago, maybe.'

'Oh, so you are God the Father?'

'You have to admit—'

'You're growing impertinent.' She had put down the little wax sun, and bent over him, her breasts were just brushing his chest. He was starting to be full of earthly concerns again.

'You do not own me. You cannot go where I go,' she said, very seriously.

'Fine.'

'Say it.'

'I do not own you, Vera.'

'Good, go on.'

'I cannot go where you go.'

'You can never go there.'

'Never?'

'Never, ever.' She had taken his lower lip between her teeth, bit him slowly at first and somehow changed it into a kiss. Outside in the stairwell he heard old Mrs Panych's son beating a carpet over the banister. In the street there was the bell ringing as a tram pulled up to the stop, in the courtyard he could hear echoing voices of the porter and his friends singing a bawdy song. Outside were the watchers, outside were conspiracies, outside was death and mayhem. A string of fireworks exploding. The cries of monsters and cascading horror. Church bells were ringing, hymns were being sung to the new year. People were giving alms to the poor, ignoring the news, drinking too much, laughing too loudly. Going to sleep in anticipation. Would the snows cover it all?

She let go of his lip, pulled away only an inch.

'No, you cannot go where I go,' she breathed.

TWENTY-FIVE

In less than a week, Tomlinovich had learned enough from the Lavrik documents, that he felt ready to have Vera and Larissa brought in for questioning. Despite Ryzhkov's attempts to set conditions for both of the women, there was no argument allowed, and because they still didn't trust him they kept him in the dark. He could only assume that Fauré was bringing them in because he had come up with possible suspects for Mr X and needed verification from witnesses.

He spent the next few days like a man in a trance, collating dead files at 17 Pushkinskaya, having dozy conversations with Zezulin about nothing. Going about his sham Okhrana business, outwardly the investigator of old, but inside dreading what he was going to have to put Vera through.

He delayed everything to the last moment; went to his barber where the talk was about the Greeks and what great fighters they were, the glory of the Spartans, the conditions of the mountain passes, too hot or too cold, the nature of betrayal and why it seemed to thrive amongst the Balkan peoples, if the Treaty of Bucharest really meant a new era of peace or if the creation of Albania complete with a grafted-on royal family, would make any difference. Wonderment over the British suffragists and their violence, over the deaths of Isadora Duncan's poor children, over the severity of the winter, the prospects for war in the new years. 'The world is going over the precipice in a basket of its own shit,' one of the barbers said and Ryzhkov had to agree.

In the cold, short afternoon he left work early, had dinner in a cheap restaurant, and then, screwing up his courage, went to the Komet.

. . . my raga, my saga, my feeling for the sea-a-a
. . . my party, my corner, my scratching at my flea-a-a

In the corner Vera and the Komet girls were going over the same chant, a ragged chorus of sopranos. Izov watching, Ryzhkov sitting against the wall peering into the rehearsal room. He had become a trusted customer and Izov regularly consulted him about business affairs when he stopped in for coffee or a konyak. They discussed finance and the international situation. The Stock Market was bouncing all over the map with speculation after the fragile peace in the Balkans. It all served to explain, Izov said, why he'd had been forced to increase the price of coffee by three kopeks.

'In the morning it's worth it.'

'Hey, those little birds, they sound pretty good, eh?' Izov remarked on his way back into the kitchen. Ryzhkov went to the entrance to the studio, stood there and watched the singers as the Professor coaxed them through the song again.

'Yes, they're getting better,' he agreed. Izov laughed as if he couldn't believe it, waving his towel at him. 'So, remember and tell all your friends—a new show each Friday! Don't forget monsieur.'

'No, I won't,' Ryzhkov called back. He wouldn't. Even with Fauré's demands hanging over him, she was the only bright spot. Vera had insisted that if he would only relax, everything would work out. It was part of her newest preoccupation, some sort of esoteric Eastern philosophy that had begun to sweep through the ranks of the city's artists.

'—Well, you may scoff, but I know that when I stop *thinking* that's when I do some of my best work.' And when he looked at her, she lifted her chin into the air, poked him in the chest with one black fingernail. 'Say *nothing*,' she warned.

He tried to follow her advice. Sat in the smoky atmosphere and made sporadic conversation with Izov, who would put in a comment and then fly away to deal with another customer. He finally got a minute with her alone. 'I need to talk to you,' he managed to say, dreading every word of it.

'Fine, but not now, I have a long rehearsal for this dog that Dmitri is trying to turn into an eagle.'

'Vera . . .'

'What?' She made a little grab his sleeve, frowned. 'What?'

'In another day or two, or soon anyway, I'm not sure when exactly . . . anyone who was there that night has to come in for questions.'

'Ahh . . .' She gave him a hard look, and then suddenly smiled. It was a tight smile with no happiness. Almost a grimace. He could see her fighting not to cry. 'And when it all happens because of the way things have . . .' He stopped. Sighed. 'When they bring you in, I can't be involved,' he said quietly.

She gave a little laugh. 'Oh, you can't be involved. Now you are no longer involved?'

'Look, I'm not even supposed to tell you, and they're not going to let me be there. So, I won't be in the room to—'

'To what, to help me? To protect me? Yes, you do a fine job at that, don't you?'

'Vera . . .'

'I'm so lucky. A boyfriend who's a real protector. I have to go to work now.' She turned and headed for the dressing-rooms.

'Another, Monsieur Ryzhkov?' Izov called to him as she left and he turned slowly in the room. A stage-door lover with no destination.

'Why not,' he said. Why not drink it all.

A man had come in and was loudly talking about how the government was heading for a crisis. The Tsar was about to sack all the ministers. Furthermore, he had it, yes, on good authority, that soon there was to be a renewed war with Japan. 'The heathens want all of Siberia! After that they're going to conquer all of China, and then—'

Izov brought him a fourth dizzying konyak, it was something new he had acquired from Riga. He took a sip of the eye-watering potion and let the conversations fade. Larissa came out and gave him a wink, Kushner a tight little nod. They were off to some revolutionary meeting. There was a time when he would have waited and followed them, discovered the address, stood in the rain for hours and, with numbed fingers, noted the carriage numbers, descriptions, and times of everyone entering and leaving.

But not tonight.

Across the room a second hysteric joined in. There was a new crisis! In order to comfort the population and quieten the strikes that were breaking out lately, the Tsar had promised to lower the tax on vodka, but, because the prime minister was worried about the finances Tsar Nicholas was about to fire the prime minister. 'Any day now . . .' the second man assured them. 'Any day, now. You wait and see!'

The world was insane. Sitting there he almost laughed, suddenly aware of the absurdity surrounding him. Everything was going crazy, he thought. The empire *was* crumbling, just like Kostya had been predicting. War and revolution were in the air and he found himself engulfed in a wave of foreboding, filled with a sudden sense of impending disaster. Let go, he told himself. Why be the only sane person in the asylum? Do what she said—think of nothing, nothing at all . . .

He finished his drink as another pair of rumour-mongers waltzed through the door of the Komet, and abruptly made up his mind to get out before he was sick all over the floor or struck somebody.

'Nothing more for you, Monsieur Ryzhkov?' came Izov's plea behind him.

'Nothing, no . . .' he said, waving the man off, walking surprisingly steadily towards the door. Vera was backstage somewhere, and wouldn't talk to him anyway even if he forced his way back there, to what? To apologize? To beg? Suddenly the atmosphere in the room was too close. He couldn't wait any longer. He had to get out, get out into the cold air where he didn't have to listen to or think about any more theories about how the world as they all knew it was about to end.

From the beginning Tomlinovich had separated Vera and Larissa, turned them against each other, pressed them to confirm every detail of each other's story. And it started to fall apart right away, even before they were shown the books of police photographs or the lists of names. Fauré had given him a free rein; short of thumb-screws he could do whatever he needed to get statements identifying the second man in the Iron Room. To demonstrate his power, Tomlinovich engineered it so that the questioning took all night. A messenger was sent to the Komet to tell Izov. Tomlinovich shrugged and said he hoped it would not be a problem.

Pyotr sat in the adjacent office, his head against the wall, smoking endlessly and listening as it all crumbled around her. At the beginning he felt like a traitor for listening in, but then even that changed. Everything changed.

Because what they found out was Vera's big secret, the one she'd kept even from him.

'Everything you've told us is a lie! We know that he came to you! To you! You never mentioned that, did you? You never told us that you're the one that got the girl in the first place, right? You knew him. You planned it with him!'

For a long moment there was nothing. Then Tomlinovich's voice. He would start quiet and build a staircase until he was yelling at her. Through the glass he saw Sinazyorksy bringing Larissa some food. He wondered for how long she'd held out, how big the deal was, what they had dealt for or threatened her with. Through the wall he could hear Vera crying.

'We know you went out and picked her up. Where did he first meet you, in the bindery? No . . .'

He unlocked his body, stood, poised, trying to hear her answer. Their voices would come in and out, get too quiet for him to hear through the walls, then they'd flare up again when Tomlinovich lost his temper.

'—*Don't tell me that! Don't try to sell me rubbish! People saw you. You're responsible!*'

He paced across the room, not wanting to hear her answer.

Her voice when it came was angry. '*I've told you everything. If I say yes, will this be over now?*'

'*It's over when we tell you. You know this fellow don't you? Where does he live? How much did he pay you? Tell me something good . . . Say it, Say it!*' Tomlinovich demanded through the wall, over and over and over again.

He didn't want to hear it, but he did anyway.

'*Yes.*'

'*"Yes," what?*'

'*Yes, I asked her if she wanted to work . . . he asked me . . . so I asked her . . .*'

'*So he could kill her, right?*'

The answer came in fragments. '*. . . doing this for years, all her life . . . I was going to be there . . . It was extra money . . . wasn't scared, so I wasn't . . . what do you think a whore does?*' She ended it by shrieking at Tomlinovich. '*No . . . I didn't know . . . I didn't know . . .*' Then he heard her sobbing again.

'*You're going to have to be a good girl, you're going to have to prove yourself, you're going to look through some pictures, help us get him. You see that, don't you?*'

Her reply was too quiet for him to hear, but after a long moment the door opened and Tomlinovich went out, crossed the big room to where they were keeping Larissa. Through the opened door he saw her stand and try to slap him, but he just put out a heavy hand and pushed her down into the chair again. A few minutes later Sinazyorksy came out and locked her inside.

When Tomlinovich saw him standing there he waddled over. They met there at the door of the office. The big man stopped a pace or two away, a little out of reach, stared at him for a long moment with a little smile. Ryzhkov tried to make his face into a mask but it was impossible now.

'It's funny, isn't it, Ryzhkov.'

'Funny?' It wasn't the word he would have chosen.

'Yes, funny. Funny in the way life works out. You try and do a colleague a favour, you trust someone, you have the best of intentions but . . .' The big man shrugged, looked over to the little room where they were keeping Vera. 'So, now we've got this little one for murder, too. Now we can use her any way we want. And we've got big plans.' The smile grew larger.

'Yes . . . now we've got both of you.' Tomlinovich pointed one pudgy finger at Ryzhkov's chest. 'Bang . . .' he said.

Then he went back into the room to torture Vera some more.

TWENTY-SIX

'I give you Mr X.'

Fauré's voice echoed in his mind as Ryzhkov watched the man, the goal of all their work. He seemed happy enough, strolling down the still-snowy prospekt, the air sharp as a knife. Pausing to eye the merchandise on display at Eliseff's. Lingering there for a few moments, pondering a purchase? Waiting for someone? Pirouetting from leg to leg. A sharp little customer, Ryzhkov thought. A paladin of the modern age, cheerfully absorbing all the pleasures the great capital of Petersburg could bestow on a perfect winter Sunday. The day was brisk with clear skies, people had flocked to the Nevsky to see and be seen. Above the throng a triangle of geese flew across the rooftops, surely the very last to leave for the south.

'Count Ivo Smyrba. He holds the post of Attaché for the Kingdom of Bulgaria. In essence, this Smyrba is a business agent. We know that he was manipulating the

*pervert Lavrik in order to facilitate the cabal's interests
here in Russia.'*

Now a smile crossed Smyrba's face. He nodded at
someone, tipped his hat. Fished in his pocket for a
cigarette. Ryzhkov caught a glimpse of Hokhodiev as he
passed them, and then paused in front of a bird-seller's
stall up ahead. Ryzhkov followed Smyrba down the
Nevsky, ambling along past the crowded Gostiny Dvor
market, matching Smyrba's pace. He thought he knew
where the man was going and then, yes, ahead of him
Smyrba stopped at the corner, and when the gendarme
blew his whistle, crossed the Nevsky at the Kazan
Cathedral and headed for the bridge.

It turned out that Tomlinovich had got a lot out of
Vera.

She finally admitted she'd met Smyrba at Madame
Hillé's. They had talked on a few occasions, although she
claimed to remember nothing of the conversations.
Probably because she did scenes he'd asked her about
procuring a child for his friend. He'd only had to bring
the idea up a couple of times before they'd set a date.
She'd been happy to take the money, she said. Such things
were normal. That was her not-so-pretty bedtime story.

Ryzhkov had seen her for about five minutes since
then. There wasn't much to say. She'd lied the whole
time. Strung him along pretty well. She'd blubbered,
she'd cried, protested and fought it all the way. Trying
to minimize her own role in the plot. Well, she was an
actress and a whore. She could get very emotional. As
far as the death of Katya Lvova was concerned, she'd
confessed that she should have seen it coming.

Maybe he should have, too.

When it was all over Fauré had let her go. Warned
her, or paid her off. Ryzhkov wasn't sure about the

arrangements. He'd tried to stay away from most of it. Maybe that was better. There were things he would never know, Ryzhkov realized. Things he would never understand. Things that he probably ought to put out of his mind.

So, maybe it was time to put some illusions aside, forget about the girl, and follow the spy.

It was good to get down to work on something that was substantial. A real human being instead of a memory or a rumour. It had only taken them a few days to develop a perfect schedule for Smyrba. So far his habits had been inflexible; breakfast at the Astoria Hotel, either in his suite or in the restaurant. From there he was driven to his office at the Embassy of Bulgaria. Often there were meetings at various locations around Petersburg. Often these took the form of luncheons at fine restaurants, mostly along the Nevsky, although twice Smyrba had been tempted across the bridge to Dacha Ernst which was located in the park near the Fortress of St Peter and St Paul.

'. . . the evidence: copies of Putilov munitions contracts, dummied-up shipping orders to Odessa . . . bribes distributed in order to secure contracts to construct an entire series of dreadnoughts. As a result of Count Smyrba's machinations, these contracts were awarded to the German shipyard Blom & Voss. Imagine! A German shipyard building Russian battleships! I'm sure we'll get the very best . . .'

Now Smyrba was strolling along the Fontanka, his little shined boots picking their way past the icy patches, tipping his hat to the younger women, nodding to the gentlemen, keeping to the sunny side of the street, a

newspaper under his arm, and Pyotr Ryzhkov stopped
directly behind him, stood there inhaling his smoke. The
cigarettes were expensive, sweet. Across the street a
horse bolted and for a moment everyone looked. A
droshky slewed sideways and a driver screamed out a
curse. As quickly as it happened, it was over. Smyrba
turned to his neighbours there on the kerb . . . laughing.

'. . . *fixing of bids from three different firms . . .*
contracts for rubber belts, tyres for military vehicles.
Boots for infantrymen. A series of orders for rifles.
Most of this matériel was purchased with Bulgarian
funds, but diverted to Serbia at a time when Smyrba's
own government was at war with them!'
'*We have military corruption, fraud, and embezzle-*
ment. Obviously this is of absolute importance.
What's Russia's situation? Do we have any guns at
all? Or is it only a charade? Only a set of tin soldiers
waiting to be led into hell?'

Smyrba's shoulder, a fine spray of dandruff on the
overcoat, or maybe it was only ash from the cigarette.
Now Ryzhkov was walking across the street, too close
he knew, but actually touching the man, brushing
against the fine woollen sleeve, all the time looking for
signals, following Smyrba's gaze, trying to think his
thoughts and see what he saw.

A sudden flight of pigeons and above them the bells
rang out in the dome of St Isaac's, calling to God for a
blessing, calling the faithful to prayer. Smyrba crossed
the street to the ornate doors of his mistress's house,
where he would while away the holy afternoon.

*'Altogether, more than eleven million roubles worth
of treason against his own nation and ours . . .'*

Smyrba was a milkmaid, Ryzhkov had told them: no
matter how far he went, he'd always come back to tend
the cows. That was the way to work it, follow him,
don't arrest him, just let him go, give him slack. He
wasn't trying to hide anything, he was too confident for
that. We watch him, we make a list of his friends, where
he goes, who he meets. We stay in the shadows, understood? If Tomlinovich wanted information, that was the
way to get it. Mark down all the dates and times, get
any observable evidence, friends, addresses or whatever
occurred that might make it easier to elevate the investigation to the next step.

The next step was Ryzhkov and Tomlinovich using a
pass key to get into Count Ivo Smyrba's fashionable
suite at the Astoria.

The rooms were immaculate. Ryzhkov looked at the
desk, checked around the edges of the drawers with a
torch to see if the count had left any 'seals'. Nothing.
Nothing in the obvious places, under the bedding or
beneath the edges of the carpet.

'The Serbs pay him, but not enough to live like this.
He's supposed to be a military attaché but he doesn't do
anything . . .' Tomlinovich went on, talking to himself.
Ryzhkov had succeeded in picking the lock on the secre-
taire that sat beside the windows that looked down on
to the plaza.

'Here we are, then,' he said. Tomlinovich came over
to look. Inside the drawer were cheque books,
stationery. The edge of something that looked like a
journal. Ryzhkov started to pick it up.

'No.' Tomlinovich moved his hand away and, extracting a pad from his jacket, diagrammed the position of the articles of everything in the drawer. Only when he was finished did he pick up the journal, grunting to himself when he encountered a particularly inept passage.

'A literary genius?' Ryzhkov had put the cheque stubs back inside.

'No . . . not at all. But a dangerous man nonetheless.'

'He doesn't seem all that dangerous to me,' Ryzhkov said. He'd found a pistol, a little silver-plated four-shot revolver, the kind of gun a woman would carry in her muff. Tomlinovich looked at it and shook his head and returned to his reading. A few seconds later he snorted, 'Now he's moaning to himself about how much he misses his fucking dogs.' Tomlinovich snapped the journal closed for a moment and rolled his eyes. 'It's people like this who are going to destroy us all.'

'This might be useful.' Ryzhkov smiled and held out a thin leather-covered book to Tomlinovich. The count had kept it sheltered under his expensive lambskin prophylactics. It was full of phone numbers and addresses.

Tomlinovich smiled for the first time that morning, raised himself from the windowseat, came over and riffled through the little book. 'Yes . . .' he said, eyes glinting like a little boy who'd found something particularly naughty. Then Tomlinovich took the book over to the coffee table, re-positioned a lamp so that it wouldn't cast a glare on the paper, reached in his jacket pocket, and came out with the smallest camera that Ryzhkov had ever seen, even more miniaturized than the ones they had used at Mendrochovich and Lubensky. 'That's nice,' Ryzhkov said, coming closer so he could see the gadget. It was narrower than a packet of cigarettes, the lens smaller than his little fingernail.

'Very special, very expensive . . .' wheezed Tomlinovich as he extracted a tiny chain from the body of the camera and began photographing the pages.

Ryzhkov watched for a moment, then finished looking through the drawers, carefully used a handkerchief to wipe his fingerprints off Smyrba's toy revolver. After he'd done all that he went into the bathroom, rolled up his sleeves, stepped up on the seat of the toilet and reached into the tank. Inside was an oilcloth package which was so heavy that it had sunk to the bottom.

When they opened it they found a thick stack of French banknotes, all in new bills, and neatly tied up beneath were three passports.

The telephone rang. It was Hokhodiev calling from in front of the Stroganoff Palace. 'Our milkmaid is on the path,' he said and rang off.

'What's our time like?'

'We're all right,' Ryzhkov said. 'We're going to do as much of this as we can and then we're leaving.'

He helped while Tomlinovich photographed the passports and leafed through the francs checking the serial numbers. The notes were nearly all new ones, they had come straight from a bank. All of comparatively large denominations. There was too much for them to count accurately. They got to up to eighty thousand francs before Pyotr stopped it.

There was a knock on the door, three, two, one, and Ryzhkov let Sinazyorksy in. Even Sinazyorksy lost his composure when he saw the pile of money on the bed. 'We're almost ready,' he said.

'Try and buy us a little more time—five minutes, eh?' Tomlinovich said.

'Yes, sir,' Sinazyorksy said. 'Don't let any of that stick to your fingers, eh?' he said to Ryzhkov and then he was gone, out the door in an instant.

'Yes, very good advice,' Tomlinovich smiled and made another exposure with his tiny camera.

Outside Sinazyorksy bought them the five minutes by holding up the rest of the cabs, so that Smyrba would have to either wait in the queue or jump into a huge pile of filthy snow. The infuriated little man finally reached his rooms and changed, dashing straight back out again. Angrily fleeing the Astoria in a state of anxiety about being late for his next engagement—a dinner meeting with business associates and embassy officials. The day had left its mark, however, and listening, Dima Dudenko heard him complain loudly about the condition of the fish, and, citing its bitter quality, return a bottle of wine to the kitchen.

The skies over the city dark and lowering, the wind rising and a fire lit in the stove in the corner of the shoe factory on Kryukov Street. Boris Fauré poised in front of a map of Europe, standing in the fading light from the dusty factory window, urging them on:

'Serbia is divided. Divided between two groups: the first—those who want to slowly build enough military power to re-claim the provinces that Austria-Hungary has taken from them. The second—a shadowy faction made up of terrorists and disgruntled militarists. This second group is actually in control of the situation. And now they will do anything for guns. Anything. They are desperate to create a war with the Austrians. They even think they can win. And while we Russians may sympathize with our fellow Slavs and agree with their natural tendencies to overthrow the Habsburg yoke, this second group is nothing more than a collection of fanatics, willing to shed whatever blood is necessary to further their ends,' Fauré said sadly.

Fauré looked directly into Ryzhkov's eyes. 'We've arranged for Smyrba to be recalled to Bulgaria. He suspects nothing, but he'll be detained, arrested, and hanged. That's something that should make you smile, Inspector?'

'Yes,' Ryzhkov said, but he didn't actually smile about it.

'So, we've found and effectively eliminated our Mr X—Ivo Smyrba: a traitor and a spy. Vermin. As reprehensible as they come, but now we see he is only one of a group of maniacs who are getting stronger every day. So, please accept my apologies, but there are still larger fish to lure into our nets, eh? Smyrba and his friends have allies within our government, those who want Russia to play big brother to the Serbs and protect all their nationalistic dreams of revenge. You know these crazy Serbs. They have long memories which go back six hundred years.' Fauré gave a bitter chuckle, 'They remember their sacred defeat at Kosovo Field like it was *yesterday*. But now the Serbian cart is driving the Russian horse.'

Ryzhkov shook his head, turned away from the coloured map of Europe, tried to get a glimpse of the street outside. The grey snow had begun again. Somewhere out there was a wonderful land where children should be safe in their beds, being given warm milk and being sung lullabies. But where was that place, he wondered?

'*Yugo-Slavia*, they call it. That's their great dream and the cross that they bear, their blood lust and their obsession. Smyrba is draining our strength to fuel

Serbian militarism, to push us into joining in a third
Balkan war, and make himself rich into the bargain.
Imagine their joy should they succeed! With Russia
standing behind Serbia, they're invulnerable. They can
get away with anything.'

'*Anything*,' Fauré said again, just to make sure they'd
got it.

TWENTY-SEVEN

In the dark of morning the monks had come.

To level the pavilion atop the ice, to ensure the carpeting was dry, brushed, and comfortable to walk upon. They had seen to the incense, to sweeping the ice around the pavilion, removing any waste paper or cigar stubs forgotten by the carpenters, twigs blown in by the wind, droppings left by animals or men. So careful had they been, that an immaculate arc had grown around the pavilion, dozens of metres out on to the river. Their brethren bent themselves to the cutting of a circular hole in the ice, its dimensions scribed with geometrical precision, sawn out and extracted with surgical care. The ice a little thinner this year, some said, quietly under their breath as they worked to ring the hole with a wreath of velvet. All to prepare for the Tsar's blessing of the Neva's waters.

Awnings had been secured, the stairs sanded and everything swept yet again. All over the city important personages were getting dressed, having breakfast, emptying themselves in preparation. Stablemen were grooming their best animals, boys were polishing the carriages. Workers were spreading sawdust on the streets.

In the barracks the soldiers were bathing, shaving, polishing, receiving their orders, checking their route through the chaos to come. Theirs was a grim celebration, the best and the worst of duties—stand there and glisten. Woe to the poor soldier who slipped in an icy puddle, whose breastplate had acquired a scuff. Appearance was truly everything today.

In the Winter Palace, now humming with activity, the Tsar and Tsarina were awake, had been fed, and were beginning to dress. A little later than everyone else, since they had the least distance to travel. From their windows, low on the west side of the building, they could nearly see the pavilion down on the quay below, curtained by the priests to waist height in an effort to mitigate the wind should gusts arise.

Ryzhkov was at his post. Hunched beneath the perfectly designed arch at the mouth of the short Winter Canal, sheltering himself from the unpredictable wind, with one eye cocked for the approach of the carriage of the Dowager Empress. At the other end of the arch three St Petersburg policemen stood shifting from foot to foot, trying to keep the circulation going inside their boots.

Hokhodiev walked in, past the flics, surreptitiously smoking a cigarette cupped behind his fingers.

'All right, then. I'm ready. Let's get it over with,' Hokhodiev said dryly.

'I'll let them know you're in place, I'm sure the Tsar will hurry right out.'

'Oh, please, don't bother the poor man. I know he has to wait for his mother to pick her teeth, breeze through the ballroom, greet a few hundred people, and to tell the truth, I'm—*ahh!*—' A particularly violent blast of frigid air whipped around the corner and interrupted him. '—I'm really in no hurry.'

Ryzhkov pulled his chin out of his collar, smiled across at Hokhodiev's dark expression. 'Someone will probably come around to check on us, you know,' he said, looking out to the embankment. Out there the wind was sweeping little bursts of freezing snow over the railing; it was a hellish place to be posted for the next couple of hours.

'I just looked, Pyotr. There's nothing out there but ice.' The embankment was closed to traffic for the ceremonies. Only after the strictly limited audience of clergy and nobility had retreated from the embankment would ordinary vehicles be allowed to use the stretch of roadway between the palace and the Neva.

'But, perhaps a submarine boat could have come up during the night, either be waiting now or have planted a mine, someone could have tunnelled over from the fortress. I'll go check again, just so we can say we're making the rounds.' Ryzhkov stepped out of the protection of the arch and walked out on to the embankment. For a moment he thought it was better once out from under the arch, but as soon as he reached the railing the wind whipped up into his face. A street away the Preobrazhensky Guards were forming.

In the other direction, the street in front of the Admiralty was completely closed by other regiments. He went out to the wall and looked down on to the granite bank to see if there was any visible disturbance; of course there was nothing. Walked for thirty metres in one direction, and then back along the other way to a set of steps leading down to a little quay. Looked around on the edge of the ice below the quay. Nothing.

Bells had begun to ring, starting with St Isaac's, spreading across the city, the echoes rolling over the river to his ears as he returned to the shelter of the arch.

He and Konstantin watched the nobility assemble themselves, their places in the throng on the embankment determined by rules of protocol more ancient than the dynasty itself. Protecting them was a ring of generals and admirals resplendent in their uniforms, and surrounding them the elite Corps des Pages—to Ryzhkov's eye, rank upon rank of pathetically young boys. The youngest didn't even come up to his belt. To be accepted as a page, particularly a page assigned to duty with the Imperial family was tacit assurance of a life-long military career that could easily reach stellar proportions. If one's family was not distinguished enough to obtain their son an appointment to the corps, the most a young man could hope for was a place in the civil service.

'Look sharp, it's fucking Tuitchevsky,' Hokhodiev hissed, snapping him out of his daydreams about military careerism. The local commander's open motorcar was approaching, veering past a knot of gendarmes at the other end of the arch.

'Nod, salute, and smile . . .' Kostya whispered as they stepped out to greet the spluttering contraption.

'What do you think you are doing inside here?' A shivering Colonel Tuitchevsky screamed at them. He obviously had a cold, his nose was wet and his words came in great spitting clouds. He looked more frightened than anything else. It took Ryzhkov a moment to recognize the man seated beside him as General Gulka, head of the entire Third Branch. His face was as immobile as a wax statue.

Tuitchevsky was dressed in his full military uniform, only the plain black car gave him away as Okhrana. The effect made him look like a children's puppet, a jack-in-the-cabriolet. Beside him Gulka looked like a different toy, a garishly painted wooden egg that might suddenly open to reveal other terrible figures growing within.

'Well, excellency . . .' Hokhodiev started.

'I checked not more than five minutes ago, sir. Nothing's been disturbed,' Ryzhkov said. He realized he was still saluting the men in the car.

'Get back out there! You won't be able to move during the prayers—go on! And no smoking, understand?' Tuitchevsky brayed.

'Yes, sir,' came Konstantin's soft acknowledgement of the order and they moved out to the railing. Behind them Tuitchevsky stood in the car, making a show for his boss, as if to follow them all the way out on to the embankment.

'It's a dog's life,' Ryzhkov said, bracing himself against the wind. 'And we are the fleas.'

'Well, at least we'll have a better view.' They took up equally spaced positions on the embankment beside each other.

'How's Lena?' he asked Hokhodiev after a while. Konstantin made a tight little smile, moved his head back and forth.

'Well, you see, they told her it would require surgery and she's set her mind against all that.'

'It's become that bad?'

Hokhodiev shook his head. 'They don't know really. These fucking doctors; one says one thing, another says something else. Every time you have to pay . . .' He spat onto the cobbles. 'She might go in for the operation if there were any guarantees, but for now she takes chamomile with her draught at night, says her prayers. She has a teacher who comes around. She claims it's working, so . . .'

'A teacher?'

'A man who is showing her the Eastern way of breathing.' Hokhodiev shrugged and stared out on to the ice. 'At least it doesn't hurt, so . . .'

'Please tell her I asked after her, eh?'

'Oh, yes. Certainly, of course. Thank you, Pyotr.' Hokhodiev stood leaning against the wall, legs tight together, hands jammed down into the pockets of his overcoat.

A blast of trumpets heralded the arrival of the Metropolitan. Ryzhkov could just pick him out in the centre of a cascade of holy men weighed down by their gold-encrusted vestments as they escorted the ikons down to the pavilion. Behind them, slowly walking in time to the music, came Nicholas II, the Tsar of all the Russias, dressed in his ceremonial uniform as an officer of the Preobrazhensky regiment. There were many stops along the way; the stairs had to be purified, the little pavilion itself had to be blessed. All of it took time.

Ryzhkov's occupational paranoia reasserted itself; a glance to the roof searching for a hidden anarchist marksman, an eye to the uniforms of the nearest men around them, searching for the detail that would reveal a terrorist in disguise. But what if the threat came from within . . .

There was the sound of a single silver bell and all the men removed their hats. Hokhodiev, nearly bald after all, groaned as he took off his fedora. The life of a policeman.

In response to a sharp command, the pages uncovered, tucking their helmets in the crook of their arms. Their colonel, satisfied, stiffly turned about and did the same. The life of a soldier.

Now the Tsar was receiving God's blessing via Metropolitan Cervenka. The Tsar knelt and Cervenka placed the cross on the Tsar's shoulder—one, two, three times. There was a pause where presumably a short, inaudible prayer was said. Ryzhkov, like everyone else, tried to avoid shuffling his numbed feet. There was the slightest glimpse of movement as the prayer ended and the Tsar stood. Then, the cry of Cervenka's voice pleading with God to accept the Tsar's blessing of the Neva. The golden cross was plunged three times into the velvet-ringed hole, a few more holy words and Cervenka stepped back, waiting for the annual miracle to occur. The life of a priest.

A bejewelled golden ladle was filled with a generous amount of river water, and poured into an equally ornate golden cup held by another ancient. Cervenka once again called upon God for reassurance, and then presented the Tsar with the goblet. Seemingly without hesitation, Nicholas drank off a portion of the contents and pronounced it good.

Ryzhkov could not help flinching at the absurdity of the moment. Why would an assassin bother trying to attack the Tsar, since drinking from the Neva might just as easily kill him. Everyone, except the most ignorant peasants, knew better. There must be doctors waiting in the palace, ready to purge Nicholas the moment the ceremony concluded. Or maybe the Tsar had just been pretending to drink; and who would have challenged him? Maybe he did drink and his personality killed the germs, or perhaps Nicholas was truly divine after all and

all the double-headed eagles were watching over him.
Ryzhkov wondered if Nicholas ever worried about
getting sick; no Tsar had ever been ill as a result of the
blessing, at least as far as the public knew. So, God must
have killed all the germs, was the obvious conclusion.

Ryzhkov looked up to the façade of the palace where
diplomats, invited commoners and their families
clustered at the tall windows. Here, safe and warm, was
everyone else, the lesser nobles, the very rich. The mayor
of the city, the members of the Duma, visiting dignitaries, the children and the elderly who could not stand
the cold. He wondered where Fauré was standing, what
thoughts were going through his head. Would the
empire hold together long enough for any of them to
witness next year's Blessing of the Waters?

Now from the Fortress of St Peter and St Paul came a
rippling series of flashes, and a moment later the roar of
the cannons' salute. As a reiteration, music began,
cathedral bells pealing across the entire city.

Thus was the Neva purified for another year.

Ryzhkov watched as Nicholas ascended the walkway,
the atmosphere slightly more informal now, the
generals, the admirals, the grand dukes, the princes, the
counts and the barons all permitted to put on their hats.
Everyone eager to get inside where the food was
waiting, everyone glad the ceremonies were over. The
life of a Tsar.

The pages assembled under a new command and
Ryzhkov and Hokhodiev trotted across the cobbles to
get out of their way as they wheeled through the arch on
their way back to the palace. Ryzhkov suddenly felt old
beyond his years, a man grown beyond the possibility of
a future. In front of him passed the regiment, bound by
oaths of loyalty to the Tsar, to the True Church, to the

Corps des Pages itself. At the moment they were just boys with beardless faces and a growing awareness of their own privileged position, but in the decades ahead they would be the chosen ones—the cabinet ministers, the generals, the leaders of industry, the commanders-in-chief of Russia's forces, the generation that held the keys to a golden Russian century. And at their head, the boy who could not kneel—Alexei.

The rhythm of their marching was hypnotic, so much so that he didn't hear Hokhodiev the first time, and Kostya had to reach out and give him a little punch on his cold shoulder.

'. . . had better come along, Pyotr. That is, unless you want to die out here . . .'

And when they turned to leave they saw that the Okhrana car had gone, leaving only the oily smell of its vanishing.

TWENTY-EIGHT

Izachik thought that he was about to lose his job.

He had come off duty that Saturday morning, awakened to find that there was an additional 'auditor' come to sift through their case books. The first 'auditor' who had been with them for two weeks, turned and looked at him as he came down the stairs from the duty officer's room and jerked a thumb over his shoulder. 'He's with me . . .' and Izachik caught a flash of an Okhrana disc before they turned back to one of the binders.

It had started with Zezulin behaving suspiciously, he was forced to admit. He should have seen it earlier. The entire station was under some great . . . threat. *Threat*, that was the only way he knew to perceive it.

Zezulin was awake all the time now. Suddenly grown alert. Serious. He'd never been like that before. He'd had a boy come and throw all the bottles in the garbage, then he'd ordered two caretakers to come around and clean his office thoroughly. He requested and returned boxes of files, folders of correspondence. He had started his own

special log, Izachik knew, perhaps two special logs, or
more . . . and he came down from his rooms and hovered
over receipt books that had long ago been properly filled
out for everything that came into their office.

Then a week later he had backslid. After having
denied himself a drink for days, Beilund found him
asleep on the couch with a bottle clasped between his
hands and another on the floor. In the morning he had
reformed and was back at work when Izachik arrived;
had his food brought up to him and left outside the door.

Whatever was happening, it must be important. He
knew it was important.

Zezulin could be in some sort of trouble; perhaps he
had been approached, offered a bribe, exposed
somehow and was now on the brink of being arrested.
These things happened, everyone knew it. Was he trying
to cover his tracks? As far as Izachik could determine,
by leafing through all the indices, there was no logic to
Zezulin's requests. Perhaps he was trying to find
something that he should have seen earlier? It was
impossible to guess. Maddening.

And then had come the auditors. Zezulin hadn't liked
it, followed the man around, made some telephone calls
immediately upon his arrival. Had the young man up for
a meeting, before letting him see the books.

And now another.

They had started with the accounts, the budget
expenditures for 17 Pushkinskaya. These were all simple
arithemetic. Nothing to worry about, everything was in
order simply because he, Izachik, had played a good
part in keeping the accounts accurately. Everything up
to snuff, he reminded himself; so, the financial books
had taken but a day to check and there was nothing to

worry about there. No, whatever they were after, it wasn't the money.

Perhaps Tuitchevsky, the local commander, was looking for an excuse to replace Zezulin; if so, why go to all the pretence, why spend the effort when anything would do. It didn't fully explain Zezulin's sudden efficiency, but then . . . what man isn't afraid to lose his job?

The next thing to happen would be something official, an *evaluation* they would call it, someone would come around, someone with more authority than the auditors, or—it would be short and sweet—a simple announcement, a pathetic goodbye party for Zezulin and a rallying speech by the new man, whoever had been selected.

Or perhaps there would be interviews beforehand, he would find himself under the spotlight, all of his actions questioned. He felt the panic rise in his throat.

It was then that he started going through the files himself. If there was any irrgularity he wanted to be the first to discover it, and, filled with guilt and anxiety, he spent the rest of the night stacking and re-arranging ledgers, file reports, dossiers, and procedural requests into their correct pigeon-holes and cabinets, trying to divine a greater logic hidden within the official logic of his office.

By dawn he was exhausted and panicky. So distraught that when Dima Dudenko came in and saw him there—rumpled, with his hair (what little there was left) hanging in greying strings from his pate—and asked if anything was wrong, he dragged him around behind the bookcases and blurted it all out to him in a stage whisper that tore at his throat, and brought tears.

Overnight he had discovered that yes . . . in horrible truth, files were *missing* or had been altered. Multiple pages had been removed, razored out of older bound volumes. It was impossible to say how long any of it had been going on, and doubtless there were official secrets that had to sometimes be . . . rewritten or various forms of evidence that, given the importance of protecting the empire, had to be fabricated. Still! There were safeguards, precautions designed for exactly this circumstance, but inevitably they had been circumvented. Case files. Different reference numbers. There's no way to trace it, of course. It could be the accountants. It could be Velimir Antonovich Zezulin.

'We must have inadvertently done something, or *he* must have—something to attract their attention! They've pretended it was about expenditures, but . . .' he spluttered into silence.

Dudenko was looking at him with a steady non-committal expression.

'The next thing is they'll want to schedule re-posting interviews . . . next week, the week after. Who knows when the axe will fall!' he said, his voice ending up in a wail.

Dudenko was kind enough to put a hand on his shoulder and suggest that he take the day off. 'Pyotr's coming in and we'll cover for you for a change, eh? Say you're sick, go upstairs and rest.'

The unexpected charity from Dudenko, a young know-it-all, a real cold fish most of the time, who had hardly ever spoken to him, caused Izachik to tear up again. He didn't even have the strength to reply, but walked quickly out of the room, and headed directly for the stairs, grateful to be told what to do. Dudenko followed him out. 'I'll bring you some tea in an hour or two, don't worry,' he said.

And, when Pyotr Ryzhkov arrived some minutes later, he told him all about it.

TWENTY-NINE

Like a princess she stepped from the Renault, remembering to cling to Fauré's arm, remembering to smile, remembering to walk, yes, like a princess up the short flight of steps. Remembering all of her instructions. Not nervous at all, she told herself. No, she was beyond all that, beyond nerves, beyond feelings. Numb.

Her smile came naturally, giddily. After all, this fabulous party was what she had always wanted. Maybe I can enjoy it for a while, she thought. Thinking too that the whole thing would be better after a few champagnes, remembering that all she had to do was stay awake. And then she was inside the doors, laughing and nodding to other guests, people Fauré knew, all the men staring. And for a few moments, yes, it was fabulous. Not everyone got to go to a ball like this, held at the Yusupov 'Palace' at the end of the Moika, one of the architectural wonders of the city, occupying nearly an entire block, splendid with its modernistic façade. It was the kind of place that you walked by and wondered what went on inside. And now, here she was.

'. . . and this is my niece, Katya . . .' Fauré was telling an old man dressed in a scarlet uniform, who chuckled politely. For tonight, she was Katya. At first she said no, but Fauré had insisted, so she would remember why she was doing it. Oh, yes. So, it would be a penance, a way of cleansing herself of not getting through the iron door a little faster, a way of assuaging guilt. After tonight she'd be free, she had told herself. But deep down she knew it was a lie.

There wasn't much rehearsing. Not enough.

She was playing the part of Boris's latest niece, a dancer who'd spent the last six years in Paris. That's where they'd met and she'd let Boris charm her. The idea was to be exotic, a rare bird. A special treat. They went over street maps, they picked out a fantasy apartment and furnished it. It was safe, Fauré said. She hated him, hated his confidence, his assurance. The way he had planned it so that there was no escape. Hated Pyotr for sitting there and saying nothing while she got a headache from memorizing the faces of the little one's friends. Why me? she was thinking all through it. Why me?

Well, because she hadn't been on her guard . . . because she, too, hated the ones who'd done it. Because she wanted to forget, and because it was a debt she wanted to cancel. Because a lot of things.

So, she'd memorized the salient events of their whirlwind courtship, listened while Fauré told stories of childhood frolics at the family compound in the Crimea. He was the writer, spinning out his fictions. 'Oh, our winters were . . . glorious! We had nine different kinds of palm trees,' he said with a gauzy look in his eye.

The fat man was the director, she decided. He was the one who took Fauré's part, rehearsed her in the dances; made her go over her French bedroom phrases. Practise how to drink out of a champagne flute. It wasn't that hard, and he was relieved. She knew all that. She had been practising for this all her life. It was just a quick run-through, a waltz across the floor of an abandoned sweatshop. A tango to take her measure, to check her abilities. She knew all the dances, they didn't have to worry. She could be Fauré's real niece if she took the notion and no one would be able to tell the difference.

She couldn't avoid Pyotr. He'd been assigned as the stage manager, sitting like a cold statue watching it all, ducking out to make telephone calls, to take care of production details. It helped to think of it that way, like a play, a great extravaganza. He kept his distance from the artists like a good stage manager. They hadn't talked since she'd been revealed as the procurer of Katya Lvova. No regret. No apology. That's the way the world turned, she decided. So . . . he did what they made him do, and she did the same. When they were all done, he'd make sure she had a cab home at night. Then she'd go to sleep and try to forget all about it.

It wasn't much of a plan.

From her studies of the portraits of the men who were coming to the Yusupov ball she knew the guest of honour—the Prime Minister of Serbia, Nicola Păsic, a bright-eyed little man with a prominent bald head and a monocle. He was in town to buy rifles and to ask the Tsar if it would be appropriate for Crown Prince Alexander to seek the hand of the lovely Grand Duchess Olga, with whom he had become friends when he was a military cadet in the city and she was just a child. A very delicate, festive mission. An attempt to bind Serbia to

Russia with bonds of steel and blood. In the nicest way, of course.

Escorting the prime minister would be most of Russia's diplomats who were posted to the Serbian capital of Belgrade—Ambassador Hartwig, (remember, it's 'Henry' to his friends) and his military attaché, Colonel Artamonov, (nothing cute, just plain 'Victor'). A few others they were interested in: Prince Evdaev, a soldier with old money, and a troika of industrialists— all of them connected to Smyrba.

'What about him?' she'd asked, pulling Smyrba's picture off the pile. 'If he's there he might recognize me.'

'He won't be there. He's out of town,' Tomlinovich said, and slid Smyrba's rodent face away.

A great screech of laughing pulled her into the moment. Fauré was making a joke, a servant came by and offered them iced champagne, she'd had two already and felt confident now, making eyes at the little knot of aristocrats that had surrounded them.

'. . . and I understand that you have been away? Living in Paris?' a man was saying to her. He was huge with twin side-whiskers that extended below his chin. A count somebody, his wife was by his side.

'It's been wonderful, the most glorious city,' she gushed.

'It is, isn't it, simply glorious . . .' the countess smiled and gripped the count's arm tightly, trying to will his eyes to elevate themselves from the altogether too-pleasant view of Katya's chest.

The revealing bodice had been necessary. Everything had been necessary. Once in the game, there was no way out, no other choice. No escape.

The fat man had taken her shopping, and she marvelled at his refined taste. They must have rejected a hundred dresses and finally left the shops, worn out and depressed. He wouldn't talk to her since he'd decided that she had no brains, that she was just Pyotr's actress-whore. Three days later a selection of dresses arrived from Paris. They hung up some blankets for her and she changed and unchanged until all the men were happy.

She did it all in a haze, exhausted from the show at the Komet, pretending to hustle out with Pyotr to her 'love nest', all the posing dropped as they went out the door, then a grim and silent carriage ride, nothing said between them. It seemed to be all right for him, but for her, after the evening's work, the real work began.

She tried on a dozen different gowns while they watched her, she walked across the factory floor, trying to stay awake. Still, it must have worked, she could tell by the way they watched her. All of them found a way to be there for the show, little Dziga and big Jekes. Hokhodiev, who was the one who'd helped hang up the curtains for her.

She ate and listened to them debate the merits of the dress, worrying up until the last minute that it would be too risqué. She had to agree, since it was nothing more than an elongated sheath of transparent silk dyed in bizarre swirls. Everything showed through depending on the light. Well, that was the idea, after all. They talked about the underclothes for hours, the underclothes must be right. All of them were the latest thing, invisible little camisoles, everything made of the finest silk. It must have cost a fortune. They wouldn't let her take them out of the factory.

'Oh, my God! Boris!' she heard a tall man call out to them. She recognized him as Prince Evdaev, Nestor, friend of the Yusupovs. Artamonov, the Russian attaché in Belgrade was there beside him. She had thought

Evdaev looked familiar when she'd been given the photographs and, now that she heard his voice—a little too highly pitched, a little strident, a little too loud—she was sure she remembered him.

'Ahh, Katya . . . someone I'd like you to meet.' Fauré neatly pulled them away from another knot of fools and across the ballroom. She moved through the crowd like a swan, like a princess-swan towards the knot of men. She didn't look at Evdaev right away, instead she smiled, let him appraise her while Fauré shook hands. 'Nestor, it's so good to see you again. It's been far, far too long. This is my niece, Ekatarina,' Fauré said with a laugh.

'Well—' Evdaev said, his eyes drinking her up. 'You certainly have a charming family, Boris.'

'Certainly,' Fauré said. Evdaev took a moment to bow and kiss her hand, and Artamonov smoothly imitated the gesture.

She stared into Artamonov's eyes for a moment, then turned shyly away from his gaze. 'It's true,' she laughed. 'We're the most charming, especially the French side of the family . . .' And all the men laughed. Just keep them laughing, keep them all off their guard.

'Katya's been living in Paris, where they grow up fast, eh?' Fauré jested.

'Well, Katya, you've made the party a success all by yourself,' Evdaev said with formal charm. She kept her eyes locked on his. Fauré had fallen silent. It was a little golden moment there, with too much unsaid. There was a blaring of music and Fauré pulled her away from them, out on to the floor to dance, but as they glided away her eyes held Evdaev's and set the hook.

'Good, we're on track so far . . .' Fauré said in her ear as they whirled their way through a waltz, and she let her head fall back, exposing the diamond collar— '. . . a

collar? Too obvious? No, he'll like that, he's the kind'—
they'd picked out for her. She let herself laugh, as if her
uncle had just said something far too witty.

From then on it was, pathetically easy. They watched
and mingled. All she had to do was have fun, drink the
best champagne from the best crystal. Laugh at things
that she couldn't hear over the music. Throughout it all,
they watched the men on her list, kept track of their
dancing partners, waiting for a vacuum that Katya
could fill.

The dancers whirled, the champagne bubbled, the
sophisticates laughed, but nothing she could do would
hold back time. It grew late, and finally Evdaev and
Păsic were striking up a polite conversation.

'Now . . .' Fauré said, and they hurried over casually.
'What fun, eh?' Fauré said, playing the part of a slightly
exhausted party-goer. 'I don't think I've danced as much
in years.'

'Come on,' she said with just a trace of disappoint-
ment. 'You're good for a few more.'

'Ah . . . ah . . . I don't think so . . . Too much time
behind a desk. I tell you, gentlemen, this girl can dance.'

'But where did you inherit such ability?' Ambassador
Hartwig had joined in. 'Most of Boris's family remind
me of draught horses . . .'

'It's so true!' Fauré managed a huge laugh, caught
sight of someone across the room. 'Oh, Christ. There's
Tippi, just a moment, will you excuse me, Katya? Will
you take care of her, Nestor. No bruises, please? I'll be
back soon, I promise.' Fauré detached himself and
vanished into the crowd.

'Do you have any toes left?' Evdaev said.

She pivoted and raised the hem of her dress to check.
'I think so . . .' Her voice was husky and cat-like.

Another man had come over . . . Victor Artamonov, the military attaché, she remembered.

'It's a lovely party,' Artamonov put in. 'Are you enjoying yourself?' he asked, trying anything to start a conversation.

She shrugged, looked bored. 'Well . . .' she said, leaving it hanging.

Artamonov laughed. 'Yes you needn't say anything. Uncle Boris is a good fellow, but . . . not exactly . . .' He made a face and it was her turn to laugh. One of the servants glided up to them with a silver tray of champagne flutes. Artamonov plucked one up and handed it to her with a little bow. The four of them touched glasses, and she looked at each man in turn, letting her eyes do the promising.

She was a little drunk now, and it was better that way. She danced with Artamonov, listened to him rhapsodize about his regiment, his horses, the nearly forgotten childhood pranks that he had sprung on his sisters in the gardens at Lillif. 'But I'll bet you were always an imp, weren't you,' he laughed, giving her a squeeze, letting his hand glide along her flank.

'Oh, yes,' she breathed. 'I'm the naughty one in the family.'

'Do you like Nestor?' Artamonov asked her, quietly, whispering in her ear. She looked around his shoulder and saw Evdaev watching them, he smiled when he caught her eye.

'He's handsome enough,' she said. It was a lie, of course.

'I think he likes you.'

'He has good taste then, doesn't he,' she giggled.

'Oh, yes. Yes, he does,' Artamonov said. And they spun away through the dancers. When they got back

Hartwig and Pašic were talking seriously about politics, and now she began her job, seemingly so simple—only to listen, to watch, to admire. To be a very pretty fly on the wall. And she did it for a few moments, until Artamonov got bored and pulled her back on to the floor. He went on and on about how he hated Belgrade, how he envied her life in Paris.

'I get there every so often, you know. Perhaps we could . . .'

'Oh, yes. I'll show you all the hot spots, we can dance the night away.'

'There is no social life in Belgrade, none whatsoever,' Artamonov pouted.

'I'd love it if you visited. You could meet all my friends, we could go around together . . . that is, if you'd like?'

'I'm sure I'd love your friends,' he said.

'I don't know, they're not like this crowd, they're not formal at all.' She decided to shock him a little, push him into a corner. 'They smoke hashish,' she said wickedly.

'Really. The artists' crowd then? Is that your circle?' She let her eyes narrow as she recounted her blissful Paris life. Oh, yes. The artists were always the ones on the edge, the artists and the young scientists. But the aviators were the best. She'd even let one of them take her up in a plane. Her eyes flickered at the memory.

'You are brave . . .'

'I'll try anything,' she said. And when his eyebrows raised—'Well, almost anything . . .' Letting her head tip from side to side with the music. 'Anything that's fun, anything that gives pleasure.'

He smiled at her for a long moment. 'I *will* come to Paris,' he said, trying to be ardent.

'I'll show you a few things. It won't be like Belgrade, that's a promise . . .'

And by the time the music ended, Artamonov was hers.

Fauré came over and took her aside, leaving the little knot to continue their political discussion. 'How is it going?' he asked her.

'So far, it's going fine,' she said. 'None of them think much about Pašic, I've learned that much.'

'No, they see him as a weak sister.'

'Evdaev said something about a party later. He wants them all to go to his place. They're getting bored.'

'Well, it's time for us to have our tiff, then. We'll be watching.' She didn't say anything. What good would watching do? Pyotr would be outside, like a dog banished to the courtyard, looking up at the windows. But he wouldn't be able to help her, he wouldn't rush in and save her. Watching. As if it was supposed to make her feel better. 'Good luck then . . .' Fauré said.

'What's wrong with *that*?' she stepped back and complained, a little too loudly.

'All right, damn it, if that's the way you want it!' Fauré suddenly hissed and stalked away. She watched him until he made it to the foyer, turned and idled her way back to Artamonov.

'Well,' she said. 'Boris is out of the way.'

'Poor Boris!' He laughed. 'And the prime minister is leaving, so that's good luck. Nestor has invited us, just a few friends. We thought we'd continue our evening, and the presence of someone so charming . . . well—'

'I'd love to,' she said, looking at him. Already she could see how the last act was going to turn out.

'We're going on, then?' Ambassador Hartwig had come over, a little flickering smile in her direction.

'You know the way, Henry?' Evdaev asked.

'Oh, yes . . . Sounds entrancing,' the ambassador said. His speech was blurred from the champagne.

'My, my . . . what an illustrious group of escorts,' she said, taking Evdaev and Artamonov and leading them towards the doors.

The carriage ride started off in a relatively civilized manner; she was squeezed between the two of them and for a few minutes the men pretended to be bored, but it didn't take long for their hands to start moving in the dim light. They mistook her squirming for enjoyment, and she let them. After all that was part of the job. She tried to joke her way out of it, 'We've got all night haven't we, boys . . .' and it worked for as long as it took to pop the cork on the champagne they'd carried away with them. She took a long drink, and as they passed the bottle between them, she let her head fall back and tried to see the stars through the window. It was cold, damp. Not yet spring. True spring wouldn't arrive for another month or so, but the cold air was her friend, it revived her with each breath, took her into her own private dream. She tried to stay in it as the men fumbled with her dress.

Pyotr was behind her somewhere, she thought. Out there following in the cold air. Could he see her face in the little window? She pulled herself away from the two men, fanned herself and laughed. It could have gone either way, then. The two of them looked at her, angry for a moment, two aristocrats who weren't used to being disappointed.

'Come on,' she pouted. 'Let's wait until we get to your place,' reaching for the bottle. 'You know, then we can make a little noise. Besides we might need a little more room, don't you think?' And the two of them settled back and laughed.

And that served to delay the third act until they arrived at Evdaev's mansion on Kronyerkskaya, the carriage entering through the back gate. And she almost thought she could hear a second carriage, clattering along on the cobbles, drive past the entrance, as the iron gates clanged shut.

When Evdaev wanted privacy he used his 'apartment' over the stables. There were no horses there any more. They made their way up the outside stairs to a little door that you had to stoop to go through, and she found herself in a long room that was partitioned off into an entry, a nicely appointed kitchen and dining-room. Her little jacket ended up on a chair in the dining-room, and she found herself being guided to the sitting-room, decorated with animal skins and guns. All leather, fur and iron. There was a gramophone and Nestor put on the music, a hissing rendition of something that was supposed to be lively. Hartwig and another man were right behind them. They'd found another girl to bring along. Two of them for four.

Artamonov had found some glasses and poured them the last of the bottle. 'Don't worry, Henry's brought some more, my dear,' he said and then kissed her, hard, before lifting his glass.

'Here,' she said. 'Have you ever had some of this?' Digging in her little bag for the hashish.

'Oh you are wicked,' Artamonov said and lurched towards her again, trying to force his tongue down her throat. When he finished, she kept her lips to his, whispering, 'It'll make it better, you'll see.'

'She's not like Boris's side of the family, thank Christ . . .' Artamonov said to Evdaev.

'No,' he replied, his voice low. Hungry.

'I'm so glad,' she said, falling into her fictional biography. 'I hate them all, they're so . . . old . . . Not like you two,' adding just a moment of tenderness.

Artamonov struck a match and watched her inhale, then passed the little pipe along.

She waited until it came around one more time and then asked for the cloakroom. It was at the end of the long garret and she took her bag with her, closed the door and snapped on the lights. Caught a long look at herself before she opened the bag, took out the vial and pulled out the sponge. Raised one leg on the lip of the toilet and pushed the sponge up her vagina, tamping it into place against her cervix, pulled her underwear back up and smelled her fingers. A little vinegary, but passable. So what, let them suffer, she thought. Another long look in the mirror, trying to remember who the beautiful angry woman was staring back at her. Oh, yes. Katya.

And then, just for a moment, she almost cracked; the tears would have come but they weren't in Fauré's script. She was supposed to be happy, she was supposed to want what the men were planning. She was supposed to stay there and have fun, and listen. And learn.

When she got out of the cloakroom, Hartwig had settled in, looking a little stiff and uncomfortable. He said no to the strange pipe with the exotic mixture, sat and tried to start up a conversation with her. Artamonov decided he was going to be her rescuer and put another disc on the gramophone. Something slower so that he could embrace her and they danced close while the others watched.

Artamonov was ready, she knew. She could feel his cock banging against her thigh. His hands were massaging the cleft in her buttocks. She groaned and he pulled away for a moment. 'Have you seen the turret?' he whispered and looked down towards the bedroom.

'I'd love too, but—' she glanced toward the ambassador. Oh yes, she could see Artamonov thinking, my boss is here after all. 'Yes . . . of course,' he said quietly in her ear.

She danced with Hartwig after that; he tried to make conversation at first, but fell silent and contented himself with staggering about the zebra skin rug and pressing his belly against her, in the belief that this would somehow be exciting.

Through it all she did what she had been told, she listened; there was a good deal of meaningless chatter about upcoming festivals in Belgrade, work that would have to be accomplished as soon as they returned to the capital. Everyone bemoaned the fact that Smyrba wasn't present, and did anyone know exactly what was going on there? They didn't seem overly worried. Evdaev had been up to the turret with the other girl. He had taken off his uniform jacket and paraded about the room in his skin-tight breeches and undershirt, the buttons opened on top to reveal the dark hair of his chest. She decided to get them all as drunk as possible, maybe they'd pass out and she could go home.

Each time one of them danced with her, she drank more champagne. They had smoked all the hashish, and at one point she found herself dancing alone to the music. It was something vaguely oriental, something languid from the south. And she swayed before the men—listening.

'. . . more dangerous than ever. Nothing is secure any longer. Did you tell him?' Hartwig was asking. She let herself turn, raised her hands above her head and repeated the dance she'd done as the Princess of Tahoo, the dance of the burning virgin.

'. . . so everything is moved up . . .' Hartwig was saying. He was a little deaf she thought. He turned his head away and squinted when someone was talking to him.

She moved away, not too far, so that she could still hear the men. All of it going into a little corner of her mind. Now she was dancing in the window, the light illuminating her dress for the men behind her. This is for you, Pyotr, this is my dance of love everlasting, my marriage dance, my dance of penance, my dance of death.

'. . . I'll let him know as soon as we get back. We don't need Smyrba, it might not be so bad. And there are only so many opportunities . . .'

'Come on . . . I don't want to wait any longer.' Artamonov had come up behind her, his hands had come around to clutch her breasts.

'What?' she said. Putting on a naive pose. Make him put it into words, make him put a label on his lust.

'Let's go, I'll show you the turret.'

'What's wrong with here?' she said, whirling in his arms, one hand reaching into his pocket. Keep on shocking him.

'No . . .' he almost growled, and pulled her away from the window and they started towards the bedroom.

'Be careful with that,' Evdaev called out behind them.

The turret was really a bedroom with a lot of stained-glass windows. A trapeze dangling there with velvet loops for your legs and a seat so that you could do all sorts of tricks.

She finished with Artamonov in a matter of minutes; he came in a short little ripple of yelping, not even making it into her. 'Oh, good Christ, you're a bloody good bitch,' he moaned in her ear. A compliment, she supposed.

She walked out of the turret first, wearing the special French underwear, the ambassador and Evdaev watching her, and then turning to each other and saying something she couldn't hear. 'Well . . . as much as I'd like to . . .' Hartwig said, and very courteously lifted her hand and kissed it.

'Stay if you want,' she said. She could hear the other girl moaning around the corner.

'No . . . no . . .' A shy man. Or maybe he was afraid, or too old, or too drunk.

She walked to the window while Evdaev saw the ambassador to the stairs, looked out on to the courtyard. It was as still as death. No birds, no breeze, no squirrels . . . Somewhere a door was closing.

'Come here,' Evdaev said behind her, and she turned to see him naked. A strong man, a flat belly and big thighs.

'You're in the cavalry aren't you,' she remembered, coming forward to meet him.

'Take this off.' He began to pull the camisole away.

'I enjoy riding too,' she said. She saw Artamonov come out of the turret and light a cigarette. He stood in the shadows and watched.

'Good . . .'

She pushed Evdaev down on to the sofa and guided his cock into her. Began to rock back and forth while his fingers pinched her. She looked down at him and his face was blank, almost dazed, as if he were trying to put together a strange puzzle. She pushed harder, pulled his hands away.

'I know who you are . . .' she said, said it cruelly, scaring him for a moment. 'I know what you think . . . I know what you want . . .'

'God . . .'

'I know all your crimes . . . I know all your secrets . . .' Artamonov had come up to the sofa and was stroking himself.

'I know both of you,' she said, looking up at Artamonov's blushing face.

And she went ahead and did what she had to do, and before the morning had arrived, she did it again. Until the men were asleep like pigs in a barnyard, curled up in a tangle, and she could retrieve her expensive foreign clothes and leave them to their snoring and their dreams.

THIRTY

They let her douche, and they let her bathe, and they let her sleep for a few hours. It was a long room with a window at the gable end with branches of trees scraping against the glass when the breeze came up. Little green buds trying to escape the chill; more promises, more waiting, she thought. The doctor came in and asked her if there was any blood. There wasn't. She'd got away easy, she told herself. They let her douche again, brought her some breakfast, and then they came in, hats in hand.

Fauré sat for a few moments looking at her. Tomlinovich looked around for a chair and then took up a post beside the window. Pyotr was gone. Who knew where. She'd been used. She knew that now. All along she had just been used. Dragged down by degrees, just look through the pictures, just play a little part, just tell me all you know. And now they were going to use her some more.

'We need to go through it all, of course,' Fauré said. She watched the young one, the thin one with the glasses take out his pad and pencil.

And so . . . she went through it all, remembering each conversation, every mundane detail of the rooms above the Evdaev stables—'It may have been one of their habitual meeting places,' Fauré explained.

So, she told him about the skins on the wall, the turret, the skylight in the turret . . .

They took a break. The woman brought her some tea. Everyone went to the lavatory. She wanted to ask where Pyotr was, but decided that she was not going to care about that any longer. She went back to the bed and got under the covers, and under the covers she just overflowed in tears. The woman came back to check on her, pulling the covers back but she knocked her hand away.

'Go down and tell them I'm ready.'

She went over it again and again. A day went by. And then another. She looked at more pictures. Walked around the woods surrounding the little clinic with Sinazyorksy to guard her. They didn't talk, which was fine with her. She dredged up everything, sometimes she thought she manufactured the details out of her dreams. Still they listened to everything. There were stenographers who came and went in shifts. She was not to worry about her job, they told her. It didn't matter, she'd almost forgotten about all of that. And Larissa who she didn't blame at all. Not really.

And so, she told them all the little fragments, tried to remember the inflections, the attitudes. Told them about how there had been a statement that things were going to have to be moved up. Everything timed for the summer, all of it arranged through someone called *Apis*.

A lot of animosity around Pǎsic, somebody named Sergei whose name kept coming up. No, they didn't suspect anything about Smyrba.

'Apis . . . The bull,' Fauré said, leaning forward.

'The bee, the bull . . .' Tomlinovich muttered from his post at the window. He must be a birdwatcher, she thought.

'Well, whoever *Apis* is, he's in Belgrade, because Hartwig was going to speak to him when they returned.'

'Speak to him?'

'That's what he said, speak. They were ready to have a meeting.'

'Speak . . .' Fauré muttered.

When they finished there were no goodbyes. They just left the room with serious expressions, and it ended with her getting dressed and being driven across the city to her place on Sadovaya. She went in and sat in the empty rooms, soaked in a bath, and then walked up the street to the club thinking that she didn't want to be alone.

Inside Kushner was lecturing them again. He called it poetry but really it was a long list detailing the many failures of the Romanov autocracy, without, of course, saying anything that might get him arrested. One had to always remember to be careful, even if there was supposedly no censorship. In front of him Tika, the cat, had been enclosed in an intricately designed metal cage, on trial for its life. Kushner explained that any animal would do; a chicken, a hawk, a double-headed eagle . . . No double-headed eagles being available, today Tika would be standing in. There were less than a dozen people in the audience.

'. . . *for those who actually do the work that causes the beast of the state to continue in its lumbering*

pace. For those whose blood is the grease within the
bloody machine. For those who, after being told there
was light, still refused to look up . . . for those who
believed they would go to hell if . . . for those
who knew they would be beaten if . . . for those who
knowing and were still afraid and could not continue
because . . . for all those who—'

No, the Komet was only marginally a political club.
Those who considered themselves firebrands might stop
by for a look-in, but the art was too artistic, the issues
too vaguely drawn, they reported. To talk about
anything substantial one had to find a place where one
could talk freely, not a café. A friend's apartment where
there were no police informers listening to your fantastical plans to bomb the Winter Palace.

She felt sick. Maybe it was the weather. Maybe it was
the life.

She went in, smiled, embraced, moved to the back of
the room. Dropped in and out of conversations, glanced
at the headlines. There had been seventeen suicides over
the weekend, including a boy who'd taken poison.

She listened to Kushner, but from the moment she
heard about the boy, she couldn't stop thinking about it.
Just the idea of it lodged in her mind. Thinking about
how it would have hurt, how he would have twisted and
writhed as the chemicals tore at his insides.

Poison.

It was not the way she would plan it. Lately she
couldn't stop thinking about death. In her latest plan she
had decided to wait until the weather got cold again,
drink her head off and then go out to the centre of the
Troitsky Bridge where there was a good current and hop
over the side. The cold would numb her, the drink

would calm her and the river would just . . . take her.
And, with a bit of luck, perhaps it would be beautiful.
Scenic, with silvery moonlight or a slow snowfall, and
warm downlighting provided by the lanterns on the
bridge. That was the way she was imagining it, floating
down through the icy water before the weight of her
clothing dragged her under, one last look at the stars . . .
tryn-trava—who cares?

Kushner did. Kushner cared very deeply and now he
had talked Larissa into caring too. They were
Bolsheviks, Maximalists they called themselves, and had
begun obsessively reading everything they could get
their hands on that was even remotely seditious. One
night, giggling, tipsy, Larissa lifted up the floorboards in
Kushner's filthy bedroom, took out something wrapped
in a remnant of red serge, started to unwrap it. For one
queasy moment as the red cloth was unwrapped Vera
saw the wooden handle like a dildo with its little iron
ring, and she thought Larissa wanted something else.
And then the cloth came all the way away and she saw
it was a pistol.

'It's called a Mauser . . .' Larissa breathed.

An ugly thing, smuggled across the border by a
student; all squares and angles, a pistol designed by an
abstract artist. Something you might use to kill
Martians. They had fourteen bullets they kept knotted
in a silk handkerchief and neither of them had ever fired
it. Well, where could they? They practised cleaning it
and taking it apart blindfolded, then they'd wrap it up
and put it under the floor again.

It didn't matter what Vera said, Larissa was too far
gone.

'Don't say I didn't warn you,' Vera had told Larissa.
'All these books could land you in Kresty with some

girls who won't be as gentle with you as I was,' she'd said, giving her a little tweak on the tit just to drive the point home. Because that was what was going to happen. Kushner was going to sink them all.

'You should think for once, think about who you are for once,' was all Larissa had said, not even laughing and that somehow made it worse.

Oh, sure, sure, it all made sense. Of course it all made sense. Did they think that she actually believed in the divinity of the Romanov dynasty? Or the sanctity of the 'pure' church? And of course something had to change, something had to give. Everybody knew that. And everyone had someone they wanted to get back at, didn't they?

It was a war, a war between different classes of people, between rich and poor, healthy and lame, smart and stupid. Kushner's solution was to hang them all from lampposts. A list that included, well . . . everybody—the members of the Duma, the judges, the lawyers, all the owners and managers, investors, bankers, accountants. But then who would be left to run things? That was easy; he'd turn it all over to the peasants, the only people who really understood the soil, the only representatives of the authentic heart of Russia.

She thought he felt that way because he'd never really spent any time with peasants. He had a picture of them in his mind that made it all much prettier than it was.

Well, she'd spent as little time with the peasants as she could. On a couple of occasions she had actually been inside a *izba*, really just a little piled-up box of mismatched logs, covered with sod. A dark, smoke-filled stinking hole where an entire family lived and died, and then the next generation did it all over again. If that was

the authentic heart of Russia, she wanted no part of it,
thank you very much.

*'. . . the bliss of making the new man who will walk
proudly among his brothers . . .'*

The cat had tried to curl up and go to sleep, but she
saw that Kushner had designed the cage to be just a little
too small. The poor animal could barely turn around,
and Kushner had the annoying habit of slapping the
podium at the end of each stanza, so the cat, with no
rest, was growing peeved at the whole exercise.

Larissa was seated at the corner of the stage. Looking
up at her man with a rapt expression, her clear, open
face almost radiant. Like a saint, Vera thought. Maybe
she was going to become the saint of the Bolsheviks.
Maybe Kushner was treating her well, it was hard to
say. They were very private.

*'. . . not shirk from the spilling of the blood of the
god . . . not to shirk from looking into the broken
mirror . . . to hold up the idols and the ikons and the
idiots and say . . .*
"Parasites! Vermin! Anathema!"'

Kushner was yelling his phrases now. Cursing and
screaming. Izov had come around from behind his
luxurious bar and was frowning at the reading. Well, it
would be over soon, she thought. And indeed after
another few imprecations, came the non-climax and the
poor cat stood condemned before them all.

There was a splatter of applause and she took the
opportunity to escape the Komet, getting out almost as
quickly as she'd come in, started walking up to the

public library, idling through the market until she came out on Sadovaya Street; steering herself vaguely towards the Nevsky. Maybe she could lose herself window-shopping for things that were impossibly expensive. She didn't want to be noticed. She was tired of being looked at and sought after. Tired of making herself into someone who was fabulously enticing. Tired of looking like someone's erotic vision; tired of trying to be appreciated all the time by people she didn't even know or care about.

Tired of being a bloody good bitch.

It was the long-promised spring come round at last. The leaves were breaking open, the rains were washing the filth of the winter away into the canals. She sniffed the air like a dog, a remarkably fresh day and underneath it all the scent of wood smoke, and the sharper tang of burning coal from the little steamers that wafted along the streets. No, it wasn't quite cold enough to jump in the Neva, she thought. The idea, the whole point, was to be numb.

She passed a dress shop and stopped for a moment looking at the mannequins and the clothes they displayed. She could wear anything up there and look good. In the weeks leading up to the Yusupov party she had made some money appearing in a really absurd show. A sort of musical extravaganza at the Alexandra Theatre of all places, and after another week she'd be able to afford anything they put up in their windows. She was doing well, she was doing just fine. Better than expected. Much better. Not as well as when she was working for Madame, but then again she didn't have to pretend to like putting her face in some other girl's ass.

She was making, what? Nearly four hundred roubles each month just for dancing. Not the top, but not bad.

Let's see, what were her choices, what were the roads she hadn't taken? She could have got a job on the looms at the silk works and after six months and fucking the boss a few dozen times she could have worked her way up to ten roubles a month. What else? Well, let's suppose God had come down and given her the skills necessary to be a metalworker, ignoring the fact that there were no women metalworkers, but let's just pretend she could work lathes and drill holes and make things square; then she would be making maybe twelve roubles a day. That was the top and she'd done better than that already. And now she was fucking princes and ambassadors, so that was a plus wasn't it?

She had to stop. There was a knot of people gathered at the intersection of Sadovaya and the Nevsky and she saw the first white-clothed mourners passing by. It was the funeral of a child, a little white casket carried in the white open hearse, the horses draped in white blankets. In the sunlight it was dazzling, an expensive funeral for a valuable child. All the faces sombre as they trudged along towards the Nicholas Station for a last long train ride back to the graveyard at the family's estate.

She thought maybe she would go ahead and die. Maybe she'd go on in this direction, turn and take a walk through the gardens and then just one last time along the embankment. Maybe she'd walk out on the bridge and just see. It was all up to her, she was free to do whatever she wanted.

She was smiling to herself as the cortège passed by. A gendarme blew a whistle, and they all broke up and crossed the street behind the mourners, the world suddenly back to normal again. Goodbye, Child, she said, saying it under her breath, almost cheerfully.

And she was still smiling when she walked right into a man who had stepped out of a little doorway, without looking. Well, she hadn't been looking either.

There was one of those moments where they each decided to avoid each other by stepping aside, and both went the same direction and the man reached out to steady her and then she looked up and saw that it was Pyotr she'd run into.

'Oh . . .' was all she could manage.

'Hello,' he said, automatically reaching for his hat. His expression was cold. Would he ever able to trust her again? Well, it didn't really matter. She brushed past him, but he grabbed her by the arm, hard. For a moment she thought he was going to hit her.

'So, you really like me now, yeah?' Reaching for a handkerchief to wipe everything away.

'I got the transcripts of your interviews. I read everything. I know what you did. I know why you did it.' He trailed off. Shrugged. Still he wouldn't be able to erase the ghost of the dead *vertika* that had come between them. How could you erase something like that? Ghosts were insubstantial, less than memories. Funny how that made them harder to get rid of.

'Just like a good investigator. Maybe you'll get a promotion.' He looked terrible, like he'd been sleeping in alleys. His clothes were neat enough, but he hadn't shaved and his eyes were rimmed with red.

'How are you?' she asked. Polite. Maybe she'd be polite right up until the last moment. They could cut that into her headstone . . . 'she was a very polite whore'.

'I came by the Komet, but they said you were gone.'

'I wasn't gone, I was helping to save the world, remember? I did just fine, thank you not at all, and I'm

going to start back working at the Alexandra.' His
eyebrows went up. Surprised that she'd recovered so
quickly? 'It's a good job and it's running for a few more
weeks unless Sasha decides to hold it over. You needn't
bother seeing it. It's a stupid show, lots of feathers.
Stupid, frivolous. Insubstantial. Parasitic . . .' she said,
tailing off. She looked at the doorway he'd come out of.
There was a brass plate screwed into the yellow
masonry that said *Volga Metals Assurance Company*.

'So, you've been busy too?' she said and for some
reason reached up to trace her finger along the letters of
the word *Volga*.

'Yes. I was just going to get something to eat. What
about you?' It was his only joke, making fun of the way
she ate.

'No,' she said and gave him the hardest look she
could dredge up. His beard had grown all grey around
the chin. 'No, I never want to eat again . . . I hate food.
I hate all food. What is this place?' she said, and pushed
the door open.

'Vera, I—' There was a little note of panic in his
voice. The front room of the offices was cramped,
closed-in with glass shelves and packing crates piled up
in the aisles between the display cases. Inside the cases
were little piles of what looked like different coloured
dirt. Crystals and strangely contorted rock fragments;
minerals displayed with Latin labels. A little yellow pile
of sulphur, four different varieties of coal, a series of
beakers of petroleum. On another wall were long
strands of different fibres, flax, hemp, twists of cotton
rope. A young man looked up from the counter, smiled
when he saw Pyotr come in behind her.

'Ahh . . . Pyotr Mikhalovich!' he said nervously.

'Do you distribute paintbrushes here? Or brushes of any kind?' she called out enthusiastically. The young clerk was frowning now. Smiling but frowning all at the same time, trying to remember what business they were in.

'I think we could order some for you, mademoiselle,' he said. A second polite person in the universe! She turned to look at Ryzhkov who was standing beside one of the cabinets waiting for her to finish having her little fit.

'Is this where you work?' she asked him. He shook his head for a second, tried to make up his mind whether or not to say something, and then only shrugged. The other man jumped in to save him.

'We're always glad to see Monsieur Ryzhkov, but I am afraid we are just closing now, so unless it is very important—' The man looked around for something to do that would demonstrate that he was actually closing his shop in the middle of the day. When he reached over to roll down the top of his desk she caught sight of the pistol stuck in the side of his belt.

'No, that's fine. I was just going.' Her brightest smile.

'Goodbye, sir, I'm so sorry we couldn't be of service,' the young man called.

'It's all right,' Pyotr said to him as they went out.

She'd started walking again. To hell with him, she decided. Men and guns. All that pretending. She was sick of pretending.

He was following along behind her as she trudged towards the river. Maybe he was going off to drown himself too. Yes! It could be a pact. People would talk, all their friends would wonder, and worry, and spin fantastic dramas about the two lovers fished up somewhere out in the Gulf. His police friends would be amazed, surprised. Who was the mystery woman? A dancer you say? What was Pyotr Mikhalovich doing with someone like that? She had no idea what they'd say, maybe he didn't have any friends.

'Where are you going?' She heard him just behind her.

'Out . . .'

She broke through the edge of the gardens . . . it had been too quick, she hadn't even noticed the people walking, hadn't even seen the colours of the leaves. Now that was all gone and she'd never have another chance.

Ahead of her was the embankment and the wide river, running high. Plenty of water out there. Boats were going up and down carrying things back and forth, endlessly. People, wood, exotic foods, fish, coal, cloth. Every damn thing you wanted and every damn thing you didn't, and never, never what you needed. Never that. Each time, each voyage someone made some money, and each time somebody else lost. Kushner laughing at the parasites and those who loved them. She was crying. Why was she always crying? He had come up beside her and was saying things, more soft talk, and she turned away so he wouldn't see she was crying. He was apologizing, and trying to get her to talk, asking her why, and she didn't know why. She was the last person who would know why. Maybe they could ask Kushner, he knew everything.

Was he pretending? That it was a coincidence, an accident? He'd been waiting for her in that doorway, she thought. Somehow events had synchronized and the two of them had been brought together. More of Boris Fauré's spy games. She certainly hadn't planned it. Now she was laughing and he was holding out a handkerchief. That was even funnier. She had to look at it for a moment before she remembered what it was. Oh, yes.

Clean yourself up Vera, be presentable again. Someone might see you, someone might see you coming apart right here on a perfect spring day.

'I don't mind if you follow me,' she said to him. 'It's a dangerous world after all.'

'It's very dangerous,' he said. She blew her nose and then handed him back the handkerchief and he took it so gingerly that she laughed. Oh, he was still the only man who ever talked any sense to her, even if he was older and infatuated. Not all that handsome . . . certainly not rich. And a liar. And married. Well, the list went on and on, didn't it.

'You know who I am, Pyotr,' she said quietly. They were standing close together and that was fine she thought because the wind had come up and he was blocking it. He was looking at her with those sad eyes. A little smile that was trying to escape. 'And I know who you are. I know what you do, why you exist. You're the one who is watching and watching, and using people up. And you say you want the truth, but all you get is lies, and you're always using people up . . . right?'

Very gently, very quietly and softly, like a child trying to pick up a butterfly, he kissed her.

She closed her eyes and his kiss seemed to last . . . for hours.

'I love you,' he said, and she watched his mouth make the words. Saying it levelly, as cold as saying two kopeks.

He bought them a cab ride across the city to her apartment, newly spacious since Larissa had moved out, made tea, and took it to her in the stuffy little bedroom where she drank half a cup and then fell asleep. When she woke up she found that he had gone out and got cartons of food from a Chinaman's kiosk in the Apraxin

market, brought it back, and contrived to keep it warm
until she came around.

Then she realized that she was hungry and that his
joke was true, and she finished the lion's share of the
strange food, and then sat back, warm and feeling
something that might be happiness, but was more like
the wonder that one feels at having survived, to have
escaped, to have turned a corner and somehow beaten
the odds. And then, not long after that, she walked
around the table and pulled his face into her breasts, and
then lifted his chin and, hungry all over again, she was
kissing him.

He tried to say that he'd better go, but she wouldn't
let him, closed his mouth with more kisses. 'No, stay
and talk.' She was still kissing him, 'Talk to me, tell me
your life story . . .' And before long they were first in the
doorway and then in the bed.

And he did, somewhere in the night, tell her his story.
A story she thought should be painted in the colours of
a Moscow winter. In tones of grey, with cinders and soft
dark shadows. Not that it was sad, just that it was
empty. A saga of the Ryzhkovs—a military family, a
mother dying too early. A father who was a natural
engineer who understood nothing of the mechanics of
the human heart or the architecture of his children, an
uncle who was a monster when he drank, an aunt who
watched but didn't see.

He told it all staring at the ceiling, in a voice as bleak
as his childhood must have been. An orderly story, a
story with no chaos or broken rules. Just an endless
logical equation that resulted in a policeman who'd
looked too deeply into the mists and thought he'd seen
something; seen the way things should be, seen how to
make them all turn out greater than zero.

'I was young then,' he said, shaking his head on the pillow. He meant 'young—like you are', but he hadn't said it. But now he sounded like he'd been wounded too many times, his young dreams battered beyond repair, as if the game he was playing had been lost long, long ago.

And still dwelling on how much older he was. As if it was important somehow, as if there was this vast gulf of experience that made it impossible for him to be honest with her. Like he was afraid she'd wake up and realize one day.

'You can never know. Maybe you made something turn out right and you just didn't notice,' she said very softly, a hand cruising across his chest.

Just as the city was waking they made love again. He was tired and she had her way with him. She didn't want him to work to impress her with his strength or his virility or his technique; she didn't want him to do anything or be anything but Pyotr Ryzhkov, the man who'd reached out and become an island for her . . .

She ground herself into him, giddy now with her own power; laughing as she devoured him, bit into him, swallowed him—and they became one mad ecstatic creature filling her little bedroom with their cries.

She could wait until later, sometime in winter when everything was exactly right. She could kill herself any time at all. After all, she was free.

There was no rush.

THIRTY-ONE

Most of the time the two teams of inspectors still maintained their professional separation, proving that there was a greater distance from the political police to justice than might be supposed. If anyone from either side talked to each other it was at the very bottom—only Jekes and Muta had become something like friends during their long waits.

On this occasion Hokhodiev was reading the *Gazette* while he lounged against an malachite column that supported the balustrade at the top of the first floor of the Imperial Biological Museum. Dima Dudenko had fiddled the lock on one of the doors and was smoking out on the balcony. Sitting in the window opposite Dziga slowly carved a slow spiral of peel from an apple. It was a warm day and he had opened his jacket to reveal the silver revolver that he holstered under his arm. Like the man it was little.

'You can hit things with that?' Hokhodiev pointed at the pistol.

'Pretty good, yes.'

'You have to get close, eh?'

'You do.'

'I couldn't hit anything with something like that. I need a rifle to kill someone,' Hokhodiev said and turned back to his paper. 'Besides, it's best to run away most of the time. And if you get caught, there's no gun and you can just play stupid.'

'I bet you could do that,' Dziga laughed.

'It works, doesn't it? And then when I get in close, I can use these.' Hokhodiev held up his left fist. It was almost the size of Dziga's head.

'Ahh . . .'

Hokhodiev just smiled at him. Dziga wound his way once more around the apple. 'And if there is some emergency and I really need a gun, I know where I can get one. I can get plenty, so . . .' Hokhodiev shrugged.

Down at the foot of the stairs, Sinazyorksy gave a whistle and Dziga recoiled the apple and put it in his pocket. Hokhodiev straightened at the column and tucked the newspaper beneath his jacket in the small of his back, walked over to the door and tapped on it three times to let Ryzhkov know they were coming, then went back to his post. 'So?' Hokhodiev whispered to Dziga.

'Don't ask me,' Dziga hissed back. 'They've both been very quiet lately.' He shrugged, and Hokhodiev saw that his leathery face was suddenly full of worry. Not a good sign, he thought as Tomlinovich and Fauré began coming up the stairs towards the doors.

The entire wall of the Cetacean Room was taken up by the skeleton of a gigantic humpback whale. Ryzhkov had to walk backwards to the windows in order to take the whole thing in from a distance. In glass cases were artefacts of other whales, models of whaling vessels, a collection of huge ivory teeth; displays of harpoons and long hoe-shaped flensing knives were mounted on the wall below the great skeleton. It was a stupid place for a meeting, he thought.

Fauré came in, apologized for being late, and then stood for a moment impassively, hands clasped behind his back. Tomlinovich was wheezing from his climb up the stairs. He went over to the balcony and threw open the doors, trying to get a breeze. He was dressed in a great yellow summer-weight cloak, a straw hat tipped back on his head. He looked like a boulevardier or a circus impresario.

Fauré looked up at the whale and sniffed. 'Isn't it ironic, Inspector? This complicated, exquisite creature is considered, quite properly, the Queen of the Seas. All lesser creatures willingly surrender their feeding grounds at her approach, so highly is she esteemed, so greatly is she feared.' Together they took another step or two along the glass cases as Fauré looked up into the long belly of the whale.

'But this position of high importance in the universe of the depths is based on illusion. A misapprehension which, if it were corrected, would mean a reversal of fortune for the great Queen. What had once been the most feared creature, would now be merely a gigantic moving target; unable to defend herself against her enemies, prey for roving packs of sharks, for—do you observe the teeth, Ryzhkov?' They had finally reached the head and Ryzhkov dutifully looked up at the long curve of the jawbone.

'You see? No lance-like fangs, no molars to crush bones. Instead our Queen is armed with nothing more than the finest of combs, constructed similarly to fans of feathers, whose function is to sieve enormous quantities of water, extracting such tiny animals as to be invisible to our land-born eyes.' Fauré turned and smirked. 'Should this great animal be attacked by some undersea menace, she, much like Mother Russia herself, is wholly unable to defend herself, and, of course, quite ill-suited to be a predator.'

'I suppose you could tell that to all the invisible shrimp,' Ryzhkov said and walked along the cabinets for a few paces.

'Mmm . . .' Fauré said, unconvinced. 'Well . . . I asked you here to discuss some international affairs which will, I can assure you, be of concern to us both.'

'All right, then. What is it?'

'It's the fucking end of the world is what it is,' Tomlinovich said from his doorway.

'It is nothing of the sort,' Fauré said, a touch of anger creeping into his womanly voice. 'We seem to be having an undue amount of trouble with our friends in Serbia.' Fauré had stopped at the end of the display cases. He was pretending to inspect a great whalebone covered with a mariner's scratched carvings, a seascape of rocks, broken ships, drowning sailors and buxom mermaids.

'Have you ever heard of the Black Hand?' Tomlinovich asked.

'The Serbian terrorists, the ones in Belgrade, the "Union or Death"?'

'Yes, yes . . .' Tomlinovich called. 'Either them or a second group called "Young Bosnia"?'

'They are the terror vanguard, they go out and recruit adolescents ready to lay down their lives for the dream of *Yugo-Slavia*. A pack of assassins. The most militant fringe of our dear brothers, the Southern Slavs,' Fauré said quietly.

'They're behind all this?'

'The arms that Smyrba has been smuggling, Lavrik, all of it. They have links to our own Slavophilic zealots: Ambassador Hartwig, Colonel Artamonov. Both have received payments.' Fauré gave a long angry sigh, his eyes never leaving the gigantic skeleton. 'Also, clear connections to our Ministry of War. Backed up by photographic evidence and banking records. Much of this we only know because of what our very courageous friend, Mademoiselle Aliyeva, overheard. I wish I could give her a medal,' Fauré said and for a moment his eyes flicked over to Ryzhkov. 'Well, perhaps one day . . .'

'The essence of the whole bloody mess,' Tomlinovich said, straightening in the doorway and heading across the crackling parquetry towards them. '. . . is that we've uncovered much more than just a financial scandal, now it's an international conspiracy, colluding with a foreign power to corrupt officials in our government,' he said gravely.

'But this is all for money, yes?'

Fauré shrugged. 'Money, patriotism, religion, power . . . money . . .'

'Well, can't you seize the money?'

'Not without a protocol, and it must be signed. Besides, now a foreign power is involved—unfortunately it is a foreign power with which we sympathize— poor little Serbia. We use the same alphabet, sing the same songs, hate the Austrians just the same. Put all that up against the bribes paid to divert Russian arms to Serbia, enough to outfit an entire corps of infantry, plus artillery to defend Belgrade from armies advancing from the north.' Fauré looked up at Ryzhkov, shrugged. 'It's espionage. Spies. If it were public, it would make a huge scandal.' Behind his smooth baby-face he looked immensely sad.

'And now, because of all that, because it's international, we have to go higher, we have to please the gods,' Tomlinovich muttered. Fauré sighed.

'I thought *secrecy* was the whole point of this,' Ryzhkov said.

'Indeed, yes . . .'

'You didn't want anyone to know, you were afraid they'd catch on to us, and now you have to *ask*?'

'Look, the whole point is to file charges, to bring a case, to prosecute,' Fauré started to explain.

'Ministry of *Justice*, remember?' Tomlinovich smiled tightly.

'But now?'

'Ryzhkov, I can't just go and arrest the Minister of War, I can't haul Hartwig in for questioning—he's the Tsar's personal friend!'

'There are rules, regulations, immunities. If we *don't* report it we are guilty of espionage ourselves, don't you see?' Tomlinovich recited.

'Yes, we have to give notice, we have to file our notice of intent.'

'It's the law. We have to ask permission of the gods,' Tomlinovich said. 'Don't look so sad, Ryzhkov, it lets you off the hook.'

'What do you mean?'

'You've done a good job for us,' Fauré said quietly, reached up for a moment and gave his shoulder a pat. 'You've performed well, you've done things that have demonstrated your—'

'Not that you had a hell of a lot of choice,' Tomlinovich said.

'We're going forward. Do what we must, do what we can. We'll take testimony formally, compile our evidence. Simultaneously we'll draft our charges.'

'He's going ahead with a Red Book.' Tomlinovich successfully resisted rolling his eyes.

'Yes,' Fauré snapped. 'I'm going to do it all legally. We will file a Red Book of Charges. I'll have to inform my minister, of course. We have to move quickly because these Black Handers and their cohorts are planning something, an operation, an action. And it will be coming soon. We shine light—'

'Oh, yes, Evil fears the Light of Justice,' Tomlinovich sang quietly. 'The White Branch isn't like you people, Foreign Okhrana only reports to one person,' he said, not bothering to name Gulka, the head of the Okhrana, as that person. 'You might be interested to know that *Apis* has turned out to be the code name of a Colonel Dragutin Dimitrijevic. He's the head of Serbian military intelligence, a real hard-liner. It's not even a code name. He's been using it so long that it's his nickname. Everybody knows it, it was in his folder, I knew I remembered it.'

'Serbia is a nation divided,' Fauré said.

'Some want to go slow, others want to go not so slow.' Tomlinovich walked backwards across the room so that he could get a better view.

'The hard-liners want to create an *iskra*—a spark that will ignite a revolution that will lead to a resurgence of Serbian power in the Balkans.'

'But standing in their way is the current Serbian Prime Minister, Nikola Păsic,' Tomlinovich called to them from across the wide floor.

'You see, for these nationalists, Păsic is worse than a moderate—he's a weakling. He appeases the Austrians, they say. So, what might be a spark for them? Well, it might be Pǎsic's assassination they are planning, it's plausible.'

'Yes, it is,' Ryzhkov said.

'So, do you understand now, why we have to properly inform the minister? And remember these are people who would stop at nothing if it means keeping their dreams alive.'

'Oh, yes. That I understand, excellency.'

'I don't like this any more than you do, Ryzhkov. But Serbia is a nest of vipers. It's a kingdom founded on conspiracies and regicides. Right now Pǎsic is an obvious target for a coup by supporters of the war party.'

Ryzhkov's eyes had turned back towards the bones, but he was seeing the Prime Minister of Serbia mounted up there instead.

'So . . .' Fauré looked at him for a long moment, then reached up and gave him another pat on the shoulder. Maybe it was a magic touch that he thought would protect Ryzhkov and Vera from harm, or maybe it was just a way of ending the conversation. 'So, we move forward, file our charges and then we'll try to stop this spark before it sets off the powder keg, eh?'

'The sharks have discovered that the whale has no teeth,' Tomlinovich said. It sounded like a chant, something said as a response during a sacred liturgy. He was standing out in the centre of the room, slowly turning his head, trying to take in the entirety of the monster.

Ryzhkov shook his head, thinking that if he ever really did get out from under Fauré's thumb he would help Vera move abroad, then perhaps he would volunteer for an assignment on the fringes of the empire, look forward to a slow death from alcoholism. He stared down at the stories the sailors had carved below him, the gigantic octopi, the broken schooners. How could they say he was off the hook?

'We'll still be using you, Ryzhkov. We'll tidy up this testimony and get everything properly collated, then I'll tear up your protocol for the murder of Oleg Lavrik. After that you can chase child-killers to hell and back if that's what you want, but for the next week or two I need you at your cold-blooded best. You and your friends,' Fauré said.

It would never end. 'All right,' he said. There was no other possible answer. 'All right. Fine. Yes . . . whatever. Thank you,' he added for reducing the murder charge to life imprisonment.

They had run out of time; there was a sudden creaking across the great room and one of the end doorways opened as a chaperone from the Smolny led a group of uniformed girl students past a shrugging Hokhodiev. Ryzhkov and Fauré stood there watching the girls, looking at their upturned faces, eyes wide as they approached the great fanned tail of the leviathan.

'They're all so beautiful, aren't they?' Fauré breathed. 'So very beautiful when they're young and innocent like that . . .'

THIRTY-TWO

The Crown was the best Belgrade could offer, the hotel where you saw everyone, anyone that mattered, and many who didn't. Men and women propelled by necessity and illusions. And by delusions, too.

Belgrade, the seat of what passed for fashion and international appeal within Serbia, all of it done over in traditional Hapsburg style, as lavish as money and convenience would allow in this, was something of a pretender among cities. Beyond the fashionable district, arrayed along a boulevard that would be an ordinary street in Petersburg or Paris, Belgrade was a hive-like mixture of cultures imprinted by each empire that had ebbed and flowed through the Balkans. It was a city that was forever reaching; architecture as practised by people who needed to display their knowledge of fashion, tea and classical music. The best of the buildings built with as much marble as affordable and ornamented in ways that sought to celebrate Serbia's sad but colourful history of victimization, a style that combined Byzantine lasciviousness with Germanic hegemony, furnished inside with dark, weighty pieces that an ordinary citizen could trust to never *fail*.

Belgrade had once been the centre of the northernmost district of Turkish control, a bloody stake driven into the ground to administer their frontier, the mark of their greatest advance, and the Slavic peoples' final defeat; hard up against the Danube, its people forever used as a buffer between the godless Muslims and their Teutonic 'protectors' across the river. It was a pitiful city, a survivor of the rape and pillage by every army that had the opportunity, but now at one of its historical peaks. Threadbare, subservient, resentful and poverty-stricken, its people were divided into classes of collaborators and frustrated revolutionaries, its streets filled with peasants and the indigent.

As for the Crown, it had never been conceived as a great hotel—there hadn't been the budget from its Viennese owners for a lavish design. Instead it occasionally succeeded to being something more practical; everything was adequate and the kitchen not bad at all, but the rooms were uninspired, the balconies were small and filled ostentatiously with flowers to screen the occupants from the street. In the distance was the old Turkish fortress, looming over everything.

'Will there be floods this year?' Andrianov asked the man seated on the tiny balcony. He could have been sitting out there beside him, but it would have meant touching knees.

'Floods?' the man said without looking around. 'Perhaps . . . It all depends if it rains upstream.'

Andrianov stared at the back of the head. The hair cut short, the skin a little whiter around the nape of the thick neck, the ears carefully plucked, the thinning hair on top macassared straight back, so that it shone in the bright light reflected off the walls of the building opposite—*Apis*.

'If it rains, if it floods? It doesn't matter really. We can cross the river in a few minutes, but here . . .' the sleek head turned towards the great castle, the terrain that dominated the city and the quays. 'Here, we wait for them to come to us.'

'What about the gunboats?' When anything happened the Austrians would send their gunboats down the river to shell the city.

'Floods would slow them down, true. And our guns are up there.' He extended a finger toward the ancient pile on the hill. 'But they have longer guns, and eventually . . .' *Apis* opened his hand, turned it back and forth to show how tenuous the military balance was.

Andrianov turned his gaze down to a pair of donkeys shitting in the street. They did it together as if one had given the other the idea. A man hit them with a switch and stepped around the piles. A buzz rose from the street; the clatter of the horses, an occasional spluttering motorcar, the bells of the trams, the unintelligible calling of the women hawking fish, vegetables, sticks of firewood and unnameable items carried in filthy, fly-surrounded baskets on their shoulders. The women were short with brown leather faces and eyes that squinted at him, who began to giggle with curiosity when ever he went out.

He had come to Belgrade on business. As usual, everything was legitimate on the surface. To any outside eye he was a speculator, an investor, a man to be wooed if you wanted to swim in the seas of serious finance. He was open about it. Advertising his presence, open for business. He had even kept up with his Viennese contacts via a flurry of telegrams, most of it harmless, some of it in code. He was alone except for Rochefort, a sharp young fellow who worked in the legal house of Rose, Steer and Duborg, the British investment firm he used in the Kingdom of Serbia.

Like any business trip there had been several appointments, a flurry of meetings, dinners, drinks, smokes, and rides in the ridiculous park. He was increasingly sought after in the kingdom. Word, or at least rumour had leaked out about his deals during the latest Balkan crisis, he was in favour, and he had made his partners and investors a great deal of money. And with success came both respect and danger. Now he was firmly entrenched, running alongside or only slightly behind the great armaments manufacturers. Now the detectives from Krupp knew what he ate for breakfast each morning. Now Basil Zaharoff, the greatest of the world's arms merchants, read a report on him each day. He did the same for Zaharoff, for Krupp, and for all the other manufacturers, so fair was fair. It was part of the game. He would win in the end.

It was such a sleepy city in the heat.

He stared down into the street and watched the Serbian version of life go by. You saw everything, but what did you miss? 'But isn't the weather of great importance to the military?' Andrianov attempted to pursue the point, but the man on the balcony gave no indication of having heard him. Perhaps he was bored. *Apis* often pretended to be bored.

'We could go somewhere . . .' he started, but *Apis* shook his head, a long exhalation of smoke. A sigh of impatience? Of boredom? The last meeting of the day was with *Apis*, and when he had arrived he had inspected the pillars for microphones, then leaned over to see if a stenographer was listening from the window below. Andrianov had watched him with amusement—as if anyone could get into the Crown without Apis knowing about it. His control over the secret police was total. If anyone was listening it would be his own people.

He had not been looking forward to the meeting. Of all the conspirators he had been forced to bring into the Plan, he found *Apis*'s independence the most disturbing, and watching him he gave an involuntary shudder. After all, the man was a killer. Only ten years before *Apis* had engineered the assassination of King Alexander and his wife, Draga, in order to put his own puppet on the throne.

Legend had it that *Apis* had arranged for his own men to guard the palace on that barbarous summer night. Explosives set into the locks had been detonated but had destroyed the electrical system in the building. The conspirators were forced to run through the palace searching for their victims, cursing and stumbling into the furniture, growing more frenzied lest the royal couple escape.

The king and his queen had huddled behind a secret panel in their bedroom, naked and terrified as they listened to the assassins prowl about and break up the furniture. Finally they were found, shot repeatedly, run-through and hacked, then thrown out of the window into the garden. Alexander, a pudgy, childlike monarch, had proven unexpectedly tough. He gripped the railing until *Apis* cut his fingers off and pushed him down. It had started to rain that night, and the bodies were left there while *Apis* took control of the city and its apparatus.

Since then he had taken total command of the hard-line faction of the Serbs. He wanted Serbian hegemony in the Balkans, and Andrianov pretended to want that as well. Well, if it happened, it could be advantageous. But putting Evdaev on the throne was his first priority. *Apis* knew nothing of that part of the Plan of course; he thought he was dealing with a fool—a Russian multi-millionaire, a super-Slav idealist ready to play at politics by funding terror. Fine. There was no need to educate him further.

Andrianov found himself thinking how much he'd like to be with Mina in France, perhaps a week at Evian. He had been lulled by the taciturn *Apis* and only suddenly realized that the man was congratulating him in his droning flat way. '. . . and the fuse is lit.'

'Yes?'

'Indeed. The invitation was made right from the top, by Potiorek, the Hapsburgs' governor of the province, and the acceptance came yesterday.'

'Ah . . . Good. Is there a date?'

'The date? St Vitus' Day, you know . . . at the end of June, but it's at the same time as the Kosovo celebrations. He's going to inspect the troops, participate in manoeuvres, ride his horse, bring his wife on a holiday.'

Andrianov turned, almost laughed. 'Really?'

'And from what is being said, he accepted because he thinks it is a gesture of peace and reconciliation. It's an olive branch to the occupied Bosnians, telling them that if they're good little boys and girls and don't blot their copybooks, one day they might get off the leash. He thinks he's a diplomat. Really, he's a fool like the rest of them,' *Apis* said.

Andrianov saw the street in a whole new light. It looked as if things were actually beginning to work. The acceptance was all he had been waiting for. Now *Apis* would carry the ball. 'So . . .' was all he could come up with to say.

But *Apis* had stopped. Already thinking about something else, perhaps the details of the action. The awning over the balcony seemed to gather the heat, rather than cast any shade. *Apis* reached up and slowly undid one of the buttons on his tunic. It was hot, the sun already betraying how powerfully it would bake these stone streets when summer came round at last.

'Well! So . . . I suppose we ought to congratulate ourselves,' Andrianov said, his tone a little forced. It was a remark designed to animate *Apis* somehow, draw him in. Now he might need encouragement, an extra push, a little motivation to carry things out to a conclusion. He might have to make him a friend, may God forgive him.

Apis shrugged. It was a rise of the shoulders, not much bigger than a breath. 'All we have to worry about is if he gets a fever, or she does, or if Franz Josef takes sick again. Who knows.' *Apis* spat his tobacco smoke at the table, reached into the box for another cigarette, lit it from the first. 'Everything is to chance. You plan, you organize, but still . . . everything is . . .' he trailed off. That gesture with the hand again.

Andrianov stood there at the balustrade, looking at him. What would *Apis* ultimately become? Where would he be in six months' time? Maybe God was on the side of the Serbs. They certainly thought so. Maybe Apis would put his new king out in front when his nation plunged into holy war and tried to claw Bosnia back from the Austrians. Maybe it would work out for both of them. He'd get Russia, *Apis* could have Serbia. If not, if things looked bad there could always be another coup . . . a few more severed fingers.

Andrianov suddenly realized that he had not thought beyond his ambitions for Evdaev. He had somehow just assumed that if he repaired the great suppurating sore that was the House of Romanov, he would be able to secure his businesses, protect his fortune and then . . . stop.

But had he miscalculated?

Once more he found himself shivering in the sweltering room. No matter what happened he and *Apis* were bound together. The magnitude of the treachery was too great. He would have to deal with *Apis* for many, many more years yet, he thought. Was there such a thing as stopping?

'Are you hungry, Colonel? Would you like something brought up?' he said, more to hide his unease than to be a good host.

There was just the shake of a head for an answer. He had no manners at all, of course. It was the worst quality of the South Slavs. The arrogance of ignorance, the honest sophistication of a rock.

He decided to order something sent up, some fruit ices. Anything to cool down. He wanted to strip off all his clothes, and run and jump into the Danube, swim away from the city and the stench of the man on his balcony. He pressed the bell repeatedly and waited for someone to respond. After a few minutes, when nothing happened, he did it again.

Apis reached into his pocket and lit another cigarette, flicked the burning match away into the crowded street.

Somehow, Andrianov thought, it was the most frightening thing he had ever seen.

THIRTY-THREE

A space of two weeks. Two weeks of waiting, fulfilling his non-duties as an Internal investigator. Two weeks of rising summer. In the sticky heat of the morning Ryzhkov went to Kryukov Street. Jekes and Dziga were packing up all their papers into pasteboard boxes. There was a boy, big for his age, smoking at the top of the stairwell. He stood up when Ryzhkov went up there. Inside everything had been torn down and was being packed up. There were trunkloads of transcripts, cabinets that were being secured by Ministry of Justice seals, mountains of file boxes containing photographic copies of the principals' personal correspondence. Dossiers full of testimony. All of it, evidence.

In the glass offices Sinazyorksy had a troika of secretaries typing around the clock. Everyone looked exhausted.

Tomlinovich was asleep, halfway dressed in his formal clothing, collapsed upon a shelf of boxes beneath the windows beside the loading lift. Beside him was a rack of clothing and Fauré was methodically getting dressed and watching himself in the mirror they'd used to tailor Vera's gown.

'Ahh . . .' he said when he saw Ryzhkov coming over. 'A very auspicious day, Inspector.'

'I certainly hope so,' he said.

'If God is willing by the end of the day we should be in the Winter Palace getting a signature from the Tsar himself. The government might fall, Ryzhkov,' Fauré said, turning from the mirror. 'Do you realize that? You are making history here. Or, actually, you aren't because I've erased you from all our records, and I've used a code name for the divine Mademoiselle Aliyeva. I hope that will be sufficient?'

'Thank you,' he said, surprising himself with the relief in his voice.

'You've done a good job in a dirty business, Ryzhkov. If this works out you might come over to the Ministry, eh?'

'I am not thinking that far ahead, excellency.'

'Can't say as I blame you. I am not thinking past lunch myself. Wake him up, would you?'

'Good luck up there this morning, I mean that,' he said as he shook Tomlinovich awake.

'Thank you, Ryzhkov.'

'What time is it?' Tomlinovich woke up groggily and took in a long wheeze to clear his head.

'It's time,' Fauré said.

'So what if the gods do shine on your proposal?'

'Let's put it like this, Ryzhkov. A trial is going to be a very real problem for all of the people in that—' He pointed to the office where Sinazyorksy was hefting one of a series of red, leather-bound volumes into a leather trunk.

'That's it?'

'Twelve bloody volumes,' muttered Tomlinovich as he took up a stance beside Fauré and began doing up the buttons on his waistcoat.

'There are no guarantees, not with this list of people. We did what we had to do, we move forward . . .'

'Forward, forward, ever forward . . .' Tomlinovich moaned.

'Do you want me to accompany you?' Both of them looked over at him, then eyed his rumpled suit.

'I think not, eh?' Tomlinovich said. 'Besides you are gone from here, you are a non-person. His supremacy General Gulka is very happy, the Minister of Justice Baron Double-Fart-fart is very happy. The only one who isn't happy is you; why aren't you smiling, Ryzhkov? Forgotten how?'

'What time is it?' Fauré said over his shoulder as he turned from side to side, checking the drape of his jacket.

'It's time,' said Tomlinovich. 'Well, Ryzhkov . . .' They shook hands and Tomlinovich clapped him on the shoulder. Fauré turned from the mirror and did the same.

'I know that this has been very difficult, a very arduous process, Inspector.' Fauré's expression was as serious as Ryzhkov had ever seen him before. 'I'm very proud to have known you, Ryzhkov. If Russia had more like you, then we might have a golden age yet again.'

'We're all very proud, proud as mother hens. Get out of here, I never want to see you or hear your name, understand?' Tomlinovich put in quietly. Then Fauré gave him an awkward embrace, stepped back, and then smiled his famous smile—the charming, confident smile that had won so much for him over his young life.

And then the two of them were gone.

He followed them out. The carriage was dark and gleaming. Jekes had dusted off his boots and was wearing a clean greatcoat for the occasion.

Just as they pulled away from the kerb, Fauré raised one finger as if pointing towards heaven, and then winked. Ryzhkov waved and watched as the carriage moved off.

A curious emptiness had come over him. He found himself staring at the street, the patterns in the cobbles, the fluttering of the awnings above the open windows, a fine view to the east and the ornate cupolas atop the Church of the Resurrection, a touch of pure Russian architecture amidst the rectilinear apartment buildings that stretched towards the river. Beyond, the Vyborg side of the city faded away to the misty horizon. For one long moment he drank in the beauty of a summer morning in St Petersburg; the warmth of the air, the clattering of carriages, the chuffing of the steamers plying the river, the factory whistles from far away, the piping of the newsboys hawking their sheets . . . all of it blending and harmonizing as the city growled and bustled into life.

So, finally it was over, and suddenly his hatreds, his horror over the girl, the visions that refused to die when he closed his eyes—suddenly it all began to float slowly away, like clouds dissolving in a clear blue sky.

He took a step, his throat suddenly constricted and he laughed. It came out sounding like a cough, and tears sprang to his eyes. He pulled out his handkerchief, blew his nose loudly, and looked back up the stairs where the new kid was laughing at him.

He stood there wondering which way to go. Spinning on the pavement like a weather vane. Back to 17 Pushkinskaya? Undoubtedly a service as big as the

Internal branch would be able to find something for him to do.

He began heading down Kryukov Street thinking that he would find Vera, try to tell her . . . Try to tell her what? That he loved her, that he wanted to marry her, to at least try. That he didn't care about her past and that he hated his own, that none of it mattered. That they could both just stop. He could resign, they could leave Russia. He could end the marriage with Filippa and the money from his share of the apartment would get them somewhere . . . somewhere else. Anywhere else. They could go to London, learn English. Settle down there. He could always translate. He was still relatively young. Young enough to start all over again, he thought.

He would find her.

And that was when he heard the explosion.

THIRTY-FOUR

He ran.

Even as the moment of shocked silence fell away. Ahead of him he could hear the screaming. The shriek of a horse in its death throes, a ripple of police whistles echoing through the streets. Around him everyone in the neighbourhood was running towards the intersection of Kryukov Street where it joined Demidov Avenue.

He rounded the corner and saw the crater where Fauré's carriage had exploded into matchsticks. Clumps of the seat stuffing had caught fire and were burning with a rancid stench. A gendarme knelt beside the dying horse. A sudden pistol shot as he put the poor animal out of its misery.

He pushed his way to the front of the crowd in time to see shopkeeper using a rag carpet to hastily enshroud a body, a large body with one leg twisted around so that it looked like a burned man trying to run in two different directions at once. A large pool of dark blood zigzagging through the channels between the paving stones and pooling in the bottom of a crater. Tomlinovich.

He let his eyes look around at the crowd, everyone riveted to the carnage. Women stricken with shrieks half-formed in their mouths. The shattered windows that had rained glass down over everything.

They had pulled a cart up there, then left it to block the narrow neck of Kryukov Street, forcing Jekes to guide his pony directly over the bomb. He remembered that there had been barricades there earlier in the week, men working on the street. It had taken some planning and they'd made a good job of it, he saw. He suddenly felt nauseous and clamped his jaws together.

They were probably watching, they would have had to be in order to accurately detonate the device. He kept his eyes down and fell back into the mob, then entered the side-door of a confectioner's shop. The place was in chaos, a woman standing in the window had been killed outright and a dozen more people were wounded by the flying glass.

Above the street a yellow cloud of smoke hung in the air; a warm, chemical smell of the bomb mixed with the sweeter smell of burned hair. He looked up at the windows and saw nothing but jagged holes and collapsed shutters. Papers were spread everywhere, some burning in the splinters—the remains of Fauré's great hope, the precious Red Book. He could not see Fauré, only portions of his clothing.

All around him there was activity. They might as well stop, it was all meaningless, he wanted to scream. He saw the scene in the street as if everything had been jerked into a double-speed parody, some kind of frenetic modern dance. There was a sudden clanging as an ambulance rushed past into the intersection. But no . . . there was no need to rush now.

Across the street he saw the local commander, Chief Tuitchevsky making his way through the cordon of police, moving to inspect another body that Ryzhkov hadn't seen at first. Tuitchevsky stepped in something and stopped for a moment to wipe his shoe off against the base of a streetlamp.

Ryzhkov spun away from the street and started walking, head down, trying to join a larger knot of pedestrians, all the time looking around for a tram. He managed to resist breaking into a run, thinking frantically about where he might go. He changed his mind and turned around on the pavement and started back the way he came, then stopped and rushed across the street and began heading down a lane that went south towards the canal.

He couldn't go back to Kryukov. He tried to remember his first moments out in the street before the explosion, tried to remember if he'd seen anyone watching. There was a sudden catch in his throat as he remembered the boy that had been minding things at the top of the stairs, wondered if he was still alive.

No one was following him, at least no one he could see.

Terrorists, they were saying. They'd be looking around the neighbourhood right now. He suddenly felt terribly vulnerable in the lane, someone threw open a shutter above him and he jumped and whirled and then did everything in his power not to run.

The busy intersection at the Yekaterininsky embankment felt like paradise, with smiling shoppers, children wailing, men smoking cigars, the braying of the cab drivers in front of the Apraxin market stalls. He moved right into the market and then cut through to Theatre Street and then around to the Nevsky, ran out into the prospekt and jumped on to a passing Number 34 that that would take him all the way down to Znamenskaya Square where he caught an *izvolchik* and drove past 17 Pushkinskaya and then back again. Then he got the *izvolchik* to drop him at the corner where he walked back up the street, watching all the time, then caught another cab to the long blocks of terraced houses in the Bozhdestvenskaya neighbourhood where Hokhodiev kept house with Lena.

He got out at the corner and looked around the street. Nothing stuck out as odd and so he kept going, walking directly to the Hokhodievs' entrance, hesitating at the door, pretending to check for an address, one last look around. Still nothing, so he went upstairs and continued past their floor, all the way up to the roof. Nothing.

He went back down to their apartment, at the rear facing the lane and a garden which everyone in the building shared.

Seeing Lena shocked him, made him go through in his mind how long it had been since he had seen her. At least a year, he supposed. Her red hair had gone a yellow-grey, and she had shrunk by a third. Her skin was waxy but when she saw him she smiled for a moment.

'Petrushka . . .' she breathed and tried to pull him inside. They embraced and he could feel the bones.

'Lena, is he around?'

'No . . . no, he's off somewhere. He's not with you?'

'No. Look, there's not perhaps much time, Lena . . .' He faltered. Staring at her, not wanting to make anything worse than it already was. 'Tell him

'*Abuschkaya*,' he'll know what I mean, and tell him to find Dima.'

'Yes, of course, of course . . .' She knew immediately what was up, Kostya had told her everything.

'Do you have a place you can go?'

'My sister, I'll go to her house, you go now—' she shooed him out and shuffled off to get dressed.

'I'm sorry, Lena—' He went to hug her once more.

'Go, Petrushka. Go—' She pushed him off and he was back out into the hall and heading for the back stairs.

He walked all the way to the river and then went into a hotel florist's and selected two dozen roses to be delivered to Mademoiselle Vera Aliyeva at the Komet Theatre as soon as possible. In the note he told Vera to stay away from his apartment, and that by looking at the morning newspapers she would know why.

Love, he wrote. Stared at the word for a long moment, and then scrawled a hasty *P* beneath it.

The vault belonged to the Abusch family, after whom Abuschskaya Street had been named.

He paced up and down through the cool long room, reading the epitaphs, noting the carved Neptunes and sinking ships that had been chiselled into the malachite plaques. A whole family of German mariners were recorded here: shipwrights, exporters, and finally accountants and canny investors; immigrants who'd prospered, owing their success to Teutonic connections and an accident of geography that had led the original Abusch to settle at the confluence of the Neva and the Gulf of Finland and begin building ships for Catherine the Great. That same original Abusch rested inside a catafalque which now supported a large canvas bag of groceries Ryzhkov had brought for the wait.

Where had all the Abuschs gone? Probably abroad, probably somewhere more fashionable, the shares in the business long since sold or placed in trusts, profits gambled away by dissolute offspring—artists without skill, wanderers without a destination.

For Ryzhkov it was a safe place, a safe place filled with death. There were no longer any Abuschs to notice that the dried flowers had been disturbed, the cobwebs had been mysteriously cleared away, that suddenly there were cigarette butts and muddy footprints across the floor. No one to complain that the family vault had been desecrated.

Hokhodiev whistled and then Ryzhkov heard him scrape his shoes on the gravel. Ryzhkov moved to the iron gates and swung them open as quietly as he could. He could tell that Hokhodiev had been walking quickly. 'Dima's coming,' he said. He had a cheese inside his jacket and a short revolver that he'd tucked in his belt. They went back and sat down in the back room.

'He's only about fifteen minutes behind me. Lena caught me on the stairs, she's gone off to Masha's place. Jesus . . .' he said, staring down at the stones. 'This is what I think it is, right? This is as bad as I think?' Hokhodiev pulled off his fedora and fanned himself.

'Fauré asked his minister, Tomlinovich asked Gulka.'

'This is, this is just what I thought. Gulka. Oh . . .' Hokhodiev said and shook his head.

'We'll get out and we'll get her out, get word to Masha.'

'I found Dima at the office.'

'I only drove past.'

'They hadn't got there yet. And . . . you know, I didn't wait to see.'

'We might be out of it. I don't know if they know us,' Ryzhkov said. 'I'd been removed from their case, that was their way of ending the deal. It might be nothing,' he said. He'd stood up now and was pacing back and forth. It was too desperate. Hokhodiev raised his finger to his lips to quieten him. For a long moment he just stood there, staring at the carvings.

'No . . . No, brother,' Hokhodiev said. 'We're not out of it. We might be a little ahead, but nobody but Gulka could get a job done like that . . . those Justice boys . . . it's a mine, they have to put it in the street like that? They'd been watching. It's probably the Parrot,' he said, meaning one of the other Internal investigators they knew who'd long made explosives his speciality.

'If they are on to us . . .' Ryzhkov had been trying to minimize it in his imagination. Now just thinking about it put a catch in his throat.

'When were you at Kryukov last?' Hokhodiev asked him.

'Before this, not for . . . three, three or four days.'

'Dima and I have been gone from there for at least a week now. When did they go upstairs to get their permissions?'

'Who knows? But probably right after the whale meeting. Three weeks.'

'Shit,' Hokhodiev said. They heard a man coughing out on the gravel and Ryzhkov moved to the gate. Across the pathway he saw Dima stop and take his hat off and shuffle about in front of a huge granite tombstone. He dropped to one knee and looked over and saw Ryzhkov nod. Dima stood up and walked away down the path for a dozen metres, then stopped and backtracked directly to the Abusch gate.

'We're all right, I think,' Dima said. 'I ran back in and pulled this before I left.' He held up an envelope that bulged with fifty-rouble notes. Part of the 'petty cash' that Volga Metals Assurance kept inside a windowsill at 17 Pushkinskaya.

'Oh, God . . .'

'The young man has balls, brother. Take your hat off to him.'

'It's fucking Fatso, isn't it,' Dima spat. He pulled off his jacket. His shirt was wringing wet.

'It's all we can come up with,' Ryzhkov said.

'It's not such a good situation,' Hokhodiev added.

'No.'

'We go, now, yes?' Dima asked him.

'Now or never. I don't know how far we'll get. If Gulka has decided to put out a description of the three of us, we're gone. We're just ahead of them.'

'Run . . .' Hokhodiev said. It came out sounding like a joke.

'It's the natural thing, the normal thing,' Ryzhkov said. Hanging around all the dead Abuschs was making him think about a boat and the Gulf of Finland as a way out. They might only have a few hours if they were ahead of Gulka and whoever he had got working for him.

'And you're sure you saw nothing when you were back there, Dima? You're sure?' It was strange that Gulka hadn't tried to raid their office. They must be a little ahead of them.

'Gulka . . . My God . . .' Hokhodiev said. Laboriously he climbed to his feet and began walking along the room, running one big hand across the surface of the stones. 'We have the top man in the secret police running this thing with the Serbs?'

'No one else knew about it that could do the bomb. It's got to be, it's got to.'

'We have to go, we have to go or . . .' Dima looked up at him. His eyes were moist, his chin suddenly trembled.

'Or what?' he asked quietly.

Hokhodiev looked at them. 'It's us against Gulka, now. I mean, maybe they've found us, maybe they find us in the next hour, maybe we have a whole day, but if they manage to pick us up, they're going to kill us, yes?' he said.

'Yes,' Ryzhkov said. 'So, if you want to leave, this is the time, Kostya. Go to Finland. Get Lena and get out tonight if you want to try it.'

Hokhodiev held up one finger for silence, just shook his head. He couldn't look either of them in the eye and his face was very red. No.

'Yes. All right, then,' Ryzhkov said quietly.

'So, we go after the bastards, I say, yes?' Dima nearly shouted, then caught himself. 'You know, what the hell, we're dead anyway.'

'No. We're not dead. We can get him . . .'

'Yes. Even with just three of us, we can do that,' Hokhodiev said. They both looked at Ryzhkov. He was right where he had been the whole time, staring at the intricately carved feet of the catafalque. For a long moment he did nothing. It was almost as if he hadn't heard himself speak. And then he looked around at them and his mouth contorted, spreading like a slash across his face as he smiled his terrible smile.

THIRTY-FIVE

Ryzhkov, Hokhodiev, and Dima Dudenko pulled their carriage behind the Kleinmichel mansion and through the trades entrance, officiously demanded from the keeper a secure place to park. Dangling from the pannier was a large sign that proclaimed 'No Smoking—Explosive Displays!'

'I didn't know there were fireworks,' the old man said.

'Oh, yes,' Dima said.

'Do you have a boy to watch this wagon? No one closer than fifty metres,' Ryzhkov called out. A member of the house staff was approaching. He was dressed formally.

'No, no. Keep away!' Hokhodiev jumped down and put himself between the man and their carriage. The gatekeeper reflexively drew back into his kiosk.

'Just no smoking! That's the important thing. If this goes, it will take half the house along with it,' he smiled.

'You can pull up over there, is that what you need?' the old man said, still sheltering in the doorway.

'That will be fine.'

'Nobody goes near this wagon, eh?' Hokhodiev jabbed a finger and the servant retreated back toward the kitchens.

And they were through and across to the far side of the lawn.

They spent the afternoon, carefully placing terracotta tubes in prominent locations around the lawn, liaised with the gardeners, and met one of the junior butlers, who was perplexed that he hadn't been informed of the display.

'Something last minute, I guess. It might be a gift, who knows?' Ryzhkov grumbled at the man. 'They told us where to go and we were up all night putting this show together.' Down at the gate a wagon was loading in an ice-sculpture packed in straw.

'And, look, they can't stop there. This whole lane all the way to the gate has to be kept open for us. I'm sorry, but the fire department makes us do that, eh?'

'Certainly, yes,' the butler agreed and turned to head back.

'And we need a place to change.'

The man stopped and turned. Hokhodiev stood on the step of the carriage displaying his costume, the armour of a fifth-century Mongol warrior.

'Oh . . . yes. I'll show him.'

And they were inside.

By midnight the colossal, fabulous party that had been so carefully organized by Countess Kleinmichel was gathering momentum. That it was a costume party made their task easier.

Ironically, for the head of the Okhrana, personal security was almost non-existent. In some ways it was a vanity, in others a mark of true confidence. Gulka had made himself a victim of his own ruthlessness; his Internal branch agents had infiltrated every terrorist cell in the empire, his provocateurs had even created their own cells of bombers and assassins in order to better entrap dissidents and neophyte revolutionaries. And besides, unless you were a member of the royal family, to show up at a society party with an entourage of detectives would be a breach of etiquette, tacit implication that the countess was not loved by one and all.

All evening Ryzhkov had followed Gulka around the party, even stood beside him at one point and laughed at his jokes.

At eleven Hokhodiev touched off the first of the fireworks. Just simple rockets they had purchased that morning. The idea was to get Gulka and get out before they had to do anything fancy.

Inside the crowd started heading toward the lawn. Ryzhkov went ahead and waited in the shadows, looking around until he saw Dima, who was in his costume and standing cloaked by the shadows of the carriage. Kostya would do the driving. Both men avoided looking at Ryzhkov, he had been nervous from the beginning.

'He's so old,' Dima said. 'What if he has a heart attack?'

'It will be lucky for him,' Ryzhkov said, and he didn't ask any more questions after that. Now he was living the angry life of a policeman, again. Waiting, wishing for it to be over. Yes, yes . . . a heart attack. Or what if Gulka simply didn't want to go outside? He'd have to go in and find him, entice him somehow. If that didn't work, they'd have to try another day. What if he got tired and took the opportunity to rest his feet, watch the show from one of the windows? What if he was with friends, or someone wanted to tag along?

'There—' Ryzhkov said as the man they were waiting for—General Alexandr Ivanovich Gulka, waddled toward them through the great doors. He was wearing an ornate costume fashioned in the style of a sixteenth-century boyar.

'Is that him?' Dima whispered.

'Yes.'

'You first. Good luck,' Ryzhkov said, pulling his mask down as he followed Dima out of the shadows, transformed suddenly into a happy drunk. Timing his approach across the yard as Gulka was coming down the stairs. 'Alexei!' a warm embrace . . . 'Alexei, my God! What are you, the devil?' A laugh to elicit an even greater exhausted laugh from those nearby. Gulka looked at him, smiled, tried to recognize the voice.

'Ay! Good heavens!' Behind them there was a sudden shriek—a woman jerking her skirts out of the way as a man costumed as Napoleon had suddenly vomited all over the terrace.

Ryzhkov took the opportunity to steer Gulka away from the mess, to call for someone to come help quickly. The sick Napoleon was causing a panic.

Behind them Hokhodiev touched a match to a rocket, then climbed up and took the reins. Ryzhkov breathed softly in the old man's ear, 'This way—this way now, or I'll cut you right here.'

The man whose name Gulka could not quite remember was dressed as some sort of demon, a sea-god, or could it be the *kikimora*, the devil who lived in the tower of Trinity Church and whose cry foretold the destruction of the city? Gulka tried to interpret it all, frowning as he was led along, searching for the name of the monstrous prankster, even laughing nervously.

'Ahh . . .' The rheumy eyes opening wide. Now he knew. Shaking his head, the eyes frowning, trying to focus after too much iced champagne. 'It's not going to work, you know . . .' Gulka whispered.

'Come on . . . one step at the time, that's the way,' hissed the sea-god, and Gulka complied with a gasp, his knees suddenly gone weak. Ryzhkov had to hold him up, thinking as he did so, that this was the worst moment, the most dangerous time, when it could all go wrong, if one of the general's friends were to call out, to look around, to see them. What if he had the heart attack now? If anything went wrong he'd kill Gulka, kill him right there on the grass. Then finally it would be done. Done and over.

'Quickly, quickly . . . everything is going to be fine.'

'Oh, I'm so sorry!' The sick Napoleon was apologizing profusely, screening the two of them as they crossed the lawn. Hokhodiev pulled the carriage around and there was a sudden flurry as they rushed toward the carriage.

'Hurry up,' he called down to them. 'The fuses are lit.'

'Step up!' a generous shove in the ass, and then they were inside the closed carriage and lurching away. Suddenly Dima jumped into the opposite side of the carriage and came up with a sharp sword stick held rigid just below Gulka's chin. Ryzhkov clipped the manacles on, ripping off the jewelled boyar head-dress, and replacing it with a cloth bag which he knotted around Gulka's neck like an executioner as Kostya pulled the carriage through the back gates, a ripple of explosions echoing behind them.

And they were away.

There was no way to know when Gulka had discovered their investigation, or how long they had been under surveillance. Ryzhkov thought that everything had probably started to fall apart once Tomlinovich had made his report but it was a gamble. He made a careful telephone appointment at the clinic where he'd been interrogated by Fauré, and, once they arrived, warned the doctor to make himself scarce. The man didn't say much, hovering in the background while they replaced the bag with a blindfold made of gauze bandages, and then led Gulka up to the bed in the upstairs room.

'When do you want to start?' the doctor whispered.

'Right now,' Ryzhkov said and watched while the man moved forward with his needle, pushed the drug into Gulka's arm, unbuttoned the beaded vestments and then put a stethoscope to Gulka's heart for a few moments. Satisfied, he stood and held the vial up so Ryzhkov could see it, pointing to a mark on the barrel of the syringe. 'No more than this, eh. You have to wait at least three hours. Too much and . . .' He shrugged and made a face. Perhaps it was supposed to be a smile. 'Day after tomorrow, then?'

'If we're here, we're here.' Now it was Ryzhkov's turn to smile.

'Good luck.' Ryzhkov waited until the doctor had left and then he moved a chair closer to the bed.

'He's not asleep, is he?' Dima said.

'We'll wake him up soon enough. The plan is I talk, you listen, if you think up questions, you pass me notes, yes?'

'Yes . . . yes . . .'

Ryzhkov went down to the kitchen, poured himself a thick coffee and drank half of it. Then he gathered his papers, and climbed back up to the attic room. Gulka tried to raise his head but Dima pushed him back down on to the pillow.

'Hello, Alexei,' Ryzhkov said quietly.

'Yes . . .' Gulka said. His voice was dreamy. The breathing regular.

'We're almost ready.'

'Good, Sergei, good . . .'

Ryzhkov looked over at Dima, shrugged. Gulka's eyes would open, then close slightly. Dreaming while he was awake.

'I just wanted to go over . . . everything, is that all right with you?' For a moment Gulka said nothing. Perhaps the doctor had given him too large a dose. Dima reached over and tapped him on the cheek.

'I wanted to check with you, Alexei, I wanted to confirm our plans.'

'Mmm . . .' Gulka breathed.

'So . . . when, exactly should we be ready?'

'Have to hurry.'

'Oh, yes.'

'Always ready.'

'Of course, but the date.'

'Everything move . . .' Gulka began turning his head to the side, like a man looking at a panorama.

'We're all ready, right now, just as you said,' Ryzhkov continued in as reassuring a voice as he could manage. Trying to mimic his mother's tones when he'd been sick as a child.

'Good . . .'

'Who should I contact?' he asked and looked up at Dima. The younger man raised his eyebrows. It was as good a tactic as any. For a moment Gulka seemed to struggle with the question and Ryzhkov asked him a second time. 'Is there anyone I should contact, anyone who needs to know?'

'I'll tell Nestor . . .'

'*Nestor?*' he said, feeling the skin at the back of his neck beginning to prickle.

'Mmm . . .' Gulka sighed.

'Nestor is right here, do you want to tell him now?' Ryzhkov said and nodded to Dima.

'Ah . . . what is the, ah . . . status of the, um . . . operation, Alexei?' Dima said rather too firmly, Ryzhkov thought. Hokhodiev had come up the stairs and was lingering there, his face looking like death.

'We are . . . sailing,' Gulka said blissfully.

'Yes, good, good.'

'So . . . everything is on schedule?' Dima asked gruffly.

'. . . dead before sunset . . .' Gulka's voice had a sing-song quality to it, like a child walking along a sunny lane, humming nursery rhymes.

'Tell me everything,' Ryzhkov said. 'Nestor wants to go through it one step at a time, just to be certain. Don't you Nestor?'

'Oh, yes. Yes, I do,' Dima said.

'Fine. Now, Alexei, where exactly is the . . . act, the *iskra*, taking place?'

There was a grumbling from Gulka's chest, a sound like a cough and a laugh mixed together. His belly shook like an Easter pudding as the spasm ran through him, beneath the blindfold the lips curled back in a wide smile.

'Clever boy,' Gulka said. 'You too, Sergei.' The rumbling went on until Gulka forgot what was so funny.

'Just tell me, Alexei. Tell me now,' Ryzhkov said quietly.

Gulka's eyes opened and it seemed that he was looking up at the ceiling. '. . . the gateway . . . the gateway to the east . . .'

'The gate?' Dima looked up at Ryzhkov and frowned.

'Mmm . . .' Gulka cooed. The smile subsided only for a moment and then he began to hum.

Dima frowned. 'What's that?' he whispered. Gulka's lips were moving, but the words were slurred.

Ryzhkov reached out and grasped his shoulder, put his lips close to Gulka's ear.

'Where, Alexei, where? You must tell me where. It's terribly important.'

'. . . sun rises, above . . . the new Sla-vi-a . . .' he sang.

Ryzhkov sat back in the chair. The blood had drained from his face. His fingers were trembling. Gulka was keeping time with one foot against the iron frame of the bedstead.

'. . . Sa-ra . . .' Gulka sang, his voice crackling with phlegm. 'Sa-ra, O, beautiful, beautiful Sa-ra-jevo . . .'

They argued but it was Hokhodiev who killed him. They led Gulka out into the green woods behind the clinic, tied him to a tree and let him watch while they dug a hole. There wasn't enough time to make it deep. Then they argued about who was going to do it, but Hokhodiev wasn't listening to reason and didn't even really reply, shoving them both away. Ryzhkov and Dima went back towards the clinic, picking their way through the underbrush and waited up on the porch while he did it.

Hokhodiev came back and they talked while he was washing his hands, a quick meeting to agree to travel separately across the border, reasoning that Gulka or Evdaev might have men at the stations.

But time was running out and the idea was to meet at the station in Riga and, from there, if everything looked clear, they would purchase tickets for the Warsaw train.

THIRTY-SIX

He was at the Finland Station by nine that night, travelling second class with a large bundle of fruit and sausages jammed into a pillowcase, unshaven and shabby, buying his ticket with coins that he counted out slowly and stupidly, shuffling past the gendarmes, afraid to look around the station to see if anyone was waiting for him, taking a seat at the very end of the car and pretending to sleep all the way to the border, crossing his fingers and using his best Polish accent when they came to check his ticket at the frontier. Taking the food to his sick grandfather, that was the story.

The train south was slow, rocking over the swampy ground, barely crawling where there had been work along the tracks. In the early hours there was a jolt and he saw that they had arrived in Rezhitsa. The engine took on water and he used the opportunity to walk into the gloom of the tiny station and buy a glass of tea. They crossed Lake Luban and went along the river arriving at Riga just as the dawn was lighting the sky red. He checked the timetable and walked into the town to find a baths where he cleaned himself and had his clothes brushed. When the shops opened he purchased a suitcase, two new shirts and a homburg.

When he went back to the station he found Dima sleeping in the corner of a bench just inside the wide doorways. He had arrived on the train that connected with the Tallinn line and was exhausted. They ate a late breakfast in the park across from the station and waited for Hokhodiev to arrive. It was eerie; neither of them had encountered any trouble along the way.

'The only explanation is that we're ahead of them,' Ryzhkov said. 'Maybe only just ahead of them, but for now that's enough.' He stood and paced away from the bench as he said it, because partly it was a lie, just wishful thinking, and he didn't want Dima to see his face.

He was beginning to get a picture of the 'conspiracy' now, beginning to understand its scope. Gulka would have been its strongest weapon—as head of the secret police he was virtually omnipotent. When, via Tomlinovich's report which Gulka would have been able to intercept, Evdaev had learned of the Fauré investigation, the Okhrana's resources had been unleashed to retaliate with savagery. But now that Gulka had disappeared, what would be Evdaev's next move?

The first sign of trouble was when they saw Kostya climbing down from the morning train, looking fit and well dressed. He carried a sample case and a travelling trunk that he reluctantly tipped a porter to put on the loading dock. Then he looked around in their direction and shook his head almost imperceptibly. Immediately Dima rose and headed for the lavatory and Ryzhkov willed himself to slump there in his seat and feign sleep.

They kept themselves separated on the Warsaw train, a long haul. He and Dima sat a row apart in the second class section, shared a newspaper as strangers might. In the dining-car they watched Hokhodiev charm two elderly Polish sisters. It was the last sitting and the three of them lingered after their meal and when Hokhodiev rose to excuse himself bowing to his companions, he turned and walked back towards their end of the carriage—'Warsaw,' the big man said quietly as he passed them and edged through the door between cars.

The Warsaw Station was crowded; Ryzhkov and Dima stood aside and listened while Kostya called for the trunk for Herr Abusch, and then they followed his carriage to the Hotel Minerva, just a few streets away. They waited a half-hour and then they went in and asked at the desk and went up to see him in his room at the rear of the building overlooking the Vistula.

'Don't get excited. I think it's nothing,' Kostya said as he let them in. The trunk was open and he had arrayed mineral samples across his bedspread. The false bottom was raised and three revolvers were fixed there with thongs. 'I saw some rather odd-looking fellows at the station, passing around some photographs at the barriers, so I thought we might take precautions, eh?'

'Good, you did the right thing.'

'I didn't see who they were looking for, I didn't go over there, but I didn't recognize any of these boys . . . amateurs, hired flics . . .'

'Still . . .'

'Still, yes, it's just going to heat up. They'll be looking for Fatso now, and soon someone is going to put two and two together and come after us. I'm just glad Lena's out of it,' he sighed.

Once again they travelled separately to Krakow, then staggered their departures, taking separate trains over the Carpathians. It so happened that Ryzhkov's made the ascent in the middle of the night. He dozed, with his head resting against the cold glass as they climbed toward the frontier. He brooded over the combination of Gulka and Nestor Evdaev. How he should have seen it all along.

After Katowice the train stopped and Austrian customs inspectors came through the carriages. He explained that he was en route to Vienna to meet with prospective clients, courteously handed over his papers to be stamped. Once the carriage had been inspected he was free to go outside. He wandered all the way up the track, paused to look up at the gigantic hissing locomotive, and then continued across the tracks to where there was an outlook through the moonlit mountains that curved away to the east.

Just ahead of him, beyond the border was the sprawling empire of the House of Hapsburg, the Dual Monarchy of Austria-Hungary, busily preserving its supremacy in the Balkans with every diplomatic and military technique in the book. All of it was born from a centuries-old loathing of everything Slavic. Their opposites, the Black Handers, were even more vigorously dedicated to establishing their independence and superiority. How could there not be a spark?

What had the great conspiracy cost Evdaev? How many roubles would have been needed to buy a Smyrba, or Russia's Ambassador Hartwig? To bring along the military attaché Artamonov? It might have come cheap; perhaps it had cost no roubles at all, perhaps they were all doing it because they were true believers in the cause of a greater Slavia. Perhaps to sweeten the bargain they would have had to toss in a few bags of grenades since nothing was so seductive to a terrorist as providing the means to his end. There was a scraping on the gravel behind him. He turned to see one of the uniformed Austrian border inspectors approaching.

'Excuse me, sir, have you been passed?' the guard said politely. Ryzhkov dug his papers out, opened them. The moonlight was so bright that the inspector didn't even need to use his torch. 'Very good, sir,' the guard said, touching his hand to his cap and clicking his heels. 'A beautiful night, yes?'

'Exquisite.'

'You are Russian?'

'Yes, from Moscow.'

'Ah.'

'Have you ever been there?'

'Unfortunately, no.'

'It is not as beautiful as this . . .'

'Bohemia is the best,' the man said with a touch of pride.

'So, you are Czech?' The guard had taken out a cigarette and Ryzhkov offered him a match.

'Yes, not quite a full-blooded Austrian, but almost as good,' the guard said with a laugh, then suddenly he turned. 'Ah! Listen!' he whispered.

From the trees came the regular hooting of an owl. 'A good night for a kill.' The guard smiled at him. His teeth were prominent and glowing; the moonlight and shadows had turned his face into a skull. Ryzhkov turned back to the mountains. If there ever was a war Russian armies would rush down this same track towards these passes, for days it would be a war of artillery and explosive mines, of repair crews laying rails while under fire. The guard began to whistle, something lilting and sad. After a few moments he tossed his cigarette out into the track.

'Good evening to you, sir. Enjoy the remainder of your journey.' A little bow and then he was gone, back to his duties.

Ryzhkov looked up into the clear sky. The moon was not quite full, washing out the stars. The owl began its calling again. An unexpected chill rose up from the darkness of the trees, cold, even for June. For a moment he thought about running, running headlong into the forest. He could make his way to a village, change his identity, leave, run away. Forget about plots and conspiracies, forget all about the victims, ignore the newspaper headlines when they trumpeted the victory of evil. Who were they to try and set the world right? Only little men. Little men fighting against the giants. Maybe he could go back and persuade Kostya and Dima to give up the quest. They could all run away together, become fishermen, or woodcutters, or customs inspectors, or drunks.

There was a long hissing sound from the engine, and Ryzhkov turned and headed back along the tracks, the great green eye of the locomotive flickering into life above him, the stinging smell of burning coal wafting over him in a sudden downdraught as he walked past the cab towards his car. No, the leopard cannot change his spots, he thought.

In Vienna they bought tickets for their own compartment.

Ahead of him in the queue Ryzhkov watched as Hokhodiev met a Swede, a mining engineer who'd been drinking and wanted to talk about bauxite. Bauxite was everything, he said. If you controlled bauxite, you could control the production of aluminium, and aluminium was the metal that was going to drive the new electro-industrial world.

'It's basic chemistry,' the Swede said. 'You have common chemicals, you have oxygen, hydrogen, nitrogen. Everybody has those, but only a few . . .'

'Gold,' Hokhodiev said.

'Correct, diamonds, things that glitter, we call them precious. There's a reason for that,' the Swede said.

'Where are you headed?' Hokhodiev asked, growing tired of the man. He'd been drinking, it was obvious.

'At the end of it all, Turkey. I don't care who knows it. If you know the chemistry, you'd be doing the same thing, eh?' The man reached up and tapped Hokhodiev in the chest with a thick finger. 'What do you do, anyway?' the Swede asked, suddenly suspicious.

'I'm a member of the secret police,' Hokhodiev said flatly. The Swede's eyes went wide and then he started laughing. 'That's good! Hah! That's good!' He slapped Hokhodiev on the back and dragged him into the buffet car to have another schnapps.

The train had barely begun to get up steam when Dima came in and tossed a newspaper on the seat. His face was drawn and he stared out at the window with a disgusted expression. 'You wanted a spark,' he said tightly. 'This is your spark, right here.'

It was a copy of the *Bosnian Post* and on the third page was an article about the upcoming military manoeuvres that the Austrian army would be holding in the mountains west of Sarajevo. Archduke Franz Ferdinand, the heir to the Austrian throne, would attend the manoeuvres himself and be in command of the 'enemy' forces. He would be joined by his wife, Princess Sophie von Hohenberg and spend a day in Ilidze, a pleasant suburb outside Sarajevo. On the following day the royal couple would make a procession by motorcar into the city and be greeted by the mayor and the governor of the province of Bosnia. Below the article the archduke's motor route into the city was detailed. There was a small map adjacent to the article so that well-wishers could be on hand to cheer and throw flowers.

'That's it, eh? Don't you think?' Dima looked at him.

'Yes,' he said. His voice was quiet, almost a whisper.

'They're insane to send him to Bosnia,' Dima spat. 'Mad. Can we warn them off? There's still time to cancel things, he could get a cold, that would do it, wouldn't it?'

'Until we get there, it will have to . . .' He had the porter get them some writing paper and began to draft a letter. It was a straightforward chronicle of the conspiracy, including the names of all the principals from Artamonov to Smyrba. The more he wrote the worse it got. He began to realize how little hard information he could include. There was nothing that could be verified, no proof, of course, that an attempt would be made on the archduke during his visit to Sarajevo. He took pains to word the letter as rationally as he could, including as a source the recently missing head of the Russian secret police, General Alexandr Ivanovich Gulka, thinking Gulka's name should strike a chord with Austrian military intelligence. When it was done he read it over with a sinking heart. It all sounded speculative, the product of a madman struggling to put the best face on his nightmares.

He passed it by Dima and Hokhodiev, who'd finally pulled himself away from the Swede, and used the last of his paper before they arrived in Budapest to add as many details as he could remember of Lavrik's corrupt business deals.

In Budapest there was a thundershower and time to kill. He walked through the dark station and posted the letter himself and purchased a copy of the Vienna paper *Neue Freie Presse*. In the society section there was an additional report on Franz Ferdinand's route. The festivities were scheduled for twenty-eighth, there were still four days to go.

When he came back to the train Hokhodiev and Dima were still talking it over. 'No, this is crazy. We're *Russians*, as far as the Austrians are concerned we're supposed to be the enemy, right? So when we get there, what do we do? We go to the police, tell them everything we know?' Dima said laughing.

'And we promptly get ourselves arrested,' Hokhodiev stopped him. He leaned forward and spun the bottle of schnapps in the ice bucket, took it out in the towel and poured Ryzhkov a glass. 'It's more simple than that,' he said to Dima. 'It's basic. It's chemistry . . .'

'Yes . . . yes . . .' Ryzhkov heard himself agreeing.

'We go and kill them. That's the magic formula, they kill us, we kill them,' Hokhodiev said. 'Russia or whether you love her has nothing to do with it, eh? If you're a Slav or a Teuton, or a Spartan or an Athenian, or a fucking Albanian or Turk or shit knows what, who cares really? It comes down to the fact that they're going to kill us if they can, they've ruined our shabby little lives, changed everything around.'

'We go on . . . we can't go back,' Dima nodded. 'I think I can adjust to that,' he said with a shrug.

'Adjust, yes. Because we cannot ever go home. Our lives are over.' Hokhodiev took a moment to let it sink in. 'So . . . I have one or two breaths left in the old bag yet,' he patted at his pockets. 'And I have my ticket on this very nice train, so . . . I don't stop until it's all over.

You—' he turned to Dima, 'you, I can understand if you start to run out.'

'Hey—' Dima complained.

'You're young, you've got a future. You can get married, have a home. Have something to be proud of. Get out at Belgrade, run away to Greece. The girls there like it in the ass, you'd do fine.'

'Go to hell, old man.'

Hokhodiev laughed. 'Here . . .' He emptied the bottle into Ryzhkov's glass. 'One last *katzenjammer* before we go and save the House of Hapsburg, eh, brother?' Ryzhkov smiled and raised his glass. Of all of them Hokhodiev, who'd lost the most, seemed the best at taking it in his stride. He drained the glass. Dima watched him and shook his head.

'Forward, then . . .' he said as the train rattled southwards through the hot, broad valleys fed by the Danube and Tisa, past the fortified city of Subotica, along the ramparts at Topola, beneath the crenellated towers of Novi Sad, and once again back to the Danube.

Forward.

Three knights on a great quest to save a prince. Three drunken knights of the brave new modern age. Forward into the maelstrom, armed with their pathetic tools (only three revolvers!) and the righteousness of their cause. Now they sally forth, now they go to their deaths. Perhaps the knight is lucky and his magic works one more time. Perhaps this is his last, final triumph.

Three knights unable to sleep. One twisting in his dreams, one having a listless conversation with the barman in the buffet car. One finding a simulacrum of love with a secretary from a leather goods manufacturer, a pretty Hungarian with nothing to do but courier documents her boss had forgotten, and Ryzhkov catching his own reflection in the window as they sped through the heat of a summer's day in Bosnia.

The rhythm of the engine changed, slowing as they entered the city, so unlike Petersburg, a chaotic tangle of yellow plaster and broken roof tiles that climbed the hills above the River Miljacka.

He saw a dividing of tracks, of points, pathways that might be taken but were not. Solitary men in strange uniforms standing about in the wilderness of the sidings puffing on their pipes, rocking back and forth on their heels.

The platform came into view. Baggage trolleys pulled by sweating boys through the dusty heat. The shrill scream of the whistle sounded as they stepped out of the carriage, through the press of the mob, a tangle of screaming Muslims, women begging in the shadow of the cathedral.

The heat slammed Ryzhkov in the face. By the time he reached the street he was bathed in perspiration.

Ahead of him was a labyrinth of narrow streets hung over with laundry and brightly coloured awnings. A dusty motorcar entered the square and the driver began squeezing the horn. Everything was noise and confusion. The Swede from the train bounded across the street and jumped into an open carriage across from them. 'Gentlemen!' he yelled, whipping off his fedora and waving to them as he drove past. 'God has smiled on you! Welcome to Sarajevo!'

THIRTY-SEVEN

They took the first place they found, rooms in a small commercial hotel, tucked in behind the station, put their mineral samples in the cupboard and then went right back out again.

Sarajevo was a maze of meandering streets, narrow bumpy lanes that twisted in on themselves the deeper one delved into the old quarter. Street signs were missing or contradictory; yellow stone buildings with crumbling tile roofs leaned precariously over the narrow lanes filled with children squalling like gulls. It was a city of mosques and cathedrals, where the Austrians had allied themselves with the infidel Muslims in their long campaign to suppress the orthodox Serbs. A city divided in a dozen directions, where everyone was on edge, watching their wallets. A city where sanity was a disadvantage, where life was running backwards.

Ryzhkov tried to shake it out of his mind, failed, and then made a sort of accommodation with the city, becoming invisible, floating through it all, ignoring the bizarre sights and sounds.

Splitting up, they walked along the entire parade route. Along with the royal itinerary, the exact route of the archduke's procession had been published in all the newspapers. Recommendations for the best viewing spots were posted in cafés and restaurants. From a security standpoint Ryzhkov thought that it couldn't be worse. Many of the roofs were gently pitched, and from the grilles and balconies of the city, behind the open, awning-covered windows, were hundreds of places where a marksman could choose his cover. For a bomb-throwing assassin there were also advantages; most of the route was along the main street that ran alongside the river—the Appel Quay, and there were few routes off it wide enough for a motorcar—the parade could easily be immobilized by a bomb, and the marksmen would have still targets for their long rifles.

By the afternoon the Okhrana men were hot, dusty and depressed. They found a café on Franz Josef Street and sat nursing glasses of warm beer. Dima was reading a greasy copy of the local newspaper. 'Well, if we assume we're thinking like the Black Handers, we can just, you know . . . follow in their footsteps . . .'

'And end up one step behind,' Hokhodiev said. He was staring at his half-empty glass of beer.

'We go forward, that's all . . . just like you said, eh, Kostya?' Ryzhkov wanted to cheer Hokhodiev up, make him happy, make him forget all his worries about Lena. All it produced was a nod from the big man, his eyes never left the beer glass.

'You know that they're coming into town on a tour tomorrow, they're going to visit the bazaar in the Turkish quarter.'

'We'll follow them all the way,' Ryzhkov said. He stood up, wanting to leave. In spite of himself, he was getting angry. So what if Evdaev's hired assassins killed the Austrian heir? So some stocks and bonds went up, so some arms merchants grew rich selling howitzers? So what . . . *tryn-trava*? He had a sudden vision of Vera twirling on stage like some dervish dressed in diaphanous silk. He could just stop, sneak back into Russia using a forged identity, find her, escape . . . A big hand on his shoulder interrupted his thoughts. Hokhodiev was smiling at him.

'Let's go little brother. We sleep tonight, for tomorrow we may die, yes?'

In the heat of the day they came shopping; the archduke and his wife, Sophie; by the looks of them, both pleasant enough. It was an 'unofficial' spontaneous gesture designed to please the mostly Muslim crowd, and it seemed to be working. It was difficult to move in the press of happy onlookers. The archduke was a tall man, with dark hair running to grey. Well fed, well groomed, with extraordinarily clear blue eyes. He seemed younger than his age of fifty-one. Today he was dressed informally, wearing fine civilian clothes that made him appear more prime minister than prince. He asked polite questions about the foodstuffs that were on display, marvelled over the work of the silversmiths, admired bolts of fabric that had been hung from sticks above the narrow lanes, shook hands, and patted children on the head. The countess was quiet, well-behaved, modest. She looked like the mother you wished you had, always with a little half-smile, happy to be out with her husband touring the foul-smelling Turkish quarter of Sarajevo.

Ryzhkov moved through it all with pained eyes and a headache that he kept pushed out to the very edge of his consciousness. He scanned the windows and rooftops, saw dozens of suspicious faces. Dozens of potential sites from which a bomber could step and throw. Everyone looked suspicious, even the children. It was like a death-watch. A macabre dress-rehearsal for a royal funeral; as soon as he saw him Ryzhkov knew the archduke was going to be killed.

It was noisy, hot, pungent with the odours of humans, animals, fruit, vegetables, spices and charcoal smoke from the braziers. General Oskar Potiorek, the Austrian-appointed Governor of Bosnia, himself a potential target, and a clutch of sweating bureaucrats hovered around the royal couple. Bespectacled transla-tors struggled with the dialects of the Muslim merchants. At times a rhythmic 'Zivio!' could be heard round the fringes of the crowd. When it got loud enough the archduke would look up, acknowledge that he'd heard the happy hurrahs and then everyone would laugh like a horde of trained monkeys.

Through the ancient market they continued. It seemed like hours. The three Russians triangulated themselves around the procession. In the packed lanes and narrow aisles the Austrian and Bosnian police were obvious in their blue and tan uniforms. They too seemed to be enjoying the day; everything was amiable, hospitable and delightful, as they all wound their way through the ancient labyrinth. At the food stalls samples were being given out and merchants were bowing to their customers. Ryzhkov even found himself trying to smile so that he wouldn't stick out.

Everything was so relaxed and secure that the royal couple took it in their fancy to explore, turning even deeper into the market. Ryzhkov, Hokhodiev and Dima turned with them. Now Hokhodiev was at the point of the triangle as they strolled from stall to stall. Ryzhkov's eyes swept the crowd, looking for the momentary predatory glance, the quickened movement of a man about to hurl a deadly object. Now they were nearing a line of ice-filled troughs with suspicious fish arrayed on them in perfect display. He saw Hokhodiev move ahead to check the street just beyond the fish stalls. Their eyes met and Kostya shook his head.

And then—

It came suddenly—only a noise at first. The sound of men's voices raised in protest. He whirled and saw that there was a scuffle in the crowd, someone shouting something in a language that Ryzhkov did not understand. He quickly forced himself to turn his eyes away, searching for someone looking, tightening his field of vision, eliminating possible threats and finally seeing Franz Ferdinand as he, too, became aware of the fracas—turning with a distracted smile across his face. His hand went to the countess's arm in a gesture of protection.

Ryzhkov desperately scanned the crowd. At the corner he saw a man on a ladder. A young man carrying his dark jacket over his sleeve. Now he was seeing the hard young faces everywhere: another flint-eyed student at the corner of a stall that was hung with carpets. Their eyes met for a moment, and the young man looked back with something like recognition, a flicker crossed his face and he suddenly looked down and away.

A diversion, Ryzhkov was thinking, his hand reaching beneath his jacket for the pistol he had tucked into his pocket, moving towards the carpet stall where the young man had vanished. He pushed his way behind the archduke, through the trailing bureaucrats. Looking for other faces, others who were watching, trying to pick out the bodyguards. Yes, it's what I would do, he was thinking as he pushed his way through the crowd; make a little noise, make a little test, see how they react, see which way they jump.

And then as quickly as it had happened it was over; the archduke turned his gaze back to the fish, the countess raised her handkerchief to her nose. No security, he thought. No security anywhere. 'A thief,' people were saying to each other, nothing to worry about, only a thief who was trying to steal from one of the jewellers.

He reached the edge of the lane that opened on to a plaza dominated by a large grilled fountain, the centre of the crowded quarter. The young man was, of course, gone.

He turned back and ran right into the chest of a blue-clad Austrian policeman.

'Excuse me,' the Austrian said, and pushed his way into the alley.

Ryzhkov headed back into the labyrinthine streets of the market, caught up in time to see Franz Ferdinand and Sophie as they were leaving. A huge covered Hispano was there in the blinding sun, its engine purring, waiting to take them back to the station. The royal itinerary flashed through Ryzhkov's memory. The archduke would return to his lodge outside Ilidze for the night; the 'official' visit to the city was set for ten the next morning. Less than twenty-four hours, Ryzhkov thought. Hokhodiev came up beside him, his face grim.

'Did you see that, brother?' he asked.

'A test.'

'Oh, yes. And our local boys failed by the looks of it, eh? Come on, I think I have them.' For the first time in

a long while Hokhodiev smiled. They pushed their way
out into the lane.

'There,' Hokhodiev said, pointing to two young men
striding up one of the twisting streets ahead of them. 'I
just saw them meet up, one was watching from back
there—'

'The boy on the ladder?'

'That's our pigeon, and I'm almost sure I remember
them from yesterday. I was on the quay in the afternoon,
they were pretending to be tourists, they had a map and
everything, asking directions, but anyone can see by
their clothes . . .' The two men were dressed in suits, but
their shoes were run down, the jackets rumpled and
unpressed. Students. Angry young men.

'They're so fucking cocky, they're not even trying to
hide it,' Hokhodiev said.

There was another great cheer from the crowd as the
Hispano lurched into gear and began to negotiate the
narrow lane. If they managed to get off the street, they'd
be safe enough for the night, Ryzhkov thought.

'Quickly . . .' He looked around and saw Dima
moving towards them. They followed the two young
men up the hill, out of the old quarter and along a
higher street where the buildings gave way to smaller
houses. Ahead of them the assassins turned a corner and
Dima rushed ahead to get a view down the lane.
Ryzhkov continued straight on and turned at the next
opportunity, Kostya had dropped back and tried to cut
around behind the pair. Ryzhkov walked along the
narrow streets. The district was quiet, only an
occasional cry from an infant, a dog's barking, the
calling of the crows to puncture the hot stillness. Women
in twos and threes passed him as he walked along.
Behind walls he heard children playing games in the

shady gardens. An old man in his chair smoking and talking to himself. Ryzhkov saw Hokhodiev coming up the hill and he went over to meet him. Together they stood just around the corner in a narrow sliver of shade.

'Dima's just there—' Hokhodiev said it without looking around. 'The house at the end of that lane. They've got rooms up there, and—look—' He pulled Ryzhkov around the corner. Down the hill another three black-clad students were making their way up towards the lane.

'Yes . . .' Ryzhkov breathed.

Suddenly Dima appeared at the mouth of the lane. He had taken off his jacket and bundled it under his arm, tied a kerchief around his head against the sun. He carried a basket in both arms, trying to look like he was doing something. He walked along pretending he hadn't noticed them.

'One at a time,' Ryzhkov said and Hokhodiev nodded and stepped out into the street, walking slowly, reading a newspaper he'd picked up somewhere. Ryzhkov stayed in the shadow and watched as the three terrorists turned and made their way to the house at the end of the lane.

THIRTY-EIGHT

'We hit them tonight,' Ryzhkov said.

Back in their rooms, he and Dima planned the raid, then Dima left to relieve Hokhodiev, and for the space of a half-hour Ryzhkov had the place to himself. He stood looking over the roof tiles. Thought about the possibility of composing some sort of note that he could send to Vera to let her know he was alive, that there was still some hope. Then he thought that perhaps he should wait for the next few hours to be over. Since he might not come out of it alive, and what was the sense of that? Hello, I love you. I'm going to be dead or in jail for ever in the next few hours. Hokhodiev came in and filled him in. Another troika of student revolutionaries had made their way to headquarters.

'These were the ones making the deliveries, I'd say.' They'd all had suitcases. 'Heavy, by the looks of it.' Together they constructed a detailed map of the house and lanes surrounding it; the building itself sat at the end of a short lane, forming a cul-de-sac. A watcher from the upstairs windows would be able to see anyone who approached via the lane. The only other way in was over the wall and through the garden of a neighbouring house, then a climb up to the roof and hop down on to the stairs leading to the balcony.

Ryzhkov shook his head and looked up to meet Hokhodiev's eye. It was a bad way in, and it was also the only escape route. 'Fine, but when we hit them, where do they run? It's good to always leave them somewhere to run. If they can't run, they're cornered, they just dig in harder. Not very pretty, brother . . .' Hokhodiev muttered.

Ryzhkov left and walked to a grocer's and purchased bread, cheese, and a bottle of red wine, counted out his dinars for the smiling assistant, and trudged back up the hill, running the permutations over and over in his mind.

Before he left to take a look at the house, he and Hokhodiev decided that Dima would wait on the adjacent roof with a view of the staircase to cut off the only escape route. Other than that there were no changes, nothing new they could come up with to give them a better chance. Dima would approach from the rear, Hokhodiev would go directly up the lane and Ryzhkov would go over the wall, through the garden, climb on to the roof. Then he and Hokhodiev would crash into the rooms through the door and a window . . .

'And then?' Hokhodiev said. A little smile was playing across his face.

Ryzhkov shrugged. 'If they fight, we kill them. If we can we take their guns, or their bombs, and then—'

'It's the "then" that I'm thinking about,' Hokhodiev laughed.

'Then we escape ourselves. If the noise hasn't brought them, we call the police. Hopefully there will be some evidence in the rooms that will lead to their arrest, but at the very least they'll be off the streets during the parade . . .' He stopped, running out of ideas. The plan was as thin as tissue.

'Ah . . .' Hokhodiev said and sat back. 'Well . . . as a master strategy, it's slightly flawed.'

'I know, I know.'

'But, still, brother, we hit them. We hit them hard. We kill as many as we can, wound the others. If any escape, we give chase, but then . . .'

'Then we go straight to the railway station. We tag along behind the motorcade.'

'Running.'

'Running. Yes, if we can. We'll just have to push our way through. We can take it in stages, like a relay, maybe.'

Hokhodiev looked at him for a long moment, the smile deepening. After a moment he reached out and put a heavy hand on his shoulder.

'Together, then . . .' he said.

Ryzhkov checked his watch. They agreed that the raid would begin at five. He checked to make sure the revolver was loaded, that his knife was in his pocket.

'I'll see the two of you at the wall,' he said and looked around the room to check. He would never be coming back there again.

'Here . . .' Hokhodiev said. He took one of the mineral cases out of the cupboard and extracted a roll of banknotes. 'It's marks, roubles, francs . . . some of everything.' He made three piles of money on the table.

'What about afterwards?' Ryzhkov said, watching him count out the notes.

'I'm going back, I think. Do whatever I can to get Lena away from her relatives. She'll be going crazy, I can't leave her to that.' He said it without looking up to meet Ryzhkov's eye. They both knew the dangers.

'You'd better go, so the boy can get some sleep, eh?'

'Yes,' Ryzhkov said, stuffed the roll of banknotes in his pocket and went through the door into the night.

In the darkness young men lay. Waiting.

Sleepless, or dreaming, staring into the blackness, thrashing about in their beds, about to become what they had always wanted.

Earlier that same day some of them had visited the cemetery to place flowers on the grave of Bogdan Žerajić, their compatriot who had been martyred in the midst of an unsuccessful assassination attempt on the governor. It was a small cemetery, meant for paupers and criminals, not at all well-tended, and the flowers they had brought were bright and artificial-looking against the parched grass on the hillside. After their prayers they looked up and saw it—Sarajevo, the gateway to the east. The heart of cherished Bosnia. Soon, yes, they had said to each other, making their young faces hard . . . yes, soon to be realized.

Oh, their names would be remembered, their fathers and uncles would nod their heads, bite back the tears, and take off their hats in pride. Girls of the village would swoon with their memory and shrines would be erected in their honour. Each one, now at the apex of this dark night, suddenly aware of his individuality, suddenly aware of the strength of their bond to the cause—the oaths they had sworn, the rituals and the promises made in blood, the obligations whose time had come round at last.

In the murky darkness the young men, unable to sleep, finally gave up, smoked, talked in whispers to their companions; admitted their passions, their fears, swore their loyalty to one another, then fell back into contemplation. Now a boy reclined, his head on the pillow, smoking, his eyes staring at the little packet on the table. Bullets enough and a little box with his cyanide capsule.

The ticking of a clock in the adjacent room, the sound of snoring, the sound of nightmares. The sound of their own breathing, struggling to remain calm, yes, Christ, to sleep, to husband their energies for what lay ahead. Death, quick or slow. Or capture and a last defiant suicide. Or the worst—failure. Death then was best. And if you die tomorrow, what then? The wait is over, yes?

Only a mile or two away, in the splendid villa that had been provided for their use, the Archduke Franz Ferdinand slept alongside his beloved Sophie. Did they dream? Did they snore? Did they find the covers too warm, did they roll over, their tranquillity suddenly disturbed by the approach of a demon yet to make himself known? In the great house others whose lot it was to rise in the very early hours had risen, were staggering to the lavatory, washing themselves, putting on their uniforms, bundling sticks into the stove, heating water—the ordinary start of an extraordinary day, for, graced by the presence of royalty soundly sleeping a few floors above them, they were nervous lest they fail in some domestic task.

In the city the multitudes were resting, clocks set to give them time to get to the quay for the morning's procession. Clothing had been cleaned and laid out, the rudiments of breakfast already on the table, the most eager of the celebrity-seekers prepared for their planned early start to secure the best places with the best view of what all were sure would prove to be a memorable spectacle.

Andrianov waited in Vienna.

Treated himself to a grand dinner, a walk through the glory of the Vienna woods. The horizon, he reflected, was a perfect one, roses pierced with beautiful elms, the artfully placed sculpture—a virgin of purest stone, a perpetual advocate of the most exquisite and holy ideals of mankind.

All around him was the great seat of the Austro-Hungarian Empire, the much-vaunted Dual Monarchy. Waltz music of course, filtering up the slope of the hill. Gaiety and the light sophistication of the smug Viennese. The growl of a motorcar with a faulty exhaust accelerating on the ring road. The dark shadows of bats flitting through the gardens.

He returned to the hotel, ignored the telegrams Rochefort brought in on a tray. The money was piling up. He had diversified as invisibly as he possibly could. Brokers across the continent were already concluding a series of sales to take place under a variety of accounts held by Andrianov or his proxies. He made his reservations on the morning train, sent Rochefort away, poured himself a glass of champagne and went in to where the girl was waiting in the other room.

And the earth spun on its axis. The stars arced across the sky. Babies cried out, dogs barked and the owls fell silent.

And men waited for their time.

THIRTY-NINE

In the dawn he watched them coming up the hill. Hokhodiev had shaved, probably gone out in the very early hours and woken some barber, made himself look neat as a pin. He smiled as he crested the hill and saw Ryzhkov sitting there beneath the wall. 'That Ukrainian fool went out and got himself a whore. He doesn't look so good, if you ask me, eh?'

Dima was trailing up the cobbles behind him. It was still cool, not quite dark, but he had his coat off with the sleeves tied around his waist and was rubbing his head. He saw them and managed to raise one arm to wave.

'This is very unprofessional behaviour,' Ryzhkov said.

Hokhodiev laughed. 'Don't get him any more pissed off than he is,' he said.

'What happened?'

'Who am I to know. Some problem with the girl. The price, who knows.'

Dudenko came and squatted down beside Ryzhkov. He had brought up a bottle, and now he hastily began to uncork it. He saw Ryzhkov's look.

'Don't worry, it's water,' he said and took a long drink, then held out the bottle to Ryzhkov. 'This might be my last time, right?'

'If you're lucky,' Hokhodiev said and nudged him with his knee so that he fell over on to the pavement.

'This is very unprofessional of you, I may have to reprimand you,' Ryzhkov said. The water was a good idea, he thought.

'Old man, I told you . . .' Dudenko jerked the pistol out of his jacket, spun it round and round his finger, and then slipped it back in the jacket.

'This is very unprofessional,' Ryzhkov said. He got to his feet and shook his legs. His back was stiff from sitting there in the dark against the wall. 'Let's go, eh?' The sky was starting to lighten. 'Are you ready?' He stepped out into the street. There was nobody down the little lane watching. He was sure of it. Everything was dark down there. He'd been on the look-out for two hours and had seen nothing. Dima stood up and came out into the street. He had his gun inside his jacket and was carrying it in his arms like a baby. 'I'll see you around the back, then,' he said and started walking down the street. His shirt-tail was out and he had his arm wrapped up in his jacket for some reason; he looked just like what he was in reality, a young man returning from a whorehouse.

Hokhodiev walked out into the centre of the street and urinated.

'This is all we need, to get arrested for public defecation . . .' Ryzhkov said. His feet were still numb and he stood there jiggling one foot after the other.

'It's very unprofessional, I agree.'

Ryzhkov began walking up the street to the wall. It was low on one side and there was a lamppost there to climb up. A great olive tree curved over the bricks and the whole site was dark. Halfway up the street he stopped between two houses, turned and unbuttoned his trousers and urinated against the wall, still watching the house at the end of the lane. Nothing.

He could see Hokhodiev down at the entrance to the lane, looking up his way. He stepped out into the street. Down at the corner Hokhodiev lifted his hand.

He started towards the wall.

He stepped up on to the base of the lamppost and then dug his toes into the bricks. The plaster had fallen away in patches and he found a place and then pushed off the lamppost and reached his fingers over the stones—just a little flick, a pat with his fingers. It was all stone, rough enough. He stepped back on to the ledge of the lamppost and then jumped again, reached over and pulled himself to the top and then lay there for a moment on the top of the wall, listening and staring down into the gloom.

Just below the olive tree was a pen for what seemed to be two goats. A little shed that looked like its roof might hold. He let himself down on to the creaking goatshed and then jumped down as lightly as he could into the centre of the pen. He let himself out, left the door open, thinking that if he'd woken anyone that they might just think it was the goats. It might give him a few seconds. He could see under the edge of the eaves of the Black Hand's house. He decided that if someone was out on the balcony he would be able to see them. He waited, watching for any movements. Nothing.

Ahead of him was the open courtyard, a series of steps up to the first floor of the house; he waited and then ran lightly across to the shadows on the far side. From somewhere a chicken squawked. Something moved in the darkness ahead of him as he made it across and started up the steps.

At the top he looked over on to the balcony, and then turned and lifted his head and tried to see Hokhodiev down in the lane. There was a shadow beneath the landing of the stairs leading to the balcony. Ryzhkov knew Dima was waiting back there to cut off the runners. He listened and gradually raised his head higher to look up on the balcony. From somewhere he thought he could hear singing. He got to his knees and stepped out and on to the wall. Stood there and counted to thirty to give Hokhodiev time to get up the steps.

Then he jumped.

It was wrong from the start—someone sleeping there in the shadows. A man he hadn't seen. He woke as Ryzhkov hit the edge of the balcony, his knee shattering the grille that had been flung open because of the heat. Ryzhkov saw him jerk awake, try to roll over on the mat where he'd been sleeping, try to curl over and get to his knees. Ryzhkov balanced there on the railing, one hand holding on to the awning, reached into his belt, took out the revolver, and shot the man straight down into his body, so that he sat down again and fell back against the wall, a big spout of blood pumping out of his neck, one, two, three.

Now someone was yelling and he heard Hokhodiev shooting, once, twice and then another sound, a shriek, someone hurt badly, and by then he was through the curtains into the front room of the apartment. Something moved in front of him and he raised the revolver to shoot before he saw that it was Hokhodiev fighting with a man. They twisted past him and he saw one of the students coming out of the back room. He had a rifle in his hands and lifted it to aim. Ryzhkov stepped out of the window and started walking at the boy who he fooled with the bolt and shot him twice through the stomach. Behind him there was a great crash and he turned in time to see Hokhodiev smash a stool into the broken face of one of the students. There was a flash off to his side and he saw that there was someone there, someone who had been sleeping on the floor, back in the corner behind the stove. He turned but knew already it was too late.

There was a crashing at the doors, it meant someone was going in or going out and he could hear someone shooting outside. Dima . . . he was thinking, thirsty Dima . . . There was another flash and he shot at a man he could hardly see standing there in the darkness, not having time to aim, turning the corner and heading into the rear of the building.

Something hit him, someone running in panic through the gloom, and he fell back on to the floor. The Serbs were screaming at each other now. He put his hand out to get up but slipped in the blood of the boy lying there in the hallway. Someone ran past and he saw that Hokhodiev was down on the floor in the front room. There was a gunshot outside the door and he turned to shoot back but saw Dima standing there. Someone was wailing outside. He finally got up, turned away and stepped into the bedroom. The grille had been torn out and the tiles broken away outside the window. He heard men yelling in the back street.

Hokhodiev was waiting for him on the landing and they started down the stairs, stepping over one of the students, wounded, who was trying to crawl back up. He reached out and tried to trip them as they went past, his touch weak as a baby's.

There were another six cartridges in Ryzhkov's pocket and he filled the cylinder as they ran around behind the building. There were three of the Serbs ahead of them. They had another with them who was limping along. There was blood all over the stones there. The street curved down towards the river and they skidded downhill. There was a great yell and he saw Dima sprint past him. The Serbs rounded a corner and Dima plunged blindly around it, his gun raised to fire.

Ryzhkov arrived at the corner just as Dima shot the wounded student who had crouched there inside a doorway to ambush them, a stupid trick, the kind of thing you would do with snowballs. Below he saw the three Serbs glance back over their shoulders and then run into the market.

By the time they had got to the edge of the market, Hokhodiev had come up behind them, Ryzhkov watched him, he was running with a limp from the fight, the gun looked heavy in his hand. He worked his way into the narrow alleys.

At the end of the lane he could see people running back up the hill the way they'd just come down; he could hear the police whistles in the distance. He walked blindly through the market. Most of the stalls were shuttered, their awnings tied down. But there were some early risers. He saw Dima a few yards away walking briskly, bending over to check under the tables. There was a crack and he turned and looked towards the end of the lane, at the edge of the market, where Hokhodiev suddenly appeared, his arm raised, carefully aiming at someone and shooting once, twice.

They ran out into the street. He could see a smear of blood across Hokhodiev's shirt. The merchants and their apprentices had woken now. An old man stepped out of a doorway in front of them. He was thin as a picked-over chicken leg and as brown as polished wood. He was dressed in a fez and a long white robe. He stood looking at them, and then bowed as they ran down the hill.

'Are you all right?' Ryzhkov asked Hokhodiev, pointing down to his shirt. Hokhodiev pulled his shirt-front up to look, shook his head. He was still running with the limp. Ahead of them the street was crowded and they slowed, he put the pistol back in his belt. The Serbs were too far ahead of them. Gone down towards the quay. In the distance there was a shrill whistle that echoed off the yellow buildings. A sudden flight of gulls lifted off the roof ahead of them.

'The station . . .' he said, and they stepped out on to the wide street that curved along past the cathedral.

They walked along now, suddenly tired, Hokhodiev taking his fedora off and wiping his brow on his sleeve. Dima ran past them, and crossed the street.

'He's wide awake now,' Hokhodiev said.

In the distance he could hear military music, and ahead of them there were the first of the crowd crossing the street to be at the quay in time to stake out their favoured places for the parade. The street was a long one. He and Hokhodiev split up and he crossed, now about fifty metres behind Dudenko. They'd been lucky, Ryzhkov thought. Only Hokhodiev had been slowed down, and if they continued to be lucky perhaps the students would abandon their plans.

There was no sight of the three Serbs. They were gone, rushing ahead to either improvise an attempt on

the archduke or to stop, retreat and plan a strike on
some safer, less bloody day.

He rocked back on his heels as a police wagon dragged
along by four sweating horses careered around the corner
just ahead of him, rushing back up the hill toward the
house of the Black Hand. By now word of the gunfight
would have reached whoever was responsible for the
security procedures for the archduke's visit to the capital.
Perhaps they would be prudent, cancel the parade . . . But
he knew it wouldn't happen. Austrian pride, if nothing
else, would cause Franz Ferdinand to walk into a hail of
bullets rather than acknowledge the Serbian threat, even
in the most fractious province of the empire.

Down the hill he heard a strange crashing. For a split
second he thought it was artillery and then recognized it
as the firing of a salute as the royal carriage arrived at the
station. He quickened his step, trying not to break out in
a run. At every turn he scanned the side alleys for the
three Serbs. Now, the task was harder. The streets were
swelling with ordinary citizens, and the men had broken
out their dark jackets even in the heat. He made his way
to the Appel Quay. He had come out at a side street near
the museum. There was a large plaza there and the
crowd had gathered and were leaning out, staring down
the street where the band was playing. He looked around
for Hokhodiev and Dudenko, but they had become
separated. His mind was whirling, trying to decide where
to go, what to do next; trying to imagine what it would
be like to be an angry, nineteen-year-old Serbian terrorist.
He stepped through the crowd, pushing his way to the
front, muttering apologies and trying to accent his speech
towards the softer-sounding local dialect.

When he got to the street he craned his neck but could
see nothing but a pair of Bosnian constables advancing

along the edges of the cobbles, one on each side of the
street telling people to step back on to the kerb. The
crowd bowed as they went, then sprawled right back
into the street. He began to edge his way along, allowing
the man to push him back when they passed, then
stepping out behind him and walking towards the
procession. He could hear the crowd cheering ahead of
him as the motorcade made its turn from the station and
accelerated along the broader quay. Ahead of him he saw
Kostya push his way out on to the street, cross to the
embankment and start walking along a few metres ahead
of the cars. Already the motorcade had slowed to accom-
modate the press of well-wishers. For a city supposedly
divided against the rule of his dynasty, thousands of
Sarajevans had come out to cheer the spectacle.

Now Ryzhkov saw the leading escorts, hussars
mounted on twin matched greys riding in advance of the
motorcars in an effort to press the crowd back against the
shopfronts. For a moment Ryzhkov stopped, standing
there in the centre of the street. Just ahead of him was a
Sarajevo police constable, a middle-aged man with a red
face and a big stomach. He was laughing with someone
he knew. He looked over and saw Ryzhkov standing
there. Ryzhkov smiled at him, nodded. Pointed down
at the oncoming parade. The old man turned to look
down the quay, and when he did, Ryzhkov stepped back
into the crowd and began working his way back up the
street. The matched greys reached him, the crowd rippled
back on to the pavement. Constables were marching
along the street, in a vain attempt to keep ahead of the
motorcade. He saw Hokhodiev across the street working
his way along, pushing people out of the way.

And then he saw the face.

A small man, hardly more than a boy, really, with a shock of dark hair that flamed away from his skull, in wild black swirls. The hint of a dark moustache, the hard eyes. He recognized him from the house of the Black Hand. He was standing only a few metres away, surrounded by the cheering crowd. The noise was deafening. The growl and chatter of the motorcars seemed to fill the universe. Ryzhkov squeezed his way through the crowd. For a moment he lost sight of the boy and when he located him he saw he had changed position, pushing his way up to the edge of the street.

Now came the first of the motorcars. Sarajevo's mayor, dressed formally, waved at the crowd; beside him was the commissioner of the police, a gloved hand raised in salute. Ryzhkov saw the young Serb step out on to the kerb.

The second car was just passing; like the first, its roof had been folded back. He saw Franz Ferdinand, unmistakable in his famous silver helmet topped with a spray of black-green feathers; seated beside him, the duchess in her immaculate white dress, smiling at the crowd.

Suddenly his eye caught Hokhodiev as he jumped out into the street; another of the Serbs was right beside him, his arm raised to throw a bomb. At the last moment Hokhodiev reached him, slapping at his shoulder. The two of them collided and the young Serb slipped down on to the cobbles.

The bomb looked like a dark ball, so small as to be almost comical. It arched above the street heading straight for the Hispano. The terrorist had been late, or perhaps Hokhodiev had spoiled his aim; the bomb fell short, bounced on the roof's leather cover and rebounded against the back of the duchess's neck. She looked startled and reached back to see what had hit her. By that point Hokhodiev had stumbled over the terrorist, thrown himself out into the street and nearly reached the back of the car.

Ryzhkov heard someone shouting; a military officer who was riding in the royal car got to his feet and was turning halfway around. Just ahead of him the young Serb had reached into his coat and stood there poised waiting for the car to come into range. Hokhodiev was trying to climb up the rear bumper of the car, slapping at the little black bomb that wobbled there, its fuse fizzing and hissing, he managed to knock it off on to the street and fell down, vanishing from Ryzhkov's sight behind the great Hispano.

From across the street people were was screaming. The bomb-thrower had picked himself up from the gutter and plunged into the crowd. He reached the edge of the quay and tried to climb the wall and escape down to the nearly dry river bed, but the crowd was on him and he vanished, pulled down into the mob.

Now the bomb exploded on the cobbles beneath the third car with a sharp crack that sent everyone in the street cowering. The car went crazily out of control as one of the wheels shattered. He saw Hokhodiev, knocked down to a sitting position by the blast, get to his feet and fall back into the crowd. Two blue-clad Austrian police constables ran up behind the stricken car and plunged in after him. The whole street was filled with the smell of burning chemicals.

Suddenly the young Serb was brushing right past Ryzhkov. For a moment their eyes met, and then he was gone, pushing his way through the mob. Ryzhkov turned and began chasing him along the quay. The boy was just a fleeting shadow, appearing and disappearing through the crowd.

He followed as best he could. There was a loud roaring and the archduke's motorcar raced along the Quay, much faster now, the crowd jumping out of its path at the last moment. He stumbled off a high kerb and looked around frantically. He was dripping with sweat. The boy was gone, nowhere, vanished into the heat-haze. Ryzhkov went back and stumbled up a side street. There was a flash of black, someone in a cheap suit veering off the street into the maw of the cathedral. He stayed over to the side of the street, trying to hide in the shadows as he ran up the hill.

Even with the doors open it was cool in the great stone building. Someone came in behind him and he whirled, thinking that the student might have come around and was attacking him, but it was Dima. His shirt was soaked and he had pulled out the shirt-tail to conceal the pistol in his waistband.

'Have you seen Kostya?' he spluttered.

'No, did the police get him?'

'I think he got away, but I saw you running so I thought—'

'He came in here—' Ryzhkov said and the two of them divided and started walking deep into the cathedral down the aisles at the side. The building was virtually empty. By the time Ryzhkov got to the apse, he was running ahead. There was a sound in front of him and he rushed forward to an exiting doorway. The light hit him as he pushed through the heavy door and immediately a gunshot rang out, it sounded doubled in his ears and a spray of rock dust and splinters flashed in the corner of his vision.

He fell to the flagstone steps automatically, pulling his knees up into a ball even as he groped for his pistol. The boy was already running away too far for a shot at the corner and over the fence behind. Dima stepped over him, Ryzhkov rose to his seat and together they ran towards the corner.

'He's a fast bastard,' Dima spat as they dashed across the street. A few old women jumped out of the way, watching the three crazy men chasing each other through the streets.

They found themselves moving higher through the city. The boy was gone now and they came upon a fountain in a square and they each put their mouths under the spigot and drank long cold draughts while the other stared around at the dark doorways, one hand on the butt of his pistol, waiting for a shot to ring out.

Now ahead of them was the town hall, and another crowd which had gathered at the steps. The cars were lined up, and Ryzhkov stood there for a moment, the archduke's itinerary flashing through his memory. He knew that the young assassin hadn't given up on his mission. On the steps the mayor was concluding his address. Ryzhkov saw the tall silver helmet, the blindingly white dress and picture hat of the countess. The words were echoing blurs against the stones of the buildings that ringed the square.

'The boy has a pistol, he'll have to get close to do any good,' Ryzhkov said and once again he and Dima began to encircle the crowd, trying to pick out a single figure among hundreds.

There was a long rolling 'Zivio!' from the crowd. Men had hoisted their children on their shoulders for a better view. The mob was well dressed for the most part, Austrians and the better-off Muslims. A sea of dark faces, red fezzes, starched white shirtfronts and dark jackets. The dignitaries had repaired inside the hall for refreshments.

As Ryzhkov meandered through the crowd, he picked up snatches of conversations. A pair of assassins had made an attempt on the life of the archduke, a man was saying. A bomb had killed one of the governor's aides. No, *two* bombs had been thrown, a lady-in-waiting had been wounded and taken to hospital. A miracle of great fortune: the crown prince himself had heroically picked up the grenade and tossed it to the safest place possible — beneath the car following his in the parade. No, dozens had been killed, including women and children. Soldiers were en route from the barracks on the west side of the city. Riots had broken out at the station. Pǎsic, the Serb Prime Minister, had made an announcement that he deplored the action of the terrorists—news of it had arrived by cable, but as proof of a gigantic conspiracy, the news had arrived before the bomb had even been thrown!

Ryzhkov moved through it all, pushing his way through the blur of conversations, the press of the citizenry gathered there in front of the huge façade. He worked his way around to the edge of the steps, looking at the crowd surrounding the vehicles. Now the police had put half a dozen constables around the cars as a cordon. According to the itinerary for the remainder of the day—the royal couple were due to visit the museum on the way back to their hotel in Ilidze. There would be another grindingly slow motorcade through Sarajevo's twisting streets. From the doorway of the town hall he could hear chamber music drawing to a close. There was a ripple of polite applause. A man in Austrian military dress appeared at the top of the steps. Subordinates rushed to confer with him, and then hurried away. A second squad of policemen rushed out and began to push the crowd further out into the plaza. Ryzhkov recognized the military man, he had been riding in the archduke's car in the front seat. Now he went along the line of vehicles, conferring with the chauffeurs; moments later the engines were started.

A flash of panic seized Ryzhkov; he found himself being pushed out to the edge of the street with the rest, his eyes travelled along the front ranks of the mob, trying to pick out the assassin. He saw Dima squirming through the crowd, earning dirty looks and elbows as he forced his way through. His gaze was dark and fixed ahead of him. Then Ryzhkov saw the boy again.

He had thrown away his cravat and grabbed a fez to conceal his appearance. He had yet to see Dima and now Ryzhkov pushed his way out past a policeman and began running towards him. Somewhere behind him a whistle sounded, someone clutched at his back. He saw the boy look up wildly as Dima charged through the crowd. At the last moment he turned and saw the young Russian plunge towards him. Ryzhkov was almost across the cobbles when a policeman spun him off balance and he slipped to one knee, another policeman was rushing towards him as he got to his feet and dived into the mob. The crowd was screaming, trumpets were sounding as behind him the archduke appeared on the steps. Now he saw the young boy savagely swipe at Dima with his pistol, connecting with his jaw and sending him to the pavement. They were only a few feet apart when the mob rushed forward to divide them.

Dima rolled over and shook himself. Ryzhkov was on his hands and knees, people were stepping all around them. Dima opened his eyes blearily, got up on one elbow. 'I'm fine, I'm fine . . .' he said, shaking his head again. Ryzhkov put an arm around him and hauled him to his feet. The young Serb was gone. Behind them there was a final cheer and the motorcade pulled away, heading back along the quay.

'Go,' Dima said, 'Go . . . I'll catch up with you. We meet at the seminary, as planned, yes?'

'Find Kostya, watch out for the flics!' he shouted but now the crowd had surged towards the plaza and they were separated like two twigs floating through a torrent.

He pushed his way to the edge of the plaza, began running down a side street leading to the quay. The route ran along the edge of the bazaar and the market was open now that the official ceremonies had concluded. Ryzhkov peered into the dark shadows, tried to remember the labyrinth of streets. Ahead of him he saw a dark head bobbing through the crowd, the face looked back over his shoulder, their eyes met and the boy turned and dug in his coat for his pistol.

Around him the crowd began to part, women screamed, a man slipped to the ground just in front of Ryzhkov. He suddenly felt naked, paralysed and terrifically vulnerable as, in front of him, the boy pulled the trigger. Something whizzed past him, sounding like an angry bee. Behind him the street erupted with screaming.

The boy dashed into the bazaar, upsetting an old woman who was tending a flower stall. Ryzhkov dug his pistol out and plunged after him, colliding with merchants and customers. All the time the screams were growing, an angry crowd forming behind them. He skidded through the debris the young man was leaving behind him in his panic, fell down, got back to his knees in time to see the Serb cut back out towards the street. Now there was the sound of car horns, a roaring of engine exhaust, and the gleam of brass shining in the sunlight. He saw the motorcade starting to pick up speed. The young terrorist must have seen it too—he was rushing along the edge of the market, his attention focused on the archduke's car. Ryzhkov began running towards him as fast as he could. He had the revolver out and the hammer pulled back, stopped and aimed at the young man and pulled the trigger once, twice.

It only bought him a second—now the young Serb had plunged out of the market and was standing there in the doorway, oblivious to Ryzhkov's approach. There was a great squealing sound as the Hispano braked to a stop at the corner by the bridge. Men's voices cursing, a rising call of klaxons. The archduke was half-standing in his seat, saying something to the driver. There had been a mistake. The Hispano stopped, rolled forward, then shuddered into reverse gear. The duchess smiled and reached over to pat her husband on his arm. No one saw the boy from the Black Hand.

Ryzhkov screamed. It was supposed to be 'Stop!' but it came out as something animalistic, a great bellow of anger and regret. The boy turned and looked his way. His face was calm, almost sad. The dark eyes alert, piercing. He held his revolver down by his leg, and now raised it. Ryzhkov aimed, risking one more shot, too late. The bullet was high, passed the boy, over the street into the low river.

And then the boy stepped out into the street and shot his gun into the back seat of the Hispano.

The sound was like fireworks, two tiny cracks, like dry branches breaking. The archduke sat back like a man exhausted by the whole ordeal, reached up to touch his shoulder. His wife turned towards him. The Hispano was rolling backwards now, slipping away from the Serb. A man reached out and tried to slap the assassin's gun away, two more were on him and the boy tried to whirl away, tried to run up the hill but now a police

constable had him by the wrist and he spun around, held
by his arms until they threw him to the ground. The
policeman stood and saw Ryzhkov standing there,
trembling, his pistol outstretched, poised and waiting to
take a shot that would never come.

'Halt!' the policeman screamed, he raised his whistle
to his mouth. There were howls from the people pressed
all around him in the market. Ryzhkov turned and saw
the sea of faces—someone was charging towards him
wielding a wooden rake as a weapon. He slipped along
the wall for a few feet; there was a sudden chorus of
police whistles, and suddenly the light was blinding, the
air in the street was like a hot pillow that had been
pushed over his face. He threw the pistol into an open
window and ran. He was crying and the street was a
twisting, blurred illusion.

He ran, harder than he had ever run before.

Terrified now, terrified because he had failed. Failed
utterly and completely. Terrified because Evdaev had
won and because . . . because nothing had come out
right, because he had left the woman he loved in a
quixotic effort to put the world straight, because he was
a fool, because he had always been a fool, because he
had led his only friends into a death trap, and because
now he was going to die there in that street, die in some
alien capital for reasons that could only sound absurd
when he would try to explain them to his final judge.

Behind him the voices were howling, 'Assassin!
Assassin!'

FORTY

Life was an afternoon in a manure bin, the gasses so strong as to nearly suffocate him. Pressing his nostrils to the cracks in the boards so that he could breathe, balanced the whole time on his hands and toes, so that he wouldn't ruin his clothes because, by God, he had decided that he was going to walk out of there.

Death was the tolling of bells that had begun while he was waiting, tolling for at least one of the royals, he knew. And death was whatever would happen next, whatever inferno would be ignited by the *iskra*. Death was the echo of Evdaev's laughing.

Life was everything he should have done, all the paths not taken, all of the happiness he'd eluded. He could have made it to Life, he thought. If he hadn't been slowed down by the guilt he'd hoarded, the fear he had tried to bury. All the mistakes. He thought of Vera to take his mind off it while he waited there, balled up in the shit-pile trying to stay clean. Vera was Life.

Death was when they came through the yard, a whole family, picking up one of their children who lived downstairs, and death was when the old woman stayed behind to talk with her friend.

Life was when the two of them went inside because it was so hot in the courtyard.

Death was when he climbed over the fence just in front of two people walking along—a woman and her son, the boy dressed in short trousers and shoes whose shine had melted in the sun, and she clothed from head to foot with only a chaste window for her eyes. He walked away from them, afraid to look back.

Life was fresh air and his shaking legs carrying him along one street, and then two, and then another without the sound of police whistles all around him. He went into a shop that was on the corner and bought some bread, some cheese and pears and asked the shopkeeper to put them in a bag. He ambled up the street feasting on the first food he had eaten that day. Life.

And life was seeing out of the corner of his vision two men lounging on a park bench in the early evening, one of them sleeping in the shade of the big trees, the second smoking in the gathering blue darkness.

He walked up, asked for a match from Dima.

'He's hurt,' Dima said quietly. 'You can't see it, he stuffed a towel in there.' Hokhodiev looked like he was sleeping, his head pillowed on a coat Dima had picked up somewhere.

'Hurt?'

'I've got it, boy . . .' Hokhodiev said. He hadn't opened his eyes. 'She's got me good, I think . . .' Now he saw that Hokhodiev was holding himself stiffly. His breathing was shallow.

'It was just a little splinter. We've got to get him to a doctor,' Dima whispered. Two elderly men walked by and they all muttered greetings to each other. They fell silent.

'Where?' Ryzhkov asked, watching the two men go. He pretended to fumble with the match.

'Somewhere down here,' Dima said and brushed the side of his shirt.

'No . . .' Hokhodiev said. 'Just walk now . . .' His voice was weak. It looked like he was trying to keep from moving.

'Let's get a carriage.'

'No,' Hokhodiev said. His voice was like a child crying.

'I'll go and find one and come back,' Ryzhkov said. Hokhodiev tried to complain again but by then he was already gone, walking with purpose now, rounding the little square. Searching the street. There was a small restaurant open at the corner not far away. He got a boy to find him a cab, then he turned around and headed back so he could be there to help Dima move Hokhodiev into the carriage.

The bells continued their mournful clanging. He smoked the last of his tobacco and tossed the remains in the gutter.

They wouldn't be looking for three men, he thought. Only one.

Hokhodiev was standing when he got back. 'I'm fine,' he said, but he didn't meet Ryzhkov's eye. He was looking off in the middle distance and kept one hand on the stone wall for balance. Dima was standing there ready to catch him. Stepping like a man with sore feet, a tight little smile, he climbed into the carriage well enough, but once the door was closed he groaned and fell against Dima and collapsed.

Ryzhkov stalled for a moment before negotiating with the driver, trying to remember the maps he'd seen, the best directions out of town. Trying to remember the nearest cities, trying to recall the last time he'd read a newspaper seeking anything other than the movements of the Archduke Franz Ferdinand during the lead-up to the royal visit. He put his head back in the carriage door. 'We're going on the road to Sofia, we'll get you a doctor along there, eh, Kostya?'

Hokhodiev shook his head. 'Get away, find some pliers, pull it out yourself. I can feel it,' he gestured to his side. 'Get over the border and then a doctor. Use your head, brother . . .'

Dima looked up at him. His face was stricken.

Ryzhkov took a deep breath, put on a smile, and went out to talk to the driver.

'Let's go. We're looking to take my friend back to his house in a little town that's ah . . . east of here, on the way to Sofia, I can't remember the name—'

'Uzice?'

'That sounds like it.'

'It's in the mountains, on the way to Nis.'

'Can you take us there?'

'It's a long way.'

'I know.'

'All night.'

'That's fine. He wants to see his mother, eh? The doctor says she's dying. It's this place called Uzice, you know that?'

'To Uzice, sure. Get some water on the way, yes.'

'He wants to talk to a doctor there, about his mother, eh?'

'They have doctors there in that town.'

'Good. And we can get something to eat on the way, I think, yes?' Ryzhkov held up an Austrian twenty-mark banknote.

'Leave it to me, excellency.' The driver smiled.

'Is this your carriage?' Ryzhkov smiled up at the man.

'Yes, excellency, I own it.'

'And the horses, as well?' The horses looked thin, he thought.

'Yes, excellency.'

'Are they strong enough to take us there?'

'Oh, yes. Plenty strong.'

'You have water?'

'Yes, plenty of water, excellency.'

'Good,' he said. 'Let's go along, then.'

And life was leaving Sarajevo by night. Passing through the suburbs, a cursory look and salute from a sleepy gendarme at the boundary of the city. And life was Hokhodiev sleeping, piled against Dima's side. Shivering and muttering in the moonlight.

He and Dima talked, planning the next few hours, the next few days. They could get out, they agreed. But a doctor first.

Death was the rocky hillside where they stopped, not yet reaching Uzice. Hokhodiev delirious and breathing shallowly. Ryzhkov reached up and tapped on the roof of the cab and the horses slowed. 'Got your gun?' he asked Dima quietly. The younger man nodded.

'It's here.' He stepped out and called up to the driver. The man looked at him; there was nothing around but a ruined stone farmhouse at the crest of the hill. The driver gave it a look, frowned. 'Not here, excellency,' he said. 'Later.'

'Just up there, that will do,' Ryzhkov said. 'My friend wants to buy this carriage from you, is it for sale?'

'No, not for sale,' the driver said, his face wary.

Ryzhkov looked at him for a moment, nodded. 'Just up there at that house. My friend wants to stop up there.'

The driver shrugged.

'You think about the price,' he said.

At the ruins of the house they settled on a price in Austrian marks for the carriage and horses. They didn't have to use the gun; the money was more than a fair exchange and the driver smiled, bowed elaborately, and pretended not to notice as Dima carried Hokhodiev out and in behind the wall of the dilapidated house. Watching them he pocketed the money, they shared out some of the bread, and he turned around and walked back in the early morning's light, down the long winding road back to Sarajevo.

They led the horses around the lee side of the hill and let them graze while they made a place for Kostya to rest in the back of the tumble-down building. It was a bad place to wait. Risky; obviously used with some frequency, the kind of place where a tired driver might decide to hole up for the evening. But it had the benefit of being sheltered from the winds which piled up against the top of the ridge—cold even in summer, and there was a place to build a fire. Dima went out to wander around the hilltop in search of wood, there was nothing left within the house itself.

Hokhodiev was breathing rapidly, then his breath would suddenly stop. He would seem to cough, or be caught in a snore, then his eyes would snap open. It must have hurt. He woke and Ryzhkov dipped his handkerchief in a little of their water and touched it to his lips.

'Sorry . . .' he said, shivering as if he had the fever.

'Kostya . . .'

'All right . . .'

'I can get Lena out, I could do that for you, eh?'

He could feel Hokhodiev shaking his head, just a little contraction of the muscles in his neck. Dima came in with an armful of twigs. 'How are you, old man?' he said with false cheeriness as he broke the twigs over the remains of a fire. 'This whole place smells like piss,' he said as he did it. He looked over at Hokhodiev again. 'You rest, then we'll get you to the doctor, eh?' It sounded like someone talking to a baby. Or a mule. He built a little arena for the twigs, crunched them into a ball and looked over and smiled.

'. . . Kostroma . . .' Hokhodiev said. His voice was quiet, eyes closed. Like a man dreaming. Dudenko fumbled in his jacket for a match.

'. . . Should go, Pyotr. Go . . .' Hokhodiev said quietly.

'I could try to get her out, Konstantin, I can go back and at least try,' he said. His voice was almost that of a child. Begging now.

'No . . . see her sooner if you don't, eh? Go . . .' Konstantin said. And Ryzhkov tried to smile, tried to hide the fact that, yes, soon it would be over. That soon, too soon now, they would go.

'Kostroma . . .' Hokhodiev said again after a moment. The twigs caught in a series of little chained crackles and Dima began fanning them into flames with his hand. 'That's where we met,' Hokhodiev said. Ryzhkov knew it, of course. Knew it well. 'Thirteen, the time we met, well . . . when I first saw her . . .'

'Just thirteen?' he said, knowing what response was expected of him.

'. . . beautiful girl . . . and . . . afraid of me, eh?'

'Mmm . . .'

'. . . swimming there . . .' he said and faded away for a moment.

'Swimming?' Ryzhkov said, trying to keep him in the dream.

'Give him a little water,' Dima whispered. The fire sputtered. It wasn't going to last long.

'. . . swimming down the river from . . . from . . .'

'Griette's . . .'

'. . . from the . . . silk works and we didn't know about that, eh?' He thought he saw Hokhodiev nodding, a little movement, as if he was laughing. Kostroma, Ryzhkov remembered, suddenly seeing the river, children playing in the waters. Wishing that Hokhodiev had stayed there. He could have worked there, he would be in Griette's huge mill right now, living in the town with Lena and maybe even children. Right now he would be hard at work on the shop floor, instead of bleeding to death in a shepherd's hut on a Serbian hillside. A big happy man bringing in steady money.

But he and Lena had wanted to see the city, he'd told Ryzhkov once. He had always wanted to live in a metropolis; even with its mills Kostroma had been too Russian for him.

And now, here they were.

'. . . and . . . then when we came out we were all blue, from here, down . . .' Hokhodiev laughed thickly, the head bobbing just a time or two. 'Blue . . .' he said again.

'Rest now, rest now, Kostya.'

'. . . and, you know, tried everything . . .'

'Rest now.'

'. . . to get ourselves clean . . .'

Ryzhkov tried to watch him now, but tears were in his eyes and he could only see Konstantin as a blur, just an outline resting against the dirty floor of the hut.

'. . . a child in Kostroma . . .' Hokhodiev said again, very slowly. Sleepily. As if he were thinking about it, considering it very carefully. Something fragile and miraculous, that everlasting blue stain from long ago.

'Ahh . . .' said Dima after a long moment, turning away. 'Ah . . .' he said again.

And then Hokhodiev was quiet. His head slowly dropping down, all his blood leaking away.

Ryzhkov sat and watched him for a long time. As if they were both caught between heartbeats, as if there was no other universe but one man dead, and another man watching. As if all the talking was gone, as if it had never happened, none of it. A void where the living used to be; the memories, the jokes, the lies. Just a life gone out with no answer from the heavens.

The fire had died out, only a few wisps of smoke curling towards the broken ceiling. Dima got to his feet and stood in the doorway for a moment and then went outside.

They carried Hokhodiev's body out of the little building, hurrying as they did it, because they were visible to anyone coming along the road from either direction. They placed him on the ground, behind a rock, took his papers, divided the money, and then covered him with stones. It went quickly. Stones were plentiful on the hillside and they both worked swiftly, wanting it to be over.

When it was done they stood there for a moment, the wind rising and chilling them through their sweaty clothes.

'Goodbye friend. God bless you.' Ryzhkov looked over at Dima who met his eye and just shook his head. 'Goodbye, old man. I'll see you soon,' he said quietly.

From the summit they could see the clouds rushing up against the hill, darkening. To the north there was a dark grey fan of rain falling against the rising ground.

'Well . . .' Dima said.

'I guess we should . . .'

'It's over now, yeah-yeah?' Dima said.

'Oh, yes. Over. Where are you going?'

'I was thinking . . . Greece. Should be able to get there from Nis, right? There ought to be a train running south from there, I think.'

'Mmm.'

'Get down there, get new papers down there, maybe go to Italy . . .'

'Mmm . . .' he said, watching the rain sweeping over the ridgeline. On the other side of the mountain he could see the curve of a river as it ran . . . down to Nis, probably he thought.

'What about you, Pyotr? You want to come along?'

'No.'

'Where are you going?'

'Back.' He turned and looked at the younger man.

'You're crazy, you know that?' Dima looked away from him, dug a toe into the dirt there by Hokhodiev's grave. 'Trying to get revenge on Evdaev or expose him, whatever you're dreaming, that's a purely crazy idea, Pyotr. No one is going to believe you.'

'I know.'

'And there's your friend, too . . . so . . . you'd better take this,' he reached behind and pulled Hokhodiev's pistol out of his belt, held it out. At first Ryzhkov just stared at it. 'If you're going back to Piter in these circumstances, you'll probably need it, right?'

Ryzhkov shook his head, then reached out and took the gun. It was irrevocable, he thought. Like a compass needle swinging back northward. 'I don't know, Dima. You're probably right.'

'I know I'm right. I'm going to Greece. Get a job mending telephones. One day, if the two of you get out of all this you can tell them you were once so lucky to know Vladimir Dudenko,' he said and reached over and gave Pyotr a push on the shoulder.

'I'll tell the grandchildren.'

'Sure, sure you will. But I understand. You're crazy and . . . it's unfinished business, I suppose, yeah?' Dima looked at him.

'Yes.'

'Well.' Dima stepped over and embraced him, surprisingly strong, stepped back and gave him a little slap on the cheek. 'Let's not grow old here, let's get to Nis, then . . . brother.'

And hurrying then, they walked down to the horses, picking their way down the stony slope like elderly men with bad joints, Ryzhkov thinking that Dima was probably right, that going to Greece was the smart thing to do, the safe thing. Going to Greece, or Italy or anywhere outside of Russia was something that he should have done long, long ago. And he found himself moving quickly now over the uneven ground, starting to panic, worried that someone, some shepherd with his dog might find the grave within the next few hours, that now his time, too, was running out.

He dropped Dima near the station, a quick wave and then the boy was gone around a corner, his coat dangling over his shoulder, a spring in his step and a last narrow smile as he headed for a new life.

Ryzhkov drove behind the station, pulled the carriage into the first lane he came to, pried loose the number tag from the back of the carriage and threw it over the railing into the brown waters of the river, walked a few streets away and pushed Hokhodiev's identity papers down a gutter.

Deeper in the city he bought a traveller's trunk, a blank journal, a box of pencils, and a pair of reading glasses. There was enough money left, so he could stop at a tailor's and have a summer suit made in the local style. By evening he had transformed himself into a facsimile of a touring poet-artist, complete with a sweet-smelling shave and haircut, and so he was ready to tell the man at the station barriers that he was en route to Belgrade where he would take the riverboat along the Danube as far as he could—a great adventure—all the way to the Black Sea and the land of the Moldavians.

The ticket-seller laughed at him. 'There's nothing but swamps there,' he said and stamped the tickets. 'A man could get lost and just end up going round and round for the rest of his life!' He pushed the tickets through the little window, shook his head and laughed again.

And Ryzhkov laughed with him.

FORTY-ONE

Men. Sometimes, most times, they are impossible. She cannot read him, and honestly, if she were to allow herself that luxury, that rare privilege mostly unknown to her, since she has constructed her life with Sergei out of a tissue of half-lies, shared flatteries and, well . . . dreams that they have both given voice to, but never taken the trouble to realize—if she were to somehow throw all that aside to let herself be honest, honest just for a moment, then she could only arrive at the conclusion that he has fallen . . . honestly, into insanity.

For instance, he does not sleep. Not for nearly two weeks. He reads and re-reads the newspapers obsessively. He spends all his time in the tiny room, his special room. The telegraph chatters continuously. She has Anna bring up food, tea, and she takes it to him herself, a girlish rapping at the door, the bookcases pulled aside—she has to put the tray down to do this, the hidden door is so heavy, and then without looking, lest he think she was spying on him, she passes him the sustenance. Sometimes he barely notices, other times he sits back and stares at her, not recognizing. And the room stinks now, stinks of his sweat and his cigars, is piled with papers and torn tapes from the machines that he's installed. She can't wait to get out, to tell the truth. But then he sits back and thanks her, smiling. Profusely. Smiling.

Of course it is all to do with the events in Bosnia. A prince has been killed, the archduke. She met him once. Met Rupert too. The whole damned family of block-heads. Thick unimaginative people, she thought. The one she's sad for is Sophie, with whom she can identify, after all she was a commoner, whom he married for love and thus began all his problems. Love. At least she had that at the end.

But today he is happy.

A man and his wife are shot down in the street and he is happy? She tries to understand this, puts on her aggrieved face, pouts, and even in her tone of voice, challenges him.

He just laughs, dismisses her. In his eyes she's a poor little ignorant ornament. Something bright and bubbly to trot out when he feels like getting dressed up. Too stupid to understand the affairs of great men of the world and their fancy machines that are so up-to-date that they have to be hidden away in a cupboard in their mistress's house.

She doesn't know anything about the world, he says. He says it outright! 'You don't know anything about the world,' with that condescending laugh he uses when he wants to change the subject. As if she had never been anywhere, as if she was a peasant instead of someone who had performed all over Europe, even toured to the United States and Brazil. That's not knowing about the world, though. That's not crafty enough for him. 'Forget trying to learn . . .' And then a furious clatter, suddenly there are more telegrams that interrupt them, and he pulls the bookcase closed.

He's made a killing, recently.

She knows that much. She knows he's sold shares, lots of shares in advance of the assassination, and he's just waiting now, waiting to pounce . . . waiting to buy. Waiting to plunge back in when the market reaches the bottom. She knows all that, she can hear all that. He talks on the telephone and she can hear, can't she? She knows he's into something with Nestor Evdaev and that it all hinges on 'making a show' somewhere over something. She knows about making a show.

Angry at him, bored with him too, she goes out for a walk, an excursion to look for a little peace but it turns out to be a mistake. Suddenly Petersburg is ugly. It comes in the form of a demonstration that interrupts her tram across town. A strike she thinks, metalworkers or newly organized peasants from one of the textile mills who want more money, better food, improved lodging in the company dormitories. Well, who can blame them? But then she sees that the crowd is massing directly in front of the German embassy, screaming repeated choruses of rhymed insults at the building. High in the façade she can glimpse embassy personnel alternately clustering near the windows and then retreating back into the shadows for safety.

As the disturbance is filling the street and preventing the tram from progressing, she decides to get out and make her way around the edge of the demonstration. Of course, men help her, a woman in distress. They can howl and shake their fists at the windows as much as they want, but a pretty face will still bring their eyes down to earth. She

wonders if it will turn violent. No one is throwing anything at the façade, although it is an ugly enough building.
The embassy is brand-new, with a headstone-like façade,
long rectangular windows with shockingly muscled
statues of naked men holding up the cornice. The whole
thing is heavy and imposing, an edifice meant to inspire
fear, and obviously designed to deliberately clash with its
surroundings. Perhaps it was the design they are disputing,
perhaps it is a mob of insulted young architects and their
parents and friends who have come out to protest. Now
that would be civilization.

Swaying in the street above her are banners calling
for an *End to Teutonic Provocation!* and *Save Our Slav
Brothers!* Many of the banners are painted on red cloth,
the mark of various union organizations or radical
political groups, she knows that much! She moves
through the crowd, who are chanting with arms linked
as they move in a wide circle around the front of the
hideous building. On the steps of the embassy a long
double-line of St Petersburg gendarmes wait for the
bravest of the firebrands to make a dash up the steps
where they will be arrested and taken directly to the
police wagons. In a way it's beautiful, invigorating.
Passionate.

By the time she walks through the demonstration she
has learned what it is all about. Everything can be read
on the front of the *Berliner Tageblatt*—a long rant by the
Kaiser, accusing Russia of deliberately fomenting a
general European war. Of course, peace-loving Germany
has no aggressive intentions or even any ill-will towards
the quaint Muscovites, but should the Tsar succumb to
his base instincts and unleash his dark hordes of
cossacks, Germany would naturally be forced to defend
herself.

She almost laughs in disbelief. The tone of the article is nasty, insulting, the kind of thing men say in bars when they want to goad each other into a fight. Full of obvious incitements and taunts, and pitched to inflame Russia's old inferiority complex about her Tartar past. On top of it is the smug assurance that should the irrational Muscovites succumb to their animalistic impulses and plunge the two nations into war, the efficient German General Staff will easily sweep the Tsar's forces from the field. The Kaiser . . . what an ego-maniac, she thinks.

Now she hears the clash of hooves against the cobbles and sees a troop of cossacks assembling at the end of the street. The crowd, if they knew what was good for them, would surely begin to disperse before the troops ride over them wielding their leaded knouts, it doesn't do to infuriate those fellows, and so she pushes her way through the masses, hurrying away, angry and wondering all the time what he's had to do with all this chaos.

And then she finally gets back, and he's still upstairs in his little snake-pit. Now all the laughter is gone and he is screaming into the telephone.

'What do you mean, you can't find him?' And then waiting for a reply. A curse. He runs one of his beautiful hands through his beautiful hair. He needs a bath. He needs someone to make love to him.

'You've telephoned, have you sent someone around? What do the servants say?' A pause, another curse. 'Just do what you're supposed to do, you know what's expected of you,' he says. His tone more controlled now, like talking to a stupid child. 'No, I am troubled too. No one wants trouble. Yes. It's very troublesome,' trying to calm someone. It must be Nestor. He only talks to princes with that tone of voice. 'I don't know. They'll have to replace him, probably, wouldn't you think?' he says, the sarcasm plain in his voice. Disgusted, she moves away into the bedroom. He hasn't even noticed. Probably didn't even know she'd gone out for a walk. Now something has gone wrong, someone is missing, someone isn't where he should be, and all the conniving in the world can't supply him with any answers. Happiness has taken flight and whatever he's been up to, it's all coming unglued.

She knows that much.

FORTY-TWO

Princip was the name of the assassin. Gavrilo Princip. A student. An anarchist. A Serb terrorist. And now he was famous, now the name Princip was on the tip of everyone's tongue all over the world. The details of the conspiracy were vague but there had been no fewer than a dozen anarchists, the newspaper claimed. Ryzhkov read the reports in a week-old version of *Wiener Zeitung* as he was steaming along the coast of the Black Sea from Rumania to Odessa. The decks were baking and the air was fetid. The fumes of coal smoke hung in the air and made a brown haze across the still waters. It was as if they were sailing across an infinite lake, on a voyage to nowhere.

In Odessa he found what he wanted, a cheap hotel where he could wait while he changed identities again. A safe-house where he stored his single bag, hiding Kostya's pistol beneath layers of his underwear.

He prowled the city until he discovered a suitable bar, the kind of place where travellers came to drink and be relieved of their money by con-men and prostitutes. On the first night there was no one suitable so he went back to the hotel. Waited, bought more newspapers.

The truth penetrated in scraps. Austria was bellicose, Serbia was looking for a way out. Rumours had it that war had already begun, that the British were on the march through Afghanistan.

The city was too hot. Empty of tourists and the sane. No one would visit Odessa in the summer unless they had some compelling reason. Because of the heat he changed his schedule. Now he slept during the day and went out at night until he found the one he was looking for.

He was about the same height, the same size. A happy fellow, a laugher and a storyteller. He was attempting to purchase land for the construction of a new hotel on the beachfront. But now, with international tensions, his investors were becoming hesitant. It was a waiting game, he explained sadly. The whole world was waiting. Ryzhkov agreed, stood him round after round of drinks. After a while they developed a plan, to visit the bordello that Ryzhkov said he had found. The best. The man smiled.

It was dawn when they escaped the bar, the light made them squint and hold their hands over their eyes like outcasts from a doomed Old Testament city. He pushed the man down in the mouth of the first alley they came too, the empty bottle spinning its frantic glassy song on the paving stones. It only took a few moments for Ryzhkov to riffle through his pockets, dig out his papers and money and get away.

He stopped at the end of the street and inspected the documents. An identity card, with a description that was close enough. A district permit to reside in Moscow.

All of it looked genuine enough. He read the name over and over, memorized his new birthdate. It turned out he was from the city of Saratov. He had never been there, he would have to look it up.

He tucked the papers into his pocket and looked around the street. The morning sun was behind him. It made his shadow long, made his legs look huge and strong. A giant, a super-man. A man ready to take on the world.

Go then *Pravdin, Pavel Vasilyevich*. Go into the bloody new world.

By nine o'clock he'd settled his bill at the hotel and was on the first train north.

A light snapped on and the bottom tier of corridors at 40 Furshtatskaya Street was illuminated. The custodian straightened his jacket and tried to wipe the sleep out of his eyes, fumbled for his pen and keys and waited until his junior was in place behind the desk. The boy was tall and gangly with a faint smear of dark hairs across his lip that had ambitions to one day become a moustache. He looked up at the fox-like man who had arrived and his eyes were unblinking with fear and awe at being in the presence of someone so lofty. Everyone had heard that the commander was missing, everyone knew that changes were in the offing. And now Baron Rudolph Nikolsky was here!

Yes there were rumours, even in such a clandestine organization as the Okhrana. Nikolsky had been recently elevated, tipped as the broom that was going to sweep the Okhrana clean, but no one knew who the Tsar would pick to replace General Gulka on a permanent basis. Changes were in the wind, but knowing it all in advance still hadn't prepared the custodian for the shock. He raised his pince-nez to his eyes, tried to find the location of the room Nikolsky was looking for.

'I know where it is, excellency,' the boy piped up.

Nikolsky looked over at him. 'All right then, you show me. Give him the keys. How do you know it?'

'I was often on duty in the early hours, and General Gulka frequently used the room at those times.'

'Do you know what he was doing there?'

'No, excellency. He would arrive, sometimes stay for an hour or two—'

'It's all in the books,' the senior man snapped. Nikolsky looked over at him, thinking that he was already on his way to an assignment on the border, he just didn't know it yet.

'Yes, it would be in the sign-in book,' the boy said, and bowed reflexively and shut up. The older man handed him the keys and they went off down the long hallway.

'Anything else?'

'Often he would ask for tea. I would bring him tea, take away the cart afterwards.'

'He came alone?'

'Yes. It would be in the book as well, excellency,' he said quietly and then fell silent until they arrived at the door. 'It is a special electrical lock, excellency. It requires a code before the key can be inserted.'

Nikolsky sighed. 'Of course. Very well, go back and call the men upstairs.' He had brought two locksmiths, and when they were stymied by the lock and mistakenly fired it, so that it fused the metal together and they had to drill out the cylinders, he sent the custodian upstairs to keep everyone out of the halls and let the boy keep an eye on the men while they did their work. The door was

sheathed in steel and to force it required a great deal of
hammering. Nikolsky tried to doze in the chair at the
end of the hall. Admittedly it was a superb chair; a
warm, well-padded leather chair meant for passing long
hours in the service of the Tsar, and sitting in it,
Nikolsky could not honestly begrudge the custodian his
lassitude. But they would all be much more fatigued yet,
before it was over.

Finally the boy came back. 'They've opened both
doors, excellency. I made sure they touched nothing.'

'What's in there?' said Nikolsky, getting up and
hurrying down the hall.

'I saw nothing, excellency,' the boy said, which
Nikolsky thought was probably not the whole truth.

The locksmiths were waiting halfway along, and
Nikolsky had the boy make them wait; if there was a
vault inside he would need them again. He went into the
first room, really nothing more than an ante-chamber.
There was a desk there, just as there would be if a clerk
or receptionist were on duty, but it had been pushed back
against the wall with no chair. Fixed into the corridor
wall was a drop-box and Nikolsky went over and looked
inside. There was a series of daily reports and he opened
the one on the bottom, the earliest that Gulka hadn't
picked up; it bore the date of his disappearance.

The second room was larger. Fitted out with a
padded chair, even more comfortable than the
custodian's, and a settee with a pillow and blankets. A
lamp for reading, a long table that held piles of
paperwork, various files and dossiers. A glance at their
spines told Nikolsky the level of secrecy. A thorough,
ongoing investigation of . . . and then he turned and saw
how Gulka had arranged the walls of the room, and the
faces of the men he had been investigating.

He recognized Andrianov immediately and had already started across to the bulletin board which held his own photographs and documents, when the other faces stopped him. Evdaev, whom he had not seen since the wedding reception at the Gorchakovs, looking as noble as a Lippizaner, a second man he vaguely remembered, a foreigner, an embassy official . . . Yes, the Bulgarian attaché, Smyrba, who had lately been recalled to receive instructions from his government. There were two more men he did not know. An older one, perhaps someone's father, with white whiskers and a bare pate, and then a panel pinned with photographs of an ordinary man of the streets. His attention was drawn to it, purely because of its poverty and he moved across the room and looked more closely at the panel, then reached up and unpinned the man's Okhrana identity photograph and put it in his jacket pocket.

He had the men install new locks while he searched through the papers, bagged what he needed, lit a fire in the furnace in the corner and burned his own dossier that Gulka had begun to assemble. When they were done he snapped off the lights and closed the doors behind him, using his own code for the buttons. The custodian had come back and stood there with his clipboard. He was wide awake now, trying to smile and look competent. He ticked the rooms off the list.

'I'll hold on to these,' Nikolsky said as he pocketed the keys and started down the hall.

'Yes, excellency.'

'My level, restricted just as before. If there's an expanded list of recipients I'll give it to you in due course.'

'Yes excellency.'

'It's pathetic, you know that?' Nikolsky said.

'Yes, excellency?'

'We recruit the best men in the service, everything is fine and then, suddenly . . .' he shrugged. The custodian nodded in sympathy, as if he understood the great tragedy of human frailty within the secret services.

'It just goes to prove that even good men, even the very best men can go bad,' Nikolsky said. 'Temptation,' he intoned 'say nothing about this, eh? You see . . . we may have a matter that goes before the special courts,' he whispered, tapping the man on the chest and inclining his head down in the direction of Gulka's secret rooms. 'There are the requirements of evidence, you see?'

'Ahh. Quite right, then entry is restricted to only you, excellency.'

'Correct. I may have to seal the rooms, who knows?' Nikolsky gave the man a smile, a reassuring pat on the back, then headed up the stairs. He would deconstruct Gulka's labyrinthine investigation and, if what he learned caused a scandal that brought down a few nobles, or shook up a few ministries, so be it. The boy was waiting at the top. He bowed and made way for Nikolsky's exit.

'You're working for me, now. You're my assistant, understand?' Nikolsky said, and took him by the arm.

'Yes, of course, excellency. Thank you—'

'Have this man brought to my office immediately.' He fished in his jacket and handed Zezulin's photograph to the boy. 'He's been reassigned somewhere I think, look it up, find him, have him arrested if you have to. Under my authority.' He stopped at the desk and signed himself out, tossed his disc down at the barrier. The boy watched him for a moment and then did the same, smiling. Nikolsky handed the boy his card, wrote

Zezulin's name across the back, signed it and gave it to the boy. 'Under my authority,' he said and started towards the doors, the new keys making a disturbing weight in his trouser pocket.

FORTY-THREE

In Pyotr's dream the world was burning.

Above the ashes of the cities he could see the dismembered bodies of the citizenry. He could see children running, miraculously spared the fires, but terrorized by fear and abandonment; running like chickens caught in a yard with a weasel, chaotically, looking over their shoulders. Above them great winged vultures were soaring. Waiting, preparing to strike.

Ryzhkov was with them, like all the rest, running away. Like all the rest, trying to escape the claws on the cobbles behind him, the hot breath of the advancing predator. Crying out, he spun away from his pursuers, and spun away into a different world, spun away into wakefulness.

And that, he thought, in some ways was worse.

The landscape was tedious, unending rolling fields of the Ukraine. The carriage was sweltering and he was dehydrated from all the drinking the night before. Pravdin, he remembered. Pavel Pravdin.

In the dining-car he met an old woman with her blind granddaughter. The girl was fourteen, straight and serious. Her eyes seemed to look in different directions at once. Her hearing was very acute the old woman said, as she told their story. The girl found her food on the plate by touch, her manners were impeccable. They were on their way to Moscow to consult a famous medium. The girl could see ghosts, the old woman said.

'Truly?' Ryzhkov asked her.

'Yes,' the girl said. 'There are many riding with us in this carriage at this very moment.'

He returned to his seat and fell asleep against the hot window. All the windows were open, and each time he awoke he felt like a dried prune. He ran into the old woman and her clairvoyant granddaughter in the station, and seized with a sudden wave of paranoia he sold the balance of his ticket in Kharkov and changed to a direct train for Petersburg.

They had only just pulled away from the Kharkov Station when the executioner asked if he could share the compartment with him.

The man wasn't the least bit reluctant to talk about his profession. He told Ryzhkov about the mechanics of hanging, how they took the one who was about to die up on to the gallows, the physics of the noose and the drop. The condemneds' attitudes towards the priests' blessings, the last words. At Schlusselburg they used a gallows installed at one end of an old stable, the man said. It was always cold in that region and it was better to perform the executions indoors. Warmer, out of the rain. There was no danger the mechanism would freeze. It made it easier on everyone.

Without his black mask the executioner was a smooth-faced man of middle age, a man who looked, Ryzhkov thought, like anyone else one might meet, a shopkeeper, or a minor bureaucrat. He had inherited the job from an uncle nearly twenty years earlier, he said, and during his career he had been called upon to hang exactly seventy-three persons, sixteen of whom were women.

He said the number with a little smile, as if it was something that he was proud of, but didn't want to boast about. The answer came easily, practised, one of the things everyone wanted to know about the job.

He was a religious man, he said. With a family. Newly become a grandfather, the result of his long marriage and six children, all of whom were doing well. The youngest girl was the wild one of the lot, his favourite, an artist who had moved to Copenhagen to study. Being an executioner did not pay all that well. The fees had gone up over the years, but he supplemented his income by taking a second job.

'Why don't you stop? All the—'

'Yes. My wife wants me to stop, she can't imagine that it does me any good. She makes me wash after,' he said with a shrug. 'I suppose she's right, but . . .' For the first time the executioner had the beginnings of a frown across his brow. 'You see . . . I can do this, it's not something that I enjoy, but it's necessary, and I can do it. Can you imagine someone doing it who loved it? Or who brought an attitude of . . . vengeance? I meet them the night before when I weigh them, I ask their forgiveness, and describe what I can do for them. I try to put them at ease.' The executioner paused, looked at the open fields that stretched to the horizon.

'I see,' said Ryzhkov.

For a long time they said nothing.

The executioner slept, snoring lightly on the seat across from him. Later in the day they ate together and the executioner excused himself. He had to get off at Kursk. Only family business, he said with a little smile.

'You said you asked for their forgiveness,' Ryzhkov said. 'Do they give it to you?'

'Oh, yes. Nearly always.'

At Kursk he helped the man with his rather heavy suitcases. 'It's been a pleasure meeting you, sir,' the executioner said, a little out of breath, after they had trudged the length of the platform. A gendarme stepped out from a barrier and blocked their way, roping off that portion of the platform. Another train had come into the station and was being given priority.

'Oh, my . . .' said the executioner. They put the bags down and waited with the other passengers while a crowd of young peasant boys, still in their rough clothes, lined up in long ranks. Perhaps a hundred of them. Looking around with their open faces, shaking off their sleep. Now Ryzhkov saw that all around them, on the lampposts, on the railings of the station, around each of the windows were garlands of bunting with little shields representing the hereditary arms of Russia.

'What's all this?' he asked a gendarme.

'Haven't you heard the news sir? The red cards are going up soon. On Tuesday they put out the call for the technical battalions. It's the start of mobilization,' the man said with a smile. Russia's peasant armies were beginning to form. 'The President of France, Monsieur Poincaré, is visiting the capital, too, eh? You know, discussing strategy with the Tsar so we can get together and crush those filthy Huns, eh?' And now the policeman laughed and walked a few paces away to patrol the other end of his rope.

Over by the platform someone screamed a command

and the lines of boys straightened up and tried to look serious.

He watched a sergeant and his officer inspect the boys. It seemed to go on for quite some time, and the scene was novel enough that gradually a small crowd gathered to watch. The boys were growing up before his eyes. Now the sly looks were gone. Now their baby faces were hardened, scowling. Their shoulders thrown back, chests open to whatever challenge was coming their way.

He and the executioner stood patiently and watched the whole thing, the sergeant and his officer walking the ranks, stopping at each boy, grilling them, encouraging them, correcting them. Soon their clothes would be shucked off and replaced with khaki. Soon, instead of carrying the pathetic parcels their mothers had pressed on them the day before, they would be shouldering their long bayoneted rifles. Soon you wouldn't be able to tell them apart.

The officer came out on to the platform, the sergeant saluted, spun around and screamed a new command. The boys all turned, raggedly, a little awkwardly. Another command and they began to march, all out of step, towards their train.

The gendarme untied his rope and Ryzhkov and the executioner continued along the platform with their bags. 'Well, good luck to you, Monsieur Pravdin. Godspeed,' the man said happily.

'And you, sir.' Ryzhkov returned his handshake and watched him cross the street and take a shortcut through a little barrier of shrubbery that separated the tracks from the houses of the city.

The crowd had begun to disperse. Whistles were sounding from the Petersburg train. For a moment he stood there on the platform with everything swirling around him. He could still leave, he could still save himself. Disappear. Buy a ticket. With the additional money he had stolen from Pravdin he had enough. Enough to run away. Go on, he said to himself. Go on, you've done what you can, you've already given your life for a Tsar who couldn't have cared less. You tried, you failed. But you tried.

Something caught his eye and he saw the executioner across the street waving to him, and he raised his hand to return a goodbye salute as the man disappeared into the throng. Ryzhkov saw that the city fathers had decorated everything with bunting. The colourful fabrics had been tied up everywhere, on the lampposts all along the street and even on the carriages that were swarming in front of the station. Everyone was smiling, a thrill of electricity had engulfed the whole station. In the distance a band was practising the *Marseillaise*. It was an exquisitely beautiful day.

It was so beautiful, he thought, that it brought tears to his eyes.

Vera caught sight of herself in the bright sun reflected off a shop window. She hated the reflection and turned away, crossing over one more street, walking along until she came to a large rambling shop that housed several dressmakers. She debated for a moment about going up to La Fleur on the Nevsky. It would be the best, but she was not shopping for the best. Just something she could afford, something more conservative, something that wouldn't stand out. She was tired of standing out. She put on her smile and went through the doors, cheerfully greeted the madam and told her that she wanted to purchase a suit.

'Something fit for travelling. Something lightweight but still . . .'

'Distinguished,' said the woman finishing her sentence. 'Elegant . . .'

'But nothing too . . .'

'Frivolous? I have just the thing,' she said giving Vera a brief appraisal and then vanishing into her stock room.

She idled along the tables and racks, letting her fingers travel over the textures of the cloth. The woman returned and in a few minutes Vera was trying on a brown travelling suit, of linen, with a wide skirt for the summer. It was the kind of thing that wouldn't show dust or grime from a long journey by rail or coach.

She put it on, while the woman made clucking noises behind her. Turned from side to side and steeled herself to meet her own gaze in the mirror. It would be better if she were blonde, she thought. She could go to Puli's salon and have her hair coloured, her brows bleached. The suit would look better then.

'I'll take it,' she smiled to the woman. And yes, the fit was nearly perfect. There were only slight alterations required on the hem, and for an extra five roubles Vera said she would wait. There were shoes to match and a hat, something that would guard against the sun. She found what she wanted almost immediately. The woman bustled away, happy at the easy sale.

Vera sat in the little foyer of the shop while her clothing was being prepared. Stared out at the street traffic. No dark carriages lurking at the corner. No men standing in doorways smoking cigarette after cigarette. No one looking through the windows searching for a secret policeman's girlfriend.

She wondered where he was and then stopped herself as soon as she was conscious of the thought, put him out of her mind like a broom sweeping across the threshold. The sun poured through the window and she watched the motes of dust rise and fall.

Now Pyotr was a dust mote, or as free as a dust mote. On the run, of course. Being pursued by his fellow secret policeman, a target waiting for his assassin. Death could come at any moment; may have come already for all she knew. He might have been captured, put up a fight or foolishly tried to run . . . that would be the lie the ones who killed him would tell—but maybe he was, for now—free.

So, maybe she was free, too. Free of all that, at least. Well, she'd lost all her family things, the half-dozen pieces of furniture she'd inherited, when she'd been made to leave her aunt's, and if she tried to made a stink Varvara was the type who would hire an attorney and tell everybody about her exciting background with her heels in the air. Get the gendarmes to talk to Izov, have someone come around and check her residency permit and maybe send her back to Yekaterinoslav.

So, to hell with the furniture and those keep-sakes, to hell with Pyotr Ryzhkov, God bless him where ever he was. She would be free, step out into the new electric world and begin all over again one more time. It was a giddy sensation. A kind of insanity. A sudden recognition and learning of something brand-new and a lot more profound than a dance step. Maybe she had never known anyone who was free, she would have never recognized them if she had.

The woman came out and apologized for the length of time the alterations were taking; Vera waved her away with a smile, she could sit there all week she thought. Sit there for the rest of her life.

She leaned her head back against the pillar that supported the window and began to dream about her escape. She had more than sufficient funds to leave the country, that was no problem. She might have enough money for a year in Italy, enough to pay the fee for a visa, enough to take classes, to become established. It would work, she thought as she closed her eyes. Smiling in the closeness of the room, with the perfume of expensive fabrics all around her.

She would leave a note for Pyotr, on the off-chance that he came back. That was fair enough. A postcard, a seascape from Capri or Corfu, or Corsica, or somewhere exotic and warm. She'd leave it in an envelope with Izov, they were such good friends. And then? Well, it was up to him. By that time she'd be on the way to something better, something where she didn't have to watch out for every last kopek. He'd be sorry, but . . . those were the breaks. He should have seen it coming, should have got out too. She would have gone with him if he'd asked. All he had to do was ask. Well, that was his loss, wasn't it?

And if he did find her? Then he'd want her to follow him, to take on a new future together, running away from men in black hats, a life of false names, forged papers that might evaporate beneath the first serious scrutiny. She would have to dance under an assumed name, move from city to city, live like a rat. The kind of men Pyotr swam with would not hesitate to reach beyond Russia's borders. They'd hunt both of them down and garrotte them if they ever discovered his hiding place.

And maybe that was why he was staying away.

Or maybe he was dead. But she couldn't think about that, couldn't imagine it. It just wasn't in the cards. Couldn't believe that someone like him, someone who knew the kinds of things he knew could . . . No, she thought.

No.

So, it was over then. And the sadness of it made her open her eyes to a summer's day turned cold and joyless. Made her aware that the cost of her freedom was losing him.

Gone.

She shifted in the chair, suddenly anxious. Angry at the delay in the back of the shop. There was a pile of old magazines sitting on the low windowsill, all of them thumbed through and dog-eared from countless readings. She was riffling through them when the madam came out and apologized again. Something wrong with the steam in their press. It had just been repaired. Her suit would be ready shortly. She saw Vera with the old magazines in her hand and an embarrassed expression crossed her face.

'Oh, mademoiselle, here is something much more current—' she handed Vera a pair of more recent magazines to look through. 'Moments away . . .' Smiling as she backed out.

The magazine on top was the latest issue of *Woman*, the popular weekly that was subtitled *Mother-Citizen-Wife-Housewife*. It took her about two minutes to thumb through. A useless rag packed with recipes and tips on how to affect the latest styles of make-up and hairdressing. All of it out of date. Who wanted to look like a Russian housewife? Beneath it was something better, a French fashion magazine, somewhat more general in its outlook. It had lithographs of fashions, the long silhouette was the newest style; she had anticipated the look with the dress that she'd worn to Fauré's big party. She suddenly choked. Tears sprang to her eyes. She dug a handkerchief out of her purse, dabbed at her eyes, tried to concentrate on the pages in front of her.

The magazine was much concerned with gossip and the doings of royalty. In the back was a long schedule of gala events planned all across Europe. She read that in June King George and the Kaiser were planning to be in Kiel for the annual regatta. The royal family of Spain had recently returned to Madrid. The King of Peru was visiting King Olav of Norway, just starting to learn how to ski. Peru had many mountains, the magazine claimed, and his serene majesty hoped to take the sport back to his country. In Austria, Emperor Franz Joseph was fully recovered from his illness, a bout of influenza which had sent shivers through the nation. At the height of the deathwatch, the heir to the throne—Archduke Franz Ferdinand—had been called back to Vienna in case the emperor succumbed.

She started at the words, the irony of what she had just read.

Now that same young archduke was dead, gunned down along with his wife, and everything had changed. It was all anyone talked about at the Komet. She'd read the papers. She hadn't even known where Sarajevo was, she'd barely even heard of the archduke. Now these two deaths peppered everyone's conversations. It was eerie to look at the magazine, written only a month before . . . before the killings. It was almost as if one could have seen it coming, could have seen it in the art, heard it in the crazy rhythms, almost as if it were pre-ordained. The newspapers were full of war fever and no one could read the future. Would common sense prevail? Diplomats were working overtime, while politicians railed against each other in print. There were conferences, notes were being exchanged and interpreted. Serbia would have to pay for her perfidy, but how much? Would Russia leap into the breach and support her brothers to the south? And how much? What was the price of peace, and who would pay it? The royal dynasties? The industrialists? Or would it be as it always had been—the peasants, the factory workers, the artists and the whores?

Maybe humans weren't so smart after all, maybe they were just lemmings with finer clothes.

'Ahh . . . Finally!' The madam whirled in, with the suit, immaculately pressed. Just for a moment Vera looked at the woman, not quite realizing where she was; absentminded and a little muzzy because of the sun, and because she had floated away with her musings on the rise and fall of the royal households of Europe.

'I'm so sorry for the wait, mademoiselle.'

'Oh, it's nothing. Quite all right.' She gave the woman an affectionate pat on the arm.

She ran her hands over the little jacket. It was good quality linen, and now that it had been freshly pressed, she would look like any travelling woman about to join her family abroad, or preparing for an excursion to Scandinavia. She smiled at the clothes. Her suit of armour, her cloak of adventure.

Her new life.

It would be better if she were blonde. Men liked blondes. They liked them because they were exotic and because they reminded them of little girls, fair and pure and unsoiled. They looked clean. If they were dangerous underneath, well, that was a plus. She would go to Puli's next. She looked at the woman. She was smiling as well, and suddenly they both laughed.

'You know,' Vera said, 'I'll change . . .'

'Yes?'

'Yes,' she said. 'I think I'll change right now.'

FORTY-FOUR

Now, for the condemned man, the city lay open. Splayed out in the summer light eyes wide, teeth bared, with not even the promise of a dark night within which to hide.

No one even looked at him as he walked, invisible, through the crowds. Why was everyone so happy? Everywhere people were smiling, there were sly looks, witticisms. Remarks that drew laughter. Arms were linked through arms. The street was a swarm of summer-dazzled Petersburgers strolling towards whatever awaited them, taking their sweet time; a sophisticated promenade of life. Not an umbrella in sight.

Ryzhkov moved through the crowds as if through a thick syrup, wafted along on the fetid smells from the canals, the reek of petrol exhaust, the sharp scent of a woman's perfume as he stepped aside to let her pass.

Boys were hawking newspapers, screaming things he couldn't decipher, important things. Things to which he should pay attention: the opening of the Panama Canal had already altered the balance of power; academics had proven the story of Noah and the flood to be true, rebels in Mexico had captured another city . . . Unrelated facts swarmed about Ryzhkov's head like gnats, thousands of things which would certainly change his life if—if only he would listen! But no one else was listening, why should he? He boarded a tram, a new electric one, for the long trip up the Nevsky. Even here, people were laughing, happy. Content, giddy, smugly satisfied—the whole range of bliss. One would never know, never suspect that . . .

The pistol was a thick lump in his jacket, grown warm from the heat of his body. His own warmth entering the frame of the pistol, the barrel, the clip of cartridges. Warming the powder, the heavy lead of each bullet. So warm that he could only feel it when he moved and it swung heavily against his chest. A part of him almost detached, then returning. *I am here, I am here with you* . . .

They waited while the Troitsky Bridge was lowered and he looked out of the window at the little white passenger steamers plying the river, the heavier cargo vessels on their way out to the Gulf. Gulls were sweeping along behind the boats, wheeling and diving for their food. Not a cloud on the horizon.

He had telephoned ahead to the barracks of the Guards.

Prince Evdaev was at his Petersburg residence, the duty officer had told him. Home awaiting orders. The operations of the army were strictly private, undoubtedly with the recent disturbances and the mobilization, the prince was very busy, and for security reasons they would tell him nothing more.

'Oh, well, I'll have to catch him later,' Ryzhkov said.

'Yes, I'm afraid he's a hard man to catch,' the officer said, his voice full of pride. Pride and defiance, Ryzhkov thought.

But hidden from all of them, from the other passengers on the tram, from Evdaev taking his midday nap with his mistress, from the squawking newsboys—the metronome was ticking. The sands were running out. Hidden from all of them, Ryzhkov was coming, an inevitable progression, coming closer. With each turn of the wheel, each house the tram passed on its relentless climb up Kamenoovstrovsky Prospekt. Closer . . . closer . . .

He watched the number plates on the buildings glide away behind him, the numbers ascending until, up ahead he saw the intersection of Kronyerkskaya. Ryzhkov stayed on the tram, got off at the next stop and walked back along the pavement. Only an old man sitting on a bench, glaring up as he walked by. Did he know? Could he see the pistol slapping into his ribs with each step?

Ahead of him was the orange bulk of Evdaev's venerable mansion; set a little way back from the street, approached through an arched gate, surrounded by modest gardens, and a finely crafted wrought-iron fence that defied the mind with its whorls and twisted leaves. He knew it well—the stable house with its guest apartments, where he had waited for Vera during her long night. He tried to put the thought out of his mind as he crossed a side street to the corner.

Pulled up beside the wrought-iron fence, a carriage, a small family crest on the side. Too far away to read, but somehow familiar. A quiet scene: the carriage waiting under the shade of the trees, the driver, even in the summer heat, smothered in his padded coat. Head dropped forward, sleeping like his horses. Everything calm.

Except for the gendarme at the front entrance. There would be another one somewhere at the back, he thought. He walked around; it was an old neighbourhood, great mansions of merchant and noble families of Russia, high walls, gardens gone to riot. New money that had moved into the occasional pile, sandblasted the walls and put in conveniences. Motorcars parked along the street in the shade, their tops pulled back. Tradesmen and their wagons making deliveries in the lanes.

He walked through the quarter for the remainder of the day, thinking it all through, stopped and ate at a modest restaurant and then tried to rest in the park. It was the white night, no darkness to hide in, just the glow that enveloped the city. He walked back towards Evdaev's street and then turned down the lane.

He had plenty of time. Time enough to walk down the entire lane and get a good look at the back of the mansion. It was older there, a wall that had been partially taken down and only repaired for a few feet of its length. To fill in the space someone had put up a rotting wooden fence there, and he climbed over finding his way behind a woodshed where he could see both the apartments over the stables and the main house, waited in the bushes, and tried to discover Evdaev's window.

He squatted there, took Kostya's pistol out and checked it, returned it to the pocket of his jacket. Thought about having a cigarette, but since he didn't have any he reached out and pulled out a strand of grass and chewed on the end of it, sat cross-legged there and watched the house and tried to learn its ways.

He sat there like that for perhaps an hour, he may have even slept. It was hard to tell, things were so warm and dreamy. Only an occasional bird crying out, trying to decide what time it was.

At some point a movement caught his eye. He came out of his reverie and saw a thin stream of smoke coming from an upstairs window on the end of the house—one of windows he thought most probable for Evdaev's personal quarters. It was early, and he realized that, like him, Evdaev must have been awake all through the bright night.

There was no one in the yard, no guards at the back doors, and he straightened and shook his legs out, like an athlete preparing for an important contest. When he could feel his feet again, he stepped out into the lawn and walked directly across to the stairs that led to an expansive terrace. It was the kind of place where you would take a girl out and look at the moonlight, but today it was a simmering oven of dark marble. He stood against the wall with his heart beating, looking back towards the kitchen and the servants' quarters. Nothing from the gardener's cottage, nothing from the garage, nothing from the stables.

He suddenly became aware that the house was empty and stepped over to the doors and peered through. Nothing. He tried one of the latches, but it was locked, tapped a pane of glass three times with his elbow until it cracked across the middle, then winkled out the shards of glass, reached in and unlocked the door.

He was in the ballroom of the great house. There was a circular settee that was covered with white dust sheets. The chandelier had been lowered on its pulley. The floor was dusty, as if the place had been abandoned or was caught up in some legal quagmire. Maybe Evdaev had left town.

He walked quietly but his weight still made clacking sounds on the parquet. When he got to the stairs he listened. Distinctly from the upstairs he heard the sounds of a gramophone. A long plaintive violin. Something tragic and Russian.

He started up the carpeted stairs, taking them two at a time. A pause at the landing to locate the source of the music, and then a few steps down the long corridor. He passed an open bedroom, the covers strewn all over the floor. A meal had been served in there and abandoned. A half-empty bottle of wine.

The music was coming from behind the next door and he fumbled in his pocket for the gun, jerking it free so that the fabric of his pocket tore, pulling back the hammer, and flinging open the wide double-doors to what turned out to be the library.

The room was darkened, only dusty light pouring in through narrow slits in the thick curtains, around the edges of the windows. The room was surrounded by tall shelves crammed with books that hadn't been read in a century; once it had been a working library, with a ladder on rollers to reach the highest shelves, wide tables to display the maps and atlases. A globe in one corner of the room was long out-of-date.

He could see Evdaev sitting in the large chair at the desk, it had been swivelled around so he could read something in the light from the window behind him. A curl of smoke from a forgotten cigarette still burning in the ashtray. A half-finished glass of brandy. Something nagged at his consciousness as he pushed through the door, and now Ryzhkov was walking, three steps over to the edge of the desk, raising his arm, planning to shoot him right through the back of the chair . . . but . . . something not right, not right at all. No . . .

'Congratulations,' said a voice from behind him, and he whirled and peered into the darkness. 'Put the gun down, please,' said the voice again and then he saw Evdaev, set up in a little hide he'd built out of books piled high around a desk in the far corner of the room, given away only by the dull silver gleam of the muzzle of his hunting rifle. Reflexively, Ryzhkov whirled again, but the man at the desk had not moved . . . and then he understood.

All done, then.

Behind the books Evdaev straightened. He was wearing a silk dressing-gown, his face stricken. Hair gone awry. He must have been living in the room for hours, for days . . . waiting. He had never actually seen Evdaev before, not closely. Now he was mesmerized by the flawless skin, the sharpened moustaches, the predator's eyes, the smile of triumph. His face like ice, shaking his head as he moved around from behind the books, the black hole of the muzzle growing larger with each step.

'Sergei, Sergei, Sergei . . . First he sends a killer, and then a new killer to check up on the first killer. He thinks I'm a fool. A coward, that's what he thinks. Poor Sergei. Now, please put the pistol on the floor, yes?'

The last grain of sand falling through the hourglass.

There was no choice, he did as Evdaev said, watching him as he walked about the room. He might have been tired from waiting for his quarry, but he moved smoothly, always balanced, the rifle held easily, confidently. Never wavering from Ryzhkov's chest.

'He doesn't have to send thugs to kill me, I was going to save him the trouble, but he wouldn't recognize something like that. He wouldn't know honour if it slapped him in the face.' Evdaev had reached the desk by the window and spun the chair with one hand. There was a body there, a man felled by what looked like one shot through the heart, a blank expression on his face, eyes open, an infinite stare like the stuffed heads that rimmed the ceiling of the room. A tradesman's face, something ordinary. And dead.

'He's starting to smell. We're going to move him out on to the balcony.' Evdaev gestured by pointing the rifle and Ryzhkov obeyed, moving to the corpse. There was hardly any smell at all, only the smell of the imagination, but the body was stiff. As he was levering the man out of the chair, his mind was racing through the possibilities. It was awkward carrying him, the legs caught under the desk and he had to push the chair back against the window. Evdaev kept his distance. He had all the time in the world. On the blotter was a sheaf of papers, as if the dead man had been writing a long letter but hadn't had a chance to finish.

'I'm here under house arrest, but . . . surely you know that,' Evdaev said with a little chuckle. He was looking away now, relaxing a little while Ryzhkov dragged the man across the carpet. He paused at the door and Evdaev reached forward to open the wide doors, used his toe to kick them open. 'Put him out there, by the flower boxes.'

The sun was boiling down. If there was no smell now, it wouldn't take long.

'Good, good. So . . . now I am trying to decide what to do with you,' Evdaev said. Ryzhkov lowered the dead man to the tiles, stood there waiting for instructions. 'Cover him up with this.' Evdaev stepped back into the library and dragged out a bearskin rug. It must have been twelve feet square, too heavy to pick up. Ryzhkov dragged it across the stones and draped it over the corpse. 'Now, what I think I am going to do, is get you to tell your side of the story, yes?'

Ryzhkov shrugged. He didn't have any idea what Evdaev was talking about.

'They called me back, they arrested me. I have no friends. What is it? Victory has a hundred fathers. Defeat? He's just a bastard.' A laugh, a shake of the head. 'After all the lies and the rumours, after all the shit that's been spread about me, the Tsar wouldn't even talk to me. He may still decide to hang me, it's treason after all. So . . .' There was a trace of a smile. Evdaev gestured for him to come in from the balcony. 'Here, sit. Pick up the pen. We're going to correct the record. You can write, can't you?'

'Yes,' he said, a touch of defiance creeping into his voice, then his knees buckled and he did as he was told. Found himself being enclosed by the soft volume of Evdaev's great leather chair.

'Excellent. Then take a blank sheet, put down your name, where you live . . . go on . . .'

Evdaev took a few steps back, leaned against one of the tables, the barrel of the rifle sinking lower. Now Ryzhkov could see the fatigue. 'It's all evidence, you see? Put down about how he first hired you, when you had your first meeting, how he filled your head with . . . *ideas*.' Evdaev was looking away. He straightened suddenly, not even really paying attention to Ryzhkov, even turning his back as he walked over and stooped to pick up the pistol from the floor, abandoning the heavy rifle on the library table. 'And make sure to include a summary of the investments he made on your behalf, how you were . . . persuaded, how you were a dreamer, a child . . . a girl listening to fairy stories.'

Ryzhkov had stopped writing and suddenly Evdaev spun screaming, 'Go on, put it all down! We don't have that much time, do we?'

He bent to the paper and started writing, trying to concentrate on his name, his address . . . he really didn't have either any more, did he?

'But be sure to write down how you got on to the train, how you were seduced, how you decided that you were going to *intervene*, that you were going to be the avenging angel . . . You don't know the *why* of any of this, do you? You don't have ideas, you don't see the future, you improvise instead of plan. You're an old woman! You're ruled by your *heart*, not your fucking head, man!' Evdaev reached out and knocked on Ryzhkov's skull with his knuckles. 'You're romantic, not *pragmatic*. No, worse!' Evdaev shook his head, laughing in little hisses. He wasn't looking at Ryzhkov any more, but around at the stacks of books, the cracked oil paintings, the antique flags dangling from the ceiling. 'Dumb as an ox . . .' He looked down to where Ryzhkov was struggling to compose his sentences.

'I love it! Sergei thinks he's so brilliant, and I've played him perfectly. You see, he knows nothing of war, real war. What it means to be a warrior. He doesn't understand the concept. A warrior doesn't mind dying, a warrior makes a pact with his God, to die on the field of battle, to give up his life for something higher. Sergei wouldn't give up anything unless it was in hard currency. He wants it all and then a percentage. And now he sends you people to hunt me down and shut me up? I love it.' Watching as Ryzhkov scribbled away on the note.

'People like him. Think you can do whatever you want, think you know what's best. And then you fall into the trap, the same trap we all made for ourselves, eh?' Ryzhkov looked up at him. 'Aren't you done yet? Use smaller words,' Evdaev said and turned away to wander through the library, still carrying the gun, walking easily like a fencer or a gymnast; a big man who was lighter on his feet than you might think. Even so, his attention would come in and out. After a moment Evdaev fell silent and there was only the scratching of the pen, then Ryzhkov would look up and Evdaev would be watching him.

'I ought to kill you like you people killed Gulka. That's what you deserve, an anonymous death, a simple *disappearance*, yes?' Evdaev said bitterly and took a step closer. 'I knew it, too. I knew it in my heart. I knew a bunch of merchants couldn't pull something like this off. You think, you really think that money and a few killers is all it takes to overthrow the greatest nation on earth?' For a moment Ryzhkov thought he was going to club him with the pistol. Then he stopped; there was a script somewhere he was following, a plan for the hunt, for sharing out the spoils and mounting the trophy. Probably there was no struggle written into it. Evdaev stood staring at him for a moment and then laughed. 'I told Alexandr Ivanovich that Sergei was soft, a fucking mama's boy, scared to go all the way. Now it's gone all wrong, and I knew it . . . *I knew it*.'

Evdaev's face contorted and then he did hit him, a sharp little slap with the side of the pistol that came so quickly that Ryzhkov didn't even see it. Everything went black for a moment and he fell back into the chair. There was a ringing in his ears that wouldn't go away; it sounded like a long continuous siren, or the howling of a dog that never ran out of breath, someone screeching on a flute . . . It didn't really hurt, but the first thing he saw when he opened his eyes were little dark circles of his own blood dripping on to his trousers.

Evdaev was still muttering. He had put the rifle down across the chart table. It was only a few feet away. A leap across the desk, a desperate lunge—across the carpet Evdaev had the pistol in his hands and was checking its action. 'Think I'm a *fool* . . . telephoning me, oh, yes . . . not to worry. We take care of our own. I'm sending someone over, Nestor. Not to *worry*. I *love* you. I'm sending money, the Andrianov companies will provide whatever is needed. After all, I'm your *friend*. I'm your *brother*,' Evdaev recited, his voice growing more constricted. Was he crying? In the gloom Ryzhkov couldn't see.

'So . . . three little letters, then. One from you, one from me, one from him out there. Everything nice and set out in good order, written clearly with signatures, and then Nicholas will know that I have not died with this stain on my honour. That I lived to serve Russia . . . and my Tsar.'

Evdaev was standing there with an ethereal smile on his face. He looked so peaceful that it happened automatically; an instinct to ingratiate, to grant him some kind of forgiveness, to speak a friendly word in his last moments, just like the executioner on the train had said. Or maybe it was just to keep him talking. To stall for time. 'Who was he?' Ryzhkov asked. 'Him? The one out there?' He inclined his head in the direction of the balcony.

Evdaev flinched. Shook himself like a dog. 'Shut up!' he suddenly screamed, and then whirled away from the view. 'Hurry up, damn it! Read it back to me—hurry up! I know there's more of your confederates watching! I know someone's out there waiting for you to finish the job. I'm not stupid!' Evdaev bellowed and then abruptly crossed behind the desk to check out the window to the gardens. 'It's a confession. Make your confession. "... and I freely admit that I, conspiring with others, did engage in acts of treason against his Most Holy Majesty"—Put that in.' Evdaev said and then turned and came back to the desk, looking at the papers, the eyes asking, *pleading* for something, whatever it was he thought would save . . . his honour. For an exit he could die with, for salvation.

'Go ahead . . . The ending—' Evdaev pushed the barrel of the gun against his neck.

'Yes, fine. I'll write it. What do you want me to say?' Ryzhkov said, a little peevishly. Maybe a little too peevishly.

'". . . and I name . . ."'

'Fine, fine,' he said, writing it.

'"Sergei Danilovich Andrianov as my associate and fellow conspirator . . ."' Watching as Ryzhkov made the name, the gun in the side of his head pushing him into illegibility.

'Good, good. Sign it.' And when his hand shook Evdaev pushed the muzzle against his neck, harder so that he was leaning over in the chair. 'Sign-the-fucking-letter!' he shouted.

Time stopped finally. Ryzhkov could see it stop. See the moment when there was *no moment*. The space between heartbeats, as he reached out with his pen to sign his name on the paper—the space between Evdaev's wheezing breath—a bird flicking from its resting place on the stonework of the balcony—his own eyes following the loops of his signature, the last act in the script.

'Here,' he said, signing the letter and gathering the papers up with one hand, as if to hand them to Evdaev and then——Ryzhkov was up now, launching himself out of the chair, his hand slapping the gun away from his own neck, pushing himself up into Evdaev who pulled the trigger an instant before they collided so that it felt like an explosion between the two of them, something bursting behind his head. The bullet slammed into the window, and then they were falling back against the doors, and the finely crafted mullions that could not hold their weight, and Ryzhkov was clawing to bend the gun back out of the bigger man's hand as they tumbled out on to the tiles of the balcony. As they landed he had turned the pistol away from himself and there was a second gunshot, Evdaev screamed and jerked away, a fountain of blood gushed on to the tiles and Ryzhkov saw that he had shot himself in the hand, losing his grip, the gun sliding away across the tiles, and . . .

And now . . .

Now, he was moving faster than light, moving faster than time. Faster than the sound of the shots.

Someone was shouting inside the house. Evdaev was shrieking for help, someone was pounding on the door. Maybe it was the confederate he didn't know about, maybe it was the servants, the gendarme, or some other friend of . . . Sergei's coming to take revenge. He stood and staggered back to the doorway. He had the gun now, the sheaf of papers was on the floor and he scooped them up. Evdaev was getting to his knees when he rushed him and jammed his knee into the man's face. It was like hitting brick, the sound was a hard crack and it echoed through the garden. His leg was suddenly numb. Behind him the door was breaking and there was no time, no more sand in the hourglass.

He stepped out on to the balcony, looked over the rail and immediately jumped into the softest place he could find, a trellis of roses that flanked a patio directly below him. The fall shook him for a moment but he recovered and began to run for the stables, only realizing when he was nearly all the way across the lawn that he must have smashed his ankle, that he was running with his legs askew, that something was wrong.

He reached the stables, there was no one waiting inside, and he staggered out into the sloping lane, and began to limp down it, trying desperately not to run.

The river was ahead of him. Across its breadth he could see the spire of the Admiralty, a golden needle pointed towards the heavens, gleaming in the bright sun; behind it the green copper roof of St Isaac's. He hobbled down the hill, gingerly testing his weight on the ankle, shaking it every step or two, as if he could mend it that way, by jiggling it back into place. Feeling like a fool, a marionette covered in blood.

He plunged his bleeding head into a trough of water at the end of the lane, threw the bloody jacket into the dark recess of a chicken coop, jammed the pistol down into the waistband of his trousers and covered it with his shirt. As he came out on to the next lowest cross street he saw a St Petersburg police motorcar whizzing past, changing gears and climbing the hill loudly, loaded down with gendarmes, one man furiously cranking the siren.

Along the street everyone had stopped, looking up the hill towards Evdaev's mansion. Ryzhkov walked into the crowd, skipped across the street and continued on, meandering towards the river, his ankle thickening up. He looked at his reflection in a shop window and then turned off the street, down the next lane.

He untied his cravat and wrapped it around his head like a sweatband, hiding the cut. Opened the neck of his shirt and rolled his sleeves up. There was a manure rake leaning against a stack of firewood and he reached out and stole it, swung it over his shoulder and walked along trying to look like a labourer. He felt weak, as if he were going to faint. Sirens came and went on Kamenoovstrovsky, two streets away now.

He continued on, his foot really hurting him now, crossed over the bridge to the Fortress of St Peter and St Paul. There was a little beach there down below the thick walls and he threw the rake aside and took his time, slowly climbed down the stairs one at a time, took off his clothes and went out into the river in his underwear and then came back and collapsed on the hot sand.

His heart was still pounding. Crazy designs floated behind his eyelids; darkness that grew red as blood, overprinted with whirling, spiralling, flickering, tessellated patterns, all of it going down the drain.

FORTY-FIVE

He bathed his ankle in the cold Neva, testing his weight until he could hobble along in the sand. Washed the blood off his face and rested on the beach until his underclothes dried, then dressed. The ankle had swollen and he had to open his shoe to its widest and leave the laces loose. He strolled away from the fortress slowly, trying to limp as little as possible, casually, like a man taking his ease on a hot afternoon.

He caught a tram back across the river and then another down the Nevsky, getting out and dodging behind a gendarme who was handing out leaflets bearing a series of photographs of himself, Dima and Hokhodiev. There was a fourth man's likeness printed on the paper and it took him a moment to recognize the portrait of a very young Zezulin. Somehow he too must have been swept up in everything, and somehow he must also be on the run. So, the sleepy old man had had enough wits to make a break for it. The thought of it made him happy.

To avoid the policeman he ducked into the Imperial Public Library. He waited there, finding himself a corner in the gigantic reading room, and, as the afternoon wore on, amassed a pile of books, notes, pamphlets, the better to understand the life of one Sergei Danilovich Andrianov.

Evdaev's confession was detailed enough to tell him most of what he needed to know and over a few hours he collected addresses, the names of the clubs to which Andrianov belonged, a list of his properties, anything that he thought would help to track him down, anything that would help him decide on the exact spot where he could wait in the shadows.

He grew colder and colder as he did it, watching the conspirators' privileged lives play out in front of him; watching them as boys, growing, acquiring knowledge, virtues, credentials, awards, titles. The inevitable accretion of greed, of vanity, the emergence of the Pan-Slavic ideology that came to dominate their class.

So Evdaev had come to his Slavist ideology honestly. After all he had been born into that world, lost relatives in the war against the Turks, nearly lost his own life fighting against the Japanese because of Russia's weakness; in reaction he had dedicated himself to the re-establishment of the Evdaev family in its position of primacy.

But to actually turn the clock back in an empire like Russia's you would need to have power, real power. And blocking him from that power was the anaemic House of Romanov. At this point his desires coincided with Andrianov's and Nestor had decided that he could get what he wanted, for himself, for his own family, for his rejuvenated Russia, and for Slavs all over the world, by taking a shortcut.

On the table in front of Ryzhkov was the class annual for the Corps des Pages of the year of 1896. In each volume were representatives of all of the ruling families of the empire. He was riffling through the book when the name Andrianov leapt out at him and he suddenly found himself staring at a young version of Sergei. Then, after a moment, he checked himself, realizing his mistake; he was looking at a portrait of Andrianov's younger brother, who had graduated from the school and promptly been assigned to the Black Sea Fleet.

There were photographs of the faculty and he saw that *Major* A.I. Gulka had been a professor of history at the academy. Ryzhkov stared at the severe face that glowered directly at the camera; hearing in his memory the dreamy voice singing to his lovely Sara-jev-ooo.

In the photograph Andrianov's mentor was stronger, leaner. The hair much darker and the moustache very dark indeed. He must have been a fearsome instructor. It was a very contained world at the top, he thought. A world where personal relationships were the basis for everything. Where family was at least as important as riches, a world where codes of behaviour meant more than codes of law. A world gushed over by society columnists, a world served by tailors, equerries, jewellers and clerics. That was the real Petersburg. The filthy streets in spring, the frozen bodies of the peasants in winter, the suicides floating downstream to the Gulf—all of it might as well be on another planet.

For a moment Ryzhkov's old bitterness surfaced and he shook his head at the injustice, wondering how different his own life would have been if he had been allowed to attend the academy of the Corps des Pages. Maybe Gulka would have been his teacher, too. Perhaps he would have learned that Slavic purity was the greatest philosophy ever invented. Maybe he could have been Evdaev's friend, something like a brother, living in the big house with the stables at the back, the mistress on the Moika. Everything would have been different; there would have been no Filippa, no rainy nights waiting in the darkness for an informer to show up. Life wouldn't have included a stint as a *gorokhovnik* on the run, that much was sure.

Paging through the year books, the faces gliding by, he suddenly had a vision of his father. It came as something only half-remembered, a flash of the old man bent over his drawing table. The characteristic way he would look up, seemingly perplexed at the slightest interruption. His calculations, his intricate designs inked out in front of him, his barrier and refuge from reality. His father looking up, startled—as if he didn't even recognise the face of his own son, as if he didn't even know where he was, once he had been awakened from his paper labyrinth.

Always dreaming up something fantastic, something no other engineer had even conceived. Fortifications too far-fetched to be constructed, barracks that would house only fantasy legions. His life a mystery of frustration, a self-created puzzle, because finally he had never understood why he had not progressed any further. He'd never understood that he aspired to a world from which he would always be excluded; an Olympus where effort and inventiveness didn't matter, where the hat one chose to wear was of more interest than the brain it sheltered. Yes, his father had craved a glittering world perpetually just out of reach; like the sound of music emanating from a spectacular party to which one had not been invited.

And he never knew it.

I'm the same way, Ryzhkov thought sadly. I've inherited his closed-mindedness. I'm just like him, blind as a bat. Tilting at windmills, pushing boulders up hills, chasing my own tail. The realization stopped him for a moment, depressed him even more, as he gazed down at the photographs of Russia's young aristocrats.

Well, it was too late to change, he told himself, as he shook the depression off. He didn't want any of it anyway. He didn't want to be like any of the men whose photographs were in the books. He'd seen too much to want any of that.

He had Evdaev's published pamphlets, nearly a dozen altogether—revisionist histories that traced the Slavic race's rise to power in ancient Russ, attempted to justify their displacement from the Mediterranean by the treacherous Moors, fulminated against their denial of the Aryan homelands of India by the British. Always surrounded, thwarted, displaced. A slow rhythm of frustration that permeated all of Evdaev's adulthood. The books were stacked on the corner of Ryzhkov's table, printed on the highest quality paper, bound in blue morocco with gilt lettering. And beneath the signature on the title page the colophon of Andrianov's publishing houses. Suddenly the Apollo Bindery made sense.

After that it was just a matter of finding the right books in the stacks; the annual of the Imperial Yacht Club. And in only a few minutes, as he opened the fine leather binding, as he turned through the heavy pages, let his gaze scan the happy faces of the members in their carefully posed photographs—Ryzhkov found the conspirators at play.

Yes, Andrianov's mentor had started in the army, in his beloved Corps des Pages. He had become an aficionado of history, a specialist in conspiracy and in the dark arts. Perhaps it was then that he began his long love affair with the sea. With the great Russian dream to possess Constantinople, to open the Black Sea. Perhaps Gulka had seen himself as a catalyst, hoping to play a part in the creation of a new Peter the Great, a great navigator, the founder of a New Russia. When Andrianov had given Gulka the opportunity to ascend to the top of the Third Branch he had accepted it at once, smoothly. Gracefully, invisibly with no pomp or ceremony.

The Third Branch had been Gulka's own personal Constantinople, the strategic fulfilment of his own ambitions. A way to shape destiny to his way of thinking. Control. Perhaps it was the illusion of being in control of the elements that drew Gulka to the sea. Perhaps it was the feeling of freedom.

He was an experienced mariner; the librarian brought Ryzhkov a dozen previous annuals that all revealed Gulka with his yachting friends, born high and low. A giddy celebration with Gulka lifting a silver plate awarded for a second place in the Petersburg to Stockholm race for 1909. Evdaev had been on the crew. Ryzhkov followed his voyages through the years, the boats getting larger and larger. A photograph of Gulka and his late wife, standing with a group of other happy sailors. In the most recent annual, for 1913, he came across Andrianov, a little too well dressed for a day's sailing, smiling tightly as he held on to one of the stays of the yacht, Evdaev and Gulka posed beside him, arm-in-arm like brothers. All of them smiling in the sun.

There was the sound of a drumroll and a clattering outside as a squadron of cavalry passed by the windows, and, as he looked out on to the dusty street, a great settling came over Ryzhkov. He had been staring out of the window for some minutes without realizing, because he only snapped out of it when the librarian came over.

'Anything else, sir? We are closing in just a few moments.'

He shook his head politely and the librarian smiled at him.

Even with his bruised face and dishevelled clothing, he must have resembled the kind of patron she liked. Well-mannered, gentle. Civilized. An enthusiastic reader who knew what he was looking for, sat quietly, and didn't fold over the corners of the pages.

FORTY-SIX

'Oh, God . . . look at you. Stay here, I'll get her,' he heard a woman saying. It took him a second or two to place the voice—Larissa. When he opened his eyes, she had gone, and after a moment he realized he was in the back lane behind the Komet. He must have fallen asleep in the rubbish. Then he thought that Larissa seeing him was a mistake, something he should have been careful to avoid. He couldn't let anyone see him. Even as Pravdin he had been too afraid to register for a room in Petersburg. Too late now . . . And then, bone-tired, he tried to get up, in order to leave before anyone else came along. And by that time Vera had come out and was helping him stand up.

'Are you crazy?' she said. 'Are you completely crazy? You can't come back here, you have to leave, Pyotr. The police come around here all the time now.' She was looking down the lane to make sure they hadn't been seen; over her shoulder he saw Larissa guarding the door. The two women glanced at each other and Larissa nodded, waved them away and ducked back inside.

'Let's go,' Vera said. 'I know a place.' And he found himself staggering down the alley in the pearly light, propped up by her strong dancer's legs.

The place she knew was a flea-bitten hotel with rooms rented by the hour. She left him outside while she made the deal with the receptionist. He went past the counter with his head down, face turned away, just another drunk, embarrassed, married man.

At the top of the steps he grabbed her, spun her around. What he wanted to do was kiss her, to hold her and beg for everything to be like it was, or like he had wanted it to be. What he really wanted to do was go back in time. He would never see her again, he was thinking. Never.

'Don't, Pyotr,' she said quietly. He had already let her go and she looked down and fiddled with the key, unlocked the door. He went into the cramped room, stood at the window, found himself reflexively watching the street. Going to the Komet had been insane, he thought, but there was no other choice. Where else could he go? But he needed her and so he couldn't stay away. One more time, that's all he had wanted. Just one more time.

There was a knock on the door, and he heard her open it and bring in the samovar. A tinkling of glasses.

'You'd better drink that tea before it gets cold,' she said.

'Yes. Thanks . . . I'm going to be leaving,' he said as he kicked off his shoes, began fumbling with his trouser buttons.

'Do you know where?'

'No.'

'Have you seen this?' She dug a sheet of paper out of her bag, unfolded it. It was leaflet printed by the police; a smudgy photograph occupied most of the page. There he was—younger, unfathomably more innocent, staring into the camera with a slight air of superiority, as if the whole thing were just a waste of time. Below it his life had been reduced to a list of dates and addresses and a warning that he was considered armed and dangerous and that any information leading to his arrest would fetch a substantial reward.

'You should grow your moustache out,' she said. 'I can bleach your hair for you, if you want.' For the first time he realized she had turned herself into a blonde.

'It's nice,' he said.

'Thank you.'

'Did you get the roses I sent? I was running. I couldn't say much of anything on the card.'

'Oh yes. I didn't try to find you, but of course I didn't know . . . I didn't know anything. I still don't.'

He gave her back the police leaflet. 'I can't stay here, there's nothing here anyway, I'm sure Filippa's lawyers have taken everything. I'd only get killed if I tried to get back my part of it . . .' He was talking nonsense.

'So?' she said quietly.

'So . . . Pyotr is dead,' he shrugged. Then he sat there with one leg in his trousers and one out and told her the long story, starting from the explosion in the street that took Fauré and the entire team, Gulka and the race to Sarajevo, Hokhodiev on his lonely mountaintop, and the blood-stained confessions he'd grabbed when he fled Evdaev's.

'Do they know about me?' she asked.

'No, I don't think so. If Andrianov really thought you were dangerous he would have had his contacts pick you up already. Gulka's gone, so he doesn't have access to all the information—' He was suddenly seized with a fit of coughing. She passed him the tea, he took another drink and the coughing stopped.

'Everyone's gone, dead, or run away,' he said. 'Everyone but me . . .' And looking up at her, he changed it to—'Everyone but *us*.' Wondering why they'd been spared; was an angel keeping him safe so that he could be God's sword of vengeance against Andrianov? After that would God need him any more?

'Andrianov the zillionaire?' She was staring at a photograph of Andrianov he had ripped out of one of the yearbooks, picked it out of Pyotr's pile of papers.

He nodded.

She looked at the photograph for another long moment. 'These people. What a life. Everybody knows you, they follow your exploits in the paper. If you stumble on the pavement, they say you're drunk, and if you are a drunk, they say you're a visionary genius. Sergei Andrianov, he's behind all this?'

'If I can find him, I'll kill him,' he said in a tired, thin voice.

'I'm sorry, I don't understand. Someone like him? He has everything anyway, what else does he want?' she said, looking at it with a little frown. 'Patron of the arts, king of the city, new, modern man. He needs more than that? I guess so. Everybody's on their own now anyway.'

'You know, once upon a time I found your name on a list,' he said. 'It was before Fauré, just a standard surveillance report. Thousands of them are written each week. I don't know why they started the file; perhaps because of Kushner. They were probably following, you know . . . someone else.'

'It was Kushner. Maybe he's right, I don't know. You look where things are heading and you start thinking he's right. All the blue-bloods are starting a war and we're supposed to rush to defend their honour? Why? What are we supposed to be thinking? Whatever the newspapers tell us? Kushner says we're building a movement, so I go along with it; I tell him things to make him go away. What do I have against German dancers, or the Vienna ballet? Are they supposed to be my enemies? Who's cooking it all up, you tell me. Rasputin? Monsters like this?' She dropped the photograph on the table.

He had fallen into staring at the pattern on the tablecloth, something intricate and oriental with repeating symbols around its borders, cleverly making knots about themselves, all somehow working out evenly so that there was no beginning or end to the maze.

'You need to sleep. Come on . . . we'll stay here. For tonight.'

'I love you,' he said. The way it came out, it didn't sound ardent, just a fact, a sad fact. Something almost gloomy, a statement of a medical condition or a boring scientific principle. So that it was equal in importance to everything else—I have six legs, I am an insect, I have a tumour in my chest. It is raining. I love you. They are trying to kill me . . . us . . .

He was sorry he'd said it. It was over now, anyway. Escape from Andrianov? Somebody with that much money could do anything, follow them to the ends of the earth even if it took years. No matter how far he ran, or how many colours she dyed her hair. For them it was over. Fast or slow, it was still over.

He would be gone, gone tomorrow. No moving in with her, no picking out wallpaper, no more blissful dreams. No furniture.

'Come on . . . you need to sleep,' she said again, and reached around and helped him with his braces.

'Vera . . .'

He was suddenly plunged into a great dark pit, a sadness so great that he thought he would begin sobbing. There was nothing for them. No matter how much he dreamed, how many romantic fables he invented with the two of them in starring roles, none of it, none of it would ever come true.

'I should be going, but . . .' he said, but he didn't move.

'You won't get very far without your trousers.' She reached across and took his hand. Her fingers were cool. The room was suddenly chilly and he shivered as if someone had walked across his grave.

'You go. I shouldn't have anything to do with you any more . . .'

'And vice versa, I'm sure, but I think it's probably too late for that, don't you,' and she had taken him in her arms. Warmth.

'You might be falling ill,' she said, and he felt her cool fingers on his battered forehead. 'You don't need a love-slave, you need a nurse.' And she led him to the bed, helped him pull off his clothes, and pushed him under the quilt. Climbed in behind and balled herself around him. Pushed her face tight against his neck, reached around and splayed her fingers across his heart and pulled him close.

It wasn't long that she had to wait. In a few minutes he had fallen into a deep sleep, his breathing slow and regular. Then she slowly slid out from under the covers, slipped his pistol into her handbag, crept out of the little room, and locked the door behind her.

FORTY-SEVEN

Is that the artist's curse? To never know oneself, one's true *self*, to spend your life with another you on your shoulder, always watching, always judging—do it better, do it harder, hold it longer, be more graceful, move a few inches into your light, speak a little louder for the balcony. Whether you're a great diva or a simple street performer, the curse is the same. Perhaps it is a way of never being alone, an even more terrifying fate for a performer.

Now enters a woman with reddened eyes, pausing at the gate, holding on to the stanchion for support, almost doubled over with the passion of her tears. She straightens, regains her composure, pats at her nose, and strides more comfortably to the door. Mina sees her coming.

Meets her there at the door, and now there are the two of them, these duped bedraggled spectres both with faces gone all to hell, tear-streaked, their perfect masks pulled by the cords in their necks, furrowed with sadness. Two women destroyed.

It is like a mirror. The stranger pauses there for a moment. A look of shock, of recognition on her face and Mina thinks . . . well, it explains so much, at least part of what had been happening over the last few weeks. This is all part of it, things begin to fall into place. Ahh . . . she thinks, this is the long-awaited *other one*.

The butler is hurrying to the door but she has beaten him. 'Yes?' she means to say firmly, officiously. Already she is poised to close the door in the girl's face. Younger, blonder, and, looking at the dress, well, that's how she has recently spent the money. His money. 'Yes?' She means to say it loudly, forcefully. A *yes* which really means no, but it comes out plaintively, more like *please*?

The stranger's lip trembles, is she going to cry again?

'Is he here? I need to speak to him,' and even as she says it, knowing what the answer will be, and that she will not see him, not ever again. Defeated.

'What is it that you want?' Mina replies, the voice a little stronger now, as the girl's eyes glaze over, her face beginning to turn away in misery.

'I . . . I just wanted to see him, to tell him . . .' and the girl is suddenly staring at her strangely, an open—yes, damn it—beautiful face, and then she is falling, fainting right there on Mina's threshold.

Of course they carry her inside.

While the butler fans her—it is hot after all—she loosens the girl's collar, a flash of perfect skin that is flushed, and her sweet long neck fallen back against the silk pillows. Mina stands back and looks at her. Younger.

Almost as quickly the poor wretch comes around, realizes where she is, looks around the parlour with the expression of a wild beast. 'Is he here?' Clutching her bag to her bosom, now all afraid.

'No,' Mina says, the fight leaked out of her. 'Bring some tea,' she calls out to Anna who is hovering in the archway. 'No, he's not here,' she repeats and then she crosses through the gloom of the parlour to her cabinets. It is always dark this room, a real cavern. She hates the parlour, never uses it except when she's waiting for Sergei to return, and now, in the summer when it's cool and she can get a good breeze through the place. 'No, he's not here,' she says, and her voice reveals much more than she wants. She finds a bottle and pours the girl a schnapps, and after a hesitation a little one for herself. The girl looks at it as if it were poison, refuses to drink until Mina knocks hers back. 'No, you've missed him,' her own lip starting to tremble.

There is a noise from upstairs, the blasted machine. The door is open now, just as he left it, papers all over the floor. The girl stands, the schnapps goes flying, she sees the staircase and sets off for it at a run. It takes Mina a moment, and she doesn't get to her until the girl has reached the stairs with a gun in her hand.

As soon as Mina sees the gun she understands, and a wave of sympathy for the creature begins to build in her chest. Watching her, following her like a dog, as she moves through the upper rooms. Wherever he's stashed her, it can't be this good, and there is the most ironic pride she feels as they walk along, and the child gawks at the oil paintings, the chandelier, the carved doors, the ferns exploding from every recess, the thickness of the carpet. They are at the bedroom now and the girl stands there at the false bookcase watching the jabbering machine disgorge its coded message. The barrel of the gun wavers, droops.

'No, he's gone. Gone to hell as far as I'm concerned. You'll probably hear from him, who knows when,' Mina says. She walks past the girl into her own room. Maybe she will change, go out. Start anew. It's no great tragedy after all. Actually, if one were to be honest, it's something she has been preparing for . . . for how long? Years. Since the first morning after, a little someone on her shoulder warning her the whole time that it couldn't last.

She pauses before the windows. She'd take off her clothes and get changed if it weren't for this girl lingering behind her.

'Gone . . . gone where?' comes the little lost voice, as if *going* were a fantastical concept, something not taught in the conservatory. A obscene new word being learnt the hard way.

'*America*,' Mina says. Unable to control her tears now, just the strange sound of the word has brought everything up again. 'America. He didn't say so, but I can tell. He had the tickets sent to the dacha, so I wouldn't know.' She almost manages to laugh as she says it.

The girl moves on the parquet behind her. She has gone inside the forbidden room. Who cares? The jabbering stops and the sounds of the street come through the great open windows, a man with his cart and donkey walking along the embankment crying out that he has melons for sale.

She collapses in the windowseat, watches the poor man going along. No one will buy anything like that here. Everyone is out of the city anyway, everyone flown except the lost ones, the drunks, the prostitutes and addicts, the soldiers and the diplomats, all rushing back because of the emergency. Still, that doesn't affect the people on her street, here everyone but the dead is on holiday. From somewhere down on the Nevsky there is what she can recognize as a long drumroll, another regiment marching by. In the last days everything is suddenly being organized, gendarmes are coming around putting forms under every door. All the men are supposed to be giving their names and dates of birth. Sergei's notices have arrived and are still there on the table.

'When did he go?' says the girl, a trace of urgency.

Mina cannot help but laugh a little. 'This morning. He's sneaking out on his boat to Finland, there's a yacht club there that he owns, or subsidizes, or . . . he's a big benefactor, an *angel* . . . something. Then Hamburg, then Brest, and then . . . away. It was in code but I still saw the itinerary, they send that around whether you want it or not. He made all the arrangements with the porters about his steamer trunks, they were supposed to pick them up at his father's house so I wouldn't know, but he telephoned from here and they got the address wrong and came here first. A mistake.' She smiles now at Sergei's fallibility.

'America. Are you sure?'

'I know that's where he's going. Look. Letters. All from some bank in America. He was planning it for the last week or two. He has codes. Some of it is in code. But I always know where he is,' she says, her voice hard now, flinty. She will not cry again, that was it. The last time she'll cry for that bastard. The girl still has the gun out and while it is pointing at the floor, she might suddenly fly out of control, jealousy can do strange things. Jealousy can push you a long, long, way and in unusual directions.

'He said that he'll send for me,' Mina informs her, and watches the girl's face, measuring how she handles it, how she deals with the revocable nature of Sergei's love, the passion that was supposed to last for ever vanished like the weakest summer breeze.

'Could you put that away, please. He's gone. It won't do either of us any good.' The girl sinks into a chair, her future lost in the maze of the carpet.

'I suppose if you love him enough, you could go after him, chase him across Europe. Perhaps if there's not enough wind, or some problem with his train connection, you could be together in Stockholm by tomorrow,' Mina says. Teasing, prodding. How hard will jealousy push this girl? Maybe she has hidden wells of strength, resources that will now suddenly surface, just as her own have. Maybe they should be thankful to Sergei for pulling the scab off their souls, making them both stronger.

Then all at once she understands the depth of the girl's dead expression. 'Are you pregnant?' she asks as gently as she can.

The question brings a look of innocent surprise to the girl's face, a grimace that almost looks like a smile, and a supreme effort to hold back the tears, a pathetic gesture to protect her womb.

'Why don't you give me that?' she asks, reaching for the revolver, an ugly thing, black and scuffed, the wooden handle held together with twine. How far can jealousy push this girl? She finally reaches out for the gun, the girl lets it go, their eyes meet, Mina puts it aside on the little table, and they embrace and the tears start all over again. Long sobs, and a moment when she can feel the girl trying to struggle out from her arms; that's her pride showing, not wanting to take anyone's charity, not wanting the pity. Well, she knows that feeling, Mina thinks. And then she surrenders and Mina has her face between her hands, like a mother herself. 'I'll give you money. He left me money. I don't want his money, but you'll need it, won't you? I hate him. He's a bastard. You can come to Antibes. I know someone who can help you.'

The girl looks at her levelly for a long time, then over to the horrible little closet, a frown creases the young brow. 'What has he . . . ?'

'Oh, he's in trouble. Selling everything he can. To hell with the loss. He's trying to put all his money in Brazil or Dublin, or . . . Chicago . . .' She reels off the exotic names. 'Selling at a loss, for a man like Sergei, that's trouble.'

'I thought so,' she says, eyes wide. Just a child, Mina thinks. Doesn't she know that's what men like Sergei do? They get in trouble, that's part of the attraction, she wants to scream. Then they go down and we go down with them. 'What did he promise you, did he give you anything?'

The girl shakes her head.

'There's not much of his, here. You can look around. If you find something you can have it, if you want. I don't care,' Mina says. It surprises her, actually, how little it hurts.

'What about all that?' the girl asks, looking back at the machine which has suddenly stuttered to life. Outside the military band is louder, the drums pounding as the men lustily play their way down the long boulevard.

Mina shrugs. 'I just wish I could turn it off. There must be some way.' She stares at the jittering keys, the long curl of paper that has piled up on the floor. It looks like it could catch fire at any moment. Stupid thing. 'I thought about calling the police and giving them all this. Maybe they could make some sense out of it. Maybe they could catch him at the station. Jail might be good for Sergei, don't you think? But now I think I'm going to burn it all instead.'

'Because of him, of what he did?' the girl asks, her eyes wide. Such an innocent, she is. The kind of girl who would never burn her lover's property, would probably not even be able to tear up one of his letters.

'Yes, of course I'm going to burn it! Certainly, I'm going to burn it *all*. You can see what's happening, can't you. He was involved in all this somehow. He did it and it's all come undone and he did it here . . . here in my house. When it all comes out, they'll say that I helped him, they'll come here and arrest me! Yes, I'm burning it.' She is laughing. The Lilac Fairy in Chains, the newspapers will scream. How absurd.

The girl is looking at her, Sergei's itinerary in her hand. She looks into the secret room for a long moment. The tears are all gone now, and she faces Mina with a long cool look. A little taller when she is not slumped over sobbing and thinking about suicide. Maybe the trace of a smile. She holds out her hand for the gun. 'I have to give this back,' she says. 'To someone, a friend.' Then, yes, a little smile to reassure her; it's so touching, she must have had to go out, find someone she knows and borrow the pistol. It's so operatic.

'You can come back here. If you need help,' Mina says, crossing the wide bedroom and picking up the filthy thing, two fingers dangling it like a rotten fish on its way to the bin. 'There's plenty of room, and I meant what I said about Antibes,' she says. 'Sometimes blessings are where you least expect them. You can visit there and even have the baby, if that's what you want. It's lovely. Right by the sea.' And she looks into the girl's beautiful eyes; there's no reason to hate her, none at all.

Why not do something good in the world, reach out with your wand and make someone's life better for a change? 'In a few days I'm going to turn all this over to the agents and they can send me the cheque when it's settled, so don't take too long to make up your mind.' She goes over to her wardrobe and stares for a moment at the treasures there, takes out one of her boxes of jewels, grabs the first thing that comes to hand, a bracelet. Rubies. He gave it to her in Venice.

'Take this,' and when the girl reacts, she pushes it on her. 'I don't need it. I'm never going to wear these again. Sell it, you'll need some money, yes?' Sergei's women all develop a taste for fine things if they didn't have it in the beginning, she knows that much about women.

'Take it, and don't be a fool.' She drops the bracelet into the girl's handbag. 'Don't ever be a fool again.'

FORTY-EIGHT

She told him all about it. Interrupting and cutting through his rage and his worry when she came through the door. Handed him the itinerary she'd been given. Still stunned by it all, really. He was silent, looking at her finally, and then setting the papers aside rather formally, uncreasing them because after all . . . they were important.

He held her for a long moment and she felt his head against her chest, the hair in her fingers. Nothing would ever erase it, she thought. She could always have that. Just that. Then she took his arms away because there was no time and they both knew it, locked the door behind her, paid the man an extra two roubles to leave him alone, and then went out to get food.

When she got back he was at the desk at one end of the room, writing with pen and paper that he must have made the porter bring up. He didn't even look around when she came in. She made sandwiches for them, uncorked a bottle of wine, tore off a corner of the butcher's paper to use as a plate, and put it on the edge of the desk where he could reach it. Watched him for a moment and then walked back, propped up all the pillows and sat there in the bed, eating and looking at him.

Eventually she fell asleep, and when she woke he was still at the desk writing. When he heard her stirring he looked around and smiled. A tired smile with sad eyes.

'This is the last thing, I'll ask of you,' he said quietly. 'I'm going to finish with this, and then . . .' Suddenly the eyes changed, she thought. They went from being sad to something much, much colder, and she saw the secret policeman emerge right before her; come out from the inside of him and take over.

'And then . . . I think after that, Vera, you'll have to go.' His face cracked for a moment, a little ripple across his mouth and he blushed. She got off the bed and went to him. 'You will,' he said weakly. 'Who knows what he's got going, if they find you, they'll kill you too.'

She buried his face against her to keep him quiet. 'You can't even walk,' she said.

Later, in the bed, they found themselves just staring at each other. Reaching for something. Trying to remember always the eyes, the mouth, the touch. As if by staring at the loved one, it would all be captured with photographic perfection, so that no matter what happened, so that even years later, it would be something, maybe the one good thing still left to them. One last good memory they might hold.

And because there was no time, she let him get up and go back to the desk and show her the papers; a series of letters, he told her; some of them necessarily lengthy, specifying everything that had been uncovered in Fauré's investigation, all of the crumpled pages he'd saved from Evdaev's mansion. It had all started with the girl, with Katya, did she remember?

'Yes . . . oh, yes . . .' She let her head fall over on to the pillows and watched him sitting there at the desk, naked. The long bones of his arms, the spine with its uneven little knots. The muscles flinching in his shoulders as he moved the pen across the paper. When it came time for her to leave for the club, she just let it pass. Larissa would say something, tell some lie and save her one more time.

When he was done, he brought the letters over to the bed and carefully told her about each one. It was like a man making out his will, she thought. And she sat there listening to him, trying to hold herself together, trying to be what he needed, which was a strong partner, an ally. Now he really was going to go, she realized. He was going to go out of her life, change his name and lose himself. She just looked at him and tried to focus on the details of what he was saying, but the whole time it was growing inside her, this frightful unerring knowledge that they would never see each other again.

'. . . this one is for the Austrian embassy. Everything I know about the assassination, about the Black Hand and who, from here, was involved. Everything . . . his visits to Sarajevo, all the names, the aliases, everything is here. Good. Now . . .' he said, putting the letter aside. 'Now, this one is . . .'

What did he think she would be able to do about it? Why was he telling her all this? Did he think that she would be able to get the ear of embassy officials if he couldn't? It was too late. The archduke was dead. Dead. Didn't he understand that? It was like the death of a thousand cuts.

'. . . another copy of all this is for our own Foreign Ministry, since it's their policy that is being . . . subverted. Perhaps if they know, then they should be able to prosecute Andrianov and his friends . . . you see?'

'Yes.'

She couldn't understand why he had come back, why he might choose to die for all this, for all these letters to other men. It was so pathetic that she wanted to scream. Instead she sat there and made her face blank, sat there and acted for him, pretended to listen.

'. . . and this one I want to be taken to the Minister of Justice, since one of their own . . . since Boris was killed for it . . .'

'Yes, of course.' Oh, yes. Yes, of course. Naturally. Whatever you say.

'He should be told about all of it . . . about a conspiracy within, how Evdaev and Andrianov were attempting . . . attempting a coup, really. You see, Vera, that's what it is—a coup d'état.' He was looking at her with those big eyes. Trusting and sad, like a dog who had found an old bone in the garden and, tired from the digging, only wanted to lie down beside his master.

'Yes,' she said. 'A coup, yes.' Of course.

He smiled and looked at her for a moment, then turned to the last letter.

'This is a copy of all of it,' he said, and by his expression, the gravity of the way he held the pages, she knew it was his last card, the most important of the letters. 'This one tells what I am doing, says who has been sent the other letters, says what they're all about. It's for you.'

'Me?'

'I want you to keep it, to hold on to it, put it somewhere safe, not in your apartment, but maybe . . . somewhere else.'

'I can hide it in the dressing-room, the place is a mess. Izov never cleans up, you can't find anything in there.'

'Good, put it there. I want you to keep it . . . for a month. If you haven't seen anything about any of this in any of the papers, I want you to take it to Kylberg at the *Kopek Gazette*.'

'That's good, yes,' she said, trying to make her enthusiasm plausible.

'He's supposed to be a liberal, if he can't actually put it in his newspaper, he might . . .'

'He might pass it to others in the Duma.' She was gradually working up to something approaching optimism, playing the part of the encouraging comrade. All she had wanted to do was kill Andrianov, send him to his dog's death and be done with it.

He put the last letter—*her* letter—on the bed covers and reached out to her. From where he was sitting, they could not properly embrace. Their foreheads touched, knocking together, but she held him there. Perhaps their thoughts could jump through that little portion of skin and bone, then she would know why all of this was happening.

'Vera . . .' he started, and she pushed forward and kissed him so that he would not say anything more. No more plans, no more words about tragically necessary things. She hadn't even made any plans and now suddenly nothing was working out right. He pulled away, held her face.

'Vera . . . I'm so sorry,' he said again. It was all going too quickly. She bit her lip so she wouldn't cry but she began to cry anyway. He was explaining how he would send her a postcard when he got his feet back on the ground, he'd send it to the Komet. It wasn't a question of money, between the two of them they had enough money to get a ticket for her. But for now . . . for now . . .

'Vera, you have to go,' he was saying. 'Go, before they find me. No one stays in places like this overnight, they'll be looking. Go—' He had pulled her up off the bed. For a moment she thought he would hit her. This was it, she realized. This was the exit.

'Go!' he said, louder, shaking her. She couldn't have left even if she wanted to, he was holding her so tightly. She nodded, said she would, pressed her mouth to his, and his hands released her. He stood there limply until she stepped away from him, afraid to hold her again. Afraid to say any more.

She stumbled about the room looking for her costume, her props. He handed her the letters to post and the other, the most important letter. She had stopped crying, a triumph of self-control, she thought. Where was the applause for that? There should be applause. There should be cheers and bowing. Flowers at the curtain call.

She jammed her hat down over her eyes, stood there with her hand on the doorknob. Turned, chin held high. A true princess.

'And you . . . where are you, what are you . . . ?'

He looked up at her and she had never seen him so pale. Now she saw a boy, a little lost boy trapped inside the body of a man.

'I'm going now, too,' he said softly. A shrug. With only the faintest of smiles to reassure her. His voice gone wistful, tinged with amazement at the words that were coming out.

'I'll come with you,' but he was shaking his head before she finished.

'No.' His photograph was everywhere and the populace had been whipped up by spy fever to suspect even their closest neighbours. 'I know where he is and I'll get him and I'll get out. I'll do it, and . . . I'll, I'll send for you. I will,' he said and then suddenly stopped. He jerked his head down, his face constricted in pain and confusion, and she thought for a moment that he was about to choke.

Then there was the last kiss; everything passing too quickly now, a ritual speeding up, out of control. She reached up and touched his poor cheek, tried to memorize his eyes, and then, before it went on too long and she ended up making a big scene out of it, she turned and opened the door and left the shabby room, not looking back, because of what it might do to him; make him weak, slow him down, blunt the edge of the sword with which he was going to smite down evil. Instead, like a good actor, she would get off his stage cleanly, wait in the darkness where no one could see her tears. Bite her lip and cheer.

That was her role, to hold his letters and his love next to her heart, and carry them to their destiny.

Khulchaev was drunk, giddy. Laughing and improvising his speech of prosecution. At the end of every clause the Professor emphasized the words with pounding chords from the newly-tuned piano. Others shouted hurrahs. *War!*

Glory was in the air. To hear them you would have thought it a grand exercise. A celebration. Something everyone really wanted to happen. Something triumphant. She'd had nowhere else to go, had come in and been given a drink right away. And another. Caught Larissa looking at her with concern in her eyes. Smiled and raised her glass in a toast of forgiveness, and to deflect all that mothering. She didn't need that any more.

Kushner was screaming at them now: '. . . working men in Germany will be killing working men in Russia so that the honour of their royal masters will be assuaged, and the only ones who will get anything out of it are the Putilovs, and the Krupps, and the Schneiders. The Rockefellers and the Rothschilds . . .'

And Dmitri drunkenly ignoring everything that Kushner had said to them, laughing it off (how smooth he was!) and going on with his little obsessive comedy, raising his voice to condemn Tika for all the death that Kushner had just foretold.

Soon there would be a verdict. It was all too ugly. She had an inch of brandy left to go, then she could leave.

'. . . and I submit that the defendant should be given a reprieve—' there were howls of protest from Kushner and his revolutionary faction. 'Yes, comrades, a pardon. A pardon based on the patriotic necessity, the necessity of protecting the soul, the very essence of Mother Russia, the strong heart of her manhood, the purity of her motherhood. Now, more than ever we need royal blood.'

'Christ,' she said, not actually meaning to say it out loud and everyone turned and laughed at her.

She shakily stood and raised the glass to her lips, toasted Tika. 'She's not pure, no one is pure . . .' It sounded very profound as she said it. Very royal in her delivery. She drank off the last of the brandy during the applause and began planning her exit through the tangle of chairs.

As she was finding her way out of the labyrinth, they decided to take a vote. Deliberations were instantaneous; guilty was the shouted response. Guilty, and the sentence the Professor intoned, standing now at his keyboard, must be death. Death so that the crime of Mother Russia herself would not be replicated, so that Tika would not breed, so she wouldn't spread her filth into the future.

'But first get her some food!' someone called to Izov, as Vera walked by. 'It's her last meal.' And there was more laughter. More applause.

She was finished with them all now. To dance while the world collapsed all around her was . . . Well, she had grown past all that now. Maybe she had listened to Kushner a little too much. Maybe some of it had seeped in. Maybe she was really becoming a Social Revolutionary in fact.

At her table in the dressing-room there were cards, little souvenirs, clippings from favourable critics. Wedged in behind the mirror, propped up behind her pots and vials. She paused there, looking at the mirror. Maybe she should take them. Just to prove she had done all the things, been all those characters. A scrap of paper to prove she really had opened at the Alexandra.

The mirror was clean, perfect except for a diagonal crack at the top right corner. Sometimes she liked to pose so that the reflection of her face was bisected by the crack. It made her look strange, fragmented. Crazy. She liked looking crazy sometimes. Liked seeing on the outside the way she felt inside. Liked having it affirmed by the evidence of her eyes.

To hell with the critics and their yellowed clippings, she thought. If she didn't believe them when they were wrong, why believe them when they were right? She had a raincoat there, it was the only thing she cared about, and she reached up and took it off the peg, thinking that she would go to the bank, take everything out, get a cab for the station. Odessa, here I come; Get ready, Roma. Maybe even somewhere really exotic, Cairo, or Japan . . .

She stood there with the coat over her arm, thinking she really should leave a note for Larissa. Give her free pick of everything she wanted out of the little apartment. Maybe she'd stop in on the way to the station, throw some underclothes in a bag.

She sat back down at her table, looked up and leaned so that her face was cut by the crack in the mirror. The vision of her cleft face caused her to smile, proved that she really was . . . well, eccentric, let's say. She tore a page out of their most recent script and began to write on the back of it with grease pencil:

My dearest Larissa—
By the time you get this I will be gone on my long-promised great adventure. There is nothing here and I am worn out . . .

She thought about Pyotr, about his going, about the pain of it and if it would ever go away. Maybe he would land on his feet somewhere safe, maybe he would write. Then again, the promised postcard might never come. She'd be sitting there waiting when she was an old woman. An old, eccentric woman, waiting for a message from the only man that she'd ever truly . . . She'd be the kind of woman everyone whispered about; yes, she used to be pretty, they'd say, and she used to be a dancer, a good dancer. A dancer in Russia, back when that meant something. No, she couldn't wait.

She couldn't, still—

. . . and it may be that I get some corres-
pondence. If so, could you do me the great favour of
forwarding . . .

She couldn't live a life counting on Pyotr, a life of
always waiting. She was going to stop all that now. She
would never wait for anyone again.

And she wasn't going to the river, either. From now
on it was going to be Vera, Vera, Vera. She was going to
be happy, she was going to feel the sun on her shoulders
in January. She was going to fall asleep in a perfumed
garden.

. . . hope you will always know that I thank you for
all your blessings, all the gifts you have given me.
And now, please do not hate me—now I am leaving
you to clean up once again . . .

Suddenly, looking up at her mirror, the carefully
plucked arch of her brows, the straight nose, the blush
of her lips, she became aware of her beauty. She was
good as a blonde, she was beautiful, yes. Yes, she was.
A man would see her beauty instantaneously, a woman
too, given the right kind of light. It was in the eyes, the
wide dark eyes. The carriage of her head, the way she
looked at herself. She was brave now. All of it had
conspired to make her brave and beautiful. She had
won.

And, then, she remembered the packet, the letters
Pyotr had given her. She took them out of her bag and
held them in her hands, turning the envelopes over and
over. Inspected his writing, the sharp way he formed his
letters. Some little thing inherited from the engineer-

father. Fine, then. For you, my only one, for you . . .

One last thing to do on her way out of town.

And so, thank you, my darling. Thank you for all the generous things you have done, all our good times. Wish me well . . . V

She stood, then. Pushed his envelope into one of the big pockets in her raincoat. Now the mirror reflected her chest, the crack splitting her between the breasts, and she took a breath, thinking it might be an omen. A sign that her heart was breaking? That she would be struck dead before she could leave, before she could break free?

At the door Izov saw her, frowned. 'What do you think you're doing? Where have you been the last few days? Remember you've got a show in less than an hour, girlie . . .'

She didn't even bother smiling at him.

As she walked by the edge of the stage they were proceeding to hang the cat. Someone had rigged up a gallows made of empty wine crates topped with a mop handle. She looked around just as the Professor sprung the trap and Tika fell and swung between the tables.

For a moment the whole room was silent, riveted on the animal swinging there, her legs stuck straight out, wriggling her hind quarters, trembling as if an electric current was being passed through her, claws extended.

And then Vera broke through the ring of 'jurors', to lift the cat into her arms, hooking a finger under the loop of string they had scrounged to make the noose.

'Bastards! Filthy bastards!' Groans from some of them, thinking it had all been a set-up, part of one of Khulchaev's elaborately choreographed dramas. A man sitting there reached up to take the cat away from her. For an awful moment Tika fell back, still knotted in the string, but Vera slapped at the man, knocked his ugly, thick hands away from her, grabbed the cat back up again and this time got the string untangled.

'Hey, damn it!' The man was trying to stand up now, drunk. Angry that a woman had come between him and his enjoyment.

She reached out, found one of the empties and smashed the bottle down on the man's head, breaking it off so that there was only the sharp neck in her hand. Turning now to Khulchaev who had managed to stagger to his feet, not laughing now.

'Please, Dmitri, just give me an excuse,' she said, poised to plunge the glass into his face. And then she was pushing her way through the crowd as the wave of protest and applause erupted, filling the club behind her.

'A miracle! A miracle!' someone was shouting behind her as she made it to the doors, moving fast so they wouldn't see her tears, dropping the broken bottle-neck on the bar as she crashed outside.

She was talking to the cat as she walked down the street, reprimanding it, giving it advice. Telling it to behave and whatever happened, to never, never go back there again. And then, at the end of the street, with nothing else to do, and no real plan in mind, she knelt and tossed the cat into an alley. Watched her skitter away, knowing Tika was just as big a fool as the people gathered at the club, and that no matter what miracles occurred, she would always find her way home.

Ahead of her, at the intersection of Sadovaya Street, was a parade. Drums were crashing, music was playing and men and women were waving little flags of France and Russia. Everything was a sea of music and colour.

There were women there at the edge of the crowd. For a moment she thought they were nuns. Their heads were covered in immaculate white kerchiefs, their aprons were spotless. Across their breasts had been stitched perfect red crosses.

They were handing out leaflets to anyone who passed by.

Vera walked closer and closer to the women. One of them smiled at her and said something, words that were drowned out by a blare of trumpets. There was a sharp crackle of hooves on cobbles as a shining regiment of hussars passed them. The girl looked up at her, reached out with a leaflet. She was young, with clear skin and dark eyes.

Vera leaned closer so she could hear.

They would be needing nurses, the girl shouted over the music. They would need plenty of nurses, to care for all the brave young men who would be wounded in the war.

They would need lots of nurses, the girl said, and pressed the leaflet into her hand.

It was something a woman could do.

FORTY-NINE

Once Vera had told him, it all made sense, made things suddenly urgent, made things turn upon themselves in accord with greater forces; the Sun, the Moon, the direction and force of the winds, the tides.

He limped across the city while everyone enjoyed the summer evening. Peaceful. The sound of music, laughter, conversations floating from the windows. As he went, he worked out which tram to take across the Neva, seeking the most crowded stations where he would be most likely to avoid detection, the safest connections that would carry him all the way to the top of Krestovsky Island and the marina where Andrianov tied up his yacht.

Finally, it was a single detail in one of the photographs that undid Andrianov, a detail he'd remembered from the annuals of the Imperial Yacht Club.

The book was formal, expensively produced, distributed gratis to the members of the club; a chronicle of race results, noted speakers, statistics, and posed photographs of the officers and members. But amateur photography was very much in vogue among those who could afford it, and the final section of the book had been given over to casual photographs. He had been following Gulka's rise, letting his eyes roam through the pictures, noting the décor in his old academy office—a posed photograph meant to depict the distinguished military academic. Gulka pretending to be looking at some papers, securely surrounded by his books, his maps, and—the ship models, their hulls intricately carved. And Ryzhkov remembering—because it had never quite fitted—the crossed oars of the rowing club, the nautical fascination, the strong attraction for the water, so unusual for an army man.

And then he had seen Andrianov in another annual, with Gulka and Evdaev beside him, all of them posed on Andrianov's new 6-metre *Firebird*. At the next stop there was confirmation: a woman was reading a newspaper as they rocked along the Prospekt, she turned her pages and he saw the announcement of tomorrow's regatta to escort Poincaré and the *France* out of the city.

By the time he got to the Krestovsky Gardens he was the last person on the tram, and when he got off the car he kept his head down, his elbow tight to his side to hide the gun, and tried not to limp.

On some ordinary occasion it would be a pleasant walk through the little resort community that had grown up along the narrow arm of the river. He walked slowly and tried to loosen his ankle. Each step brought a sharp pain and a misstep nearly sent him to his knees. Vera, as usual, had been right. In a fight he would be hopeless, running away would be suicidal.

So, he moved cautiously, sitting down, taking his time, thinking about how it would be. Meandering towards the river—the Nevka it was called, to distinguish it from its huge parent to the south. He had all night to get to the dock, and thinking that he would be more likely to meet a gendarme along the embankment, he cut through the unpaved streets, walked down the back lanes until he found a path that led more or less in the direction of the yacht club.

There was a wide creek that cut across the island. You could row along there. It was a popular diversion for lovers, with dark little overhangs where one could tether the boat for an afternoon. The creek was too deep to cross without swimming and so he turned and kept to the bank, heading towards the river, until he came through the brambles and saw a footbridge that paralleled the road that led to the yacht club.

It was a magical walk, like something a character would take in a fairy story, the white light streaking through the trees in rippling threads of silver. Each step down the path sent animals scurrying away from his approach, little rustlings in the flowers and shrubbery, skitterings in the canopy above him.

It seemed entirely appropriate that animals would flee as he strolled along. Yes, run away, he said to himself. Run away fast, because here comes a man carrying death.

He tried to think about exactly what he would do at the docks. How hard it would be to find Andrianov, if there was a guard or a watchman he might have to avoid, or if there was even a way to postpone it all and wait for a better chance. Or if he might have to track Andrianov across Europe and on to a liner for America. It all swirled through his mind, but somehow on the eve of this last fatal act he really couldn't concentrate as he walked along the long swath cut out beneath the trees. There were puddles that reflected the silver light, a breeze stirred above him and made the leaves like mirrors. It was as if he were shedding a skin and with it his thoughts were sloughing away into the white night. Perhaps I died in Sarajevo, he thought. Perhaps this is another world.

At the edge of the forest he paused, stood there and fanned himself with his hat, tried to look as much as possible like a birdwatcher who'd forgotten his binoculars, or an artist who had left his easel at home. He moved along the bank, towards the mouth of the river. The ground was wet there, and marshy. He moved into the bushes and waited out of sight. Loitering was dangerous and he thought he would only get one approach to Andrianov's boat. He leaned back against the trees, checked the gun. In the white night everything was illuminated in a flat silvery glow. He waited there in the bushes until after midnight and then he stood and tested his weight on the ankle before he started off towards the boathouses at the edge of the docks.

Going off the paths was too painful, his foot would turn over in the mud, and it was implausible. The thing to do was to fit in. There would be a watchman, maybe more than one.

He took off his jacket, and put it over his shoulder. He came to a shed and looked around until he found something that he could carry along the docks, to make it look like he had some purpose other than death. He found a canvas bag and a coil of rope, looped the rope over his shoulder and walked around the corner of the little building. He carried the bag along, both his arms wrapped around it, holding it up to his chest, trying to act like it was heavier than it was, stopping to adjust the rope, the jacket, looking around, always looking.

When he saw it, the yacht looked just like the photographs he'd studied in the club annual for 1913; low-slung, fine lines, a modern design with an undercut transom. Small enough to be crewed solo, large enough to sleep four on an overnight excursion.

Firebird.

He stopped for a moment, put the bag down. Turned away and looked down the marshy river, the Nevka gleaming in the flat light, a long view all the way across to the point of Yelagin Island, and the Finnish coast beyond.

He felt for the gun beneath his shirt, stood and took a short hard breath, turned and picked up his props, then continued down a gangway on to a narrow floating dock where the yacht was moored. He heard a noise, a kind of hissing and then saw a tendril of smoke coming from the galley chimney, took another few steps and then he could smell Andrianov making his breakfast.

When he got to the yacht he set the bag down, as if it had been a gruelling task. Taking the time to look at all the other boats, most of which were smaller, perhaps with no facilities for sleeping aboard. He saw no more smoke, heard no other noises. Stood up, stretched and gave an exaggerated yawn and scratched his neck while he scanned the boathouse at the top of the pier. No one.

He reached into his pocket and pulled out the pistol and stepped on to the deck. 'Excuse me?' he called out in a stage whisper, at the entrance to the cabin. 'Excuse me, excellency?' sounding as much as he could like a man who was lost, a man who was worried, scared that there might be some irregularity, afraid to make a noise, a busy-body who perhaps had seen the smoke and worried if it was breakfast being cooked or was the immaculate *Firebird* actually on fire?

He could feel him moving inside the boat, fiddling with the catch on the bottom of the hatch and pulling it open, starting to say, with a touch of anger, a touch of gruffness in the voice, 'Yes, what is it?' but instead, opening the hatch to see the dark little hole in the end of the pistol, the brusque enquiry stopping in his throat, the eyes travelling up to see who was holding the gun, the beginnings of a frown, and then the moment of recognition when he remembered the face on the handbills.

'Ahh . . .' was all Andrianov said, stepping back now, a spatula in his hand.

Quickly, before he could slam the hatch, Ryzhkov stepped down into the cabin, sat at the top of the stairs on the narrow threshold, levelled the gun at Andrianov's chest. He was still standing there with the spatula in his hand, looking empty.

'You'd better do something with your eggs,' Ryzhkov said. Andrianov blinked and looked towards the tiny stove. Reached out and turned the eggs over. Stared at them for a moment. The smell was making Ryzhkov hungry. There were two sausages on a plate.

'Put those in too,' he said, and Andrianov looked at him for a moment and then did it.

'Is there anyone else here?'

'No.'

'Are you sure?'

'Yes.'

'All right, get dressed. Hurry up.' Andrianov stood blankly for another moment and then put the spatula down on the edge of the skillet, turned and began to walk toward the narrow bow of the boat. There was a triangular bed built in there. Fine wood panelling, polished brass fittings, shelves tucked into every available space. Even a little ikon in the corner. Andrianov unlatched a cupboard and took his jacket off a hanger.

'No, not that,' Ryzhkov said. 'Something else. Not so formal, something so you look like everybody else.' Andrianov had to think about it for a moment. He closed the door and started towards Ryzhkov. Stopped, looked up at him with his eagle's eyes, a little anger coming out of him, habitually not used to having someone standing in his way.

'Excuse me,' he finally said, and Ryzhkov stepped back to let him pass. Andrianov pulled out a set of raingear, thick canvas trousers and a jacket that had been treated with rubber, held it out.

'That's good enough. Give it to me, first.' He took the clothes one at a time and went through the pockets looking for a knife. Handed them back. Andrianov paused for a moment and then opened his robe, turned slightly, letting Ryzhkov see his nakedness, the flat belly, the spray of fair hair across his chest and around his penis, shrunk now with fear and the morning chill.

'You'd better turn that cooker off,' Ryzhkov said, once Andrianov had put his jacket on.

'I have money . . . if you want money. I can get you out. We can get out today, we can sail out and . . .' Andrianov turned from the stove and looked at Ryzhkov, shrugged.

'Money? How much?' Ryzhkov said, wondering how far Andrianov would go, wondering if he would bargain for his life or just cough everything up at once. Watched his eyes flick towards the drawers behind the chart table.

'There's maybe ten thousand roubles here, on board—' and thinking that it wasn't enough to buy his life back, Andrianov blurted, '—but we could get more! We could go to a bank.' As if Ryzhkov had never heard of that peculiar institution.

'I thought you'd sold everything. I thought you were running away?' he said, and when Andrianov stood there, saying nothing— 'All right get it then,' he said, and watched while Andrianov got down on his hands and knees and reached up under the galley sink. 'Slowly . . .' Ryzhkov said, pushing the muzzle down so that it was inches from Andrianov's face.

'Yes . . . here. Take it. I can easily get more, if you—' Then stopped when Ryzhkov shook his head.

'Do you have a fork?'

'Yes, of course.' Andrianov pushed himself back up and got him a fork.

He took the money, reached over into the pan and started eating the sausages. 'Finish with your boots, we're leaving,' he said between bites, and pointed with the gun towards the hatch.

They walked along the dock, Andrianov in front and Ryzhkov quietly steering him towards the boathouses. It was bright now, the gulls were swooping above them. They walked along a muddy path that led out toward the marshes at the end of Krestovsky.

'You can't escape, you know. Everyone has your photograph, at the border, at the stations. You should listen to reason,' he heard Andrianov say to him over his shoulder. And a few moments later, 'You should be practical.'

A few metres later he tried again, 'I have people, later they're meeting me, they'll see I've gone missing.' His voice floated back to Ryzhkov. It seemed like Andrianov was walking faster, trying to get some space between them, thinking about making a break for it. Ryzhkov, right behind him, could see him looking from side to side. Maybe he thought a magic door would appear that he could walk through.

'No, you don't. You don't have people, you don't have anyone,' he said and they walked along a little further.

There was a low buzzing sound, the sound of an engine growing louder and they both turned to watch an aeroplane with floats attached to its landing gear, take off from the river. Speeding along with its pontoons slapping on the water, lifting into the sky just opposite them, the fragile wings carrying it steadily higher, banking in a long gradual turn that would take it over Kronstadt.

'That's Sikorsky,' Andrianov said and looked back and smiled. 'Now there's a real hero, eh?' His eyes were full of admiration.

'Keep going,' Ryzhkov said and pushed him on the shoulder with his free hand.

'You think you know everything,' Andrianov said after a few paces. His voice was sullen. The anger was starting to well up; any minute now he'd run, Ryzhkov thought.

'I know enough.'

Andrianov laughed at that, shook his head. 'You know nothing. People like you. Pansies like Fauré, people that think they're patriots. People that believe that because they've become vegetarians they have ideals.'

'I know that you've started a war. I know you did it to get rich.'

'You think that's it?' Andrianov lifted his hands like a criminal who had been arrested for breaking a shop window. 'Everything I've done has been for Russia, but of course you're so caught up in your own notions of what it means to love your country—'

'You're saying you did it for Russia?'

'Of course. Look at us, limping along into the twentieth century with a Tsar like Nicholas? He thinks he's an autocrat? He'd choke if he ever met an autocrat. Don't make me laugh. People like you can't see the future . . . Money? I'm insulted.' He turned around so that he was walking backwards. Andrianov's face was clear, handsome and perfect, his chin held high, a slight smile. 'What are you going to do, shoot me?'

'Yes, why not? Because of a little girl, a little girl named Katya. That's enough of a reason, isn't it?'

Andrianov's expression suddenly changed, he looked at him blankly, the beginnings of a frown. 'What?' he said. His voice was weak, lost.

'Just a little girl. A little *vertika*. Ekatarina was her name. Say it.'

'I . . . don't know what you're talking about—'

'Say it,' Ryzhkov said. He was getting angry now, coldly furious and he tried to tamp it down, tried to regain control. They hadn't got far enough out on to the marsh yet. 'Say her name . . .' he growled raising the pistol so that it pointed to the bridge of Andrianov's aristocratic nose.

'Ekat-Ekatarina . . . Look here, I don't understand—'

'Just someone you used and threw away, just a little angel that fell to earth one night, remember?'

Andrianov's mouth opened and he went pale. 'You can't be . . . serious,' he breathed.

'Oh, yes. I'm serious.'

Andrianov gave an involuntary laugh. 'This is . . . look, this is truly absurd, I'm sure we can make some kind of arrangement, the idea of you coming after me because of some whore—'

Ryzhkov pushed the pistol out so that it was almost touching the rubber sleeve of Andrianov's jacket and pulled the trigger. Andrianov's eyes opened wide with surprise for an instant and then he crouched over with the pain of it, not quite falling to his knees.

'Keep going, it's not far,' Ryzhkov said, and slapped the man hard against his ear. When he stood up he had tears in his eyes. Blood was running out of the sleeve of the rain jacket.

'You fucking bastard . . . you fucking little shit,' Andrianov said between his gritted teeth. 'You think you have any idea at all about real justice? You think you can even begin to *appreciate* true morality or what is right and wrong? You're a child, an infant!'

And that was when Ryzhkov shot him again, low down, through the kidney. So that Andrianov fell into the mud with a great moan and rolled over, sighing, the game over, his face gone white. 'Oh, God . . .' he puffed.

'Get up. Keep going,' Ryzhkov said, standing above him. Andrianov looked up at him for a long moment, the face slack, like a child waiting for the lights to be turned down. Ryzhkov reached out and prodded him with his shoe. The second shot would kill him, but it would take a while. 'Go on.'

Andrianov rolled over, braced himself with his good arm, and managed to get to his feet.

They only walked a couple of steps before Ryzhkov heard him say something, something garbled that he couldn't understand, and then Andrianov finally decided to make his run.

Ryzhkov let him go, watching him lumber down the pathway, Andrianov taking his hand away from his bloody shoulder so that he could keep his balance. He let him run off, opened the cylinder of the pistol to check how many bullets were left.

Enough.

Andrianov was crashing along, stumbling through the bushes, trying to find a place to hide in the reeds. There was enough blood and stamped-down vegetation that Ryzhkov could follow along easily. Ryzhkov could hear him groaning, the labouring of his breath as he tried to slog through the marsh by the side of the raised path.

He walked through the crushed reeds until he found Andrianov, stood there watching him, sunk in the mud up to his mid-thigh. Watched him struggling until the man looked over his shoulder and saw Ryzhkov waiting. Then the fight went out of him and then he stopped, knowing that in the end there was no escape.

'Do you want to say a prayer, before?' Ryzhkov asked the man in the mud. Andrianov stared at him for a moment, looked out towards the Gulf, towards the place he'd thought he would be sailing this morning. Towards all the different banking houses in which he had hidden his monies, towards the promise of an America beyond the gathering storm.

From a long distance away there was a rumbling of the salute being fired to cement the alliance between France and Russia, fireworks for Poincaré's departure.

'Well, all right then. It probably wouldn't do much good anyway,' he said to Andrianov, who was just planted there in the mud, slumping over now, his head slowly bowing as if he were falling asleep. He looked like he was inspecting some tiny plant that had just emerged from the slime.

Ryzhkov checked Kostya's gun to make sure there was a bullet in the chamber, stepped down and squatted on a hummock of grass and watched Andrianov die. It was as if he had gone to sleep and then he would suddenly wake up and have to figure everything out anew. Then he would try to pull himself out of the muck. He did it three or four times, but it didn't work. Behind him the mud was stained red from his bleeding.

'There is nothing . . . nothing . . .' Andrianov said. His voice was almost a whisper and he was staring down at the mud as he spoke. Maybe he was already gone, Ryzhkov thought. He remembered the way the gendarme had put Fauré's horse out of his misery, and he raised the gun and pointed it at the crown of Andrianov's blonde head. His finger tightened on the trigger.

'Nothing . . .' Andrianov moaned. Maybe that was all he was left with, or maybe it was all he could imagine. A horse pulled loads all day, never complained. A horse could be your friend, would run itself to death under you if you asked for it. Had Andrianov ever done anything to deserve the mercy you gave a wounded horse?

Ryzhkov uncocked the hammer and stood up, thinking about it.

He stood for a long, long moment without coming up with a single thing, watching the man go through his feeble swimming motions, listening to his muddy whispers.

He climbed back up to the path and looked out over the Gulf. There was a cacophony of whistles, horns and bells as the low angry silhouette of *France* steamed past the forts. There was a gargling sound; below him Andrianov had sagged over, his face pressed into the mud, his arm outstretched, trying to reach something that would always be beyond his grasp.

So . . .

The walk back seemed longer. There was a low fog that kept rising over the little Nevka. He heard a low rumbling and the sharp screeching of metal and he looked over to see a train easing through Staraya Derevnya, just across the channel, the shabby little fishing town where most of Petersburg's smugglers lived.

He thought about going back to *Firebird*, maybe untying the boat and seeing how much of his nautical expertise came back to him. He thought he might be able to make it out past the Kronstadt forts, lose himself in the exuberance of the regatta. But Andrianov might really have friends on the way, and with the extra money in the pocket of his jacket Ryzhkov had enough; enough to see him into the woods, to see him on his way beneath the darkness of the firs, to see him across the border. Enough for bribes, for fresh documents, for anonymity. Enough for a future.

He knew the future. He could see it, see himself walking all night into the darkness of the forests. Yes, he would take Andrianov's money and escape first to Finland and then . . . Then . . .

He would never be able to go back, he would have to be shut off from her, for her own safety, eventually he would forget about her, lose the memory of her face. It would all be decided by the end of one more day when he sneaked across the border, and he finally would run, limping blindly through the trees, terrified of the shouting of a too-alert guard, the sound of gunshots in the white night.

He caught his breath for a moment as a vision of Vera came to him, unbidden, invading his imagination, nearly causing him to stumble. His eyes were smarting and he tried to make his thoughts reach out to her. Tried to frame his love into a picture postcard.

'For you,' he said to the sky. 'For you and Katya.'

He reached into his pocket and threw Kostya's gun into the water, skipping it like a stone for a single hop before it tumbled into the murk. Made himself keep walking away. Now there was nothing but the screaming of the birds, the regular pulse of the locomotive across the water.

Away out there he could see the amazing aeroplane, the sound of its engine coming to him erratically on the wind. Buzzing like an addled honeybee, circling over the crowds of boats, above the fireworks and the cheering; high above all the whistles, the bunting, and the flags, as Petersburg wished Poincaré *bon voyage*.

Sikorsky in his little silken aeroplane, defying gravity, cheating death as he hovered above the heavy black dreadnought.

A real hero.

EPILOGUE

These are the fiery mornings of August.

His manservant, Zonta, wakes him, his gentle purring 'excellency . . .' A light touch on the shoulder. But Evdaev rarely sleeps. He does not need sleep any more, he has become free of the need for sleep, free of the dreaming.

Why dream when each day is unto itself such an ornate dream? A dream of millions of men rushing to meet each other, a dream of urgent messages being delivered, sweating horses, exhausted couriers. Blood and steel. Things burning.

And on the roads, all sorts of people—peasants, farmers, merchants, priests, Jews, local dignitaries with their hats in their hands, poised, looking up as his regiment rides through their miserable hamlets. Old people, children, their hands held aloft so that you cannot divine what they want; is it a salutation, a wish for Godspeed? Is it because they are already starving? All this strife about, and they have only been at war for a week or two!

He is on his way to decapitate Prussia. The mobilization has gone perfectly, no, better than 'perfectly'. The armies have been assembled with unbelievable speed. And now the Russian steamroller is driving westward, to divert the Germans from their meticulously planned invasion of Belgium. They are rushing forward, always forward. Forward to save France. A fantastic, glorious, noble gesture. It will be like Tannenberg in 1410 and the destruction of the Teutonic knights all over again. Ha! Yes, history is doomed to repeat itself. And, yes . . . those poor, poor German boys.

And afterwards there will be time for adjustments, for the memoirs and the alibis, for promotions and forgiveness, for the historians to remark on the ironies, to reflect on the Tsar's gallant, sacrificial gesture. Time to set the record straight for once.

They have been billeted in a series of houses, this latest a large farmhouse that smells of generations of Polish grime. Every corner, every wall and door betrays clumsy attempts to modernize and repair the sad dwelling. The most you can say is that it is a hideous pile, devoid of character, for decades repaired and maintained on the cheap. The people who lived there, one notch above their own animals.

Still . . . he is rapidly becoming used to such quarters. He shares these spaces with the officers of the 133rd, an honourable regiment, but nothing, nothing like the Life Guards. He floats through the days like a ghost. Naturally enough there are rumours which swirl around him; lies, misconceptions, fantasies that rarely touch upon the truth. He says nothing. It's only through Nicholas's benevolence that he has escaped the gallows.

Undeserved charity from the man he'd planned to kill; the nobility of the Tsar's gesture brings tears of shame. But he says nothing. Honestly, he is still feverish, recovering from his 'accident'. Naturally the doctor attends him each day. There are a series of pleasant nurses, some who are interested, some of whom only feign interest.

They have advanced rapidly, outrunning their supplies, their communications, their plans, their maps. A headlong rush towards Danzig, a thrust, a coup that will divide Prussia from the shoulders of Germany. It is all according to plan. Timetables, schedules. Oh! These modern tools of warfare! The telegraph, the railway. It is terrible to contemplate. Opposing them are children and old men. They are so victorious it is worrisome.

Everything is confusing and miraculous in this land of Polish swamps and briar-patches. And all of these poor sods on the dusty roads! Everyone is afraid of being left behind, for in times like this whom could you count on? Some of them would be friends, some enemies, some would give you water if you were wounded, and some would steal your eyes.

A day passes. Another. Zonta's gentle touch. Another. He waits for orders. Chats with the younger men. They look up to him with respect, measuring themselves against what they imagine him to be. Of course he is a legend, a kind of god. But his fingers, it is absurd, they refuse to heal!

Like an ikon bleeding tears, the fingers are just some mushy substance. They leak, they throb, they stink of infection. The doctor does everything he can, advising salt baths. Zonta makes one for him every night. He bathes his fingers in the hot water until they throb with pain. Each beat of his heart is something joyous, a divine flagellation, a rhythmic blood-pulse chanting to God.

That's what this bloody hand is, a talisman. He has become proud of it.

To the other officers he offers no opinions, he says nothing that is in any way disagreeable, or controversial, no matter what the topic of discussion. He drinks only a toast to the Tsar, a toast to Samsonov, the commander of their army, a toast to the defeat of the Hun, and then the sad fingers are his excuse to crawl off to bed.

Under the covers he is happy, in a state of bliss, even though his sleep is feverish. Those fragmentary dreams he might have are only nonsensical screaming matches between factions in his mind that he can never identify. The wrong words coming out of the wrong faces.

Zonta touches his shoulder and he wakes confused, not knowing where he is, strange bed, strange house, strange town, strange country. Poland. According to Andrianov's mad Plan he should have been in Galicia, cutting a swath through the Austrians, becoming a heroic legend by now, and after the short little war, placing himself on the throne. But now, here he is! Lucky to be alive, lucky to have escaped the noose or a cell in the Fortress of St Peter and St Paul. Here he is, an honorary colonel, in charge of nothing much, not even in charge of his own hand. Here he is, a gleaming, embroidered dragoon, a handsome man on a great steed.

Well, whatever happens Khalif must be fed, watered, groomed, everything must be explained to him . . . yes, everything must actually be explained to his beautiful war horse. It is like a confessional, these talks he has in the stables. Or does the animal know everything already? Why not? It is a mystery, Evdaev thinks. Only the latest mystery, but . . . sometimes you look into those eyes and . . .

Each day is the same, another rapier-like thrust into the countryside. Each day there is the smell of burning. Someone's home, someone's crops. Someone. The people on the roads lift their arms, reach out. Old women in tears. A dead child.

Well, the days of luxury are long gone, aren't they? Only a few weeks and look how the world has changed! A breakfast set for him, a meal planned to be light, but he is surprised how hungry he is. That's a good sign, isn't it?

And so . . . the prince contemplates his sin. Each turn of the strap on the harness that simultaneously binds his fingers and holds his sabre in a locked grip, drives home the lesson. His sins are in multitudes. With each spike of pain he prays to his God, to the Virgin, to the Tsar, to Russia, to the men whose lives are his responsibility. He reiterates his warrior's bargain: I pledge my life for the salvation of my homeland. If only it may be.

Outside he can hear the sounds of the regiment forming up.

He is helped into Khalif's saddle. He is sweating, hot enough that he worries he will faint and have to be carried away. Wouldn't that just take it all? To have come so far only to fall apart on this most glorious morning.

They ride. Fifteen kilometres or more. All the while the sound of the artillery grows. The general and his staff consult the ridiculous maps and Evdaev stands politely to one side, nods his agreement. It is all a confusion of woods and nondescript towns, creeks that are called rivers, marshes that are endless, fires, burned-out sheds and farmhouses, weeping women and bad food. Corpses like sacks of spilled rotten fodder pouring out of doorways, splayed out across the rutted roads, stinking in a ditch. The map shows none of it.

Ahead of them is a long valley, a field. Some fences that might slow the horses. Ground higher on the slope where they wait under the cover of the trees. There are names that he can recall if he wanted give a title to this battle. A boy looks over at him and smiles. He is smiling too. There is music running through his thoughts, a martial symphony, a compelling rhythm of cymbals, of bugles, the sound of boots marching, of Russia moving forward into the glorious century.

He looks down at his . . . hand. What's left of it. All of it bound into a long bloody stump. The remains of a man's fist. Smelling and swollen and festering. Bound into a hard leather stump to which his sawn-down sabre's grip has been bolted.

There is a screamed command. His reverie, and his memory have carried him away for a moment. But . . . thankfully he has returned. Yes, he is here. His men surrounding him, the magnificent beast nervously trembling between his legs, nearly uncontrollable, muscles rippling spasmodically along his flanks. Now there are sudden explosions in the treetops as German artillery tries to disrupt their attack. And now that they've been discovered, the only response is to commit to the offensive, to charge down into that promised field, yes?

See it there? Dappled with sunlight, the wind gently swaying the wheat, not quite ready for harvest. All of it green, as green as one's youth.

More shelling in the treetops. There are screams, and men are shouting over the din. Yes. It is time to make a charge. Forward to the field, forward to meet the enemy in a bloody embrace. At the very least it will take them away from the horror of the screaming shells, the screams of the terrified horses, their mouths foaming, their eyes rolling towards heaven.

Is that some mysterious music he hears? A chorus of deep men's voices, all of them chanting, war, war, war, war, war, war, war.

He has only to touch the spur—

Sources and Acknowledgements

I would like to thank Helen Heller who sparked the creation of this book, who worked with me throughout the process, and whose contributions can be found all through these pages. My sincere thanks go to my editors David Davidar at Penguin Canada, and Susan Watt at HarperCollins UK who have much improved my manuscript. I owe a great specific debt to my partner Suzie Payne who listened, read, and helpfully nudged me along during the entire project, from idea to finished manuscript. My brother, Richard Miller, the one with the imagination in the family, has contributed a great deal to the entire Ryzhkov story, and deserves much more than my thanks given here. I also must acknowledge the very valuable input given by Fraser Gabbott, Suzanne Nairne, Daniel Conrad, John Maclachlan Gray and Irina Templeton-Trouchenko in the middle stages.

The Anna Akhmatova quote is from *In the Year 1913*, my own translation; the translation of Glinka's *A*

Life for the Tsar is by Pamela Davidson taken from the notes to the Sony Classical recording by the Sofia National Opera, *S3K 46 487, 1991*.

Apis was the code name for Col. Dragutin Dimitrijevic, head of Serbian military intelligence —who hatched the plot to assassinate Franz Ferdinand. The Russian diplomats Hartwig and Artamonov were probably involved. They are, along with other historical characters, fictionalized in this novel. The *Apis* plot and Russia's complicity is steeped in almost a century's worth of obfuscation, and any truth-seeker approaching this incident should do so with caution. More on *Apis* can be found in David MacKenzie's *Apis: The Congenial Conspirator, The life of Colonel Dragutin T. Dimitrijevic*, published by East European Monographs, Boulder Colorado, 1989.

A bibliography of the books, newspapers, videos, recordings and magazines consulted in the writing of *The Field of Mars* would itself fill a small volume. Below are some English language titles that provided good background, plus some harder-to-find sources which were especially useful as I was researching the book—a labour of love which did not stop until the last day; cited in no particular order. Any missed attributions are honest mistakes, and my apologies are sincerely offered.

Ruud, Charles A. and Sergei Stepanov—*Fontanka 16*, McGill Queen's University Press, 1999. This is the only English-language general history of the Okhrana in print.

Baedeker, Karl—*Russia* 1914. Arno Press reprinted it in 1971. Rare. The original copy I used was discovered at the Perkins Library at Duke University. Baedeker has everything between its covers. The maps alone were crucial.

Fitzlyon, Kyril and Tatiana Browning—*Before the Revolution: A View of Russia under the last Tsar*, Penguin Books, Harmondsworth, 1982. Photographs and insightful text; widely available.

Ometev, Boris and John Stuart, compiled by Olga Suslova and Lily Ukhtomskaya—*St Petersburg: Portrait of an Imperial City*, Vendome Press, New York, 1990. Stunning photographs throughout this absolutely splendid book.

Troyat, Henri—*Daily Life in Russia Under the Last Tsar*, translated by Malcolm Barnes, Stanford University Press, Stanford, California, 1961. A fictionalized Baedeker of everyday life. Set primarily in Moscow.

Fay, Sidney B.—*The Origins of the World War*, Second edition, The Free Press, New York, 1966.

Lincoln, W. Bruce—*In War's Dark Shadow: The Russians Before the Great War*, The Dial Press, New York, 1983. Also his Sunlight at Midnight. Lincoln is always thorough and readable. One of the basics.

Gilfond, Henry—*Black Hand at Sarajevo*, Bobbs-Merrill, New York, 1975, Hertha Pauli's *The Secret of Sarajevo*, Appleton-Century, New York, 1965, and Lavender Cassels's *The Archduke and the Assassin*, Dorset, New York, 1984. All were good for details of the assassination.

Morton, Frederic—*Thunder at Twilight, Vienna 1913–1914*, Charles Scribner's Sons, New York, 1989. Dramatic portrait of Austria in the months before the war.

Taylor, Edmund—*The Fall of the Dynasties: The Collapse of the Old Order, 1905–1922*, Doubleday, Garden City, New York, 1963. Especially good on the Hartwig–Artamonov–Apis plot.

Vassilyev, A.T. and Rene Fullop-Miller—*Ochrana: The Russian Secret Police*, J.B. Lippincott Company, Philadelphia, 1930. Fullop-Miller, the co-writer, points out that Vassilyev must be taken with several grains of salt. Self-justifying memoir of the Okhrana by its last commander in St Petersburg.

Volkov, Solomon—*St Petersburg: A Cultural History*, The Free Press, New York, 1995. Excellent.

West, Rebecca—*Black Lamb and Grey Falcon*, Viking Press, New York, 1940. For background of Balkan struggles and later perspectives on the assassination.

Bely, Andrei—*Petersburg*, translated, annotated and introduced by Robert A. Maguire and John E. Malmstad, Indiana University Press, Bloomington, 1978. Bely's novel came out in serial form during 1913, but was neglected during the Soviet era. Bely's appeal rests on his intricate wordplay which is lost in most translations, thus *Petersburg* has been underrated abroad. Maguire's and Malmstad's extensive notes were invaluable.

Finally, the first draft of *The Field of Mars* was completed shortly after the death of my father, Wendell Richard Miller. A fine man, my father was a history buff; his interests spanned mostly American history from the Revolution to World War II, and it is from him that I derive my own love of the past. 'Spud' was a larger-than-life character, a man with a multitude of interests and multitudes of friends. I find that I miss him very much as the years go by, and one book is not enough to dedicate to his memory.